MW00880495

To Murder a King
Book 2
in the
Struggle for a Crown Series
By
Griff Hosker

To Murder a King

Published by Sword Books Ltd 2018

Copyright © Griff Hosker First Edition

Cover by Design for Writers

Prologue

I had been a gentleman for three years. Born the son of a member of the Free Company, I had been elevated far higher than I could possibly have imagined. I knew that my father, even though he had treated me badly, would be proud. Stony Stratford was a small village and I was the only gentleman. Sir Robert Armistead, Lord of the Manor of Stratford, was the lord to whom I owed fealty. He was not a warrior but he respected me. I had been King Richard's bodyguard. I had fought in Spain and Aquitaine. We got on. He was a vassal lord of the Earl of Northampton. The feudal system was complicated but, thanks to my title, gentleman, I had slightly more rights than when I was a commoner. It was all due to Robert de Vere, Earl of Oxford I had been dismissed as King Richard's bodyguard. I had been a threat to the young Earl. The Earl had seemed to mesmerize the young king and he dismissed me and the guards I had assembled to protect him. Men made lewd suggestions about the King and the Earl. I did not believe them but many men did and the King was unpopular. Those years I spent away from the King changed that impressionable young man. He became a different King to the one I had known and trained to be a warrior. I felt that I had let him down. I had made an oath to his father, King Edward, that I would watch over his son. I could no longer do so and that bothered me.

I had been forced to become a farmer. It did not come naturally to me. I was lucky that Eleanor, my wife, was a natural. Her family had been farmers and when the plague had taken her village I had found and married her. We were happy. We had two children, Tom and Alice. I promised myself that I would be a better father to them than he had been to me. I knew that Harry of Lymm had meant to be a good father but he chose the route of making me tough. I had been beaten and treated badly. Perhaps he had been right for I was able to endure great hardship and I did not expect much out of life.

In the three years since I had returned to the farm, I had tried to be a farmer and failed. I did not understand the rigour. The seasons were different to me. Spring, summer and autumn were for fighting battles and winter was when you hunkered down in a billet and drank and ate as much as you could. A farmer used the seasons. I was lost. Luckily my wife had those skills in abundance and she made the farm so profitable that we were able to hire three men and their wives to help. They lived in cottages close to the hall which we had extended. There might have been a time when we would have had serfs and slaves but the plague had killed so many in England that men who could work were valuable and so we gave the three of them a share in the crops they produced. The lack of farm workers had driven up the price of animals and grain. The country's loss was our gain and we made money. That was nothing to do with me and all to do with my wife.

I became a real gentleman. We had men we hired to work the land and I could ride my horses and practise with my weapons. Even without my farm I was well off and still had coin. When I had been a sword for hire I had husbanded my money. Others wasted it away on women and drink. I had not. The spare weapons and treasure I had collected on the battlefield I had sold and stored the precious coins in a chest. The King, when he had dismissed me, had given me the manor and money. He felt guilty for he knew what he did was wrong. I cursed Robert de Vere. I was still a soldier at heart and I made certain that if I had to then I could protect my family, my farm, my country and my King. I had good horses. I had the local smith make me armour which was of the best quality. I no longer wore a simple mail coat. I had a breast and back plate and I had cannons for my arm, with cuisse, poleyn and sabaton for my legs and feet. I was well protected. My arming jacket which I wore beneath my plate was the finest in the county. I did not like the helmets which enclosed my face and so I had a basinet and aventail. I did not bother with the besagews which some men wore under their armpits or the fauld to protect the lower abdomen. I found them both restrictive. My best horse, Goldheart, was not a destrier. I could not justify such an expense. She was a courser. She was still the best war horse I had. Jack was my hackney. He was a gelding and good workaday horse. Of all my horses I loved Jack the best. We understood each other and I rode him far more than the expensive Goldheart.

I practised each day. Sometimes it was on my horse and sometimes on foot. I knew that a day without training might, one day, cost me my life. I used my sword and shield to fight imaginary opponents. It was not perfect but I developed techniques which still improved my skills. The three men who worked land which belonged to me had too much to do to practise and so I was forced to work alone. I built up my strength and I made sure that my horses would respond to my commands, knees and hands. One day King Richard would need me and when he did then I would be ready. I was a true gentleman farmer.

Chapter 1

The King married Anne of Bohemia. It was a good marriage. Her father was Holy Roman Emperor and the young king was allied to the most important house in Europe. It was not a popular marriage. There was a great deal of expense and some people objected. It was a shame. I was not invited to the wedding. I like to think that the King might have wished to invite me but Robert de Vere would not. He both hated and feared me. All that the King now needed was children. I wondered how Robert de Vere would feel about the King's children, when and if they were born.

My eldest child was born the year after the wedding. The King, three years later, still had no children. People began to wonder if the couple was cursed. Michael de la Pole was the new chancellor. He appeared, from a distance, to be as bad an influence on the King as Robert de Vere. I only learned of the goings on at court when I travelled to Lincoln. Captain Tom lived there now and ran an inn. Lincoln was on the main road to the north and travellers told Old Tom of the goings on at court. Some was rumour and some was conjecture but Captain Tom knew how to sift the wheat from the chaff and most of what he told me was accurate. Certainly, the King was unpopular. The halcyon days when he had put down the Peasants' Revolt by sheer willpower were long gone. The Queen was not popular and his two advisors were hated. I feared for his future. He was hanging on to the crown by his fingertips and there were many, his uncle, the Duke of Gloucester included, who were unhappy with his reign. In the heart of England, the place they called the garden of England, I was happy. I had a good wife and a fine family. Robert de Vere had done me a favour by having me dismissed but it was not good for the realm.

Sir Robert Armistead liked me. I had been given the manor and he should have resented that but he was not a warrior knight. His son had died in Gascony and he had raised his grandson, Henry, himself. His grandson was coming up to fourteen. He was a man. As the son of a knight, he had responsibilities. The Reeve of Sir Robert came to see me.

"Sir, my lord asks if you and your wife would care to dine with him and his lady wife this evening?"

"In Stratford? It is many miles hence."

He smiled. He was a typical retainer. He was both old and wise. He had never had to raise his hand in anger and had lived a peaceful life. "No, sir, he is at his hall at Towcester."

The invitation was a surprise. The knight liked me but he had never yet invited me to dine. I said that we would. Eleanor had servants who could care for the children, Tom and Alice. When I told her, however, she was mortified at the thought of dining with nobility. "I am no lady, husband. How can I dine with Sir Robert and Lady Anne?"

"You are a lady for you are married to a gentleman. Come, I had already accepted the invitation. You would not wish to make me look a fool, would you?"

She shook her head but I could see she was unhappy. "What shall I wear?"

I sighed, "I am the wrong person to ask. Wear your best garment."

"That is the dress in which I was married."

"There, you can wear that then!"

"I cannot fit into it. I have grown since the wedding."

I sighed, "Then let it out! God's Blood, my lady, I am a warrior and know nothing about dresses and the like! We have money! Buy a new one!"

"It is too late for tonight."

"Then let out the one you have!" She nodded and scurried off.

Sir Robert had a number of halls and castles. He invited us to Towcester. It was the closest one to my home and I suspected he had used it for that reason. It was not his best residence. That was on the Avon but was many miles to the west of us. However, it was far enough away that Eleanor would have to ride. We had a docile rouncy, Nell, and Eleanor could ride. She was a farmer's daughter. I had my groom prepare the horses. A good brush and comb would make them look better. I would wear my best tunic. My wife had been outraged when she heard how much I had paid for it to be made in Lincoln. She was convinced that she and her ladies could do a better and cheaper job. However, I thought it a good investment. If I was to rise beyond a gentleman to the rank of knight then I needed to look like one. Captain Tom had negotiated a good price and the black staff on the blue background was striking. The needlework was exquisite. One addition to my coat of arms was a red and blue quartered shield over the heart. As this was the design of my shield it was effective.

My wife looked beautiful when we rode into the courtyard at Towcester. She had a simple cap adorning her hair but she had plaited fresh summer flowers into her long locks. I was proud of her. I had been lucky to marry such a beautiful woman and such a practical one.

Lady Anne was of an age with her husband. Both were approaching their sixtieth year. With a son who had died in battle and a daughter in law who had died in childbirth all that they had in the way of family was their grandson, Henry. Their servants must have warned them of our imminent arrival for they were waiting for us in their courtyard. It was a wooden hall with a wooden palisade. There were few such buildings left. Most lords had learned to make their castles from stone. I saw Henry for the first time. He was tall but he had no muscle to him. His training to be a knight had been neglected. Perhaps he would be like his grandfather. He would be a lord who sent others to fight for him. Over the last fifty or so years it had been common. Knights were now allowed to have others serve for them. It was how the free companies had grown.

As we dismounted Lady Anne allayed all of my wife's fears by gushing over her. She became almost tearful. "Lady Eleanor you are most welcome. You must come and see us more often."

I saw the relief on my wife's face. Sir Robert smiled and put his arm around me, "My wife is keen for the ladies of the manor to get together more. She has missed the company of refined women. It is good to see you. May I introduce my grandson, Henry of Stratford. I would have him become a knight."

I studied the young man. He was all arms and legs. His arms showed that he had not had much physical exercise. He had been indulged. He had eaten well and done little exercise. I was not sure that he would be anything other than a priest or a merchant. I had never seen such a condition until I met the children of lords. Growing up in the camps meant that we were at best lean and often emaciated.

"Henry, this is William Strongstaff. He was King Richard's bodyguard and champion."

"In fairness Sir Robert, I never had to fight for the King's honour."

Sir Robert laughed, "I believe that is because none would face you. I have heard of your prowess. Come let us go indoors. I have some fine wine from Castile. I do not know if I have mentioned it before but John of Gaunt's first wife, Blanche, was my cousin. I hold this manor thanks to the King of Castile's good offices."

I knew that John of Gaunt intended to go back to his realm of Castile, held by right of his second marriage, as he could not have the throne of England. I liked Sir John. He was a good soldier and had always treated the Free Companies well. If he asked me to go with him then I would. There was good money to be had in Galicia. With two claimants to the Castilian throne it would be a profitable war. The youth seemed a little shy. "I look forward to hearing, sir, some of your experiences while we eat."

Sir Robert said, hurriedly, "I pray you make them ones which do not upset my wife. When Henry's father was killed it scarred her."

"I will try to keep the tales tasteful for the feast table." In truth, I would find it hard to do so without resorting to lies and exaggeration. There was a misguided belief that knights and their battles were somehow noble. Nothing could be further from the truth. If a knight allowed an opponent to surrender it was because he thought the man rich enough to be worthy of ransom. Those of the Free Companies had no such qualms. They fought to kill and took what their opponent had. Some took everything, including their underwear!

It was a cosy hall and I could see why Sir Robert had chosen it. The hall was little bigger than my own and the five of us were close enough together to be able to chat easily. "This will be the last meal in this hall, William. The hall is old. Tomorrow we empty it of all that is within and then demolish it. We will build a more substantial home, in time. My home in Stratford is much grander and we now have greater trade there. We are allowed to have two markets a week and the town grows each day. I fear I will be spending less time in the land hereabouts." Sir Robert was more of a merchant than a knight!

"And what of the Earl of Derby and Northampton lord?"

"As you may know Humphrey de Bohun was Earl and was murdered more than ten years since. The title has been restored and given to John of Gaunt's son, Henry Bolingbroke. He has yet to visit Northampton. I have not met him."

"I know him, a little, or at least I did. He and the King were under my care for a time." In truth, they were of an age and I had trained them both. Henry was the better warrior. This was a coincidence. I would owe fealty to one who had a claim to King Richard's crown.

The wine had been served while we spoke and delicacies placed on the table. I recognised a couple of them but my wife, who ate plain fare at home, looked a little mesmerized. I chose one I recognised, a small pastry stuffed with delicately flavoured meats and chopped dried fruit. I caught my wife's eye, nodded, and she chose one too. She nibbled and smiled. She was clever and I knew that she would now watch that which others ate and try them first. The wine was a good one. Sir Robert had money and spent it well.

I could tell that his grandson was keen to speak with me, "Grandfather, the meat of the matter?"

Sir Robert smiled and shook his head, "My grandson is impatient." He sighed. "It is this, William Strongstaff, you are not a knight but you have a reputation as a soldier. I know, from the time I trained as a squire, that it was the men at arms who taught me my skills. My grandson would learn from you."

"I am not a knight and cannot dub him!"

"But you can give him the skills so that when he is ready then I can give him his spurs."

I nodded, "To speak plainly, lord, you could do that now. He is old enough. A knight does not need to fight these days. There is always scutage." Sir Robert did not fight. He paid others to do it for him.

Sir Robert shook his head. I noticed that Lady Anne had stopped speaking and was listening intently. Henry was hanging on to every word of the conversation. "When there was no Earl of Northampton there was not an issue. Who would call for swords to fight for Northampton? Now we have Henry Bolingbroke. He is Earl of Derby and now Earl of Northampton. He is ambitious. His father is gathering men to fight in his Kingdom of Castile. What if his son joins him? No, William Strongstaff, my grandson needs skills before he becomes a squire and begins his journey to knighthood. If the Earl calls him then I would have him know one end of a sword from the other. Would you train him?"

I looked at the youth. I needed to do much with his body before we could even consider the training to be a knight. When I was his age I had already killed men. I had been twice his size and had skills with sword, spear, sling and even bow.

Sir Robert took my hesitation for doubt, "You would not be out of pocket, William. I know that you would have to neglect your farm and I would pay two shillings a day for you to train him. In addition, I will furnish all of his weapons and armour not to mention horses and servants."

I saw my wife's eyes light up when she heard that we would have an income of fourteen shillings a week. We would be able to bear a poor harvest or a disastrous winter with such an income. I smiled at Sir Robert and squeezed Henry's arm, "Armour is the last thing we need for he has to become stronger and more muscular. My only reservation is that this training might be a little late. Most knights start to train at the age of seven."

"I promise, Master, that I will heed all of your commands and I will eat for England if I have to," Henry spoke for the first time. He was earnest and I saw no deception in his eyes. He wished this to happen.

I laughed at the image, "I will take you on, Master Henry, but know that you can return home at any time you choose. There is little to be gained from training a reluctant warrior."

My wife looked up, "Master Henry will live with us?"

I had understood this already, "Aye wife and his servants. Fret not. I had thought to have more rooms added to our hall and stable."

Lady Anne said, "And I would ask that I may come and visit regularly. Since my son was taken Henry is all that I have. I have been as his mother and he is dear to me."

"Of course, although you may find my home plainer than that which you are used to."

"William, it is not the home which is important it is the heart which beats within the house and I can see that yours is a good one."

And so Henry, his manservant, Peter, and his horses came to live with us. Peter had been one of his father's warriors. A greybeard, he had a limp from a war wound. He and I got on well for we could talk a common language. In fact, he made Henry's presence that much easier. He had known the boy all of his life and was able to advise me when I was pushing too hard or not hard enough.

Young Henry was surprised when the first thing we did was to build a training ring. He was even more surprised when he became a labourer to help with the work. Hewing wood with an axe, digging holes, driving posts into the ground all built up his muscles. He also ate great quantities of bread, eggs and cheese. We gave him beer which was not watered. For the first week, he began work when the sun rose and stopped when the sun set. Peter and I used humour to make the work seem lighter than it was and my wife fussed over the young man. By the second week, we were able to start his training proper. That, too, involved Henry manufacturing that which he would need. I had him cut and shape wooden swords. They were twice the weight of real swords. Then he had to make shields. I had him make square ones. Once again, they were heavier and more awkward to use than real ones but by making a shield he understood the structure of one. I knew that helped when it came to fighting.

Once we had the basics we began his proper training. I sparred with him at first and gave him instruction. I taught him the basic sword moves he would need and how to block with a sword. When I deemed he was ready I handed over the wooden sword and shield to Peter so that I could observe his technique. I had to teach him to use his feet.

He had grown up alone. Jack, one of my tenants had a son, John. Although a little younger than Henry he was as big as the young gentleman. He was not cut out to be a farmer. His father told me that he had been involved in scrapes in the local alehouse and he needed discipline. It suited me. My tenant was more than happy to allow his son to help in the young lord's training. We made them play a game I had seen squires enjoying. Henry was on Peter's shoulders and John on my mine. The two of them had to wrestle and throw the other from our backs. It was the best way I knew to get used to fighting from the back of a horse. Henry was thrown ten times before he began to learn. After two days honours were even.

Then we began the work with a lance. I sat, mailed and armoured, with my shield. Henry was given a lance and told to run at me and spear me. If he thought it was easy then he soon found that it was not for the lance was heavy and the end wavered up and down too much for him to control it. It took him six passes before he hit the shield and even then, it felt as though a fly had landed upon it. It was two months before I even contemplated a sword. We worked hard. Henry did not even wish to return home for Christmas and we worked through autumn and into the first frosts.

After a month or two of working with weapons, I took him riding around my tenants to assess his skills on a horse. I discovered that he was not a good rider. He had developed bad habits. He slouched in the saddle and a knight had to have a straight back. Part of the problem was that he was not muscled enough. I had to set him exercises to build up all of his muscles. That began the moment we returned from our gyration.

When we reached the home of Richard of the Stonebrook we met the priest, Father Abelard, leaving. His face told me that there was sadness. Worryingly it might also mean a return of the plague. "Trouble, Father?"

He nodded, "Richard's wife, Anne, is ill."

I waved Henry away and dismounted. I said, quietly, "The plague?"

He shook his head and made the sign of the cross. "No, thank the Good Lord. She lost a child a month since. She lost much blood and she is struggling to recover. I believe she has lost the will to live. Richard is a good man. His fields might end up being neglected but not his wife."

We did not bother the yeoman. He had enough to worry about. When I told my wife about it she went over the fields to give what aid she could. My wife had a kind heart.

A month later and we had a visit from Sir Robert. I sat in the main room of my hall. Henry and Peter were there. Eleanor left to fetch wine. Sir Robert looked concerned. "William, I have had a summons from the Earl of Derby and Northampton."

"Henry Bolingbroke?"

"The very same. He demands service from me. I owe him four swords. He needs them for service in Castile."

"And how many knights can you summon?"

"Three. Sir Walter of Blecheley, Sir Richard d'Issy and Sir Ralph Fitzjohn." He shrugged, "I suspect they may pay scutage to have others do their service for them."

Scutage was almost a fine. A knight could pay someone to do their service for them. "Then pay someone to fight for you, Sir Robert, and the summons has been fulfilled."

He looked uneasy. "The Earl has learned that you are one of my tenants. He would have you as one of the swords." Eleanor had entered while we were talking. She said nothing but poured out the wine. "I will pay you the two shillings a day for the forty days you are required."

I sipped the wine. It was good. "But you believe the contract will be extended?"

He nodded, "It will take two weeks to get to Castile and to return. The Earl has said that his father will pay the scutage after that."

Eleanor said, "Eighty shillings for forty days?"

"No, Mistress, eighty shillings for a month. The contract is for service on foreign soil." My wife had been almost destitute when the plague had taken her family. She liked the security of coins in a chest beneath the bed. I saw her nod. She would have me accept the contract. "The rate for the men should be a shilling a day." I heard the doubt in his voice.

"If men are scarce then that may not be enough."

He rubbed his chin. "I could manage fifteen pennies a day."

I nodded. "And is there security for horses?"

"Yes William, any losses will be made good by the Earl."

"And you say four swords; what else must you provide?"

"Ten sergeants and ten archers."

"You have them?" His shrug told me that he expected me to find them. "And when are we needed?"

"The muster is at Southampton in one month from now."

"And how long are we expected to serve?"

"Six months."

The contract was not excessive. We had signed for longer before but a month before departure: that was not long. I turned to Henry, "I fear, Master Henry, that your training will have to wait until I return. You will have to practise with Peter."

The young man had changed in the time he had been with me. It was not just the physical changes. He had matured. He liked the rigour of training and he was handy with a sword. He had been a little vacuous when first I had met him. Perhaps being with old people all the time had done that. My house was filled with life. He spoke quietly but firmly, "Grandfather I would go as Master Strongstaff's squire. My training has just begun. What better place to learn my trade than on the field of battle?"

Sir Robert's face fell. He had given his grandson freedom and he knew he could not confine him yet his wife, Lady Anne, would be distraught. "But you are not yet ready, Henry. Tell him, William."

"You have made great strides in a short time Henry but, as Peter will tell you, the battlefield is unforgiving."

"He is right, Master Henry, and Master Strongstaff would not have time to watch over someone who lacked experience."

"But you could, Peter. You have often said that you miss the cry of battle."

"But I am now slow. I could not guarantee that I would be able to protect you."

"If I am meant to die then so be it but I believe that I will return. Grandfather, you must let me do this. My father would have wished it."

That was the one argument which worked. His grandfather nodded, "William Strongstaff, bring my grandson home alive and there will be a one hundred pounds bounty waiting for you." I saw the look of joy on my wife's face. She had an eye on more land. With that amount of money, she could buy it.

I nodded, "Then we need to get mail for you and Peter. You will need an aketon, hauberk, sword, shield and helmet."

"Aketon?"

Peter explained, "A long padded garment worn beneath mail. And for me Master Strongstaff?"

"It is an expense, Sir Robert, but if you wish your grandson to be safe then you will buy Peter the same. They will not need a courser but they will require a hackney and a sumpter."

"Of course. I will have my steward arrange that and Henry, you must come home for your grandmother will need to see you every day now until you depart."

He looked at me, "Aye, for I will be busy trying to hire ten sergeants and ten archers. It will not be easy." I looked at Sir Robert, "And it will not be cheap!"

"I will send Peter back with coin for the men, the equipment and the horses. He can stay with you for I know that you will need his help. I will be at Towcester for another month. I have to supervise its demolition."

When they had gone Eleanor hugged me, "This is for the best, husband. We both know that you miss the clash of steel and the smell of war. You are no farmer. The money for your service will pay for more men to help around the farm and more servants. You just need to make sure that you return from Castile!"

She kissed me. She was right but there was no guarantee that I would come back from Spain. I knew many men who had gone for the riches and stayed to feed the crops.

Chapter 2

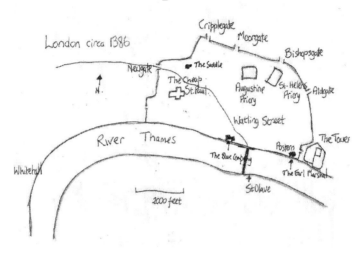

We left to find the men the next day. I rode my hackney, Jack. We would ride to Lincoln first. Captain Tom would know of good men. Then I would head to the tavern in London called 'The Blue Company'. Two members of our company had opened it after they had left us. John and Tom felt they owed me their lives. Certainly, I had allowed them to keep the purses from the dead we had slain at the bridge at Lussac where Sir John Chandos had died. I did not like London but I might find the men I needed there. Alice was too young to even know who I was but Tom became upset when I left. I promised him that I would bring a present back from my travels but it was a sign that I had changed. Before I had met Eleanor, I had only had to worry about myself. Now I had to think about others. I was not worried about my wife. She was hardy but my son and daughter were different. I needed to be a better father than mine had been. I would complete this task and then stay closer to home. I had a job now. I was training Henry of Stratford.

We headed to Lincoln. "How old are you, Peter?"

"I have seen forty summers."

"Why no family?"

He shrugged, "I know not, sir." His silence suggested something other.

"Come, Peter, we will be going to war. You and I both know that there can be no secrets on the battlefield. A man has to trust his shield brothers."

"I will hardly be that, sir. I am a cripple."

"You cannot move as quickly as some, that is true, but oft times we will be fighting horsed and I have seen you on a horse. You ride and fight as well as any. As for fighting on the ground, you are here to protect Henry and I do not intend to allow him to get close to blades. My wife is already spending the bounty for his life!"

Peter laughed and looked around. I know not why as there was no one with us, "Sir, when I was wounded the blade not only crippled me. It made me less of a man. I cannot father children."

Now I understood. "You could still marry. The plague took men and left widows and children. There is comfort in a woman."

"And yet, sir, you are leaving the comfort of your home."

I nodded, "That is true but I am a soldier still. I have spent my whole life wielding a blade. I cannot be a farmer."

"Then you have many problems to solve, sir."

Running an inn was a popular occupation for those who had been soldiers. They knew how to give orders and commands. They understood the need for supplies and they usually had money from the wars in which they had fought. Captain Tom had led a company for many years and he was rich. He could not be an idle man. He had worked and fought for all of his life. He had tried to sit in the hall he bought and found himself bored. Now he ran an inn. That is to say, he hired people to serve beer and food, keep it clean, muck out the stables and change the bedding. He sat and talked.

When I walked in and was framed in the doorway he jumped to his feet. For a man who was the wrong side of fifty, he was still remarkably fit. He grasped my arm, "It is good to see you, Will! I am running out of tales to keep my customers enthralled!"

One old man with a stump for a left arm, snorted, "You get more truth from a lawyer and I would not trust one of those further than I could throw him!"

"Don't listen to Edgar Stump Hand. He only ever fought the Scots!"

I smiled, "I have few stories these days, Captain Tom. I am a gentleman farmer now."

"And that is a step your father dreamed of. You have done well. Come, sit." He looked at Peter. "And who is this?"

"He is another old soldier and he is here to help me recruit."

Edgar Stump Hand quipped, "If you need a hand, young man, I am your man!" He laughed as he waved his stump.

I smiled too. Often those with such disabilities mocked themselves. "And I daresay you would be better than many with two!"

Edgar Stump Hand shook his head, "He cannot be your friend Old Tom; he talks sense!"

From their banter, I gathered that they were the best of friends. "This is Peter, Captain Tom. Have you a room for us and stables for our horses?"

"Of course. The stables are at the back. Tell Tam I said to give you the best stalls." Peter left. "Dolly!" A plump woman with cochineal on her lips and rouged cheeks came from the back. "Find a room for my young friend."

She smiled lewdly, "Does the young master wish me to warm his bed?"

"Away with you, doxy! He is a friend and he is married!"

She blew me a kiss and left. "She is new."

Captain Tom nodded, "Aye, Hilda Plump Buttocks caught the pox last year. Dolly Ample Breast means well but she has a mouth on her." He gestured for me to sit next to him and he poured me a beaker of ale. "So, you need men?"

"Scutage. The Earl of Derby and Northampton wishes men to fight for his father in Castile. The lord of the manor wishes me to go in his stead and find ten archers and ten men at arms." I sipped the beer.

"Men are easy to find. It is quality which you need. I would have said Red Ralph but he, like you, is married and living comfortably in Middleham. As for the rest of our company…"

"Aye, I know. I am going to 'The Blue Company' in London. Perhaps Tom and John may have men for me."

"Oh I can get you men but it will take time. How long do you have?"

"We sail in less than a month."

"Go on the morrow to London. See Tom and John. London is full of men for hire. They are our brothers and they will not see you cheated. How long is the campaign?"

"Six months."

"Then I may have men for you. This is the home of the best of English archers."

Peter came back in carrying the bags. Dolly Ample Breast appeared at the door and nodded to him. "I will show you to your chamber."

Tom and I were alone but I still lowered my voice, "Have you heard much about the King?"

"He continues to make bad decisions. He has made de Vere the first Duke of Ireland. The man is like a spider. He grows richer and more bloated day by day. Some say that it is he who rules England. France still threatens war and the King's marriage has yet to produce the allies his advisors hope. The Chancellor squeezes the land dry to pay for a war we cannot win."

"Cannot win?"

"We have no Black Prince. Who will lead the warriors to war? One uncle prepares to go to Spain and the other plots to control how his nephew rules the land. Richard is young and has not been to war. Had you still been his guide…"

"But I am not. Then I wonder that his uncle is busy in Castile."

"John of Gaunt is King of Castile. The lords chose Richard. He is letting the boy make mistakes. By going to Spain, he distances himself from any accusations of treachery. Perhaps he hopes that he will be recalled to be regent. Now his son…"

"The man to whom I now owe fealty."

"The very same; he is ambitious. Unlike his cousin, he has more experience of war. When you serve him, watch yourself."

"Watch myself?"

"You trained the two young men when they were boys. Henry knows you and your loyalty to Richard. Do not allow yourself to be used. It would not be the first time that a lord used someone from a lower station to be a scapegoat. I am suspicious that this Earl asks specifically for a man he knows was loyal to King Richard." Tom had survived as a Captain amongst men like John of Gaunt for years. He understood their world and their motives far better than I did. Peter returned. Tom smiled but he put his finger to his nose. "Remember my words."

It was not that Tom did not trust Peter he just did not know him. Peter was Sir Robert's servant and not mine. I could be just a tool to be used. We, therefore, spent a pleasant and lively evening in the tavern. We spoke, as all old friends did, of the men we had known who had died and those who were still living. We spoke of politics. Those who used the tavern each had a view. Opposing views rarely ended in blows. A man's opinions were his own and each man was entitled to hold them. Peter and the others in the tavern told tales of men they had served with and characters they had met. Many reeves came in for harsh judgements. Corrupt millers were recalled. Even Dolly Ample Breast spoke of some of the whores with whom she had worked. The conversation was as far from the ones I had had with the King and with Sir Robert as it was possible. I was a creature of two worlds.

When we left the next day Captain Tom had told me he would find as many willing men as possible. We would choose the best once I had been to London. As we rode down the Great North Road I counselled Peter. "London is a dangerous place. Do not confuse it with the capital of England; it is not. The people there serve London and self-interest." I told him of the revolt. In the country, he had witnessed unrest but my stories of theft from the Tower made him blanch.

"Then, Master William, why do we come here?"

"Because there will be more men at arms and archers seeking employment than almost anywhere else." I thought about the men who had served as the King's Guards. They would have been ideal but when we were dismissed we had all gone our own ways. They were good men but they could be serving anywhere. They all had skills and I did not doubt that they would have been employed quickly after our dismissal. It took three days to travel to London. I did not wish to thrash our horses and the time would allow Captain Tom to find my men.

London never failed to daunt me. It was so big and filled with so many people that I often thought it would burst. The King was not in the Tower. He was with his new bride at Windsor. I stayed away from the Tower. 'The Blue Company' was by the river. It was just two hundred paces from the bridge across the Thames. We had dismounted when we entered through the Newgate. Walking our horses was easier than riding through the throngs in the streets. We could keep them calmer and avoid having our heads struck by the signs which protruded into the streets. The inn had a stable. Leaving Peter outside with the horses I walked in.

I chose the wrong moment to enter. I saw one of the men who owned the inn, Tom. He lay on the ground. His head was bleeding. Another man, I could not see his face, also lay close by. I saw a pool of blood. John, the other owner, was in a crouched position and had a short sword in his hand. His left hand held a rondel dagger He was facing three men. They had leather jerkins and looked to be ex-soldiers. None saw me as I had just slipped into the room and stood in the shadows. This was like war and in war, you did not rush in. You assessed the situation first. There were just five other people inside. Three of them looked to be women of the tavern and the other two were older customers.

One of the men whose back was to me spoke, "Now then, old man, we have tried to be fair about this. You know the way these things work. You pay us and we make sure that your customers don't end up like that one there. Your mate was stupid. You might have been soldiers once but you aren't any more. This will get ugly. The two of you might just slip into the river and be never heard of again. All we want is half of your profits."

I slipped my ballock dagger from my belt. I was not wearing my arming sword. I had just brought my workaday short sword and it slid easily out of its scabbard. I moved from the darkness next to the door. John saw the movement and his eyes flickered to me. I shook my head slightly. John stood and lowered his weapons slightly. He shook his head, "How can we make a living if you are taking half of our profits?"

I took a step closer as the leader, the one in the centre laughed and said, "I don't give a cow's titty how you make a living, my friend. That is not our business. Our business is the collection of coin."

I put the edge of my sword under his ear, "Then my friend, you will know that the blade which is next to your ear is sharp and one push will end your life." I heard the door open behind me and I prayed that it was Peter and not another of the cutthroats.

The other two whipped around. I used my ballock dagger to slash across the sword hand of one of them. As John lunged at the other man the leader made the mistake of turning. I had not lied. My blade was sharp enough to shave with. It scored a line across his neck and then his throat. It was as though he was drowning in blood. I saw his hands go to his throat. His eyes widened and he gasped for air. He fell in a heap at my feet. It was a while since I had fought and my reactions were slow. The man whose hand I had slashed lunged at me with his dagger. Peter's short sword hacked deep into his neck. The man who had been stabbed by John lay on the ground trying to hold in his intestines.

"Peter, watch the door!"

"Aye, Master!"

John turned Tom over, "Angel, bandages!" One of the whores raced out to the back. "Well, Will Strongstaff, it seems that Tom and I are even more in your debt now and your fellow there."

"How is Tom?"

Tom opened his eyes, "Better for seeing you. I thought we had done with killing when we came back from Aquitaine."

I sheathed my weapons and went to the other man. As I turned him over I saw that he had but four fingers. When I saw his face, I saw that it was Harold Four Fingers. He had been one of my guards. I could not see a wound.

"What happened to Harold?"

"You know him?"

"He served under me when I was the King's bodyguard."

"When Cruel Jack, he is the one you killed, began to demand money your friend remonstrated with him. The one I slew," he kicked the writhing body, "smacked him on the back of the head with a cudgel."

I nodded, "What about the watch?"

"The men of the watch are useless. They would not dare to take on the gang. As for us?" John waved a hand at the handful of men in the tavern, "These are friends. They saw nothing. When it is dark we will weight their bodies and slip them into the river. It is one advantage of being so close to the river."

"Who are they?"

"We have had gangs before who tried to make us pay protection. We dealt with them but these arrived about a month ago. I am not sure how many are in their gang but they have control of four alehouses by the Cripplegate."

I bent down and picked up the leader's sword. It was an arming sword. It was a soldier's weapon. I checked his buskins. The leather boots showed no evidence that he had ever worn spurs. He was not a knight. I pulled down his jerkin and shirt. His neck was brown but his chest was white. He had come from hotter climes. Taking his purse, I emptied the coins. There were Castilian coins as well as French ones and one from Gascony. I saw that they all wore a cloak pin. It was a crudely cast skull.

"He could be from one of the Free Companies. If he has friends then you may be in danger."

Just then Harold Four Fingers groaned. He rubbed the back of his head. His eyes were closed as he said, "I must be slipping! Taken like that." Opening his eyes, he saw John. "Sorry friend, I thought I could talk them out of it."

I said, quietly, "Men like that only understand one thing Harold, cold steel."

His eyes widened, "Captain William! I never expected this."

I helped him to his feet. "John, how about ale for us?"

"First, Will, we will put these in the back room. Angel clear up the blood."

"Here I will help you." Peter put his hands beneath the shoulders of one of them and dragged him away.

Harold and I sat at a table. Angel had finished bandaging Tom's head and he sat with us. He poured ale from a jug. "What brings you here, Harold?"

"Work. I need an employer. I was working for a merchant. He dropped dead one day and his wife decided that it was my fault. I was thrown from the house and they owed me pay. That was a month since."

"Well, you are employed again."

"The King?"

"No, scutage. We go to Castile for six months and at the end of that time I am sure I can find work for you."

He raised his beaker, "Then my life is looking up!"

Once the floor was cleansed and night fell we disposed of the bodies. Their purses yielded coins which we shared. The weapons we took too. They had no horses and their clothes were too soiled to be of any use. After we had eaten I told them of my task. Harold gave me good news, "Captain, Wilfred of Loidis and Edgar of Derby are here in London. They have just finished working for Sir Richard Fitz William. They escorted his daughter to Southampton. They are also seeking employment. They are in the 'Earl Marshal' by the Tower."

"Then tomorrow we will seek them out."

"Why not tonight, Captain?"

"Tonight, we will be on watch. These three will be missed. Their comrades will wonder why they have not returned. They will know where they went and I am guessing they will come after you have shut up for the night." I saw them nodding. They were all soldiers and knew that the dark would suit attackers. "Do you know how many are in the gang, John?"

He shook his head, "I would guess less than ten. We have seen them walking around. I think they all wear that skull brooch you found. I have not seen many of them."

"Then tonight we keep watch. There are four of us and…"

Tom said, "There are five of us William! This is my home too and I am not going to let some piece of filth take it from us. The wound is nothing."

I nodded, "You have an upstairs?"

"Aye and a basement where we keep the ale."

"Then have your whores wait upstairs. This will be bloody."

In a well-run town or city, we would have been able to go to the mayor but John had told me that he was a corrupt man. His election had been fraudulent and he seemed to be trying to make as much coin as he could before King Richard turned his eye inwards. It did not help that Michael de la Pole was in charge of the finances of England. He was robbing all and so the mayor's theft went unnoticed. Why worry about a smaller thief when the King's Chancellor is stealing openly? It would be dangerous but if my old comrades in arms, John and Tom, were going to save their livelihood then the five of us would have to stop them.

Harold and I sat on either side of the front door. Tom sat next to the glow of the fire. Peter and John would hide at the side. Tom would be bait. They would see him when they entered through the door. We guessed that they would come soon after the last customer had left. Tom's practice was to go out, bar the stables from the inside and then return to the tavern before, finally, barring the main door. John and Tom thought that the attack would come once they had given Tom enough time to return back into the tavern. They would open the door and see him drinking ale by the fire. With their attention on him, they would enter. It would be up to John and me to deal with them once the last one had come through the door. We each had a dagger and a sword. I wore my mail as did John and Tom. Harold's was at the 'Earl Marshal' and Peter did not have any yet. I felt guilty that I would have protection while they would not.

The watch had been set when Tom went outside to lock the stables. The stable boy who looked after the stables left each day at sunset. Tom was bandaged and he limped. Cruel Jack's men would assume that their leader had been partly successful. As I took my place by the door I speculated about the events which would have followed the non-arrival of their leader. Someone would have taken charge. Cruel Jack would have taken hard men with him but someone would have been ready to take the reins. I had no doubt that one had been sent to spy out the tavern and, seeing that all appeared normal would have assumed that Cruel Jack's efforts had been in vain. Perhaps they had an arrangement with the Mayor and discovered that the three men had not been apprehended by the watch. The uncertainty would give us a slight edge but I was under no illusions. These were hardened bandits and criminals. They would show no mercy.

Tom came back in through the door. He said, loudly, "John I am going to have a warm by the fire and finish off my ale." To me, he said, quietly, "They are outside."

I said nothing. I had my sword and dagger on my lap. I put the sword on the table before me. My dagger would be an easier weapon to use at first. I caught sight of Harold on the other side of the door. The glow from the fire gave us enough light to see. Coming from the dark Cruel Jack's men would need time for their eyes to adjust to the relative brightness of the tavern. I had the hood of my cloak up and my cloak covered all but my hands and dagger. I was hiding in plain sight. Red Ralph had taught me how to do this. I controlled my breathing and I listened.

I heard, from beyond the door, the sound of murmuring. I could not make out words nor how far the speakers were from the door but they were close. I caught the sound of the faintest jingle of metal. Daggers and swords slid silently from leather and wooden scabbards. Metal meant helmets or mail. I doubted that they would walk the streets of London with helmets. Someone was wearing mail. I smelled one of them before they entered. There was the hint of a perfumed aroma. Some French men affected such smells. They used oils infused with herbs to shape their beards. The door opened slowly. There was the slightest of creaks.

Tom played his part well. He had looked as though he was dozing. He raised his head and said, "Is that you, John?"

The would-be killers raced across the tavern. We had placed the tables to make obstacles. Two had passed me when I slid my leg out and two men fell to the floor. I stood. A fifth stood in the doorway. There was no one behind him and he turned to flee. I used my left hand to grab the coif about his neck and pull him back into the room. He hit the two men who were struggling to rise from the floor. I heard the clash of metal on metal as John, Tom and Peter dealt with the two who had first raced into the room. Harold brought his sword down on the back of one of the men trying to rise. I swung my boot and connected with the jaw of a second. The third drew his sword and swung it at me. As I had suspected a sword was not the best of weapons for a room with a low ceiling. The tip caught on the ceiling and my left hand was able to grab his wrist. I brought up my dagger. It came up under the short hauberk the man was wearing and tore up into his ribs. I must have struck something vital for he went limp in my hand and fell to the floor.

I switched hands with my dagger and grabbed my sword. The one I had kicked in the head was rising and I pricked my sword into the side of his neck, "You have to ask yourself the question, friend, can I manage to hurt this man whose sword is already cutting into my neck or should I surrender? Let us see just how clever you are. Drop your weapons and put your hands on top of your head!"

The man who had been struck by Harold lay on the ground. He was moaning. The other two were dead. Tom lit a candle and the room became brighter. "Anyone hurt?"

No one answered but the five of us were still standing. I gestured with my sword, "On your feet." He rose and I saw that he was almost as tall as me and was muscular. My kick had broken his nose and he was missing teeth. His eyes glowered at me. "What do they call you?" He said nothing. "Let me explain something to you, my friend, your life and that of your companion here are in our hands. Cruel Jack is gone." His eyes widened. "Ah, you did not know that. He and the other two are now feeding the river fish in the Thames. Three of your companions are going to join them. Two more will not bother us. With a hauberk like that, you will sink to the bottom so I ask again, what is your name?" To emphasize my point, I put the dagger's tip to his eye.

"Alan of Southwark."

"And him?" I pointed to the man on the floor.

"Jacko."

"Good. You may yet live although I have not made that decision. Which of you was chosen to be the leader when Cruel Jack did not return?" He pointed to the man who had first come through the door. I saw that he had a well-groomed beard. He was French. "The Frenchman?"

He looked surprised, "Yes, Philippe of Poitou."

"And how many of your gang are left?" he hesitated. "And we were getting on so well." I suddenly moved the dagger down to press into his groin. You can still talk without your manhood. As you can see we will have to clean the floor anyway." The one who had been hit by Harold still groaned. "What is amiss with that one?"

Harold shrugged, "I fear my blow did not break flesh Captain. It did break bones."

"So he may die too." Harold nodded. "Perhaps it will not be worth our while to keep you alive. Tom, strip the mail and weapons from the Frenchman and his companions. It is dark and they can join Cruel Jack. This one will join them soon enough."

"No, no, let me live and I will tell you all."

"Carry on Tom. So, you were saying?"

"There are six left. They are in the inn called 'The Saddle'. It is between The Cheap and Cripplegate."

I surmised that they would be the weaker members of the gang. I nodded. "Take off your mail, your sword belt and your buskins."

I removed the dagger and stood back. He took off his belt. The scabbard was decorated but it had seen hard wear. This man had been a soldier. The hauberk was an old one and I saw that some of the links had been damaged. This man had fallen on hard times. Perhaps that was why he had fallen in with Cruel Jack. His buskins, however, were well made. I pointed to a chair, "Sit there. Peter bind his hands and feet to the chair."

Harold had rolled over the injured man. He looked up in terror at Harold, "I cannot feel my feet! Where are my legs?"

Harold said, gently, "I fear that my blow has injured something in your back. Can you move your arms?" The man called Jacko raised them. Harold nodded, "Then you can live. So long as you can use your hands then you can make a living."

"Doing what?"

"I know not but you will no longer prey on others that is for certain and you will need the help of another." Harold looked at me. "I know that if I was in such a situation then I have friends who would watch over me as I would watch over them. You choose your friends carefully in this life."

The watch had been set and there was no point in leaving while it was dark. "All of you, get some sleep. I will take the first watch. Peter will relieve me." The man who could not walk began to weep. "Stop that! You are a man. If you wish a warrior's death then ask now and I will give it to you. Otherwise, reflect upon your sins and how you can change your life!" He became silent.

The others curled up and slept. I sheathed my dagger but kept my sword on the table. Alan of Southwark asked, "What will happen to me?"

I shrugged, "That depends upon you. You were a soldier once?" he nodded. "Then, at some time you had honour. If, when we have visited 'The Saddle', you swear to leave London and never to return then I will let you go."

"Without weapons, mail and buskins? Kill me now!"

"Those will be returned to you when you have sworn and we have dealt with those in 'The Saddle'."

"What is there for me then?"

"There are men like you all over this land. Harold here was a soldier and he has fallen on hard times. He did not resort to brigandry! All men make choices. Whether they are good or bad depend upon what is in here." I tapped my heart. "Reflect on that!"

Chapter 3

We left as soon as the horn sounded and the watch was set down. We put Jacko in a cart. I returned all but the sword to Alan of Southwark and he pulled the cart. It was early and the only people about were those hurrying to the Cheap to begin work. We were ignored. 'The Saddle' lay north of the Roman thoroughfare, Watling Street. They had not kept a good watch for we had to bang upon the door. When it was opened I burst in closely followed by Harold who brought Alan of Southwark with us. The man before me was in a sleeping shift. I shouted, "I am William Strongstaff come now and you will live. If we have to seek you out then you will die!"

A couple of men appeared and three women. One man looked old and grey. I did not think he was a member of the gang. "Who are you?"

John said, "That is Old Peter. This is his inn."

"Who are you, sir?"

"We are rat catchers and today, Old Peter, we rid you of the vermin who have infested your inn. Harold, Tom, John, go and find the rest of the gang."

One of the men who had appeared from the back tried to run. Peter's hand swung and knocked him to the ground. He did not move. Old Peter clapped his hands and kicked the man in the ribs for good measure. The rest of the gang proved to be four sorry looking characters who came into the room in their breeks. They were not the warriors. They were the ones who fetched and carried. We had slain the warriors. I sheathed my sword. "Your days in London are finished. Outside in a cart is another of your company. Take him and leave London. I will be here for another couple of days and if I see you then I will have you given the brand of a malefactor. You have the opportunity to regain some dignity in your life. Start anew." I turned to Alan of Southwark. I had his sword and scabbard in my hand. "Your mail is on the cart. Do you swear on your sword that you will quit London?"

"You do not ask that I swear not to seek revenge?"

I smiled, "Feel free to seek revenge for I see nothing about you to make me fear you. In fact, if you wish we will try a bout now? What say you?" I handed him his sword.

He shook his head, "I know my limitations. I swear that I will quit London. More, I will quit England!"

"Then, in future, make better choices."

There were other members of the gangs in the other two inns the gang controlled. After we left 'The Saddle' we visited them too. They were soon evicted and control returned to their landlords. The ten men who fled were opportunists who had latched on to Cruel Jack and been privy to the breadcrumbs he threw their way.

The three landlords tried to press money into my palm. I shook my head, "I helped out two old friends and their friends. Next time, I would keep a sword handy and defend what is yours. Tom and John can teach you how to use weapons. Band together. If you were a guild you would have the protection of colleagues." I saw realisation fill their faces. They had power if they were of one mind.

Peter, Harold and I left them and walked across the city to 'The Earl Marshal'. Edgar and Wilfred had been concerned when Harold had not returned. When they saw the two of us they were overjoyed. Of course, they were more than happy to join me. It meant employment and guaranteed pay. More than that they knew that they would be well led. We moved their war gear to 'The Blue Company'. I had been delayed but now I could begin my search for ten archers and seven more men at arms.

Fate had taken a hand and our action in dealing with Cruel Jack and his gang yielded unexpected results. Word spread about the trio of handy warriors who had rid the city of bandits. I dare say the Mayor heard too but he was too wily to risk confrontation. Publicly he spoke of how the city had been cleansed of criminals. He took credit for our actions. He was a typical politician. I would not be in the city long enough to risk his wrath. Four warriors arrived at the tavern late in the afternoon. They wore the signs of their trade. They each had a pot helmet over their shoulder and a shield slung on their back. Their swords and daggers were well maintained. One had a mail hauberk. The others wore aketons beneath brigandines. That told me much. A brigandine was a leather faced canvas jacket lined with metal. It was almost as effective as mail. These were warriors. Their buskins were scuffed and badly worn. They had walked more than they had ridden. We would need horses for all of them. I had not considered that problem.

"Captain, we have heard you seek men at arms to serve in Castile. We would like the opportunity to serve with you."

"How do you know me?"

It was the sergeant with the mail who answered me, "I knew you in Aquitaine. I was with the White Company. I remember you at the battle of the bridge at Lussac. We heard in the tavern that you were in the city and that you had bested Cruel Jack."

"How did you know him?" I was suspicious. Had these four been part of the gang?

"He approached us when we reached London a month since. He robbed us of our horses and made life hard. He wanted us for his gang but we are not bandits."

"Did you not appeal to the city council?"

Another of them snorted, "They are just bandits who wear fine clothes. I swear, Captain, there are more thieves in London than honest folk. I would I were gone from here."

"Then fetch your war gear and I will draw up the contracts."

Peter nodded, "They look like good fellows, Master."

"Aye and I think we will get no more here. I have seen neither hide nor hair of an archer. The city is the wrong place to find them. Mayhap Captain Tom has had more luck in Lincoln." I decided to head straight back to Lincoln. I had seven of the men I needed. I had not yet tried to find men locally around the county. I drew up a contract. Tom had parchment and quill. Not all of them could write but I read it and they made their marks. The four new men: Joseph Woodman, David of Welshpool, Natty Longjack and Geoffrey of Gisburn had all served in France and Aquitaine. Most had returned to England when the work dried up.

"You will need horses but I will fetch those when I come to Southampton." I took out eight shillings. "Here is a shilling each. Harold Four Fingers I give you two. Walk the men to Southampton and I will join you there in fourteen nights. You need not leave straightaway. I will pay John and Tom for your accommodation. We took boots from the men we slew. If they fit you then take them. There are also weapons. They are yours. I will see you in Southampton."

"I will be there Captain as will the others. Have no fear."

Peter and I left London but this time we rode and people moved out of our way. All had heard of the confrontation. No one spoke openly about it but it appeared to be common knowledge. Those who had liked Cruel Jack made certain they kept their distance and the ones who had feared the gang kept away for they did not want to be singled out after we had left. The name Strongstaff and the blue surcoat would be remembered in London. I wondered how many knew that I was the same Will Strongstaff who had been King Richard's bodyguard.

"You did well, Peter."

He nodded, "I enjoyed it, Master. It has been many years since I was called upon to fight. It is good to know that I have not forgotten those skills."

"That you have not and Peter, call me Captain. I have never owned another person in my life."

"Aye Captain and it rolls off the tongue easier."

Now that we had some of the men I needed I felt easier in my own mind. I was almost halfway there and I hoped that Captain Tom would be able to deliver the rest. We managed the journey back to Lincoln in three days. Captain Tom was in the middle of an inevitable story. His back was to us and so we stood in the doorway and listened. It was the story of me at the Bridge of Lussac. Each time he told it the numbers we had killed grew and the death of Sir John Chandos took longer. When he had finished I clapped, "I should like to meet this Colossus. He sounds like a formidable fighter."

"William!" He shrugged as he stood, "What can I say? If the story changes then it is because I look at it through time's glass. Were you successful?"

I handed my cloak to Peter who followed Dolly up the stairs, "We were but the tale is so interesting that I will tell you with a beaker of ale!"

Peter had come down from the room and joined us by the time I had finished. He nodded, "I have heard about such gangs. They would not try it here for there are fewer inns and we have a good watch. I fear, however, that I have not done as well as you. The Earl of Derby and Northampton has already taken all of the men at arms who might have served with you. However, I do have eight archers who are willing to serve but there is a problem."

"What kind?"

"They are outlaws."

Since the Charter of the Forests had been signed almost a century and a half ago there had been far less need for men to resort to outlawry. I frowned.

Captain Tom held up his hand. "They have good reasons for their choice. They served with Sir Richard de Montfort in the campaigns we fought for the Black Prince."

"I remember de Montfort. I never liked him. He was a mean-spirited man. He was a leader who led from the rear."

"Aye, well he had a manor at Bolsover and when he returned he said his archers had not served him well enough in the campaign and he dismissed them, without pay. Even worse, when they appealed to the Bishop of Lincoln, he took their lands from them as punishment."

"And he got away with it?"

"He is a friend of Robert de Vere. The archers were forced to flee to the forests which lie north of here. That was three years since. Many have left the life and the forests but there are nine there still. They live not far from the hamlet of Askham."

"And how do you know them?"

"Their captain, John of Nottingham, was a friend of mine. He died last year. These last nine visit my inn. They know that they are safe here and I look after them." He shrugged. "It was not right what de Montfort did to them. I would have mentioned them before now but I wanted to be sure they would serve. They have had enough of life in the forest. They see this as a chance to redeem themselves and make a fresh start. Six months would allow them to do that."

I nodded, "When can I meet with them?"

"They will be here tomorrow after dark."

"I will take your word for their suitability and if they will serve then I will take them but we shall need horses. You know what Castile is like."

"I know a horse trader. He lives just outside Lincoln. They may well be little more than sumpters."

"Then that will have to do. If we can get rouncys so much the better."

"Has Sir Robert given you the coin for the animals yet?"

"No, I still have coins we took from the bandits. I will get it back."

The aptly named Ralph the Horse proved to be more than helpful. He had a surplus and that might have been the reason. He was too far from the embarkation port of Southampton to make real money and the midlands and north were both quiet. Horses were expensive. The country was still recovering from the plague. I bought four sumpters and eight rouncys. He only had eight spare saddles. That was not a problem. There was a saddler close to the castle. They just had to be a simple one. Archers rode to war and then dismounted to fight.

The archers did not arrive until after dark. They did not bring their bows and each came hooded and cloaked. They wore simple galoches on their feet. They were home-made and wooden, carved from the timber of the forests, and their tunics and breeks were well darned. These men had seen hard times. They all looked lean and fit. Their skins were a nutty brown and each of them moved gracefully despite the wooden shoes. Captain Tom had a small room he kept for nobles or gentlemen who stayed in the inn and required privacy. We used it and Peter stood guard on the door. He sat with Dolly on his knee but he was alert to any who might eavesdrop.

Their leader was a man who had cropped hair. He was also the biggest of them and he spoke after I had introduced myself and told them what was required. "Captain, I am Stephen the Tracker. John of Nottingham was my elder brother and I have led the band since then. We came back from the wars over twenty-five strong. We are all that is left and we deserve more. We had a treacherous lord and we should not be punished for his perfidy."

"No, you should not. If you accept this scutage then I can guarantee pay and food for six months. I hope that we can continue after that but I am a man of my word and I will not promise that which I cannot deliver."

"Captain Tom has told us about you and we have heard your name. Six months will let us become men again. We will not have to hide and eke out a living. We will not have to wear wooden shoes nor darn our clothes. We will drink ale more than once a month!"

"Then I will shake each man's hand and tomorrow we ride to my home. You will be well fed and I will have you clothed by Sir Robert."

Each man came in turn and said his name. The handshake was more than a gesture. These were archers and the handshake they gave to me were promises. To them, the handshake was as sacred as an oath.

"Stephen the Tracker. I lead this band."

"Alan of the Wood."

"Jack War Bag."

"Simon the Traveller."

"Lol son of Wilson."

"Walter Longridge."

"Silent David."

"Garth of Worksop."

"James Warbow."

The one who stood out was Silent David. He was a huge man. I am tall and broad but he was taller and broader. I learned that he could send an arrow fifty paces further than any other of the archers. Yet he rarely spoke. We spent an hour getting to know one another. We drank ale and I paid for food. They had gear to fetch from the woods and would not be back until noon the next day. Some had swords. Some had hand axes. All had daggers. Two still had helmets from the wars but all had caps. Most important were their war bows, arrows and arrow bags. As Stephen the Tracker told me they had neither war arrows nor bodkins. They had been reusing and repairing the hunting arrows. That would be the first task. We would need shafts and feathers as well as heads. They would have to fletch enough arrows to take with us. We would get none in Castile.

It took three days to reach my home. I knew that the archers, following our words on the ride home, were not expecting a castle. They knew that I was just a gentleman. When they saw the extent of my buildings they were impressed. Stephen the Tracker nodded, "And you were just one of the Blue Company?" I nodded. "Then there is hope for some of us. I thought Captain Tom was as high as a man could go but you have gone further." Tom saw us returning and ran to greet me. He was still not as coordinated as I might have liked. He often fell when he ran and so I reined in and handed my reins to Peter. "Take the men to the barn."

"Aye Captain."

I swept Tom up. He stared in awe at the archers. "Are they your men?"

I nodded, "I will lead them, for a while at least."

He whispered in my ear, "They have no mail and they look poor!"

I said, equally quietly, "They are but that is not their fault. Your mother has a couple of days to fatten them up and for me to make them look less like vagabonds."

We walked to my hall. The new buildings were all finished and I saw that Stephen the Tracker had been correct. I had come far. Who knew how much further I might travel?

I heard my wife shouting commands to the two servants as I entered the house. Alice was now crawling and when I put Tom down he ran to stop her climbing up the wooden chair which lay close to the fire. I knelt down and picked her up. She rubbed her hands in my beard and giggled, "Now then trouble! I can see we shall have to have a halter for you."

She made a sound which my wife said was dada. It did not sound like the mama she used for Eleanor and so she might have been correct. Eleanor came in from the kitchen. Her hands were covered in flour. She leaned up and kissed me. "You have found men?"

"I have some, almost all of them, in Southampton. These nine are my archers. We have but three days at home and then I must go to the muster."

She nodded, "Make sure you have the coins from Sir Robert before you leave."

I laughed, "You should have been born a reeve!"

"The plague took everything, husband. I shall not allow my family to suffer." Her eyes became sad. "Anne of Stonebrook died three days since. We buried her yesterday. You should see Dick, her husband." She shook her head. "I played with Anne when we were children. I fear that when she lost the child she lost the will to live. I pray that her husband does not follow her. He is in low spirits. He is speaking of giving up the tenancy."

I nodded, "I will visit with him. I will go with Peter and after I have spoken with Sir Robert I will spend some time with Dick. Is Sir Robert still at Towcester?" She nodded. "It may be dark before I return. The leader of the archers is Stephen the Tracker. He is a good man but these archers have lived rough. They were outlaws in the forests around Worksop."

She made the sign of the cross, "Poor men. If you will let me get about my work then they will be fed. Tom, watch your sister. If she falls in the fire then you shall be punished."

"Yes, mother!"

I took Star from the stable. My former warhorse was now too old for war but a short ride to Towcester might be just the thing for him. "Come, Peter."

"Aye, Captain."

We reached Towcester sooner than I might have hoped. Star enjoyed the opportunity to gallop. Peter's poor horse had already ridden far that day and was lathered and sweaty when we arrived. Master Henry must have spied us from afar. He came to the gatehouse. I could see that some of the older buildings had already been demolished.

"Well?"

"Well, Captain."

"Sorry, well, Captain? Did you succeed?"

"We have men. Is your grandfather within?"

"He is."

I told Sir Robert of the men I had recruited but not the manner nor their stories. He did not need to know. "Can they be paid fifteen pennies a day, my lord?"

"Aye."

"I have laid out money for twelve horses but I will need another six at least. I should have eight in case I manage to get another sergeant and archer."

Sir Robert said, "Peter, tomorrow I would have you ride to my tenant Thomas of Towcester. Tell him that in lieu of service to me he can provide eight good horses otherwise he will do service as an archer."

"Aye, lord."

"The men I lead are yours, Sir Robert, and should be attired accordingly. The Earl may already be unhappy that he does not have knights to follow his banner. We should ensure that they are all dressed well."

"I have already thought of it. When do you leave?"

"In three days."

"Then I will send over the tunics in two days' time. I have ten surcoats being made for the sergeants. They are pale blue and yellow with my crest and the archers have the halved tunics also in blue and yellow. I have pale blue archers' caps for them. Will that do?" I knew not how to mention the fact that they needed leather shoes nor that I was short of saddles. There also remained the question of arrows. He smiled, "Do not be shy with me, Captain William. I know that war is expensive. I have a duty. I am no warrior and if men go to fight on my behalf the least I can do is to make sure that they have the equipment." He took coins from his purse. "Here is ten pounds. Use this for whatever else you need."

"Thank you, lord. The men will need arrows. And you, Master Henry, are you equipped?"

He nodded, "Aye Captain and I am ready to come now."

His grandfather shook his head, "Your grandmother wishes to make the most of each moment. You and Peter can take the surcoats and tunics in two days."

He nodded.

As I prepared to take my leave I said, "And you, Master Henry, have two days to continue with your exercises and training for once we reach Southampton then we are warriors for the working day!"

I headed towards Stonebrook as the sun began to lower in the sky. I reached it at dark and the farm was already in darkness. It looked abandoned. I led Star to the trough and tied my horse there to drink. I shouted, "Richard of Stonebrook, it is William Strongstaff. Are you within?"

The door opened and I saw that my tenant farmer had been weeping. "Aye, sir, I am within but not for long."

I said, "I am sorry for your loss. What will you do?"

He shook his head, "I cannot stay here. I pray you release me from my tenancy. If I stayed here then the sadness would eat away my heart and I would not wish such a slow death."

I saw, in the corner of the desolately empty room, his war bow. I spied hope for both him and for me. My father had been torn apart from within. He had been deeply unhappy and that was because of a wife. If I could save Richard from such a life I would do all in my power. "You are an archer are you not, Dick?"

"Aye, sir. I served for six months with Sir James of Buckingham. Why?"

"I have need of an archer for six months. We go to Castile. It pays fifteen pennies a day."

He said, "The pennies do not interest me. Castile? Is that abroad?"

"It is in Spain."

"Then I would be far from here. I would have no memories to tear at me. I would not have to look at the green trees and the brooks. I would not see an English sunrise. I will join you, sir. I may find some relief there from the pain which eats me from within."

I looked around. "I think it best if you leave this night. The others are in my barn. Fetch your gear. Your new life starts this night."

He nodded, "Aye, sir, and I hope that the next tenant has more good fortune than I did. I lost a child and a wife on this farm. I leave it and my name. I am no longer Richard Stonebrook. I shall be Dick Stone Heart for that is how I shall be."

As we left to walk through the dark to my hall I hoped that I would be able to change both him and his mind. My father had found redemption at the end. I would try to give Dick a new life which would save his soul.

Chapter 4

Sir Robert was as good as his word. The pale blue and yellow tunics, along with the caps and arrows arrived with Henry. He had a sumpter to carry his war gear as did Peter. I had bought the leather and my archers had made their own shoes as well as arm protectors and archers' gloves. There was enough left for Stephen the Tracker to make a leather arrow bag. The others used canvas ones. When my wife discovered how much the leather had cost me she determined to tan our own hides. She was ever practical. Dick's recovery began as soon as he met the other archers. He learned of men who had had misfortune which was almost as bad as his and discovered that they could recover. For their part, they were pleased to have another archer in their ranks. We left for Southampton. Stonebrook would remain empty for there were no other tenants. Eleanor determined to hire men to work it. She saw the opportunity to make even more coin.

"Come back safe, husband. You are of little use as a farmer but your wife and children need you."

"And you take care. May God watch over you all."

And then we were gone on the one-hundred-mile ride to Southampton. Master Henry was excited. He wore my surcoat rather than his grandfather's. I wondered how his grandfather felt and then I realised that it had been Henry's father who had been the warrior. When Henry became a knight, he would have his own livery. He was riding better these days. He had realised it was an important skill. His sword work had improved but he could not use a lance at all. He seemed unable to coordinate his shield and the lance along with a horse. That training would need to wait until after we had fulfilled our contract. He led Goldheart and that helped his training. My courser did not like being led and Henry had to learn to give commands to a war horse. Peter led our sumpters. He, alone out of our company, had no livery. His faded red cloak covered his tunic and mail.

My archers wore their new tunics but they too were covered in a faded cloak. The former outlaws had used natural dyes and their cloaks were a muddy green. In the woodland, they would be hidden. Sir Robert had meant well buying arrows but I knew that my archers would rather have made their own. Livery arrows were unpopular because they were mass produced by men who did not have to rely on them. I had purchased some shafts for them. Most were poplar although some were good ash which my archers preferred. We had goose feathers and we had bodkin and warheads. My men would only fit the heads when we knew the target and the heads would be held in by wax. I had served with the Free Companies in Spain and I knew that arrows became as valuable as gold. If we could recover the arrows then new heads could easily be fashioned. We had also purchased a number of hemp strings. The archers kept these under their hats. We had spares of all that we needed now. Our spare sumpters carried the arrows and feathers. We had a long voyage which would take at least eight days. The archers had more than enough time to fletch their arrows. My only worry was the lack of swords. We would need to buy some but I remembered that Spain had better swords and, normally, they were less expensive than in England. Dick Stone Heart rode next to Peter. He was melancholic. Peter's humour and stories helped Dick to dwell less on his dead wife.

Henry bombarded me with questions. My father would have given me a clip or worse for annoying him but I remembered Peter the Priest and Red Ralph. They had been patient and answered all of my questions. I had to explain the hierarchy of a campaign. I was just above the sergeants and men at arms. My men would call me Captain but often the archers would be taken from me to form massed banks of bowmen and I would not lead them. I think he was disappointed that I would not be privy to the counsels of the lords. I think he believed that a campaign would be well organised. He saw long columns of men marching with precision. Nothing could be further from the truth. Armies moved from one town to the other as best they could. Some would be given the most unpopular of tasks, guarding the baggage train. Stuck at the back with the slowest animals and surrounded by horseshit and piss it was a duty my men would not enjoy. The Blue Company had been with the vanguard. Although more dangerous it was more popular. The vanguard reached towns, water, shade and treasure faster than others.

I explained to him how he should address others. He would be called sir as he was an esquire. All above him would either be captain or my lord.

"I would that I was a knight! How long will it take?"

"Your grandfather could knight you now." He brightened. "I would tell him no. You are too inexperienced and would die in your first battle. If you have to draw your sword on this campaign then I fear I will not earn the bounty for your survival. You watch and you learn. You see how others control their horses, use their shields and swords. A battle is a frightening place. It is not like a tourney. There are no rules. You do all that you can to survive."

"And what of ransom?"

"It is for fools. While you wonder if you can disarm your opponent he kills you. If they surrender all well and good but otherwise, if you have to fight, fight to kill."

Our last stop was at Newbury. We had not stayed in inns each night. Some were too expensive and others were full. The roads were filled with men heading to the muster. We were tired for we had ridden over thirty miles. We were close to Bishop's Clere when I felt the horses were getting too weary to continue. There was a small village close by and normally they would not have had an inn with stables. This one, perhaps because of the Bishop of Winchester's residence, did. It did not look large but there was a barn and a stable. We later learned that an enterprising farmer had added the inn to his farm. There were just two horses in the stables and I entered to negotiate a price for the night. I took Henry with me.

I had just stepped into the warm and inviting inn when a familiar voice said, "Captain William! What brings you here?"

I saw, by the fire, Roger of Chester who had been a guard with me. Another sergeant sat opposite. "Roger of Chester! This is well met! I take a band of sergeants and archers to the Earl of Derby and Northampton's muster."

"Then this is truly well met."

I saw the farmer-landlord hovering close by, "I have men and horses. We need beds and stables."

He shook his head. These fine fellows have one of my rooms. I have another. It could accommodate two as for the rest…"

"How much to sleep in the barn?" He made the mistake of hesitating. I said, quickly, "A groat for the stables and barn what say you?"

"Aye, sir."

"We will need food too but I will account for that at the time. Henry, go and tell the men they sleep in the barn. You and I will share the room. When you have seen to the horses then you can join me."

Roger had stood and clasped my arm. "It is good that you are heading for the muster, Captain."

"You are heading to Southampton too?"

He nodded, "This is John Bowland. He is also a sergeant at arms. We fell in together in Chester. I was visiting my family."

I waved the innkeeper over. "Ale for us and also for my men when they enter. I will settle at the end."

He saw I did not wear spurs and he said, "Yes, sir."

"Sit, Roger." I took in his threadbare cloak and buskins which had seen better days. John of Bowland looked little better. "You have a lord to serve?"

They both shook their heads. "To speak truthfully, Captain, since I left the King's Guards I have had little luck or perhaps it was poor judgement choosing a lord to follow. I was in Chester as I was able to help my parents around the farm and I was fed."

I looked at John Bowland. He shrugged. "My lord was from Lancaster and we were ambushed by Scottish cattle raiders. He fell from his horse and broke his neck. We beat off the cattle raiders and recovered his cattle but his wife blamed us, his men, for his poor horsemanship. She let us go without the money we were owed. When we appealed the Sheriff threatened us with imprisonment. I headed south and met Roger. We heard of this muster and thought to seek a lord."

"I am no lord but as Captain, I can offer you fifteen pennies a day for forty days and then thirty-seven shillings and six pennies for each month after that." In truth, I had yet to negotiate with the Earl but we were only bound for forty days from the moment we boarded the ship.

Roger said, "For my part, I will take your hand Captain. I know you for an honest man and as good a warrior as I have met."

John of Bowland nodded his agreement, "And I will take the handshake, Captain."

I shook their hands, "I have surcoats in our baggage. You fight under the colours of Sir Robert Armistead, Baron of Stratford. His son is my squire. I am training him to be a knight."

Roger smiled, "Scutage! That was what we hoped. And which lord do we serve?"

"The Earl of Derby and Northampton. You know him as Henry Bolingbroke, the King's cousin."

He frowned, "Did I not hear that they had fallen out?"

"Let us not worry about that. You and I know, Roger, that the Royal Household is a treacherous place. The Earl of Oxford and Michael de la Pole are the two counsellors who wield the real power."

John Bowland lowered his voice, "I have heard of English lords who oppose the Earl and the Chancellor."

"Do not tread down that road, John Bowland."

"It was common talk in the inns of York. I tried there before Chester. Thomas of Woodstock, the Earl of Arundel and Thomas de Beauchamp, the Earl of Warwick are involved. Thomas Woodstock is

Duke of Gloucester and the King's uncle. They do not oppose the King but his chief ministers."

Suddenly Henry Bolingbroke's decision to go to Castile and help his father made greater sense than before. He would distance himself from any hint of rebellion. He aspired to be King. "I will thank you not to mention such things before my squire. He is young and impressionable. All of us need to serve in Castile. We may have differing reasons but the purpose is the same. I speak no treason."

I heard the noise from outside as my men entered. With ale and food inside them and the prospect of just one more night in England, it was a merry gathering. Henry sat and listened. He was amongst warriors. They exchanged stories of campaigns and battles in which they had fought., They spoke of weapons they had used.

Only Dick Stone Heart remained silent. He just drank. I sat next to him, "Eat, Richard. That is a command. I cannot have an archer who cannot draw a bow."

"Never fear, Captain, I will not let you down."

"Then eat! It is good food and I have eaten in Spain. The food there is not the same. Make the most of good food while you can."

He nodded and ate. I caught the eye of Stephen the Tracker. While my former tenant ate I went to speak to my chief archer. "He is a troubled man, Captain." I told him his tale. He looked again at Dick. "He is one of ours now. We will tease him from his troubles. My father's heart was broken when my mother died of the plague. He went to the brink. I would not have another suffer as he did."

As I lay down to sleep that night I reflected that the Good Lord had sent me men of character. I had men who were of one heart and that was good. When things became hard in Castile then our fellows were all we had.

As we rode into Southampton during the late afternoon we looked less like brigands and outlaws. Wearing their new liveries, they rode proudly through the streets to the harbour. I saw the standard of the Earl of Derby and Northampton at the castle. I had, in my saddlebags, a letter for the Earl. It explained Sir Robert's commitment. Sir Walter of Blecheley, Sir Richard d'Issy and Sir Ralph Fitzjohn had all sent scutage money to the Earl. I had thought it was both foolish and lazy. The cost of men would have been less than the money they paid to the Earl. If the men died in the campaign the lords would have saved themselves the money. I had their money on a sumpter. I rode at the fore and it was I who was recognised by Harold Four Fingers. He waved me over to an inn.

"Here, Captain!"

We reined in at 'The Scallop'. It was an old inn and I could not see a stable. I dismounted and handed my reins to Henry. "No stables, Harold?"

He shook his head, "Sorry, Captain, all the inns with stables are full. Southampton is fit to burst. It is lucky that some of the ships sail on Saturday."

I frowned, "But I was told we had another fourteen days before we left."

"Aye, Captain, but a rider came in yesterday morning and went directly to the castle. It was as though someone had smacked a wasp nest. The Earl's herald came galloping down here. We have a good position here and heard most of it. We can't find out why they are leaving early but half the ships will be going then."

"Then where do we put our horses?"

"There is a field just a hundred paces down the river. The farmer will let you keep them there for a groat a day."

"We will need a watch."

"I will arrange that, Captain. Did you get all the men you needed?"

"I am one sergeant short."

He grinned, "You are not. We found Robert son of Tom when we were on the road. You remember him from the Guard?" I nodded. "He had fallen on hard times and was acting as a whore's watchdog in an inn in Andover. He threw in with us. He is inside now."

I clapped him on the back, "You are the best of fellows." I turned, "Henry, fetch the horse with the chest. I would be rid of it. Roger, Stephen the Tracker, Harold will tell you where to tether the horses. Do not wait for me to eat. I daresay the Earl will have a lowly Captain such as myself cooling his heels."

As we wound our way to the castle I counselled Henry. "You are a squire. You say nothing and keep your ears open. If you are asked a question feign that you are simple. The creatures amongst whom we go are dangerous."

"Yes, Captain."

The roads were packed. Whatever news had been brought had begun the embarkation. I saw chests on carts trundling down to the waiting fleet. From the inn, I had seen that every berth was taken and there were others waiting at anchor. John of Gaunt had to have hired or commandeered every ship on the south coast. The Cinque Ports would be ruing their special position for they were obliged to provide ships. I vaguely recognised some of the men heading to the ships. One or two had been men at arms I had known but there were others I had met

when I had been the Captain of the King's Guard. Then I had been a
man of importance and now I was just a gentleman.

The sentry who rose did not recognise me. "Your business sir?" His
companion sat in the guard room warming his hands on the brazier.

"I am one of the Earl's tenants here to speak with him. I have a letter
for him and I have coin."

The sentry nodded slyly. "Then leave your name, your letter and
your chest. I will see that the Earl gets them, sir."

I leaned forward, "Do not take me for a fool. Tell the Earl that
William Strongstaff of Stony Stratford is here to speak with him."

I wondered if he would dismiss me but he must have seen the steel
in my eye. He was part of the garrison. He was not going to war and, as
such, was not a warrior. He was an elevated member of the watch. He
nodded, "Nym, go and tell the Captain that we have a Will…"

"William Strongstaff."

"Aye, sorry, sir, William Strongstaff to speak with the Earl."

I dismounted, "Dismount your horse, Henry, and pass me the chest."
He gave me the chest and I gave him Jack's reins.

A sergeant led a line of carts from the outer ward, "Mind, sir."

We stepped back to the bridge and watched the ten carts wend their
way down to the river. I saw that these were barrels of food. It took time
for them to pass. When they were gone we re-entered the barbican.
Nym puffed his way to us. He was overweight. He spent too long sitting
in the guard room. "Follow me, sir."

He led us across the outer ward and through the gate to the inner
ward. I saw a pursuivant waiting for us. The young man waved for Nym
to depart. "If you leave your horses and this fellow here, sir, then I will
take you to the Earl. I am sorry that you were delayed."

I saw Henry colour. I said, "Take no offence at this popinjay's
words. That is all that they do. They talk, retire and then real men do the
fighting." I turned and saw that the pursuivant was now red-faced. He
could not meet my eye.

Henry said, "Thank you, Captain."

I smiled as we made our way through the castle for the slightly built
young man had to move out of the way of those coming along the
corridor. I wore mail and I was a big man. They avoided me. We
reached an antechamber. Inside the hall, I saw the great and the good. I
recognised John of Gaunt and several other Earls. There were also
Castilian and Portuguese lords. "Wait here, sir, and I will fetch the
Earl."

Henry Bolingbroke had grown since I had last seen him. I had
trained both cousins when they had been squires. Now both King

Richard and his cousin Henry were Knights of the Garter. I was not sure of my reception. Henry and King Richard, famously, did not get on. I suspected that de Vere had encouraged the rift. When the Earl smiled and grasped me about the shoulders I was surprised. "Will Strongstaff! You came!"

"I was summoned, lord."

"Come let us away from this cacophony of cockerels. I need to speak with you!" He led me down the corridor to a second antechamber. There was one page seated at the table. He leapt to his feet when we entered. "Guard the door and let no one enter, Geoffrey, and close your ears!"

The young boy scurried to the door, "Yes, lord."

"You and I know that you could have refused. My cousin does not like me and had you appealed to him then you could have stayed on your farm." He shook his head, "The mighty Will Strongstaff a farmer!"

I nodded, "It takes some getting use to lord." I handed him the letter from Sir Robert and the chest. "This is from Sir Robert, lord."

"It is immaterial. Put it on the table and I will read it later. I take it Sir Robert stays at home?" I nodded. "I expected that. It was you I wanted. Even though I was driven from court by my cousin I never held it against you. You treated us equally and the skills you taught me have stood me in good stead. When I became Earl and discovered that you were one of my tenants I saw that God had sent to me a staff upon which I could lean."

"Lord, you are the son of the King of Castile. You need no staff."

"Will, my father is King of a land in name only. We go to take back his land. I am not confident. I go reluctantly. England is the land where I shall be King."

I looked at him, "Lord should you be telling me this? It sounds remarkably like treason."

"I speak no treason. King Richard has no child either male or female. By Salic Law, I am the next heir. Until King Richard and his bride, Anne of Bohemia, have a child then I will be the next King of England."

Anne had shown no sign of becoming pregnant. A child was a lifetime away. I was still dubious. I had sworn an oath to protect the King of England. Although Richard had released me from that oath it did not sit well with me.

Henry Bolingbroke saw my hesitation. He added quietly, "William Strongstaff you hold a piece of land which is part of my fiefdom. You have a lovely wife and two children. The manor prospers. It is your choice. You can serve me or give up the land and vacate it immediately.

Richard let you go. You are either my man or landless. What will the title gentleman gain you then?"

I was beaten and I knew it. "In which case, I am honoured to serve with you on this campaign, lord." He did not detect the cynicism of my reply.

"I would have you do for me what you did for my cousin. I would have you watch my back."

"But the campaign..."

He waved an arm, "Is to get me out of England. The French are banging their swords against their shields and de la Pole is raising taxes. England will be filled with men in an ugly mood. I would not be here if they rise." He saw my face fall. "Do you think that my cousin is well advised?"

I could not lie. It was not my way. I shook my head. "No, lord, the Earl of Oxford is the reason I was dismissed and I fear he leads the King astray."

Henry lowered his voice. "It is worse than that. I have spies in de Vere's household. He has ambitions. He would be King." I was not surprised. He was a clever young man and he manipulated King Richard. "To that end, he has put a bounty on my head. He sees a way to smooth his path to the crown by having the next King of England murdered. With me dead then the succession becomes a murkier issue. It will be easier for you to identify assassins in Castile than in England."

I saw now why I had been summoned and this made perfect sense. If de Vere had hired killers then they would probably be of noble birth and would either be English or Norman. Although the army we were taking would be large, the number of potential killers would be fewer.

"How many men do you have?"

"Twenty-two, lord, including a squire and his servant."

He nodded, "You always had a good eye for men. They are good sergeants and archers?"

"Four of the sergeants served with me when we protected King Richard."

"Better and better. There were none who could exceed them. De Vere feared you and the guards and that was why they were dismissed."

"And when the assassins are dead?"

"I will still need you." He saw my crestfallen face. "Do not worry. I will allow you to return home from time to time but you serve a King in waiting. Was this not what the Black Prince wished of you? Was this not the oath you took?" I could not say that I had sworn to protect Richard only and so I nodded. Henry would not need to harm King Richard. The King had no children and he had chosen friends badly. He smiled at me, "And another reason I sought you out was that you know Castile. Most of those who fought with the Black Prince are dead. Your knowledge can be invaluable. You and your men will be paid double the rate while you serve me. If a lord wants the best then he must pay for it. It will be money well spent."

"Then we will do our best."

"I will send my page with you. He will show you your ship. You sail on the morning tide."

"I thought we had until Saturday, lord."

"That is when my father sails. I have less than three hundred men with me. I would have us take the best accommodation in A Coruña and give our horses more time to recover from the sea voyage. I told Sir Robert six months for a reason. I will return to England in six months no matter what my father has achieved. You have six months to find the assassins."

We hurried from the castle to my men and the river. The *'Maid of Harwich'* was a large cog. This one had a deck. I had travelled on those which did not. The deck had been removed to allow cargo to be loaded. The captain, Jack of King's Lynn, was a dour man. "How many horses do you have, sir?"

"Twenty-eight."

He sucked in his cheeks. "That is a might large number for such a small vessel. Are they well-schooled?"

"My men can handle them but I am guessing that they will have to be tethered on the deck."

"Aye, sir. The crew have the aft castle. You and your men will need to use the forecastle."

I saw that the forecastle was smaller than the aft castle. "How many crew do you have, Captain?"

"Eight and a boy!"

"Then myself, my squire and our servant will share the aft castle with you," I said it in such a way that there was no argument.

He nodded, reluctantly, "Aye sir. We will be ready for the horses at midnight. We leave on the tide that will be three hours after midnight. We are travelling in convoy with the Earl. We leave then even if the horses are not all loaded. Your men can put their war gear below the deck. The accommodation is tight. The less baggage they have the better."

"There is no way to access the hold during the voyage?"

"No, sir."

My men were in the inn. The landlord came to me with a wax tablet. "Here is the bill so far sir."

I nodded and took out my purse. "We leave at midnight. I will pay this and then you make another reckoning up to our departure."

I saw the disappointment on his face. We were good business and we were leaving. "Aye, sir. Do you need food?"

I saw him begin to scratch out the bill with the spatula side of the stylus. "Aye, and at the prices you are charging I expect a meal worthy of a lord!"

"Aye lord. You will not be disappointed."

I gathered my men and told them about the arrangements. "Make the most of the food and ale here. Those who have served in Spain know the problems. The good news is that the Earl has doubled your pay and we will be back in England within six months."

They cheered. I had given them the best of news. For myself, I was worried that we were heading down a road which might bring me into conflict with King Richard. Henry Bolingbroke had ambitions. Where did that leave me?

Chapter 5

A Coruña rose from the sea. It was surrounded by forests and cliffs. We were landing in Spain and that might spoil the plans made by the Spanish. King John of Portugal was an ally. Logic suggested that we would land in Portugal and use Portuguese allies. The other claimant to the Castilian throne, John of Trastámara, was caught off guard. We were landing in Galicia. There the people did not like John of Trastámara and John of Gaunt hoped to conquer Galicia quickly. It was an astute move by the Black Prince's brother.

My archers had filled the time productively. They had spent each day fletching arrows and we now had enough to last for six months. The heads would be fitted later. Getting to Galicia early meant that we would have more chance of acquiring the wagon we would need for our war gear.

Roger of Chester and Stephen the Tracker would lead the archers and men at arms of Stratford. I had made the choice but both were popular with the men. During one of the calmer evenings, we sat and spoke of the campaign on the open deck. "The Earl fears for his life. He is not a coward but he believes that murderers have been hired to kill the man who one day might be king. We will participate in the battles but the archers will not be with the other archers. They will defend the Earl. The men at arms will be as a bodyguard. When in camp then I will have to sleep close to the Earl's quarters or tents. I will have to rely on you to watch the men."

"And what of me, Captain?"

"Good question, Henry. If you were to sleep close by me then you would be in danger. You would be outside the tent and that would mean Peter would have to endure that too. I believe it is better if you stay with the men. You will have plenty of work to do with the horses."

He looked uncertain. Peter said, "It is for the best, Master. You have not yet been in a camp on campaign. I believe the Captain has spoken aright."

"But I get to fight with you."

"I hope not. We are fighting with the Earl who is the son of the King of Castile. The fighting will be fiercest around him." He looked crestfallen. "But as my squire, you will be needed close by me. You will require quicker wits and better skills than you possess now."

He looked disappointed but he had grown in the past months. He saw it as a challenge to prove to me that he was ready.

As a result of that meeting, my men at arms took it upon themselves to train him with the sword. I confess that the techniques they taught were much the same as mine. He learned skills hidden from most knights. They taught him to have a dagger in his shield hand so that when he knocked a sword aside he could stab under the arm. Unless his opponent had a besagews protecting his armpit then the blow would be fatal. They showed him how to slice through the sinews at the back of the knee. They sharpened a rondel dagger so that it was little wider than a bodkin needle. It would fit through the eyehole of a helmet. He was not totally trained when we stepped ashore at A Coruña but he was better than he had been.

My men and I were not the first to land. The Earl and his household knights stepped ashore and quickly took the better accommodation. I was unconcerned about my comfort but I made certain that my men had a good roof and stables for the horses. My Spanish was rusty but that and my full purse ensured that we were relatively close to the Earl and the horses had a roof. It was not to keep out the rain and the cold but the sun's rays. The Spanish sun could kill horses. The horses would take at least four days to recover from the sea voyage. As the Earl and his men had been the first to land that meant that we would be the first to be able to ride and the Earl was keen to begin the war as soon as he could.

I had barely finished speaking with the owner of the inn we would use when Geoffrey the Earl's page came for me, "Captain, the Earl wishes to speak with you."

Leaving my men to see to the horses I hurried to the Earl's side. His knights were studying the maps and, moving to the doorway, he waved me over. We climbed the stairs. They were ornate. This was the house of a rich merchant. He opened the door to his chamber. There was an enormous bed. His squire was already putting a cot next to it. "Your men are accommodated?" I nodded. "Then you sleep here." He pointed to the floor outside his chamber. "You had better find some bedding. I will be eating here with my household knights and I will not need you until after the meal. Geoffrey tastes my food. I want you back here well before I retire. You will search my room and then the outside of the house before I actually retire."

"Yes, lord."

As I headed back to my men I reflected that the Earl was treating me as something less than a gentleman. When I had served King Richard, I had felt that he liked me. I did not get that impression from the Earl. I had a job to do and I would do it. No one would kill the Earl while I was his guard but the sooner I could get home to my family the better it would be. We were lucky in the inn we had chosen. It was barely big enough for us and yet it was quiet. I heard as I headed back to the Earl's residence, the sound of blade on blade as other men who had arrived after an eight-day voyage, drank too much and fought. I would not have that problem. We were towards the outskirts of the town and I knew that Roger and Stephen would keep the men inside the inn. The last thing we needed was blood feuds. I walked back down the hill to the port. The Earl had not hired the Free Companies. That was a mistake. He had asked his lords of the manor to send men. They were a mixed bag. I was lucky. My men had been in the Free Companies and brought their attitudes with them. There would be blood feuds between the men in the other contingents. It would make it harder for men to fight together.

I spoke with my men and gathered some bedding. I reached the house while they were still eating. The Earl had not had too much to drink and he nodded as I entered. The same could not be said of the rest of the knights and lords who were gathered. Most were drunk. There would be fights and violence here. I took a goblet of wine from the servant. I would sip it and I would observe. I was watching for those who were not drunk. If there was a killer then they would remain sober. Of course, the killer might arrive with the main army and John of Gaunt but I needed suspects and I began to gather them. There were just three men, apart from the Earl, who were sober. I noted their liveries and I would watch them. When the daggers were drawn by Sir John Arkham and Sir Roger de Lacey the Earl stood. I wondered if he would use me to break up the fight but he did not.

"Stop now! This is most unseemly! If this is how you behave when there is no danger what can I expect when your lives are threatened?" Silence filled the chamber. The two young knights stood panting and, I daresay, feeling foolish. "All of you go to your beds. We have three days and then we will leave A Coruña to head towards Ourense. My father has tasked me with securing the town. We will do so. Any man who draws a sword against a fellow knight will be punished. And the same goes for your men. Now go! You have displeased me!"

For a nineteen-year-old, he showed great poise. He might be cold but he had presence and, more than that, he knew how to command. I could not help reflect that as much as I did not like him, he knew how to lead and King Richard did not. I slowly drank my wine while the lords, barons and knights left. There were just the Earl's squires and pages. I assumed that I did not need to check those.

"Lord, I will walk around the building."

He nodded almost absentmindedly. I put down my goblet and drew my sword. The Earl had picked the best building. There was a wall which ran around the building and there were just two gates. The Earl had two of his own guards there. I had met them earlier and they knew me. I left the main gate and said to Edward Tilbury, "Did the lords all leave?"

He laughed, "Aye Captain. They cannot hold their ale can they?"

I did not comment. "If any return let me know. Once I have returned inside, if there is anything which worries you then wake me. I will not be angry at losing sleep."

"We know Captain. The Earl has impressed that upon us."

The merchant whose house had been commandeered had sense. He had the undergrowth cleared for ten paces around the walls. As I walked I listened for alien sounds. The insects and birds I heard were not those of England but I knew them. I listened for men. I smelled for men. I went into the undergrowth and made water. When I had finished I listened. Silence. I reached Walter Codsall at the rear gate and all was quiet.

"Captain, the servants have all left. I counted them."

"Good. Be vigilant.," I returned to the main door and barred it. I walked through the empty house. The servants had quickly cleared the table. The kitchen was empty but they had not cleaned it well. That was not my problem. I barred the back door. We were now secure. I headed up the stairs. I knocked on the door. Geoffrey opened it. I saw the Earl in bed. Richard, his chief squire, was making a bed on the floor. There was a young Spanish woman with the Earl. His other squire, Harold, was hanging his clothes from a rail.

"The watch is set, lord."

"Good." He waved a hand and I was dismissed.

Geoffrey shrugged as he closed the door. I took off my sword belt and laid it next to the blankets I had brought. I took off my mail. I would sleep in my aketon. I took off my buskins. I placed my sword and buskins where I could reach them and then I wrapped myself in my blankets. I went to sleep quickly. I did not think that the Earl would be in any danger until we were close to war and then his death would be easier. I wished to keep my farm and so I did it all as he would expect; perfectly. The Earl and his doxy cavorted but it did not keep me awake. The silence, when they stopped, did. My eyes were open in an instant and I listened to the silence. Gradually the noises from within the room could be heard. It was the sound of people sleeping. They snorted, they snored and they broke wind. Satisfied that all was well I returned to my sleep.

I woke early. It was still dark but my bladder told me that it was time to rise. I donned my sword belt and descended. Unbarring the door, I stepped out into the cooler morning air. I walked to the guards at the ornamental gate. They had been changed and it was Richard of Doncaster who was on duty.

He nodded, "Morning sir. All well within?"

"All well within and the watch?"

"There was some trouble in one of the camps but other than that it was quiet. Will we be here long, do you know?"

"My guess is that we will not stay here any longer than is necessary. A camp is an easier place to guard."

He shook his head, "The Earl likes a roof and a bed, sir. The lords might have to endure canvas and the men hovels but his lordship will have a house, sir."

I made water and went back into the house. I washed and drank some ale. Although the table had been cleared and most of the uneaten food thrown out there was still a local ham and some day-old bread. I cut a healthy chunk of ham. I poked the fire into life and added more wood. Sticking the day-old bread on to a long kitchen knife I toasted it and when it was brown smeared it with local butter. The ham and toasted bread were like a feast. As I washed it down with more ale I smiled. When last I had been in Castile the amount of food I had just eaten would have fed my shield brothers. I unbarred the kitchen door. The servants would be arriving. After donning my mail, I returned to the kitchen.

The first of the servants arrived. They nodded deferentially. I was a soldier and the Galicians knew to stay on the good side of men with swords. I spoke to them and told them that I was watching over the Earl. The man who spoke to me was obviously the one in charge. His name was Raoul. He asked what the Earl would want to eat when he broke his fast.

I shrugged. I did not know. I smiled and said, "Food and lots of it!"

He smiled, "That I can do!"

He rattled out orders. They began to busy themselves and I went back into the main chamber with my ale. I thought that when I became a gentleman then my life would improve. The Earl had set it back to worse than it had been when I served in the Free Companies. I heard movement and stood. The Earl was descending. The young Spanish girl was tiptoeing behind him. She slipped out through the front door. "All quiet Will?" Geoffrey suddenly ran down the stairs and went into the kitchen.

"Aye Earl."

"Well Geoffrey can taste my food and as we leave this morning you may return to your men. Do you have any who know the land in your company?"

I shook my head. "Just me, lord."

"You know the roads?"

"I tramped them almost twenty years ago. I daresay they will come back to me."

"Then you will be the van. As much as I would have you close to me I feel that I need your skill and eyes to help us gain a quick victory."

"Do we fight all the Galicians, lord, or is it the men of Castile?"

"The men of Castile of course!" His tone was scornful and then his face changed. "What do you mean?"

"As I recall the lords of Castile who rule this land are like those on the Welsh Marches. They are not local. If you wish the Galicians to be on your side then find those lords and remove them. The Galicians will then see you as saviours and not enemies."

"That is sound advice. Then find me a Castilian that I may have a speedy victory. We head south. I would sleep next in Santiago de Compostela."

"Lord, the roads are not English roads and it is thirty miles or more. Besides, the horses need rest after the sea voyage. We cannot leave for two, perhaps three days."

Geoffrey brought him a goblet of the local wine. The Earl drank it. I saw him thinking about my words. The Earl was a thoughtful man. He liked to do things his way but he was less than twenty years old. He understood others knew more than he did. "My father will not be here for four or five days. He will have the same problem that I do. The delay will give me an opportunity to plan. William, get me some maps." He took a small purse. "Your horses may need rest but you and your men do not. Buy local horses. If they will not sell them then take them! I would have the road to Santiago de Compostela scouting out. Speak to the locals and find where the nearest Castilian lord is. I would have a victory."

I took the purse. "Aye, lord." I would be away from the town and that could only be good. I went, not out of the front door but into the kitchen.

"Raoul."

"Yes, lord."

In my crude Spanish, I told him that I needed maps of the area and horses. "There are maps in the master's desk. It is in the small room off the dining room. Horses? Just along the road south of here, there is a horse breeder, Pedro A Coruña. He is not a pleasant man but he knows his horses."

I went back to the Earl and told him where to find the maps. I then returned to my men. They were up. "Roger, fetch the men at arms. We go on a horse hunt. Stephen the Tracker, when we return we scout for the day. Find food, skins and ale."

Peter and Henry came with us as we marched south down the road. I had not been told how far south but a short way south the horses grazing in the field was a good sign. There was more forest than field in this part of the world. We turned up the farm track. It was wheel rutted. When we neared the farm ten armed men appeared. Peter said, "Well it looks like we may have to fight for the horses, Captain."

"Keep your weapons in your scabbards. I will try to talk us into a sale." It is hard to face men with bared weapons without drawing your own but I knew that it would be a bloodbath if we drew ours.

One of the Spaniards spoke English. It was heavily accented but far better than my Spanish. "Whatever you wish to take from me Englishman know that you will have to fight for it."

I spread my hands to show that I was unarmed. "I come not to fight but to trade."

"Then why do you need men of the Free Companies with you?"

"You know the Free Companies?"

"I served with the Yellow Company in the war against Peter the Cruel."

"Then you know that if we came to take them we would have sneaked up on you and already be riding your horses away."

"Perhaps. What do you want?"

"Twenty-two horses!" I held up the purse. "I have gold."

"That is almost half my herd."

"We need them for a day or two. We can sell them back to you when we are done."

I saw him calculating a profit. "The other men are as big as these? Mailed?"

"As big but not mailed."

He turned and spoke to the men around him. His Spanish was so quick that I did not catch many of the words. They sheathed their weapons and hurried off. "You need saddles, reins, stirrups?"

I shook my head. "We have those and we have horses. The horses have been at sea for eight days."

"Give me the purse and I will take what they are worth."

I held the purse before me. "This gold comes from the son of the man who would be King of Castile, John of Gaunt. I know you know the name. It would not do to cheat the Earl of Derby and Northampton."

"Nor will I do so. I served with Englishmen. I know that you do not cross them but I will be honest, Englishman, I would you were gone from my land. Free Galicia and then go. Your John of Gaunt is only welcome here if he rids us of Castilians."

I gave him the purse, "Amen to that."

He did not take all of the money. "If you wish to sell them back to me I will give you a good price. These are not war horses. If you scout with them then they will serve you well but they are not battle trained."

"That is all we need. And some information." He cocked an eye. "I believe that you will be happy to furnish me with this information. If I were to look for a Castilian lord between here and Santiago where would I go?"

He smiled, "Ah, if I were to tell you where an English lord who supports the usurper to the Castilian throne should avoid, would that suffice?"

"It would."

"North of Santiago de Compostela is a castle. It is not a large one but it controls the road. It guards the bridge over the Timbre river. Don Pedro is the lord there and he is related to Henry, the Lord of Santiago. He has the sign of the red hawk on the yellow field." He smiled. "Does that help, Captain?"

"It does indeed."

My men at arms took the largest horses. I sent two men back to my archers. They led the smaller horses. We spent the time they were away getting to know our horses. As I had expected my squire was the one who struggled to control his new horse. The rest of us had all been sergeants at arms. Until I had become a gentleman I had not actually owned a horse. We learned to ride new horses all the time. As Henry was deposited on the ground for the third time I reflected that he was having a painful lesson in horsemanship. He was sweating already. That was no surprise. The erstwhile King of Castile had chosen the hottest months in which to campaign. I was using the hood from my cloak to keep my head cool. As we waited I advised the others to do the same. Henry had lessons to learn but so had the others. We were in a hot country.

My archers soon rejoined us. As much as anything I was assessing the road south. Even though the Earl had a relatively small number of men the Spanish roads were not the best. Small obstacles could slow the wagons which carried the war gear of our men. The sun became hotter. I saw men drinking from their waterskins. "Do not drink until we stop and then drink sparingly. This is not England. Respect the land or it will punish you."

We saw few people as we headed south. The Galicians might want rid of Castilian rule but we were still foreigners and they hid. When we won we would be welcomed as heroes. Now we were a threat. The road climbed and I knew that might slow down the wagons. The horse trader had told us that it was more than thirty miles to the castle. I knew we could not reach Santiago and return. The Earl would have to make do with the news we brought.

We were, by my estimate, just seven miles from our destination when I decided we would stop. My men had obeyed my instruction but we all needed water: man and beast alike. We crossed a river. There were thick stands of trees along the side. We left the bridge and descended to the river. I left Lol son of Wilson on watch on the far side of the bridge. I watered my horse and swam her across the narrow river. It would cool her off.

I dismounted and led her up the far bank. I would relieve Lol. Suddenly he ran towards me, "Captain. Ten men. They have a yellow livery with a red bird on it."

It was Don Pedro's men. "How far?"

"The road is flat. Less than four hundred paces."

"Tell Peter and my squire to watch the horses. Have the rest of the men come up on both sides of the road. Ambush!"

"Aye Captain!"

I drew my sword. My shield was on my horse but I did not think I would need it. I tied my horse to a branch and hurried through the woods to the road. I could hear, in the distance, the sounds of hooves galloping down the road. I stood behind a tree and peered along the road. They were four hundred paces from me. I heard movement behind me. It was James War Bow. Harold four Fingers was also there. I gestured for them to move south and line the woods. I heard the hooves coming closer. I had to trust that Stephen the Tracker and Roger of Chester were on the other side of the road. I did not risk peering out. I felt men moving behind me and following James and Harold.

When I deemed that the horsemen were close I stepped out and said, in Spanish, "Stop!" The first two riders jerked their reins. Their horses reared. Every man's hands went to his weapons. "Stay your hands or you die!" My men were well hidden. I said, "Men at arms show yourselves!"

It must have looked a pathetically small number to the horseman who led the nine other riders. He shouted, "Kill them!"

Ten arrows flew and six riders fell. Two of the horsemen came at me. One was then struck by two arrows. I swung my sword two-handed at the other. He had leaned from his saddle to take my unprotected head. I was a strong man and he was not. Our swords cracked together. There was a scream and he dropped his sword. I had broken his wrist. Before he could escape Wilfred of Loidis had grabbed the reins of his horse. The rest of my men ran to grab the horses and secure the four wounded men.

"See to their wounds." I walked back to the bridge. "Henry, Peter, bring the horses."

The Spaniard with the broken wrist was cursing at me in Spanish. I understood some of the words. My men were busy moving the bodies from the road and taking any weapons and treasure which might be of use. I heard John Bowland bemoaning the small size of the Spanish feet. Roger of Chester said, "These Spanish have good steel, Captain."

"Good. We will share it out later. For now, bind the wounds. Harold Four Fingers. Pick two archers and another man at arms. Take these prisoners back to the Earl. They will have valuable information."

James War Bow had already made a sling from a piece of one of the dead men's shirts. The Spaniard said, slowly, "You will pay for this Englishman."

I smiled, "That I understood!"

"I am Roderigo, the nephew of Don Pedro of Sigüeiro. He is a powerful man!"

"Good, then he will pay ransom for you." The horses had reached us. "Henry, Peter, help this wounded man on to his horse." I turned to Don Roderigo. "Know this, my archers can pluck a hawk from the sky. If you try to run they will kill you. Do you understand?"

"I do and I will laugh when you die!"

We remounted and as Harold led the prisoners north we continued south. We had spare horses now from the dead Spaniards and we could afford to ride them hard. We stopped just half a mile from the castle. We stayed in the trees which were on a level with the hall. It was an old-fashioned castle. They had merely rebuilt wood with stone. It stood on a mound and the ditch had not been improved since it had been built. There was one gate in and no sally port. I could see that it was there to protect the bridge and the river crossing. Already a plan was in my head. We could cross the river upstream and the Earl could attack from two directions. The small hamlet was outside the castle walls. I counted twenty men. Some walked the walls and manned the towers. There were a couple by the bridge. I saw a rider leave the castle and head south. I wondered if they had been alerted to the arrival of the Earl. It seemed likely.

I turned my horse's head and we rode north. The afternoon was half gone and we would arrive back after dark. The men were in good spirits as they rode along the quiet Spanish road. They would all have coins and some weapons from the dead. We would have ransom for the living. As we passed the bridge I saw movements in the woods. Animals were already feasting upon the dead flesh.

It was dark when we rode into A Coruña. I sent my men back to the inn with my horse and I went to speak with the Earl. It was Edward on guard again. "You had a good day we hear, Captain."

"We were lucky."

"Good soldiers make their own luck Captain." I nodded. Soldiers were superstitious. Luck played a great part in their lives. "Will you be on duty again this night, Captain?"

I nodded, "I will be glad when we are in camp! Life will be easier."

"The lords left a while ago. I think the Earl has decided that he is better alone."

Geoffrey greeted me and I was taken to the hall where they dined. He looked pleased to see me. He was the youngest of the Earl's servants. I put his age at no more than ten or eleven years. The world seemed so big when you were that age. "The Earl is happy at your success, Captain. He learned much from the prisoners."

"Where are they?"

"He had them taken to the Abbey. The monks are looking after them. He has a guard on them. He said that you had earned whatever ransom there was to be had."

There were just five lords with the Earl when I entered. The atmosphere was totally different to the previous night. All of the knights were little older than the Earl. I wondered at that. Where was the wisdom and experience?

"William, you have done well. That arrogant young Spaniard told us much. They have heard of our landing and it has taken them by surprise. Their army is gathered much further south. They have gathered their army at Badajoz. It will take weeks to bring them north. When my father arrives we can subjugate the whole of Galicia."

"Good."

He shook his head, "Do you not see? When we have Galicia then I will have fulfilled my promise to my father and I can return home to England. My father will have his crown and I will be a step closer to mine."

"Lord, King Richard lives still."

"But he is unpopular. He should have gone to France to recover his lands. De la Pole has taxed the very lifeblood from England and there is nothing to show for it!" He gestured to a seat next to him. The young knight who had been seated there moved. "Now tell me of this castle. This will be my first siege and I need to know all."

"You will not need to besiege it lord. It is small. The ditch is not deep enough. We can take it in one day."

I saw the disparaging looks from the young knights at the table. I ignored them. "How so?"

"We send archers and men at arms across the river before the main force arrives. The bridge effectively seals off their escape. The men have a day to make hurdles. We use the hurdles like bridges and the walls can be scaled easily."

One of the knights, an arrogant young knight called Jocelyn d'Aubigny, drawled, "That sounds like a fantasy! It cannot be done. What does a commoner know of war?"

I turned and gave him a cold look. "When I served under the Black Prince that is precisely what we did. If you have a good shield then the crossbows they use are ineffective and our archers can make their walls into charnel houses."

"Jocelyn you are a good tourney knight. William knows how to win battles. Shut up!" The young man scowled at me. I prayed he would challenge me. He had a good war horse and if I defeated him then it would be mine. It would be worth over seventy pounds! His father was rich. "We can leave the day after tomorrow?"

"Lord, if we leave before dawn then we can reach Sigüeiro by noon. The advance guard can have cut off the castle by then. Santiago is just a few miles away. From what I have learned it is weakly held. They rely on the fact that pilgrims visit it. They believe that no one will attack it."

He frowned, "I would not upset the church. When we have taken Sigüeiro then you must find me a way in."

"And what of my other duties, lord?"

He waved an irritated hand. "I trust my men. My squire, Richard, will sleep outside my door. When my father's men arrive then I shall worry. Get me Santiago! That prize is worth a crown. The crown of England."

Chapter 6

We sold the horses back to the trader. He made a tidy profit as did we and we were both satisfied. I had learned lessons since I had first joined the Free Companies. It was better to make friends in the hostile lands in which we campaigned. Had I taken the horses as the Earl had suggested we might have made another enemy. As it was we made a friend.

Of course, it was my men who were the advance guard. I was given another twenty men who had been sent by their lords. None were knights. That suited me. I had forty good men to take and hold the bridge and we left well before dawn. I had gathered my men the night before we left. I knew how to talk to these warriors. All were professional soldiers. "No matter what your station you obey Stephen the Tracker and Roger of Chester. This is my company and we follow my rules. Whatever booty we take we share between all of us. We already have ten good horses, swords and mail. My men's purses are full. Obey me and you shall all reap the reward." My reputation ensured that there were no arguments. I had been the champion of a king.

We knew the road better after our first ride and we left the road when we reached the bridge. Stephen the Tracker did not know this wood but he knew woods and he found a hunter's trail which brought us four miles to the east of the bridge at Sigüeiro. It was an hour after dawn when we reached it. We easily forded the narrow river. That is to say all but Henry forded it easily. He fell from his horse and Peter had to rescue him. I think the laughter from the others was worse than any physical discomfort he suffered. We tightened our girths, donned helmets and rode west along the river track. Stephen the Tracker and Alan of the Wood disappeared. They would ensure that there were no unwelcome surprises at the bridge.

It was Alan who halted us. "Captain, Stephen the Tracker is at the bridge. There are four guards there."

I waved the other archers forward, "Go with Alan of the Wood. Eliminate the men on the bridge."

"Aye Captain."

As they rode off I pointed to John of Sheffield. He had brought the other men at arms. "Ride south and block the road a mile from us. If enemies approach and you cannot hold them off then return to me."

"Aye, Captain."

Turning to the others I said, "When the Earl attacks they will send for help. We stop them. Our only task is to prevent any from escaping Sigüeiro. Ride."

By the time we reached the bridge, the four guards lay pierced with goose tipped arrows. My archers were already recovering their precious missiles. We tied our horses in the woods. "Stephen the Tracker, I want archers in the woods on both sides."

"Aye Captain."

The rest of you form a double line across the road. Henry, you and Peter will be the reserve. Hopefully, we will not need you."

As we formed our lines and I hefted my shield before me we were visible to those in the castle. I saw that we had caused a commotion in the castle. The villagers ran to the castle but the gates were barred. I saw the fighting platform fill with men. The Earl and the bulk of the two hundred and fifty men he had with him would be approaching the castle down the road. We had succeeded. We had drawn Don Pedro's eye to us. I heard horns and then the gates opened. Twenty mounted men with spears appeared. I realised that they had not seen our archers. Their eye had been drawn to the twelve men at arms who blocked the road. Twenty horsemen would easily brush us aside.

I said, quietly, "These horsemen do not know whom they face. Our archers will thin their ranks before they can strike. Stand firm and lock shields. Trust in your shield brother."

The bridge was wide enough for five horsemen only. They could deploy wider once they had left the bridge but we were just ten paces from the bridge. The yellow liveried horsemen all wore an open sallet which covered a coif and ventail. They had a surcoat over their armour. None of the horses had armour nor even a caparison. The riders bore a lance. They were confident.

I shouted, "When they hit the bridge then release your arrows."

My archers did not reply. They did not need to. The bridge was but fifty paces from my men. At that range, even a levy archer from England could not miss. These were not the levy. These were the finest archers in England. The narrowing of the bridge made the riders bunch and slow. They made an even more inviting target. Twenty arrows flew as the first five horses reached the bridge. Before a man could count to ten five more flights had left the bows. It was carnage. Horses and men were hit by multiple arrows. The Spanish wore mail but bodkin arrows were made to penetrate mail links. Unarmoured horses had no protection. The animals fell and brought down more mounts and men. None made the middle of the bridge. Four men at the rear managed to turn and gallop back up the road to the castle. Arrows plucked them from their saddles. Not a single rider made the walls mounted. Three wounded riders crawled and dragged themselves through the gates. The four horses galloped, riderless, through the gates.

"To the bridge!"

We raced to the bridge. We had to clamber over dead and dying horses to do so but we made it within three hundred paces of the castle proper. We were within two hundred paces of the fighting platform. One foolish crossbowman raised his head to send a bolt in my direction. It struck my shield. Three arrows knocked him to the outer ward. No bolts followed.

"We hold here. Henry, fetch John of Sheffield. We may need him and his men. Peter put the dying horses from their misery. I would not have an animal suffer. Take the other horses to join ours." Our wagon and our spares were with the baggage train. The Earl's pages and servants watched them. My men were too worldly wise to leave their treasures with the baggage train. Our saddle bags contained what they had taken already. Spare weapons had been sold and they were all better equipped. The exception was Henry. He refused to take from the dead. He spoke of dishonour. Roger of Chester had rolled his eyes. Young nobles were ever thus.

A Spaniard, I took it to be Don Pedro, came to the gatehouse and shouted, "Is this all that you have, Englishman? My cousin will come from Santiago with an army to defeat you."

I smiled. I had the information I sought without having to ask. We would not need to besiege the city for the garrison would march to us. That would suit the Earl. Even as we had been leaving A Coruña the ships of John of Gaunt's fleet had been arriving. Son and father would have been able to speak before the Earl had to leave and within a few days, we would have more than four thousand men joining us.

I shouted, in English, pointing to the houses behind me, "Good for we quite like this pleasant little village!"

I wondered if he would send more men to shift this handful from the bridge. We were safe from bolts but a charge by horsemen might shift us. And then it came to me. He did not have enough men. I moved back from the bridge and taking off my helmet said to my men, "Move beyond bolt range. Eat and drink. He will not come. Stephen, keep four men to watch the gate."

Henry's eyes were wide when I spoke with him. He had fetched me bread, cheese and ham from his saddlebags. "I thought you were all dead when I saw men with lances charging you! Was that not foolish, Captain?"

Roger of Chester put down his ale skin and wiped his mouth with the back of his hand. "Master Henry it would have been better to have had lances but our Captain chose a position where they could not charge in a line nor could they charge at speed. If you add to that the deadly arrows of our archers then it was not a fair fight. We had all of the advantages."

Henry looked disappointed, "You mean an archer will always defeat a knight?"

Peter said, "That was the case at Poitiers and Crécy. English bowmen are the best that draw a bow." I saw my archers as they heard a man at arms praise them. Half had been outlaws scorned by all that they met. Here they were heroes. Their heads were held higher. No matter what happened at the end of the six months the men I had taken on in Lincoln would have their lives changed for the better.

As my men ate and bantered Henry came over to me. "What is the point of training to be a knight when a common yeoman can slay you with a bodkin tipped piece of ash?"

"A knight has many calls upon him. Fighting battles is a rarity. Many knights never have to fight against archers. However, if they do then it is possible to minimise the chances of death." I picked up my shield. "I made this shield. I cannot make mail nor armour but I can work with wood and leather. Feel the weight."

He picked it up. It was heavier than his own. "It is too heavy!"

"No, for that weight can save my life. I have told you that you have improved and so you have but you are still not strong enough. The Earl was like you when I first met him although he was younger. He heeded my advice and is much stronger. This shield has two layers of wood and the grain of the two pieces goes in opposite directions. The two pieces are cut from one tree and it took me many months to shape them and make them the thickness I desired." I did not tell him that I had done this to avoid working on the farm. "Between the two pieces, I have packed shavings mixed with glue. The face is made from good, thick leather. It was an expense but it is worth it. You see the staff upon it?" He looked and nodded. "There are small nails there. The staff goes down the centre and the nails afford protection. Finally, there is a padded part behind the shield. A bodkin could penetrate through the leather, nails, wood, shavings and glue and the padding but the force would have gone." I held the shield above me. "If an arrow storm came towards me then holding the shield thus would protect most of me. The fletch of the arrow would stop the missile coming through."

Harold Four Fingers laughed, "And there, Master Henry, is a free lesson which will save your life."

"But my shield is not the same! It is not as good!"

Peter smiled, "Then we will make it so, Master Henry. Instead of carousing at night we will make a new shield."

"New shield?"

Peter held one of the Spanish shields from the dead horsemen. "We strip this one and use this to make a shield like the Captain's. It will take a month but I do not think that the Captain will risk you in battle before them."

"No indeed."

Suddenly we heard horns. Half of the faces disappeared from the fighting platform. The Earl had arrived. We did not see the battle, we heard it. I knew, from my words with the Earl, what he would be doing. The wooden bridges would be laid across the ditch. Ladders would be placed against the walls while the Earl's archers kept the defenders busy. When the last of the men on our side of the castle disappeared I knew that they were racing to defend the breach.

"Come, we march to the gates!" I picked up my shield and donned my helmet. If the gates opened and the Spanish tried to flee then we would have to fight them.

When we neared the gates, I heard the sounds of combat within. The clash of steel and the cries of wounded and dying men filled the air. I heard the bar on the gate as it was lifted. "Shield wall!"

I heard Peter say, "Master Henry out of the way!" My men formed around me. We had three rows of seven. My archers formed a double row behind that. When the gate creaked open I saw a mass of women, children and old men. Their faces were filled with horror as they saw a wall of steel. They had not been on the fighting platform. They thought to escape. Their shoulders sagged. A horn from within told me that the battle was over.

Harold, one of the Earl's squires, forced his way through the villagers. "The Earl says you can let the villagers go, Captain, but not the men. They are to be kept within. He desires conference with you."

Taking off my helmet, I turned, "Roger of Chester, let the women, children and old depart. Stephen the Tracker, we will make camp in those woods on the other side of the bridge. Henry, Peter, come with me."

There were fewer dead than I had expected. The crossbowman slain by my archers still hung awkwardly from the roof of the oven. The oven had been lit and steam rose from it. "Peter, pull that poor fellow's body from the oven."

"Aye Captain."

The main fighting appeared to have taken place close to the hall. I saw the Earl. He was speaking to a disconsolate group of armed men. Don Pedro lay dead at his feet. The Earl had a bloody sword. I had trained him well.

"My plan worked! You did your part too, Captain. Now we can march on Santiago tomorrow."

I frowned and looked at the disarmed prisoners. There were three knights there. "Did the prisoners not tell you, lord?"

He shook his head, "Tell me what?"

"Henry, Lord of Santiago de Compostela is marching north to fight you."

"How do you know?"

"When we scouted the other day, we saw a rider heading south. That and the words of Don Pedro. He told me that an army was marching north to defeat you."

The Earl walked up to one of the knights. "You, you spoke English to me. Why did you not tell me?"

The young knight looked shamefaced, "Lord you did not ask me." His words told me that he was French.

The Earl backhanded the French knight across the face. He still had on his mail gloves and the knight's face was raked. "Now tell me!"

"I protest, lord! I surrendered. I should not be mistreated like this."

"Unless I am satisfied with your words then you will die!" I saw the hard side of Henry Bolingbroke that day.

"Don Pedro sent to Santiago two days since. Yesterday we had word that an army was marching north to send you back to the sea."

The Earl turned to his knights. "Sir Jocelyn, send these prisoners back to my father. Tell him that he should come with all haste, even if it is on foot. We have a battle to fight!"

Sir Jocelyn said, "Let me stay close to you lord."

"No, my friend, I need someone I can trust. There will be no fighting until you return."

"Aye lord. Come, gentlemen. We have far to travel."

When they had gone the Earl said to the knights around him, "Now we have the chance for a single victory which will give us Galicia and the honour will be ours!" He rubbed his hands. "And the treasure of Santiago too!"

I rejoined my men at the camp. The Earl had been busy and he had not asked for me to guard his body. I took the opportunity to make certain that my company were safe and secure. I need not have worried. They had cut down saplings and sharpened them to make a barrier around our horses and our camp. James War Bow and two archers had gone to fetch our wagon. We were lucky in that we had two horses to pull our wagon. The four horses we had just captured would be added to our horse herd. I knew from experience that horses were more vital in this unforgiving land than in England. My men had used the cloaks from the dead Spaniards to rig a shelter from the sun. The trees and the cloaks made it almost bearable.

I handed my sword to Henry. "When the wagon comes put an edge on my sword. Tomorrow or the day after we will need spears and lances. Sharpen those too."

"Will I need one?"

I shook my head, "You will be needed to bring me a fresh one if mine breaks." In truth, I had never had a squire and to have someone fetch me a fresh spear was a luxury. I was mindful of the need to train Henry to become a knight.

The Earl and his squires rode down the road. He waved cheerily, "I will ride just half a mile this way. If you hear the sound of combat then be a good fellow and rescue us."

"Shall I come with you, lord?"

He shook his head, "I can outrun my squires. They will protect my back. I will not be long."

I fretted for the short time he was away. When he returned he was in high spirits. "God must have smiled on me eh, Captain?" He and his squires galloped towards the castle. After he had gone I took the opportunity to wash in the pail of river water Peter had brought. I was lucky. There was no blood spattered on my surcoat.

The wagon had come and my weapons had been sharpened when Geoffrey, the page, ran into our camp. "Captain, the Earl holds a council of war and you are invited."

I saw Henry looking at me with a desperate pleading look in his eyes. "Come Henry you might learn something today. If you can keep your mouth closed and your ears open."

I saw that the Spanish dead were being interred by the priest. The Earl was being sensible. In this heat, the smell of the dead could be more than oppressive and it would calm the Spanish. We were still few in number. The earliest that the Earl's father could reach us would be the following day, after noon. His household knights were in ebullient mood. They had taken their first castle without the need for a siege. It had been swift and relatively bloodless. I did not say so but our elimination of almost thirty horsemen must have been of considerable help.

I was one of only three Captains who joined the Earl and his four senior knights. I was honoured. Captain Thomas of Northampton commanded the men at arms and archers from the Earl's town. Captain Black Jack, so named for his black armour, commanded the archers and men at arms from the rest of the army. He had the hardest task for they came from different parts of the land. His four senior knights had all served with his father and were older than I was: Sir John Fitz Edward, Sir Thomas d'Issy, Sir Richard Cheyney and Sir Walter Hood all had experience in battles. As I later learned none had more experience than I did.

We had captured good wine and there was fresh chicken for us to eat. The Earl was in good humour. He raised his goblet, "Here is to the King of Castile and England!" The toast should have mentioned King Richard but no one commented on that.

"King of Castile and England!"

"Already we are all richer. I shall send your share of the booty when time allows. Captain William, I fear you will have to wait for the ransom of the young cockerel you captured."

"No matter, lord, there will be more."

It was the right thing to say and all banged the table in approval. "Now we need to prepare for the attack by the Spanish. Although my father will doubtless reach us by the afternoon of tomorrow, I fear it will either be on foot or on horses which are too weak to fight. We must face the very real possibility that we have to fight a battle against a superior Spanish army."

I was unhappy about our lack of intelligence but I was loath to volunteer my men again.

The Earl smiled and used our goblets and the jugs of wine to illustrate his plan. "We will fight on foot tomorrow. Our horses are almost recovered but we are too few to guarantee victory in a battle on horseback. I intend to emulate the Black Prince at Crécy. I plan to use three blocks of men at arms and archers and one block of knights. We will fight with the river at our back. My knights, as they are the fewest in number, will be the reserve."

The Earl had just one hundred knights and their squires. Although that represented two out of every five men we had, the squires would not be of much use in a battle. Fighting on foot meant that they merely added to the illusion of numbers.

"We will fight a mile from the bridge. If things go awry, which I doubt, then we can retreat down the road and slow them at the bridge. I have found a piece of ground which should suit. There are woods to guard our flanks and the cleared fields are just big enough for three battles." He turned to the three captains. "I would have your men march there this evening and prepare the defences. We need stakes to be embedded. You should leave a guard there to warn us of the enemy's approach. I confess I would be happier if I knew the exact position of Duke Henry's army but as we have seen no scouts we must assume they are still well to the south of us. I want the army in position by dawn. We can eat once we are assembled. Let the enemy march in the heat. We will move in the cold. I hope that Sir Jocelyn arrives back this evening to tell us of my father's dispositions but he may not." He sat back. "Any questions?"

"This is the first time we have fought together, lord. What signals will you use?"

"A fair point William. Two horns to retreat and four to advance. That should suffice. I will be behind you and I would not have you crane your necks to see the standards."

Black Jack said, "They will see that there are few banners amongst our men. As you say, lord, you will be slightly behind us, they will think to ride over us as we are not knights."

It was a cold smile which spread on the Earl's face. "And you will hold them for the men you lead are here to serve me. They are all well paid. If that is all I will see you on the morrow."

Henry had been listening and when we walked through the town he shook his head, "It sounded like the sergeants and archers are not as important as the lords, Captain."

"That would be right. Most of my men know that. Sometimes weak men will run but the men I lead will not. Tomorrow you and Peter will be the third rank again. We will be using spears for defence. When they are shattered then you will replace them. You will be safe from the bolts of the enemy for they would have to pass through two ranks of men at arms and one of archers to reach you."

I saw that my words had an effect for he was silent. If bolts did get close to him then it meant that the men he had come to know were dead!

Chapter 7

We fought in the same battle as Captain Thomas. We were on the left of the clearing with a wood to our left. I disobeyed orders. I did not want to leave the woods without defence. We had plenty of archers and so I sent my woodsmen into the woods. The forests were their home and they knew how to use cover. If the enemy attempted to outflank us they would have a shock but, equally, we could launch a flank attack on them. We had also had time to add a shallow ditch before the stakes. That done we sat and ate, watching the sun rise in the east. It was cold but we knew that it would be unbearably hot by the tenth hour of the day. The experienced men made shelters of spears and cloaks.

Captain Thomas and I shared some bread and cheese. "You were the King's man, Captain Will?"

"I still am but I think you meant I was the King's Guard. Aye, I was."

"You know our master has ambitions to be a king." He held his hand up. "I speak no treason and I do not believe for one moment that he would try to seize the throne but you were Richard's man. How does this sit with you?"

I had thought on this. "Here we are no threat to the King of England. I will not raise my hand against an anointed king."

"I will ask no more for I hear a 'but'. I only ask because I know of your reputation and what I have seen thus far impresses me. I would hate to be on the opposite side. That is all."

"None of us can see the future. We deal with whatever we see before us. When last I was here I was a commoner. Now I am a gentleman. I did not see that. There may be events in the future which change my life. That is the future. A good soldier lives in the present."

The Earl arrived before the sun was fully up and he sent four knights and their squires down the road. He rode his horse as did his squires. He came to speak to us. "I doubt not the strength of purpose of your men. Know that when we reach Santiago then you and your men will be well rewarded."

He did not say any more but I guessed that meant his father would not arrive until the battle was decided one way or another. The Earl meant to be the first to Santiago.

Captain Thomas said, "These Spaniards have yet to meet an army such as ours, lord. We may be small in number but our archers have enough arrows to darken the skies."

He nodded. I pointed south, "And the Earl has a good eye for defence. When they emerge from the woods they will almost be in range of our arrows." The Spanish would be just two hundred and fifty paces from us when they saw us. I could see that he did not understand what I meant.

"Enlighten me, William. Tell me what I am missing!" There was an edge to his voice.

"With respect, lord, there will be many young knights amongst the Spaniards. If we loose our arrows as soon as we see them then their horses and the knights will be the ones who are struck. It will annoy them and may spur them to charge. We are set up to defend and an impromptu attack will only aid us. This is not like Crécy. There will be no rain today to make the crossbows less efficient. Our archers are better than their crossbows but they can still do great damage. A hurried attack will negate their effect."

He grinned, "Then let us make it so. I will go and tell Black Jack!"

It was almost noon when the knights and their squires returned. They galloped to the Earl and he became animated. He rode towards us and placed his horse where he could easily see us and be heard. "The Spanish host comes. They are a mile down the road. They outnumber us but they do not have bows. Their crossbows are used by mercenaries. Stand firm and know that my father will be here to relieve us soon. God is on our side!"

I turned to Captain Thomas, "Has no one told him that we fight for pay too?"

He laughed, "Ah but we are English and that makes a difference." He turned and shouted, "Ready your weapons, boys. Archers, know that when you see the enemy then is the time to release. Let their scouts alone. Wait not upon an order. You are all men skilled in the art of the war bow."

I went to my archers. "The same goes for you. Aim for the knights and their horses. We wish to goad them to come within range of our spears. When they get too close then draw your swords. I have no doubt you are skilled with the sword too. Sergeants, we will sit and take the sun awhile. It will afford our archers a better view and might make the enemy wonder what it is that we do!"

They all laughed. Happily, they squatted on the ground. They were seated in their battle lines. It was the work of moments to rise and present shields and spears.

Scouts appeared first. They had to have seen our knights and followed them. While four stayed and watched us the other four galloped back down the road. The road bent a little and we could not see the men but their banners fluttered as they approached.

I heard Captain Thomas shout, "Right boys! On your feet! Present shields."

My archers bent their bows to string them. They always left that act until the last moment. It added to the power of their arrow. They had already jammed into the ground ten good arrows. They now chose the best one. The knights began to appear and we heard a Spanish horn. They began to deploy into line. Their shields were still either hung over their cantles or draped over their legs. Their spears and lances were with their squires. I had counted one hundred when the first arrows flew. The Spanish were closer to the archers of Black Jack than us.

The first flight took them by surprise and eight men fell from their horses. Not all were badly wounded but they were dismounted. Two horses galloped back through their lines, maddened by the arrows sticking in them. Then the archers on our flank let fly. The effect was even greater. Some of the nobles realised that the archers were on the flanks and they spurred their horses towards us. It made others join them. That suited us for they came without spears. They were angry and an angry warrior is always at a disadvantage. I waved my arm and my men rose. Our archers switched targets to the centre and more knights and their horses fell. Their most dangerous weapon, the crossbowmen, could not get sight of us and our archers had free rein.

There were so many men charging towards us that not all of them could be struck by the arrows our archers rained upon them. We had locked shields and spears which were planted against our right feet. Our left hands held our shields and supported our spears. Had they had spears or lances then we might have been at risk but they had swords and we outreached them.

"Prepare to receive horses!" My words were not for my men but for the others I did not know. Stephen and the archers in the woods now had the opportunity for a flank attack. They sent arrows at the unprotected right sides of the horsemen. There the horsemen had no shields. They were less than eighty paces from them. The Spaniards did not have cannons upon their arms. They wore surcoats and mail. The bodkin arrows slid through them into arms and their sides. When they struck us half of the men had no weapon to use. They had raw courage and a horse. Horses baulk at a wall of steel. Roger and my men at arms were strong. They were able to thrust their spears, one-handed, up under the mail and armour of the young knights. As the horses wheeled the

Spaniards fell. A horn sounded but it was to no avail. The knights refused to fall back. Now the knights had friends to avenge. The ones who had not been struck by arrows slashed down with their swords.

They approached me. I was not afraid of a Spaniard on a war horse for I had a spear, a good shield and armour. I saw a Spaniard with a red surcoat and a horse with a red caparison. I rammed my spear at his horse's head. He hacked my spear in two and he then tried to rear his horse to flail me with its hooves. I rammed the broken spear up under the helmet of the knight. He began to fall backwards. I hurled the stump in the air. I hoped it might strike another and then I whipped out my sword. As the horse fell backwards I stepped forward. The knight was young and agile. He slipped his feet free from his stirrups. He landed somewhat awkwardly just a couple of paces from me. Although his horse did not fall upon him my sword was at his throat in an instant. "You are brave but surrender or die!" To emphasise my point, I pushed and blood trickled down his neck.

He nodded and reversed his sword.

"Henry, we have a prisoner." I pulled the Spaniard behind me and into our lines.

The Duke had managed to control the rest of his knights. They had rallied out of range of our men. I saw that others had been wounded by the spears of my men at arms. Disconsolate, riderless horses walked before us. I saw that forty knights and horses had fallen. Not all were dead. Some knights stumbled back to their lines. One or two horses lay kicking in their death throes. Others limped back to the Spanish lines. Many more than forty knights remained. We had not won but we had hurt them. The Genoese crossbowmen began to form ranks. The problem with crossbows was that you could not protect them. Our archers were behind a wall of shields held by men at arms.

Captain Thomas shouted, "Shields!"

We held our shields before us. They covered our heads and bodies and we braced ourselves for a bolt in the leg. I hoped that my leg armour was well made. Our archers sent their arrows into the air. They were fresh and they were fast. Ten flights before a man could count fifty sailed into the air. Even as the crossbow bolts hit shields and struck the gamboised cuisse the men wielding the crossbows died. This was not like Crécy where they had wet strings and were tired. Here they were facing a superior weapon and they lost. Some of our men at arms were hit but the men with the crossbows suffered more. A bolt in the leg was not life-threatening. Our archers were protected and they had no one attacking them. The Genoese ran. It was getting to the hottest part of the day and I felt the sweat running down inside my aketon. How much harder must it be for the men marching towards us?

A horn sounded and ranks of horsemen charged towards us. Of course, it was no longer a clear field. There were dead horses and men littering it. There were discarded crossbows and swords. The field was littered with obstacles and our small line stood intact. The horses thundered on the field but they would not be able to generate enough speed. Riders would have to negotiate obstacles. The stakes and the ditch before us were yet to be breached. The knight I had captured had managed to wend his way through. He had been lucky. Now there were more knights and horsemen in a smaller area. Horses and knights would have to die in greater numbers if they were to break through.

The Spanish were brave. Perhaps the paucity of our numbers made them think that they could break us. However, we were Englishmen and we were stubborn. We stood and we did not flinch. This charge had spears. I had none. I had sent Henry back with my prisoner. I would have to rely upon my sword. I took the opportunity to put my ballock dagger in my left hand. The archers were tiring now and the rate of arrows slowed. More of the knights would reach us. As the horses closed with us I saw that some of those who had fallen were not dead. They tried to rise. The metal plates they wore on their arms, front and backs were protection against blades and arrows but not against horses' hooves and I saw two knights crushed beneath the hooves of the horses thundering towards us. They slowed the horses down.

The first knight to reach me struck at my face with his lance. It was an optimistic strike. The knight had had to concentrate on negotiating stakes and bodies. He saw me and urged his horse on. The wavering head came towards my face. I wore a bascinet without visor for I found it easier to judge weapons which came at me. I pulled up my shield, angling it as I did so. The head of the lance slid towards Natty Longjack. He had no foe before him and he, like me, had a bascinet upon his head. He moved his shield to shatter the spear's head. At the same time, he whipped up his sword to strike at the horse. The horse had a crinet around its neck. The crinet was a metal plate designed to protect a horse from such an attack. Natty's sword found the crinet. He did not break skin but Natty was a strong man and he hurt the horse. As the horse's head jerked to the right the knights' left leg was exposed. The cuisse covered the front of the knee and the poleyn, the knee. The back was just guarded by his chausse. I hacked my sword hard. The tip scored a line along the already maddened horse's side and the edge tore through the mail. The bending of the knee always weakened mail links. I struck flesh and ripped through the stirrup. The rider fell off to the right. His horse tried to return to the south and dragged the rider a few paces before his other stirrup broke and he lay inert on the ground.

All along our line, the single riders who had made it through the morass of men, horses and stakes had suffered a similar fate. Some of our men had spears and our archers, releasing their arrows at twenty paces, drove bodkin tipped arrows through the Spanish plate cuirass as though it was cloth. Two more knights lumbered up on their weary mounts. The wounded and panicked fleeing horse had forced them apart and slowed them down. Their lances came for us. As one stood in his stirrups to strike down at Natty an arrow hit his unprotected face. The force was so powerful that the arrow came out of the rear of his head and helmet. The second knight raised his shield to protect his face as he struck blindly down at me. The lance's tip was easily deflected up by my shield and I lunged with my sword. The knight wore a surcoat and I could not tell if he had on a cuirass. I punched with my sword and it hit him hard in the middle. He was not expecting it. The sword's tip went through the surcoat and the mail. The aketon stopped it penetrating flesh but the damage had been done. His horse was stopped by the wall of shields. Geoffrey of Gisburn grabbed the reins of the horse and I reached with my shielded left hand to grab the knight's gauntlet and I pulled him over my head. He landed behind me.

I heard Peter shout, in poor Spanish, "Yield or die!"

Geoffrey pulled the horse through our lines. It was a destrier. In England, it would have cost me more than eighty pounds! I knew some manors which would not yield that amount in a year.

I heard the Spaniard shout, "I yield!" He had learned that much English.

There were still many knights before us but they were no longer charging. Some had charged and been rebuffed. They were milling and trying to reform. As the captured horse was moved behind us I saw gaps. Many of the Spanish knights had been killed or wounded. Just then, from the north, came the sound of a horn. It had to be John of Gaunt. I glanced up at the sun and saw that it was well after noon. We had been fighting for some time. The hottest part of the day had passed. I was desperate for a drink but that would have to wait.

The Earl was close enough for us to hear his words, "Knights of Northampton, my father comes, we are few in number but we have enough for glory! Mount your horses and let us drive these Spanish from our field! Our sergeants and archers have shown us what to do, let us complete their work and win this battle!" There was a cheer from the knights.

I shouted, "Ware right!" Our knights needed a gap through which to move. They were pursuing and would not need to use a solid line. The Earl's horse had a caparison. He bore the royal arms of England: quartered red and blue with the three lions of England on a field of fleur de lys it was differenced by a label of five points ermine. It was a distinctive and colourful livery. It made him a marked man. He led the line and his squires and household knights, with banners flying charged the Spanish knights. Our archers continued to send arrows over the heads of the charging Earl and his men. The Spanish fled.

When the last knight had passed I shouted, "Charge!" The knights would pursue the mounted Spanish but there were still crossbowmen and dismounted men at arms who needed to be eliminated. I had learned from Captain Tom that you had to be thorough when finishing a battle or else you left men alive who would fight you a second time. If we could defeat them now we might not have to besiege Santiago. We lumbered through the bodies and the stakes. Our archers, unencumbered by mail, quickly passed us. Their bows were left behind and they ran with sword and hand axe. The Spanish crossbowmen had been badly handled by our archers. The charging knights had made the crossbowmen take cover. Our archers reached them before they could bring their crossbows to bear. Knights might be taken prisoner. The ordinary men who fought us had no such luxury. They were butchered. Archers took at least ten years to train. Their muscles and bodies were far stronger than men who learned to use a crossbow in months. It was an uneven contest.

The Spanish sergeants were mailed. They had no plate save for an occasional cuisse. They were professionals too and knew that if they ran and presented their backs then they would die. They faced us. My investment in good armour on my arms, neck and legs paid off that day. I blocked the blow from a gisarme. The gisarme had a conical axe head attached to a pole. It was more effective against a mounted man but it could still deliver a mighty blow. Although I took the strike on my shield the head was so large that it came towards my upper arm. The cannon held it and the Spaniard was left defenceless. His shield arm also held the pole and I slashed my sword in a long sweep at his side. His mail held but not the bones beneath. I cracked and broke his ribs. He sank to his knee. I raised my sword and drove it through his open helmet down into his body. I kicked the dead man from my blade and followed my men. The same combats were taking place all along our front. It was a brutal battle. We were still fewer in number but we had the advantage of having repulsed mounted knights. My men were confident. I saw Stephen the Tracker as he stabbed a man at arms through the eye hole with his sharpened rondel dagger. Harold Four Fingers used the dagger in his left hand to strike under the armpit of a Spanish man at arms. When we reached the woods I shouted, "Men at arms, hold! Archers the woods are yours!" The open battlefield was somewhere we could fight but not the woods. Archers would be in their element. I needed a drink and fighting in armour was tiring.

Eager for the chance to take purses and weapons from mailed men who could not move easily in the woods they hurtled after them. I slung my shield on my back and sheathed my sword. I saw that one of the dead Spaniards had a skin on his belt. I took it and sniffed it. It was ale. I drank and peered around the field as I did so. I saw that the men I led still lived. Others had died. Captain Thomas was kneeling next to one of his men who had been badly wounded. I saw him make the sign of the cross and then end the man's suffering with his dagger. I walked back seeking the men I had slain. I took their purses and other treasures. If they had a good sword then I took that. Later we would collect the mail and helmets. Nothing would be wasted. I saw other companies stripping the bodies of buskins, tunics and breeks. My men did not.

I had almost reached our starting point when I heard horses clip-clopping over the bridge. I looked up and saw John of Gaunt, King of Castile and Leon, as he and half a dozen knights rode towards us. I took off my helmet and bowed as he approached. I saw Sir Jocelyn with him. "You are Captain Will Strongstaff are you not? I remember you."

"Yes, lord."

"Where is my son?"

"He and his knights drove Henry of Santiago and his knights south. We have had a great victory, your majesty."

He nodded. "We hurried to come to your aid. It seems we might have saved ourselves the trouble. My son and his men are resourceful." He turned to Sir Jocelyn, "You should have returned to your lord. You have missed the opportunity to have glory!"

"I am sure that I will have more, majesty."

One of the two who claimed the title, King of Castile, turned to head back to the castle. I headed back to our men. Peter and Henry had the prisoners gathered. There were six of them. Those I had captured would be ransomed to me. The others ransomed to the company. I saw that there were two squires amongst the prisoners. One looked to be little older than Geoffrey, the Earl's page. I went to examine the destrier I had captured. I would sell him. I was not a knight and I did not need such a magnificent creature. My courser was good enough for me.

My men returned and we piled up that which we would share. Peter and Henry would be given some of my treasure. Men drank from their ale and water skins. Food could wait but we all needed a drink. When the archers returned my men took off their helmets and went amongst the dead to collect weapons, helmets, plate and mail. Captain Thomas' men, as well as Black Jack's, did the same.

I stood with Henry, "Peter there are some dead horses out there. Go and butcher some. We will light a fire."

The evening would bring welcome cooler air. John of Gaunt and his men would take the castle's accommodation. We would use the camp we had had for the last few days. I pointed to the Spanish, "Bring the wood." Disconsolately they picked up the wood Henry had gathered. Henry led the horse laden with the weapons I had taken. We headed back to our camp. I gave the captives water to drink and then lit the fire. That was the difference between me and a knight. I had been the dogsbody around the camp of the Blue Company. I knew how to light a good fire. I needed no servants. When the fire was going I said, "Henry, watch the fire and do not let it falter."

I began to take off my armour. Knights would have waited for a servant to do so. I saw the Spaniard who had first surrendered to me. "You are not a knight!" He spoke in French.

"No, I am a gentleman."

"Yet you have the skills of a knight and you lead men."

"A knight has a title and spurs. I am content." I knew that the Spaniard was unhappy that he had to yield to a commoner and not someone of the nobility. "Your family has money for ransom?"

"They do."

"Good!"

Peter had hunks of horsemeat roasting on the fire when the Earl and his men returned. They led twenty prisoners. One, I saw, was Henry Duke of Santiago. The Earl had done well. He reined in and smiled at me, "You and the other captains upheld the high standards of the Free Companies. I thank you. You shall be rewarded. Send your prisoners to the castle. Geoffrey will see that you receive their ransoms." He saw the war horse." Whose is the horse?"

"Mine, lord!"

"It is too valuable for a commoner to own. I will buy it from you. Edward, fetch it and the prisoners!"

And then they were gone. Henry, my squire, said, "That is not fair, Captain, you captured it."

"And I would have sold it. This is better. The Earl is now indebted to me and I have coin in my purse."

We ate well and I was not summoned to sleep inside the Earl's room.

My sleep was interrupted in the middle of the night. There were the sounds of a commotion in the castle. My men and I were awake in an instant. Had the Spanish launched a sudden attack? We armed ourselves. It was better to lose a little sleep than to lose a life.

Geoffrey, the Earl's page, came rushing from the castle. "Captain William the Earl has need of you. Treachery!" He turned and ran. I followed. Had I been needed? Had an assassin done the deed?

Chapter 8

The castle was awake. Geoffrey waited for me at the gate and we rushed through to the hall. There I saw Sir Jocelyn and the other household knights. They parted and I saw two cloak covered bodies. The livery of the hose of one was that of the Earl. I saw his father, John of Gaunt. He was white. I could not work out if it was anger or grief. The Earl's voice came from behind me. "I was too confident, Captain, and filled with the joy of the victory. My squire, Harold, has paid the price."

"I am sorry I was not sleeping in your chamber, lord."

John of Gaunt said, "From now on you will. Has no one found the squire of this vermin?"

He kicked the other body. No one answered.

The Earl said, "Sir Edmund de Ufford was one of the knights who accompanied my father. He tried to gain entry to my chamber in the night. He slew Harold and would have slain me had not Richard slept with a sword."

The squire said, "I am sorry that I was unable to keep him alive, lord."

"It would have been useful to know who sent him to murder me but better that he died. Besides we may yet apprehend his squire."

John of Gaunt turned and glowered at the rest of his household. "This is not over! Each of you will swear on a bible. I would know all there is to know about this Edmund de Ufford."

It crossed my mind that I would have learned all there was to know before I left England but I was not a lord. I was a commoner. Perhaps we had more common sense.

The squire was not found. He had fled. I had no more sleep that night. The Earl and his father spoke for an hour. I was present and heard all. Both his father and the Earl feared for his life. Young Geoffrey fetched Henry, my squire. "Henry, have the men ready to ride. We accompany the Earl and the King to Santiago de Compostela." I added quietly, "We ride in close company. Have two men to drive the wagon. When you have told them then return with Jack and your horse. Peter can stay with the wagon and our spare horses too."

John of Gaunt left half of his knights at the castle. He had his senior lieutenant, the Earl of Southampton, stay with the remainder to discover their loyalties. The victory of the previous day now seemed hollow. As we headed south the Earl felt obliged to confide in me a little more. "I know who sent the killer. It was the Earl of Oxford. His mother is a de Ufford. I have no doubt that he promised the young Edmund power if he succeeded."

"But how did he think he would get away with it?"

"He used a poisoned blade. You did not see Harold's body. It was most dreadfully contorted. Richard was lucky or highly skilled. Newly arrived de Ufford did not know of the arrangement of men sleeping within my chamber. He thought I was alone. Had I been alone he would have succeeded."

"I am sorry, lord. Perhaps I am foolish but I cannot see what de Vere has to gain by your death."

"A throne. The crown of England. I am the next in line. He has duped my cousin and is now incredibly rich. Robert de Vere has a vague claim to the throne. His wife is Phillipa de Courcy. She is my cousin and the King's cousin. He is ambitious. With Richard and myself out of the way, he would have a clear path to the crown. The fact that he is not of royal blood would not stop him. We would have a second anarchy and with the coin he and de la Pole have accumulated then he could buy the crown for himself."

"Then why not fight de Vere?"

"You know him, do you not?"

"I do and I do not like him. Go to your cousin and tell him your suspicions."

"My cousin does not trust me. He trusts de Vere and de la Pole. I do not believe the rumours about de Vere, the Duke of Ireland, and my cousin but I do believe that my cousin is under the Duke of Ireland's power." He lowered his voice. "We will leave for England within this three month. We take Galicia for my father and then return. I will fight de Vere but I will do it my way. I trust you to watch my back from now on. Your men I trust. My squires and pages I trust. As for the rest? Let none near me."

As we headed south the few miles to the most important town in Galicia we saw the evidence of the Earl's ride the previous day. Bodies still lay where they had fallen. These were not the knights. The knights had surrendered and would be ransomed. These were the poorer fellows who had been ridden down and slain. It would be the fate of my men and me if we lost. It was up to me to ensure that we did not lose.

Richard, the Earl's senior squire, Edward his second squire and Geoffrey were all in serious and sombre mood. A poisoned blade gave a man no chance. It did not seem like an English weapon. Henry, my squire, also seemed preoccupied. The life of a knight had seemed so glamorous back in England. Now he was on campaign he saw the reality. He had eaten his first horsemeat the night before. My men had laughed at him for he approached it as though it was poisoned. Roger of Chester had laughed, "I am just pleased that it is cooked. Raw horsemeat is not as pleasant. I ate it but I did not enjoy it. This? It is well cooked and delicious."

"But it is a horse!"

"Aye, Master, but it is not mine and it is Spanish!"

We had Duke Henry with us. John of Gaunt knew that it would gain us the keys to the city. I knew that he was pleased with his son. Had we besieged the city then we would have lost many men and risked damaging a city to which pilgrims flocked each year. Rome was the only city which could rival Santiago. Once men had gone to Jerusalem but that was now lost to the Christian world. John of Gaunt sent his own men ahead so that we would not have the embarrassment of having to have the King of Castile beg entry to his own city. His knights left the inhabitants in no doubt about their fate should they resist. The result was that the gates were open and we rode through the streets triumphantly. The ones loyal to John of Trastámara had fled south. I knew, from the Earl, that our stay in Santiago would be brief. He intended pushing on to the borders with Portugal to ensure that we held Galicia. Once that happened then the Earl would leave for England.

The palace was huge and my men had the luxury of a roof over their heads and stables. Henry and I were given a room which adjoined the Earl's. To get to him any killer would have to pass through our room first. I would no longer have to sleep on the floor. The King of Castile, John of Gaunt, had the largest chambers. The Earl did not mind for he wished to be away from the country sooner rather than later.

John of Gaunt had to wait for his army to arrive. He received visitors. These were the Galicians who wished independence. They would happily support the Earl's father but only until they got that which they desired. We took the opportunity to bathe, wash our clothes and have wounds tended to by the doctors who accompanied John of Gaunt. The attempt on Henry Bolingbroke's life had made the Earl less keen to go abroad and he stayed within the palace. When he moved he had me and two of my men with him. We were like his shadows. He became almost a recluse. We still had not moved a week later. The army had arrived within two days and I thought that he would move quickly. John of Gaunt did not. He blamed the weather but, if anything, it was slightly cooler than when we had first arrived. A few days later and the ransoms arrived. There were chests of coins. We were all rich! Yet still, we did not move.

The Earl became impatient with his father and they had words. I wondered if his father feared that he would not be as successful as his son. Certainly, our victory had made everyone take notice of the Earl. He was a general!

It was a month after we arrived that we finally headed south. My men formed a protective layer around the Earl and we rode just behind King John of Castile. The Bishop in the cathedral had anointed John of Gaunt. There were two Kings of Castile and Leon. Of course, the other King John ruled far more of the land than did the Earl's father but we now had legitimacy as we headed south. We also had Galicians in our host. The Earl was unhappy about that as it meant there were more potential killers.

When we reached Ourense, it became clear that we had reached the limit of John of Gaunt's ambitions. He set up court there and Galician nobles flocked from all over the land to pay homage to what they saw as their saviour. The Earl became despondent. As we waited in idleness he fretted about missing opportunities to gather more gold and victories. He began to confide in me. He no longer trusted his own household knights and they resented me. It was as if they blamed me for the Earl's attitude. The Earl opened up his heart to me. We had good rooms and life was good but he was unhappy. "Come, Will. Bring your men and we will ride. I need to get away from this stifling court and false courtiers." I knew what he meant. I could see that the Galician nobles were merely using the English King of Castile to their own ends but John of Gaunt seemed to enjoy the flattery.

"This is not what I wanted, William. I thought we would defeat the enemies of my father and my men would become skilled in war. We have fought one battle and my men now grow fat and lazy."

"Lord, why do you need an army? Are you going on crusade?"

"I may do but not just yet. I need men who are all like yours. This is costing me money to pay for an army which does nothing."

"Then ask your father for coin to pay your men. The cost should be borne by him for this is his country and not yours." He looked at me. I saw the question in his eyes. "You would not be King of Castile would you, lord?"

"King of this fly-ridden land? Never! When I am king it will be King of England."

"Which cannot be yet for King Richard lives. Perhaps you could take your men to Aquitaine or Gascony. King Richard might like someone to regain his lost lands."

"He might do but I will not get them for him."

"Then the only alternative is a chevauchée. The lands to the south of us are not Galicia. They are Castile. Ask your father for payment and then let us raid. The weather is cooler and I have seen nothing to fear in these Spanish armies."

"Go on, elaborate."

I told him how we had raided when serving with the Free Companies. I told him all; the good and the bad.

He liked the idea and we rode back to the palace. The Earl was a clever man and he sought information from some of the Galician lords. He thought it amusing that he used them much as they used his father. After a few days, he was ready. He asked me to come with him when he spoke with John of Gaunt. I knew why. I had fought alongside the Black Prince. I was respected.

"Father I would have you pay my men. This is your land we defend and I am spending English money to do so."

Surprisingly his father nodded. "That is a sound suggestion. Give your account to my chancellor, the Count of Ourense. It will all be paid."

"And I would like to raid east of here. I have spoken with some Galician lords and they say that there is a town called El Bierzo. Although it is in the Kingdom of Leon it is ruled by a Castilian lord. From what I hear he is a cruel and unpopular man. If we raid him it will endear you to the people."

"How far away is it?"

"More than a hundred miles. My small battle might just be able to sneak through this land and raid before anyone knows."

I saw King John weighing up the advantages against the possible problems. A hundred miles away meant that he would not be risking annoying a wasps' nest. He nodded. "Then do it but be careful, my son. There may be more assassins out there."

"Until the Earl of Oxford lies dead that is a certainty, father, but I have Will Strongstaff. I will be safe."

As we left I asked, "Have you ever been on a such a raid, lord?"

He shook his head. "It cannot be difficult."

"There are corpses lying yet unburied in both France and Spain which will argue with that. You have to travel light. You do not use your warhorse. You need a hackney or palfrey. You do not take servants. You do not take tents. You make hovels. It is one hundred miles to El Bierzo, we need to reach that in two days. To do so we do not travel in the heat of the day. We leave well before dawn and we continue to travel in the cool of night. We use scouts and they must be the best of scouts too. If we can reach El Bierzo unseen then we have a chance. If they are forewarned and close their gates then we lose. It is as simple as that."

"Do I take all of my men?"

"You take the best, lord. How many knights are there in El Bierzo?"

"No more than thirty."

"Then we take your best fifty. We take all of the archers, lord and the fittest men at arms. We lost some in the battle in the north. There are wounded men. We take the best. Two hundred and fifty men is almost too big a force."

"And what of the plunder? How do we get that back?"

"That is the easy part. If we win then we have the town and we use hostages to drive wagons back. That way it is unlikely that we will suffer retribution. Besides this town is many miles from Valladolid. It would take three days for word to reach there that we had attacked and by then we should be safely back here."

"Then I will choose the men."

My squire Henry was delighted at the prospect of action until Peter explained what a hovel was. "You mean I sleep beneath a shelter of twigs and leaves?" Peter nodded. "On the ground?"

"Aye master. The Captain and I have done this in England where it is cold. It will not be so bad here in a hot clime. Of course, the spiders, insects and snakes may cause a problem but we will make coin."

I smiled at the crestfallen look on his face.

Those who were not chosen felt slighted. I wondered if the Earl was storing problems for the future. We had already unearthed one killer. What if the Earl created more malcontents? I began to study his knights more carefully. I now knew that if there was another killer then he was amongst the household knights of the Earl. De Ufford had shown us how easy it was to get close to the Earl. A household knight would be able to judge the time to kill to perfection. Now that we knew of poisoned blades we were looking for a knight who had travelled. The poison had been from the east. There were ten knights who had either been on Crusade or pilgrimage to the Holy Land. Those ten were the suspects. Six would be on the chevauchée. I confided in no one. I did not want to risk my men. I would watch them and, if they tried to strike, then I would stop them. When I had enough evidence, I would present it to the Earl. I knew that despite his words he could not believe that one of his household knights was a traitor.

We left in the middle of the night for the sun during the day still burned. All knew that we would be raiding but the Earl and I had told no one where. I had my ten archers as the scouts. The fact that they could not speak much Spanish was irrelevant. They were seeking enemies. Enemies were armed and mailed men. We would ignore the ordinary folk. Most were Galicians anyway. So long as we did not bother them they would ignore us. We made thirty miles before the sun became too hot to ride. My men had found a small village with water and shade. I had persuaded the Earl to use coin to ease our passage. We paid for the food we consumed and the water our horses drank. I did as the Spanish did. I slept beneath the shade of my cloak. When we left, in the middle of the afternoon, we were both refreshed and cooler. We made another sixty miles. When we stopped there was no village but there was a stream. We had food and we had oats for the horses. It was not the perfect diet but it would do.

We set guards and hobbled our horses. We were less than forty miles from our objective. The Earl was being guided by me. My plan was simple. We would reach the town after dark. The Earl had envisioned a charge on horses through the town. I planned to scale the walls, kill the guards and take the town while folk slept.

Once again, we made thirty miles before we stopped and I advised the Earl to take a longer break. We had but ten miles to go. The August days were so hot that Roger of Chester swore that an egg dropped on a rock would cook. All the way east the Earl and his squires had been surrounded by my men. As we rested before the last ten miles I said, "Do you wish this raid to be a complete success, lord?"

He nodded, "Of course."

"Then when we reach town I must go with ten chosen men to gain entry to the town. That means leaving you to be guarded by Henry and the rest of my men."

His face fell. "But why you?"

"Because I have done this before and I know what needs to be done. My men are good warriors and I trust them implicitly but this requires decisions to be made which are not in their experience. If you had a good knight then he could do it."

He nodded, sadly, "But I have not!"

"Then do you want victory and will you trust my men?"

He looked into my eyes. His eyes were not the eyes of a callow nineteen-year-old. They had wisdom beyond their years. "Aye, I will." He smiled at Henry. "Tonight, squire, you hold the life of a future King of England in your hands. Guard it well!"

We reached the outskirts of the town an hour after sunset. The watch would be set. There was a wall around the town but it was not a substantial obstacle. Stephen the Tracker and Lol son of Wilson had ridden ahead and spied it out before dark. I knew what the town would be like. We walked our horses to within half a mile of the wall. I spoke to Roger of Chester as well as the Earl. "We will move quickly to the walls. The rest will lead their horses slowly until you are within four hundred paces of the wall. When we have secured the gates, we will open them. I will signal with a light. You will ride as though the devil is at your heels."

"You make it sound simple, Captain."

"It will be far from simple but if I did not have the men I have then it would be impossible."

"From what I heard a chevauchée was a raid deep into enemy territory by mounted men."

"And that is what this will be, Earl. The difference will be that we will attack at night. They will not expect it. Spies will have told Castilians that you were going to raid. They will be watching for a column of mounted men. If they see us during the day they will bar their gates and then send men to deal with us. We can do this once. I do not think anyone has tried this for many years. For that reason alone, it stands a chance of success."

I left my shield and helmet on the cantle of Jack. Peter would lead my horse. I would fight bareheaded. I had chosen the tallest of my men. We hurried down the road but we kept to the shrub-covered side. There was no moon and we would be shadows only. I wore my buskins. They were silent on the cobbled road. When we were just two hundred paces from the gate we stopped and Stephen the Tracker led us through the scrubby undergrowth. The town had a grazing area for animals. I saw the stakes they employed to tether the beasts. There was a trough of water too. The ground was flattened and, as it was August, there was little grazing left. We watched for sentries. They appeared to have them just on the gatehouse. We saw the glow from their brazier and heard their conversation. It was a dull buzz in the distance. We crossed it and reached the ditch. The ditch was not well maintained. This was northern Spain and this was not the wet season. The ditch was dry. Stephen had noticed that the stone walls had been made with large pieces of stone. It was common in Spain. Peter the Priest had told me that the Romans had used the stones for their forts. The people who came afterwards simply reused them. The mortar was old and had crumbled. It afforded places we could use to climb.

Natty Longjack and I stood with our backs to the wall and cupped our hands. Stephen the Tracker and Silent David used the four paces between the ditch and the wall to get enough speed to launch themselves up the wall. Stephen managed to grab hold of the crenulations. Silent David put his foot on Natty's head and he too reached the top of the wall. The next two were not as agile as Stephen and they used Silent David's technique. I wished I had worn my arming cap. When the last men had scaled the walls Natty and I drew our swords and ran around the outside of the wall to the gate. Above us, my nine men would be creeping along to eliminate the watch and open the gates.

We could hear nothing. I took that to be a good sign. Something clattered to the fighting platform and then I heard the bar on the gate being removed. The gate opened. Lol handed me a lighted brand. I waved it from side to side and then laid it next to the gate. Stephen took his archers back up the stairs to the fighting platform. The four of them would use their bows to protect the Earl and the rest of our men as they galloped through. I led my six men through the town. There was another gate large enough to be used by wagons at the far side of the town and we had to secure that one.

The town was asleep as we raced through but behind me, I heard the thunder of hooves. There would be a captain of the watch and he would hear it. There was a glow from a building close to the town square. Someone was on watch. We sped through the square. The noise behind us grew and I knew that it must have been heard. Sure enough, when we were just thirty paces from the far gate, I heard the sound of a bell. The alarm had been given. Then I heard a clash of steel and cries from the gate we had already captured.

"Now we run even faster!" My tall men all had long legs and we reached the gate even as the two watchmen appeared. They had seen us and had pikes. There was a small guardhouse next to it and men began to spill sleepily out. I used my left hand to fend off the pike and I punched the hilt of my sword into the face of the watchman. He dropped like a stone. I still held the shaft of the pike and I threw it towards the men racing from the guard room. They were half asleep and they raised their hands as the pike sailed towards them. My men all had a sword and a dagger. One of the watch had descended and he was both mailed and armed. He ran at me. I pulled my ballock dagger from my belt and used it to block his sword strike. I swung my sword in an arc and it connected with his mail. We were too close for me to generate enough power to hurt him. He pulled his own dagger and, with incredibly quick hands, lunged at my eye. I barely managed to move my head out of the way. I stepped closer to him and ripped my dagger across the back of his hand. He wore no gauntlets and blood spurted. He pulled his helmeted head back to head butt me. Red Ralph had taught me that trick. Without a helmet, I would stand no chance. I pushed off from him and prepared to end the combat.

Behind me, I heard the sound of screams and cries as the Earl led our men into the town. Unless we could secure this gate then the townsfolk would open it and escape. We needed them penned. The sergeant at arms I fought had a bleeding right hand and I used that weakness. I swung my sword backhanded and he was forced to block it with his sword. I used my dagger to thrust at his eye. My blade scraped off the nasal of his helmet and missed his eye. I scored a long wound beneath it. He had to step back. I feinted with my sword for another back-hand sweep and as he brought up his own sword, switched to a strike from above. I hit his helmet. It stunned him and I took the opportunity to bring my dagger up under his right arm and into his body. He fell and I knew he would not rise.

Whipping my head around I saw that people were running towards us. I sheathed my weapons and picked up a discarded pike. I swung it before me. The people stopped. As Natty slew the last of the watch I shouted, "Stop! We have the town! If you wish to live drop to your knees." The time we had spent in Ourense had improved my Spanish. My men all took a step forward as I spoke and that had the desired effect. The ten people dropped to their knees. More people ran towards what they saw as an escape to freedom. I waved the pike and they too dropped to their knees. I could hear fighting in the town square. This would be a test of the Earl and his men. The sun began to edge over the eastern walls before the sounds of fighting died down. Henry and Peter rode towards us leading my horse, Jack. I saw that my squire's sword was bloody. I frowned. I had instructed him to stay at the rear. The people squatting before us parted and my squire and his servant dismounted.

"The Earl sent me lord. The town is ours. There was hard fighting in the square and he lost some knights but all is ours."

"And what of my instructions to you, young Henry?"

Peter dismounted and came to hand me my reins, "Captain, he did but two fellows came from the shadows to try to attack us and take the three horses. I fought one but Master Henry had to defend himself."

I looked at my squire. I could detect a change in him. "You killed a man?"

"I had no choice. He tried to kill me."

"Then you have learned a valuable lesson. The next time you fight you will find it easier to kill but I hope that you have more skills when that day dawns." I mounted my horse. "Natty, take charge here. There should be food and drink in the guardhouse. Henry, Peter you can remain here too. I will find the Earl."

Already men were searching buildings and fetching forth the treasures from within. When I reached the square, I saw the scenes of fighting. There were scattered bodies. I saw four men at arms from Captain Thomas' company and two dead household knights. The defenders had fought hard. The intensity of the fighting could be seen when I met the Earl. His surcoat was spattered with blood and his sword was notched. He managed a wan smile. "They fought hard, Captain, but we prevailed. I have my men searching for wagons and horses. I have the family of the dead lord under guard. I thought we might use those as hostages for good behaviour."

"Aye lord and I would have our men fed. It will take until noon to discover all that there is to take and then we can leave in the late afternoon."

Sir Jocelyn said, "Why not stay here for the night? Better a comfortable bed than a night under the stars." I noticed that he spoke to the Earl and not to me even though it had been my suggestion.

I answered for the Earl, "Lord, this is an important town. People will visit it. We cannot move back as swiftly as we came south. The journey which took us two days will take three. Valladolid is three days away but there will be other lords who are closer. We do not want to lose any more men or treasure. Better a night or two on the ground than a battle to get home."

The Earl looked from me to Sir Jocelyn. "We will stay here the night and leave on the morrow before dawn. We travel in the cool of the day."

Sir Jocelyn smirked. He had won but I wondered if it would cost us. We would have to mount a watch on the walls. Our men would be tired. However, I was merely a captain. I nodded, "As you wish, lord. I will find my men."

I rode to the gate where Stephen the Tracker waited. "Gather my men. Find somewhere close to this gate where we can rest. We stay the night."

Stephen shook his head, "That is a mistake, Captain."

"I know but the Earl has decreed it so."

The chevauchée had been successful. I knew that if we left immediately there was a good chance we could reach Ourense without any further fighting. The Earl's decision now placed us and our gains in jeopardy.

Chapter 9

We had ten wagons with treasure. There was not only gold and jewels taken from the people of El Bierzo there was their wheat and their animals. The animals would slow us to a walk. We had to use our own men to drive the wagons. We used archers. If we were attacked then they could become mobile castles. Captain Black Jack's archers were our scouts for we were back to protecting the Earl. His torn surcoat had been a warning to him of the parlous nature of a battle.

We camped forty miles from El Bierzo. The family of the dead lord were guarded by Sir Jocelyn and the household knights. Captain Black Jack's men kept watch. The forty miles we had travelled had been tortuous. We had had to move at the speed of the animals we had taken. We tried to persuade the Earl to slaughter some of them. A carcass was easier to transport than an animal was to drive. He refused. I knew why. He wished to impress his father and the other lords when he drove them into Ourense.

The Spanish horsemen found us when we were just thirty miles from Ourense. It was a mixture of knights, squires and mounted sergeants. There were two hundred of them and they looked to be armed with spears. We had parity of numbers but we had prisoners and animals to guard. Even before the Earl could react Captain Thomas of Northampton had ordered the wagons into a square with the animals in the centre. I shouted, "Archers into the wagons!"

The Earl stared at us. Black Jack said, "Time is of the essence lord. We should charge them with our own mounted men."

Sir Jocelyn said, "We will be outnumbered!"

Black Jack said, "Earl, trust your men. We can defeat these Spaniards."

The Earl looked at me and I nodded. When he spoke it was with authority, "I agree. Form up our knights Sir Jocelyn. Captain William and his men will protect me in the centre."

"But, my lord, they are sergeants!"

I turned, "And all the better for that, Sir Jocelyn. Do not insult my men again or you and I will have words."

"Stop this bickering. Sir Jocelyn, I have spoken!"

We quickly formed up. We had a hundred and twenty men. We used three lines of forty. I noticed that it was Captain Thomas and his men who were to our left and Black Jack to our right. The knights formed the third rank with the squires. We had not had time to fetch our spears but I gambled that if these horsemen had caught us they had ridden hard. Carrying a lance or a spear was tiring and the ground over which they were moving was not flat. I could tell that the Earl was worried for he kept glancing at me as the men formed. I knew that we had time. The Spanish were just under half a mile away and they were forming into a double line. They would overlap us.

"Whenever you are ready, Earl. The men are formed."

The Earl raised his sword, "For the honour of Northampton!" He spurred his horse. Despite what I had said the Earl had brought a destrier. It was the one he had bought from me. It was the best horse we had and it showed for it began to outstrip us.

"Lord, rein him in!"

"I am trying!" We just had to ride faster and that would weaken our horses. It also meant we would strike them like an arrow point and the Earl would be the tip. I remembered training him but that had been many years ago. Would he remember all that I had taught him? I had my shield held high and my sword held behind me. The Earl's shield was a little lower than I would have liked. He was not as strong as me and my men. We had well-made shields but they were heavy. I took heart from the fact that the advancing Spaniards were also more ragged than they ought to have been. They had many banners. That denoted knights. The knights were in the centre and I saw that the leader and the men around them had full face helmets. Those in the centre also had destriers.

The Earl kept reining back and we gradually caught up with him. Once we drew next to him I knew that his horse would want to gallop ahead again. He was a war horse and a leader. We were less than sixty paces from the enemy and almost at full gallop. I saw the spears begin to lower. The ones in the centre had lances and they were, generally straight. Their leader was riding for the Earl. Roger of Chester was to the Earl's left and I had the right. I kicked my horse hard when we were just twenty paces apart. It would be too late for the Earl's horse to respond and I wanted to distract the leader.

I saw the four knights in the centre pull back their arms to punch at us. I was aware of a lance coming at my right side. I did the only thing I could do. I swept my sword from behind and up. I managed, somehow, to deflect the lance in the air. Behind me, David of Welshpool would have an easy strike for the lance was still in the air as the Spaniard passed me. Then the Spanish leader's lance cracked into the Earl's. He was saved by two things. My shield was on his side and his horse chose that moment to try to bite the Spanish horse. There was the sound of cracks all the way down the line as lances and spears hit shields and mail. The Earl brought his sword over and it hit the Spanish leader's helmet. It was a good blow and the blade slid down and into the aventail. Roger of Chester swung his sword and the distracted Spaniard was hit in the middle. He began to tumble over the back of his horse.

The Spanish second rank was closer to us now but these had brigandines and mail hauberks. More importantly, they had long spears which they were struggling to control. I did not even have to move much as the Spanish spear came at me. His shield was on the opposite side and when my swinging sword hit his middle I cracked mail and bones. He reeled and I knew that David of Welshpool would finish him.

We were through their lines and I shouted, "Wheel left!" I thought for a moment that the Earl's horse was going to bite my mount as I turned quicker than the Earl. Thankfully, he did not.

Now we held the advantage for we were riding behind men with spears. They could not defend themselves. The mail hauberk of the first sergeant at arms did not completely cover his leg. I swung hard and cut through to the bone. He screamed and, as he fell, pulled his horse over. His horse barged into the next one and confusion reigned in the disordered Spanish lines. Some of the sergeants turned right, away from us and fled. The loss of their leader had weakened their resolve.

It became a confused mêlée. Our ranks were now intermingled. Roger of Chester and I still flanked the Earl and we protected him from any attacks from the front or side. Two horses suddenly burst through. They were riderless. Two of our men had fallen. The knights of the Earl were still close behind us. We had won. However, in that moment of victory, I saw the Earl throw his arms in the air and drop his shield. I reached over to grab his reins and Roger of Chester placed himself between the Earl and danger. Natty and Geoffrey of Gisburn spurred their horses to place them behind the stricken Earl who leaned over in his saddle. I saw blood. Our swords had won the battle but the Earl, somehow, was hurt. The more experienced Spaniards threw away their spears and drew their swords but in the time they took to do that many were either wounded or forced to surrender. When the Spanish horn sounded there were thirty Spanish riders on the ground. Many were dead or dying and another twenty knights had been forced to surrender. The Count of Valladolid was not one of them. When Roger of Chester had struck him, he had fallen over the back of his horse and a rider in the second rank had crushed his skull.

I nudged my horse next to the Earl, "What is it, lord? Where are you hurt?"

He shook his head, "I know not. I felt a sharp pain in my side. Where is Richard? He should have been behind me."

I looked and saw Richard's horse wandering riderless. "Natty, find Master Richard!" I kicked my horse and led the destrier back to our wagons. "We must get your wound seen to. Roger, find Captain Thomas and tell him to take command," I looked around and saw that none of the household knights were close. Had this been an attempt at murder? As we rode back I saw blood trickling down the cuisse of the Earl's armour. I now regretted not bringing a healer with us. As we neared the wagons I saw horses and sergeants at arms littering the ground. Some had tried to attack the wagons and our archers had slaughtered them. It explained why we had been able to defeat a superior number.

As we entered the square of wagons I shouted for Peter and Henry. I helped the Earl from his horse and then they reached me. "The Earl is wounded. Get the healer's satchel. Find Geoffrey, his page." My men and I knew how to deal with wounds. The nobles had doctors and monks. We relied on ourselves. Peter the Priest had taught me much. I wasted no time after I had shed my gauntlets, in taking off the armour of the Earl. His squire Edward rode in. He had a wound over his head. "Edward, help me. Your lord is wounded."

As we undressed him he said, quietly, "This was treachery, Captain. Richard and I were knocked from our saddles."

Geoffrey ran up. "Get your lord something to drink." The Earl had not spoken since we had returned. I hoped he was not dying. When we took off his undershirt I saw the wound. Geoffrey poured some wine in the Earl's mouth and Peter handed me the satchel. I nodded towards the Earl's mail. "Look at the mail for me."

"Aye Captain."

The wound was bloody. I poured some water on it and saw that the puncture mark was very narrow. "A rondel blade!"

Peter said, "Aye, Captain. I can see the links which were forced apart."

"Say nothing. Light a fire. We will seal the wound. Henry, hold onto this cloth and press it against the wound."

"Aye Captain."

I leaned into the Earl. His eyes were open. "One of your men tried to kill you. You were stabbed in the left side by a rondel blade. Had you not had such good mail then it might have been fatal."

"But who?"

"Perhaps we can work it out from the words of Edward and, if he lives, Richard. But for now, let me try to heal you." We looked up as there was a huge cheer when the Spanish prisoners were brought in. "Earl, say nothing. We want the assassin to be off his guard. I have narrowed it down to four knights. When I speak with your squires we might get closer to his identity."

"His?"

"My mistake, lord, it might be more than one. "Edward, Peter, stay close to the Earl. Geoffrey, go and watch the fire." I handed him by ballock dagger. "Put this in the fire when it is hot."

"Aye Captain."

I shouted, "Stephen, we need room here. Keep all from us, no matter who. We trust none save our own."

"Aye Captain. It was a fine victory."

"Only if the Earl survives." The Earl looked up at me. I saw fear in his eyes. "I will not speak false to you, lord. A rondel dagger has a long and round point. I am no doctor and I do not know what lies beneath your flesh. I am guessing, and hoping, that there is nothing vital but I know not. I will seal the wound and when we reach Ourense seek help from a doctor. If they have one then an Arab might be the best. They may be infidels but they know their medicine."

I heard Stephen say, "I am sorry, lord, but the Captain and the Earl are busy."

"And I am Sir Jocelyn! I do not answer to the scum of the forest."

I heard a scuffle and a thud. "I care not if you are the King of England. If my Captain says you stand clear then you do so. Come at me again like that and it will be more than a clout I fetch you."

I saw the Earl smile. He said weakly, "Your men are stalwart. Give me a thousand like that and I can defeat any army sent to me."

"Aye, lord. They are good."

"Captain, it is ready."

"Peter and Edward, hold his shoulders. This will hurt, lord. There will be no shame in crying out. Curse me if it will help."

He nodded. Geoffrey gingerly handed me the hilt of the knife. I could smell the heat. "When I say, Henry, lift the cloth."

"Aye Captain." I knew my squire was worried. He had done nothing like this, ever.

"Now!"

He had done a good job but blood began to ooze. Even as I pressed the flat of the blade against it I hoped that there was not a deeper wound. If I sealed it and the wound still bled he would die. There was a hiss and then the smell of burning hair and flesh. He cried out. I heard men murmur behind me.

Stephen said, "Peace, lords. It is just a wound being sealed."

I held it for a moment or two and then pulled it away. The Earl had passed out. I looked at the wound. Nothing seeped from it. I risked, while he was unconscious, pressing on the sides of the wound. No blood came from it. I handed a bandage to Edward. "I will apply a salve. When that is done I would have you wrap the bandage as tightly as you can."

"Aye Captain."

I stood. I saw Sir Jocelyn and Sir Humphrey. They were off to the side casting evil looks in my direction. Black Jack and Thomas stood with Stephen the Tracker. "It is sealed but I know not if it is healed."

"It is good that you have the skill."

"I served with a priest and he taught me a few tricks."

Captain Thomas gestured at the hostages. "So much for them. We would have been better without them."

Black Jack shrugged, "We demand more ransom!"

I nodded towards the two knights. "They could cause trouble."

"There are fewer of the Earl's knights, Captain. Another four were wounded. Only one looks likely to live. Their squires are with them."

"We will put the wounded in one wagon and the Earl in a separate one. I will have his squires with him. Where is Natty?"

I looked up and saw Natty leading a horse with Richard slumped over it. Was he dead? "How is he, Natty?"

"His coxcomb is bloody that is all. He has a tale Captain."

"Put him next to the Earl and I will look at him. Stephen, have a bed made in your wagon. If we have to get rid of treasure we will do so."

"You take charge, Captain." I looked at Black Jack. He smiled, "It was not a question. We need someone to take command. I would not trust the ten knights who are left to command a sumpter! You know this land better than any and you are the Earl's man. Command and we will obey."

"Then we leave now. I would have us get as close to Ourense before dark. I will send two riders to Ourense to tell the Earl's father the news." I gestured for the two captains to come closer. "The Earl was stabbed by one of his men, it had to be a knight or a squire. When I have spoken with Edward and Richard I might have an idea who."

"You are sure? It is a serious allegation."

"It could have been no one else. It was not a mêlée at the moment he was struck and it was a rondel dagger in the back. I cannot see a

Spaniard being able to do that and besides the Spanish were all to our fore. No, there is a killer and I will find him."

We buried our own dead. There were few in number and the wounded were all loaded in the wagons. We took the decision to make the hostages ride the newly captured horses along with the captured knights. While we were doing that I spoke with the two squires. They were still somewhat shocked by the events. The Earl slept and Geoffrey tended him.

"Who was behind you? I know that the two of you flanked the rear of the Earl's horse. Tell me of your battle."

"Roger of Chester, yourself and Natty Longjack managed to keep all danger from us, Captain. We kept our swords ready and our shields were there to protect the Earl. The biggest danger we had was of our horses tripping over the dead. Behind us were eight of the Earl's household knights."

"I need you to be specific. I need names. I also need you to tell me who was immediately behind you and then work out."

"Sir Jocelyn and his squire, Sir Humphrey and his squire, Sir Richard Laidlaw and his squire."

I held up my hand. "I will assume their squires were with them."

Edward nodded, "Sir John Fitzcreke, Sir Robert Hatherley, Sir James Fotheringhay, Sir Gilbert de Bois and Sir Ralph of Helmsley."

"Good. And did you see who struck you? Either of you?"

"No, Captain. We feared no danger to the rear but Natty said that I was struck by a mace." He showed me his helmet. There was a distinctive indentation. That narrowed it down even more. Few young knights use the mace. I picked up Edward's helmet. He also had the marks of a mace. I could see now that two knights had ridden between them and swung their maces at the same time. It explained how the two had fallen instantaneously.

"The three of you will be the Earl's armour until we reach Ourense. Come let us lift him up."

Along with Peter and Henry, we lifted the Earl. As we laid him down he woke. "Do you know who did it, Captain William?"

"I think so but I will need your father to judge for these are nobles. I will send to him…"

"No! We keep this here. No one should know what has happened to me!"

"But, lord!"

"Listen, William, someone, de Vere probably, has paid men to do his bidding. I do not want him to have the satisfaction of knowing that he almost succeeded. Let us keep him in the dark. I owe you my life.

Now help me to make it a longer one. Wait until we reach Ourense and I am on my feet again before you confront the killer."

"Killers, lord, there are four, at least, involved. Of that I am certain." While they made him comfortable I waved over Roger of Chester. "Our men at arms guard the Earl. Let no one approach."

"Aye, lord."

"And watch for any man with a rondel dagger."

We headed west and I watched the men I suspected, the two knights and their squires for I had the household knights in the van. All eight who had been behind the Earl were there but I knew which two were the guilty ones. Even as I had listened to the accounts of the two squires', pieces began to fall into place. I remembered conversations which now made more sense. The attack in the castle became clearer once I knew who it was. Looking back always afforded perfect vision and I cursed myself for my blindness. I rode with the two captains and told them what the Earl had said.

"He is a brave man, William, but foolish."

"He is young. He is entitled. Whatever he is we swear never to mention the attempt. He was wounded in battle. We leave it at that."

"And the killers?"

"The Earl and I will deal with them in Ourense."

We were weary when I finally called a halt to our progress. We made camp just twenty miles from Ourense. The town was close enough that had we just had our men at arms we would have pushed on but we had wounded and we had women. We had one in three men on guard and the Earl's wagon had a wall of steel around it. The three Captains took a watch each. I had the first one and when I crawled beneath the Earl's wagon I was weary beyond words.

I was woken by Stephen the Tracker when it was as black as coal. "Captain, two knights and their squires have fled. They killed two of the guards at the treasure wagon and they have fled."

I knew who it was without asking but I needed confirmation. "Who?"

"Sir Jocelyn and his squire, Sir Humphrey and his squire."

I nodded, "Get a horse and fetch your two best men. We hunt knights!"

Chapter 10

Captain Thomas was angry for one of his men had been killed. He wanted to go with me. "No, Captain. I have the best trackers and I can speak some of the language. More, I know this country. You two return with the Earl to Ourense. You will be there by morning and a healer can look at the Earl. We have spare horses. I will take my men and we will find them."

"And bring them back?"

I shook my head, "We will find them and there will be an end to it."

We did not tell the Earl. He was sleeping and I had heard that sleep was always the best medicine. Along with Stephen's two archers, Lol and Silent David, I took Roger of Chester, Harold Four Fingers, Natty Longjack and David of Welshpool. We took four spare horses. The riders had, according to the sentries, ridden north. That made sense. If they could make A Coruña they could take ship and get to Ireland. The Earl of Oxford now ruled that island for the King. The four would not risk Ourense and would take smaller roads. We headed north and west looking for signs.

They had at least three hours start on us but had only taken one sumpter and that for the two chests which they took. They would not be able to travel as fast as we would. I also doubted that they had ever had to husband a horse. I had and knew that there was a fine line between making the most of a horse and killing it. I worked out that they would head for Lugo. We had avoided it on our way south. The two knights would have to travel on the east bank of the Minho river which ran all the way from Lugo to the sea. They could either cross it at Ourense or Lugo. We headed along the road to Lugo. Road was not the best description of the surface we travelled upon. It was stone but not cobbles and the dust, even in the dark, flew up. During the heat of the day, it would be unbearable.

When dawn broke we found evidence that the knights and the squires had passed along the road. They had ridden close to an acacia bush and a piece of material from the dark blue cloak worn by Sir Jocelyn and his squire was clearly visible. The first dung we found was relatively cold. We stopped to change four of the horses after we had travelled twenty miles. We ate. I had not thought to bring food but my men had and we ate well. With horses refreshed, we continued north and the sun began to beat down upon us. I dared not rest during the heat of the sun. We had to catch them before they disappeared into Lugo. When we found the warm dung, we knew we were closing and we changed horses again. This time we rode for two miles or so and then walked for a mile. It slowed our progress but kept it steady. We found the dying horse towards the middle of the afternoon. Stephen put the sumpter out of its misery. We saw the two empty chests. They had spread the treasure out between them. They were carrying it in their saddlebags and giving their mounts a heavier load.

Silent Dave rarely spoke and when he did it always came as a shock. He pointed to a hoof print just off the road. "The prints are deeper. The horses are struggling."

Stephen said, "Captain, they cannot reach Lugo by dark. With laden horses and after the abuse they have given them they will be lucky if their horses survive another couple of miles."

"Then let us continue to save our own."

It was as we were walking that Lol pointed to the boot print. "Captain, they have begun to walk too. Their horses are not as laden."

Roger of Chester suddenly darted to the side, "And they are fools. They have finished an ale skin and just tossed it away!"

"Then we are closing. I do not wish to lose them in the dark. We will walk too. Keep your eyes, ears and noses open. They may light a fire."

We trudged along the road. Despite the fact that the sun was setting the day did not appear to be getting any cooler. It was an hour past sunset and I was contemplating resting when we smelled wood smoke. We could not see the fire and that confused us. I let Stephen and his archers lead. He knew how to track. It was a short while later that he held up his hand. There was a tree nearby and he tied his horse there. He gestured for us to do the same. I trusted my men and we obeyed. He mimed taking off our helmets and we all did as he suggested. He pointed north. Slinging his bow on the saddle he drew his sword and led us off the road. I knew that there were animals out in the scrub. There would be rabbits and hares, foxes and wild cats. They had enormous spiders, lizards and geckoes out here. They were alien to men from England. I wondered how the four fugitives were coping.

Then we heard a scream. It was the scream of a woman or a girl. I sniffed the air. The smell of smoke was stronger. Had the fugitives found a house in which to shelter? The scream was replaced by the sound of laughter. We moved slowly towards the house for it was now obvious that it was a dwelling. A faint glow could be seen and we heard a horse neighing. Another stamped its hoof. I waved for Roger and

Natty to go to my left and for David and Harold to go to my right. My three archers disappeared and I walked towards the house. I heard sobs. There was little point in trying to make any sense of what we could hear. I was now convinced that the men we pursued had stopped at this remote farm which lay off the main road. Perhaps they thought we would go galloping northwards. Then I stopped. They were not that foolish. They would leave someone on guard to watch and listen for our horses.

My four men at arms had also stopped when I did. Where had my archers gone? The noises in the farm suggested that the knights were behaving badly. I do not know how long I waited but I realised we would have to move. If there was no guard then whatever was going on in the farm would get worse. I waved my arm and we moved. Suddenly there was a movement ahead. I heard a brief scuffle and then there was a sigh. Stephen the Tracker waved his arm. I almost tripped over the body of the squire who had been watching. It was Jack, Sir Jocelyn's squire. He had been old for a squire and by all accounts a thoroughly unpleasant man. I saw Stephen shrug apologetically. He had not intended to kill him. The seven of us spread out. I had no idea how many entrances there were but I guessed more than one.

I waved David, Harold and Natty to go around the far side of the building. Fate intervened when we were less than ten paces from the door. It opened and the light from inside bathed us. Sir Jocelyn stood in the doorway. He was unfastening his hose. He was going to make water. He saw me and shouted, "Run!"

He threw something at Silent David. Whatever it was it caught my archer and he fell. Even as I glanced down Sir Jocelyn raced into the dark. "Lol see to David." I ran after Sir Jocelyn. I had seen which direction he took. Behind me, I heard the clash of steel on steel and shouts. My men would deal with Sir Humphrey and his squire. I concentrated on the man who had tried to murder Henry Bolingbroke the would be King of England. There were two dead men who would still be alive if I had acted sooner. My prevarication had been responsible. We were on a path which ran away from the road. It was not perfectly straight but appeared to run south to north. Would Sir Jocelyn leave the path and head left to the road? I debated second-guessing him and running to the road first. I dismissed the thought as soon as it entered my head. Red Ralph had told me that overcomplicating things often made them worse.

I sheathed my sword. We might soon leave the path and be running across rough ground. I needed my balance. To the side of the path, we were on lay the slopes of the valley in which this remote farm lay. This was mountainous rocky country with sudden drops and hidden rocks. I needed my balance. I wore my leather riding gauntlets. If I had to fend off a blade then they would have to do. I counted my steps to help me estimate how far we had come. When I reached eight hundred I heard, from ahead, the sound of slithering. Sir Jocelyn was scrambling on rougher ground. The noise came slightly from my right. Was he trying to run in a circle around me? I stopped. Where was the knight going? The simple answer was that he needed a horse and the horses were behind us. He did not know just one man pursued him. He thought to lead us into the night and then cut back and take a horse. He had seen just myself, David and Lol. I turned and listened. I could hear movement in the dark. It was the sound of a boot on stones. Chausse brushed against leaves. I turned and I followed the sound. I was still on the path and it was flat. More importantly, it was without stones. I was silent. My feet had stopped pounding. Even if Sir Jocelyn was running the rougher ground would make him slower. A fast walk would keep pace with him and my boots would not make a sound.

We were moving back to the farm. I could see it in the distance. The door was open and a shaft of light shone out. The sounds to my left drew closer. Sir Jocelyn had seen the light and was returning to the path. I looked away from the firelight of the farm and into the dark. I kept moving. I was looking for shadows which moved. My hand went to my sword as I saw, just twenty paces from me, a shadow drawing closer to the path. It was at that moment that Roger of Chester chose to shout.

"Captain! Where are you?"

The shadow stopped. It confirmed that this was Sir Jocelyn. I drew my sword and slipped my ballock dagger into my left hand. Sir Jocelyn suddenly ran on to the path. He turned to look north and saw me. His hand went to his sword as I stepped forward and swung my own sword. I was under no illusions, Sir Jocelyn was more than a competent swordsman. I had seen him when he had practised with the other knights and he was the best. I had learned how to use a sword in battle. Sir Jocelyn had learned the tricks which would win him duels and tourneys.

He batted away my sword with his dagger. It was almost contemptuous. "You have crossed me for the last time, spawn of the gutter. When I have killed you those two men you brought with you will take but a moment to slay."

He then spun his sword and lifted it to strike at my head. I had fought enough times to know how to spin and I did so. My foot slipped on a stone to the side of the path and I fell to my knee. Sir Jocelyn saw his chance and he seized it. He lunged with his dagger. I had something Sir Jocelyn did not have. I had survival instincts. My hands had learned to react to blows from a violent father when I had been a child. I did not even have to think and my sword came up instinctively to block the dagger. It was almost a punch which struck his left hand and the dagger flew into the air to strike a stone in the dark. I rose and lunged with my own dagger. His sword came around in an arc to deflect it but it gave me the opportunity to rise and to recover my balance.

His left hand slipped down to his boot and pulled a rondel dagger from it. My eyes were now accustomed to the dark and I saw that it was a long one. It was almost like the bodkin sailors and leather workers used. It was the weapon he had used on the Earl. I needed to end this. I brought my sword around in a long arc. It was a ploy. He knew it was coming and his dagger was already coming around to meet it. I was using the move to step close to him. I kept my own dagger out to the side as I stepped closer with my left leg. His dagger easily blocked the blow and his own sword came down diagonally to strike across my neck. My movement meant that even if I did not fully block the blow then he would hit me with the blade closest to the hilt. It would hurt but it would not break the skin. My dagger locked with his hilt and my face was almost level with his. I could smell the perfume on his oiled beard. I had taken him by surprise. His widening eyes told me that. I had stepped forward on my left leg and my right knee drove up between his legs. It was a trick I had learned when fighting in the camps. Growing up I had often had to fight bigger boys. The knee to the groin always brought me victory.

Sir Jocelyn grunted in pain and he stepped back. He was now off the path. He was hurt and I did not allow him any respite. I swung my sword. He was forced to bring across his own sword to block it and he did so without any strength. I drove his sword against his face. This time it was the blade next to the tip which struck him and that was sharp. His own sword sliced a line from his forehead to his cheek. Sir Jocelyn had ever been a vain man. The Earl had told me that. He became enraged and lunged with his dagger. My ballock dagger blocked the blow and I was able to turn the rondel dagger away and to strike upwards. I felt the blade slice through the surcoat and brigandine. When it reached his mail it was stopped and so I pushed hard. He slipped and began to fall.

From the direction of the farm, I heard Stephen the Tracker shout, "Captain! We are coming!"

Even as his eyes flicked to the side I brought my sword down across his shoulders. He was overbalancing and could not protect himself. My sword hit him hard enough to break the bone which lay beneath his mail. He swung his sword as he was falling and it caught my leg. I lost my footing and I fell. My dagger was still in my hand and my weight drove the dagger deep into his thigh beneath his hauberk. He screamed in pain. I pushed myself to my feet with my sword and looked down. The dagger had caused a mortal wound.

"Who is your master?"

He laughed and he closed his eyes briefly. When he opened them there was a fire within them, "You know nothing! You think I just have one master? There are many men who wish the line of the Plantagenets to end! When Bolingbroke and the foolish boy, Richard, are dead there will be a new dynasty ruling England!" He coughed and I saw that the black pool of blood was bigger. The light just went from his eyes and he was dead.

Roger of Chester and Stephen the Tracker ran up. "Captain, that was foolish. You should have waited for one of us."

"And then we might have lost him. Fetch his body back and we will search him at the farm." I picked up the rondel dagger and the knight's sword as my two men lifted his body. "Are the others dead?"

"Aye Captain. They gave us no opportunity to take them alive."

"You have not searched them yet?"

"No, Captain."

"And the family?"

"The farmer had been beaten and the wife… Sir Humphrey was about to defile her. The two children were terrified. I think they fear us too."

"And I would not blame them."

Roger of Chester shook his head, "They were fleeing for their lives and yet they took the time for that! I do not understand it."

I nodded, "I do. They thought they had escaped us. There was no sign of pursuit and they were but a short ride from safety. They were arrogant men. They were traitors. Once you have contemplated treason and regicide then no crime is too great."

"Regicide Captain?"

"Aye, it was not just the Earl who was in danger but King Richard, Roger. This plot was one to end the Plantagenet dynasty and it is bigger than I thought."

We reached the farm and I saw that my men had tended to the farmer but the children and the wife looked terrified. My men laid Sir Jocelyn's body on the ground next to the other four. I spoke Spanish to them. "I am sorry for what this knight did." I reached down and took Sir Jocelyn's purse from him. "This is for your trouble. With your permission, we will sleep in your barn. I know that our presence might offend you. We will take the bodies and burn them." Our time in Ourense had not been wasted entirely. My Spanish was much better.

The farmer, heavily bandaged about the head said, "Thank you, sir. We have such evil men in our land. I came to live here as it is such a poor piece of land that we thought no one would desire it. I can see that there are other dangers. Thank you for coming to our aid and burning this offal." He handed me a skin of wine. "Here, sir, we have little food but we can offer this." I nodded my thanks and he closed the door.

I turned to my men, "Take what you can from the bodies and place them over there. Silent David, fetch firewood and a brand. We will burn them first and then search their belongings."

"Aye Captain."

I was weary. The ride and the combat had taken more from me than I had expected. When I reached my home, I would have earned every penny that was coming to me. We made the pyre large enough to accommodate four bodies and we used dry wood. There was plenty of it. Once it was burning well we laid the bodies upon it and then piled more dried wood on the top. When we smelled flesh burning we retired to the barn. The four horses which the fugitives had taken were in a bad way. Sir Jocelyn's courser would not recover fully for months. It was a pity for it was a fine horse. The treasure was still in the saddlebags. We would return that to the Earl but that which was carried by the three dead men I gave to my hunters. They had earned it.

As they divided it Roger said, "Captain, there are a large number of French coins here."

Stephen the Tracker said, "That is not a surprise is it?"

Roger said, "This is for they are freshly minted. If I was to take a guess then I would say that Sir Humphrey was paid these since we reached Galicia."

I nodded. That made sense. A change in dynasty meant another family wished to take over England. French kings claimed England just as English kings claimed France. I had much to ponder on the ride to Ourense. It was a long day's ride to Ourense. The rest of our chevauchée had already reached the city the day before. Henry was watching for us from the gatehouse. Henry ran to greet us when we entered the castle and stopped in the outer ward.

"Captain, the Earl is desperate to speak with you."

I nodded, "Henry go with my men. Roger, take the treasure and place it with the rest of the booty. Sell the horses and weapons we captured. All save this." I handed Sir Jocelyn's sword to Henry. "This is yours. It is a better sword than the one your father had made for you."

"But he paid a great deal for it."

"And he was robbed. Sir Jocelyn might have been a treacherous traitor but he knew his weapons. This is as fine a sword as mine. Take it."

I saw that my men still guarded the chamber of the Earl. They looked pleased to see me. "I will take over now. The Earl will be safe enough."

Inside were the two squires and the Earl's page. He looked up from the day bed on which he reclined, "Well?"

"They are all dead and the treasure recovered."

"Thank God and thank you, Captain. The best day's work I did was to employ you."

"If I might have a word?"

He nodded. "Guard the door and Geoffrey, fetch wine and sweetmeats for the Captain." They scurried out. "Sit for I see from your face that the danger is not yet passed."

"No, lord," I told him what had happened and what we had discovered. "It seems, lord, that the King's life is also in danger."

Henry Bolingbroke would be king. I knew that for a certainty but he was no traitor. Regicide was not in his heart. After he became king there were rumours but I knew that they were unfounded. He showed his nobility with his next words. "Then you must ride to him now and warn him."

"But, lord, what of you?"

He smiled, "I did not say you should take your men. I trust them and I will keep them about me until we reach England. Do not worry, Captain. I have done enough to please my father. He thinks the wound came from war and he does not wish me to risk my life further. I will rest for a month and then return home. You need to leave now. Rest today for I would have further conference with you. You have a mind which is most agile and I believe that we can tease out whence the threat comes. Leave on the morrow. I will have a letter drafted for you and you can prepare our ships to take us home in three or four weeks' time." I nodded. "Now fetch my squires and Geoffrey. I will celebrate this brief interlude of safety."

The Earl was easier with me now. When first I had joined him, he had been distant. It had been as though I was a new suit of armour; functional but without attachment. We had fought together and as with all warriors that made us closer.

"My father is a ditherer. He squats here in Ourense enjoying the flattery of the Galician nobility. His army grows indolent and lazy. If he wishes Castile he should take it."

He was speaking to me of his father and I was uncomfortable. He was right. John of Gaunt might have been a warrior once but now he was old. I could not believe that his brother, the Black Prince, would have dallied so long. He would have struck and Castile would have been his.

"I will be home as soon as my doctors tell me that I can travel. My wife, Mary, is with child. I know that it will be a boy and I will have an heir. England will have an heir."

That was the difference between the Earl and myself. He put his ambitions before his wife. I had been there when my wife gave birth.

"Congratulations, lord. You had not spoken of this before."

"Perhaps I did not know you well enough to confide such matters."

"And where is your wife, lord?"

"In my castle in Wales. The journey from Spain to Wales is much the same as the journey from Spain to Southampton. It will take but ten days and I shall be with them both." He smiled at the memory of his wife and I smiled with him. He rarely smiled and it changed him when he did. "William, I have a mind to ennoble you. You deserve a knighthood for what you did. You have saved a future King of England from death."

"Lord, King Richard still lives."

"I know and I pray that it continues but…" he waved a hand so that the squires and page moved away, "you served with my cousin. Did you not see the flaw in him?"

"Flaw lord?"

"De Vere could not have manipulated him if he had a strong character. Sir Jocelyn tried to bend me to his will but I resisted. I do not believe the rumours that the two are lovers, as Walsingham suggests. He is vain and de Vere has appealed to that side of him. Did you know that when we grew up together Richard accused me of all manner of slights, none of which were true? I need do nothing, William. Richard has the seed of his own destruction within his own breast."

I had much to think about as I headed home.

Chapter 11

The journey through Spain was peaceful. There were just three of us and we had six horses with us. They carried the treasure we had all gained. I had the letter for the captain of the ship which would carry us home and the one to Richard from Henry Bolingbroke. My squire was delighted to be going home. "Will I soon be knighted, Captain?"

"You are far from ready. I confess you have improved. You have been blooded but there is still much for you to learn." I smiled, "Are you so keen to leave my service?"

"No, Captain. I am still learning but I am impatient to be a knight. I believe I know some of the pitfalls. I would not be as Sir Jocelyn and Sir Humphrey."

"And I am sure that when they were your age they did not believe they would turn out that way. Life throws obstacles in your path. A real man who is a true knight learns to deal with them and emerge stronger. The two traitors chose the easier, quicker course. Be patient and you shall be a better knight for that."

There was just one English ship in A Coruña when we arrived. She had brought more knights for John of Gaunt's army. The captain was more than happy to take us home especially when I told him of the impending departure of the Earl and his men. He was happy to sail to Wales. The profit would still be the same for him. The cargo was being loaded as we arrived. Wine, oil and other goods were being stored below the deck. Our horses would be the last aboard and they would have slightly more freedom than on the outward journey.

The voyage home took longer than the one on the way out. It was ten days before we reached Southampton. On the voyage we learned that King Richard had taken an army north for the Scots were becoming active. Nothing had happened. There was neither a battle nor a skirmish. It had done the King's reputation no good whatsoever. He had raised the levy and knights had been mustered. There had been a cost and nothing was gained. Once more the King had been badly advised. The Earl of Oxford, or as he was now titled, the Duke of Ireland, had managed to absent himself and spent the time in Ireland. Thus, he was not tainted by the ignominy. I now saw the plot in all its fullness. The King was under de Vere's spell. De Vere was working with others, probably the King of France, to bring about the fall of King Richard. With murderers seeking the cousins and the Duke of Ireland able to use the revenue from that land to fund an army, he would be able to take power when Henry and Richard were dead. I was uncertain if I could persuade the King of the veracity of my words but I would have to try. I had been ousted from court by de Vere. I hoped that in his absence I might help the King to see a little more clearly.

It was past the end of English summer by the time we reached Southampton. We had only been away for a few months and yet I detected the first fingers of autumn gripping the land. Leaves had begun to fall and the harvest had been collected. There was a chill in the air. We had to get to Windsor quickly and so I just allowed our horses one day of rest. We now had more and we could afford to change them if we had to.

We took it slowly and stopped in Basingstoke at an inn. We had coin to spare and I paid for two rooms. Peter was happier since returning to England. He preferred English ale to Spanish ale and he was not fond of their wine. He also liked the English style of cooking. The Galicians cooked dishes such as octopus and heavily spiced it. The only food he approved of was the mutton and lamb.

Replete after the meal we sat in the largely empty inn and watched the fire flicker. Henry asked the question which had been on his mind since we had left Ourense. "Is our service to the Earl done, Captain?"

"I fear not. There is still danger to his person but I hope we can have a month at home at the very least. He still has to recover and then he will sail to Wales to be with his newborn. Do not forget, young Henry, that we still have much training if you are to progress and become a knight." He nodded. "You have acquitted yourself with honour. The Earl both values and trusts you. He has learned his lesson. He will judge his household knights more carefully from now on. If you wish more land and power then you could do worse than ally yourself to the Earl. He will go far. A household knight of Henry Bolingbroke, if he is true, has a bright future."

"Richard and Edward said he would be King of England one day." The squires had spent much time together and shared secrets.

"He might well be for King Richard and the Queen have been married for four years and there are yet no children."

"They are both young, Captain."

"And they need an heir. Even as we speak I suspect that the Earl will be a father. He and King Richard are the same age and yet the Earl has managed to get his wife with child." As the first King Henry had discovered not having enough male children could be disastrous.

There was a squall as we headed to Windsor the next morning. It was the first rain we had witnessed since we had landed in Spain. It was a sign we were home. As we neared the castle I wondered if I would be admitted. No doubt de Vere had ensured that the guards at the castle were loyal to him. When we reached the castle, I saw that there was no standard fluttering there. There were few guards but, luckily, I recognised the sergeant at arms who was at the gate. He had been one of the guards at the Tower during the Peasants' Revolt. He was happy to volunteer information. "The King and Queen are in London, sir, at the Palace of Eltham."

"Trouble?"

"Not for me to say, sir, but I daresay he will be pleased to see you." His response was guarded. De Vere would have men planted to report back to him.

There was a hidden message in the sergeant's words. We hurried east. I knew that we would not reach Eltham Castle in a day and so we rode to London first. We stayed in 'The Blue Company'. We knew that we would be safe there and that John and Tom would be able to furnish us with the information we needed.

We did not talk but we listened. This was not a quiet little alehouse in Basingstoke. This was a tavern in the heart of the capital. Men here knew when was going on in the world. I learned much from Tom and John. The King was in trouble. He needed money for the French were not only threatening to invade they had renewed their alliance with Scotland. That explained the King's abortive visit to the borderlands. His Chancellor was in Parliament trying to get the Commons and the Lords to approve taxes. Taxes were always unpopular. When they were for a King who had yet to win anything then they were doubly hated. The alehouse became busy and Tom and John had to serve customers. We drank and listened. I heard John of Gaunt's name spoken. Men wondered why he was in Castile and not supporting his nephew. Had I spoken it would have fuelled their suspicions for John of Gaunt was delaying in his attempt to reclaim his kingdom. Had he abandoned his nephew? My opinion of the Henry Bolingbroke rose. I had a letter in my possession which allied him to the King. It seemed to me that most people were doing the opposite. King Richard was being abandoned.

When the alehouse had emptied John and Tom were able to speak more freely. "You see, Captain, they are holding the Parliament in Oxfordshire. Clever move that is. The King would have to leave the protection of his guards. Between you and me his uncle, the Duke of Gloucester wants to be regent. John of Gaunt isn't here to oppose him."

"What do you know of the King's guards?"

"Little, Captain. When they are at the Tower then they drink in 'The Earl Marshal'. He has household knights but they are men like Sir Simon Burley. If you remember he was the one upset the folk in Kent so much they began the Peasant's Revolt. If you don't mind me saying so he needs someone who has common sense close by him. He needs someone like you."

I shook my head, "Those days are gone for I was dismissed. I serve the Earl of Northampton now but I will use what little influence I have with the King. I owe him that much." I did not mention that the Earl had threatened me with losing my land and my farm. The title I had been given was a shackle. I was tied to the Earl and my family tied me to the land. I was no longer the young warrior who could go wherever he pleased.

We left the inn as soon as the gates to the city were opened and rode hard for Eltham Palace. It was to the south of the Thames and had been given by the Bishop of Durham to the crown. It was more luxurious than the Tower and also further from the unpredictable London mob. When we reached Eltham we were not recognised and there was a heightened tension amongst the guards. I had been one of Richard's guards and I understood their predicament. They did not know me and knew that there was a mob close by who would wish the King harm. The Peasants' Revolt had scarred King Richard. "Just tell the King that William Strongstaff, gentleman, brings a letter from the Earl of Derby and Northampton."

"Then give me the letter!"

"Sir! I am a gentleman and I will take no insult from you. The letter is to be delivered to the King by me personally." I smiled but it was a cold humourless smile, "Of course I can leave and not deliver the letter but when the King discovers that the man who was his Captain of the Guard was denied admittance then I fear you will not be one of his guards for much longer. I will wait here!"

I saw the sergeant chew his lip. His companion appeared amused. Eventually, the sergeant left. "He is new sir. The Earl of Oxford sent him three months since. I do not think the Queen likes him. I have heard your name, sir. My father served with the White Company."

"And you chose this life?"

"I had little choice, sir. The Free Companies are not what they were and this post pays good money. I fear we will earn it now."

"How so?"

He lowered his voice, "The King and Parliament, sir. They cannot agree. Some speak of the Lords and Commons ordering the King to speak to them. It will not happen, sir. I am just grateful that the Queen is here. She offers him good advice." He suddenly looked shocked, "I am sorry, sir. My father always told me that my tongue would get me in trouble. I should not have spoken."

"And you should know that I never betray anyone. Your words are safe with me and I am honoured that you should trust me."

The sergeant returned and he looked a little abashed. "The King will see you. Tom, take him to the King. Your servant and squire can wait in the guard room, sir."

I smiled, "He remembered me then?"

"Aye sir and sorry for any misunderstanding." I knew there was no misunderstanding. He was just trying to use the little power he had.

I was taken to the hall where there were clerks and clerics along with the King, a lady I took to be the Queen and then a grandly dressed lord. I knew without being introduced that he was the Earl of Suffolk, Michael de la Pole. He was no knight. A wool merchant elevated to rule the finances of England he had misjudged the mood of the land. I knew that from my travels from Southampton.

When the King saw me, he leapt to his feet, "Will Strongstaff! You have not abandoned me!"

I dropped to my knee. "My liege as I recall I was dismissed but I am ever at your beck and call."

"Rise." He turned to the Queen. "Anne, this is the man who saved my life and helped me to become the warrior I am."

Anne of Bohemia was a lovely young thing. When I met her, she was but nineteen. She was stunningly beautiful and had a quality of inner peace. She was a calming influence upon her husband. Although the marriage had been arranged I never saw a couple more in love. The King held his wife's hand and looked adoringly at her. He held her other hand for me to kiss. "Majesty, I am honoured."

"Rise, William Strongstaff, I have heard much about you. I beg that you stay with us here." She glanced nervously at de la Pole.

The King said, "A splendid idea. Have you brought people with you?"

"A squire and a servant."

"Excellent!" He clapped his hands and a herald stepped forward, "Ralph see my Steward and have rooms made available for my guests." He, too, glanced at the Chancellor who nodded.

He came over to me. His voice was heavy with suspicion. "I am the Earl of Suffolk, Chancellor of England. This seems a strange time to arrive. The French are preparing to invade and we have an army of ten thousand men preparing to repel them and you, Master Strongstaff, arrive from nowhere."

If he thought to intimidate me then he did not know me. I smiled, "It is pure coincidence, my lord. I was serving with the Earl of Derby and Northampton in Galicia when…" I put my hand into my satchel and brought forth the letter. I waved it tantalizingly in front of the Chancellor before handing it to the King. "I believe your majesties should read the letter. I can attest to the veracity of the information it contains for I was the one who obtained it.

The Chancellor held his hand out. "I believe that I should read it."

I stepped between the Chancellor and the royal couple, "I was charged with delivering the letter to the King and the King alone." My eyes made it clear that I would brook no interference. He nodded but I saw resentment on his face. Another enemy made!

The King read it and then handed it to the Queen. She studied it as though it was the murder weapon itself. He turned to me, "You serve my cousin."

"Aye, Majesty, but it was you placed me in his hands."

"Me?"

"You gave me the manor in Stony Stratford and then gave Northampton to Henry Bolingbroke. I owe service to the Earl and he claimed it."

His face softened and it was the King Richard of old. "I would you had not left me. You always gave sage advice."

The Chancellor said, "May I?"

The King nodded and the Queen handed him the letter. "Henry lives then?"

"He is lucky to be alive, my liege. The rondel blade almost killed him. He will barely make it back to England in time for the birth of his child." I saw a look of pain flash across the Queen's eyes.

"And you killed his would-be killers?" There was still suspicion in the voice of the Chancellor.

"I did."

"Then you must have an idea who is behind it then?"

"An idea but an idea only. The King of France is an obvious suspect but whom has he suborned?" De la Pole and de Vere were confederates. I dared not give my suspicions voice in such a public place.

The Chancellor was white with shock. "Assassins? In England?"

The King looked genuinely worried. "You must return to my side Will. I need you."

"And I will stay as long as I can my liege but I still owe the Earl service and when he summons me…"

"You would reject me for the Earl?"

"No, Majesty, I would ask the Earl to release me from my service."

The Queen smiled, "That shows honour. You are a true gentleman."

I did not mention that the Earl had said I was to be knighted. Was I throwing away my chance of a knighthood? I could not think that way. As my men at arms might have said, the bones were cast and whatever numbers I saw would be my fate.

The Chancellor handed the letter back to the King, "Your Majesty, I have to go to Osney Abbey where I will address Parliament. They are due to convene on the eighth of October. I must be there beforehand to attempt to win over some of those who would oppose you." He looked pointedly at me. "We need to speak."

The Queen linked my arm, "Come I will show you the Palace. I prefer it to the Tower. This is a warm and friendly old place."

Once we were outside she whispered, "The King needs you. Do not abandon him."

That word 'abandon' again. I had done no such thing. I smiled. "I will do what I can but the Earl of Oxford does not like me."

"He fears you."

I was surprised. He was probably the most powerful man in England and he was afraid of a mere gentleman? "I do not think so."

She nodded and looked sad, "I am but a woman and have no power but if I were to give the King a child then I know he would fear me too and drive a wedge between us. He tolerates me but he knows that you helped to form the King into the man he is. My husband often speaks of you and the things you taught him. They are the good side of him but when the Earl of Oxford is with him he brings out the worst in my husband or perhaps he is a mage and makes him do the things he does. My husband is a good man!" She buried her head in my shoulder and cried.

I was not certain of the protocol but I put my arm around her. "I know he is a good man for I saw the boy. I saw the man who faced down Wat Tyler. I will do what I can." Her words disturbed me. Was the Earl of Oxford somehow responsible for the barren nature of the King and Queen's marriage? I did not know if that was possible but I would not put it past the evil Robert de Vere. Suddenly Henry Bolingbroke's words made even more sense. The unborn son of the Earl of Derby and Northampton was now important to me as well as the Earl.

When she had regained her composure, she led me to our chambers. There were two rooms. They were not large and they were in the cold northeast corner but I did not mind. She pointed down the corridor. "My husband and I sleep in the south range. It is, however, on this floor. I pray that you can keep watch. It will make us both sleep easier."

"I will, majesty."

Henry and Peter were taken aback by the presence of the Queen of England. They both bowed so low I thought they would fall over. She smiled. The daughter of the Holy Roman Emperor had inbuilt grace and nobility, "Rise for you are in what is, temporarily, my home. I hope that you two, like your master, will protect the King."

"We will lady! I swear!" I smiled at the earnestness of Henry's words. They made the Queen giggle. "And it will be pleasant to have such youth at our table. I fear that the Chancellor, whilst he is a good man, is dull beyond words. We would have tales to raise our spirits."

I was not sure we could do that but I nodded, "We will try, my lady."

"And I will leave you now. I will send a servant to fetch you when the food is ready. Refresh yourselves after your long journey."

When she had gone Henry sat on his bed, "That is a Queen? She is so beautiful and yet she spoke to me as though I was her equal."

"All the great monarchs have that skill. Did you learn anything while you stabled the horses?"

Peter nodded, "Aye lord. The King refuses to go to Parliament. The Chancellor will go but the King will get no money. The King's uncle, the Duke of Gloucester, is on the side of Parliament. The rumour is that John of Gaunt might have sided with his nephew but he is in Galicia."

This was a conspiracy and poor Richard was caught in the centre of it. He was clinging on to the crown by his fingertips. What I did know was that Henry Bolingbroke was innocent. He did not want the King dead nor removed from power. Sending me to London with the letter proved that. He wanted the crown but he would have it through a natural process. I had to stay with the King but I needed to let the Earl know why I was doing it. I should have brought some of my men with me.

Poor Henry was very much out of his depth when we ate with the King and Queen. He had been used to eating at feasts but they were local lords. I had come from much more humble origins but I had experienced this more than he had. I could see that the Chancellor was put out when I was seated next to the King. The Queen had Henry at her side and Michael de la Pole had to make do with the Bishop of London for conversation. The King, despite the news I brought and the news from Osney Abbey, was in a good mood. He spoke quietly to me as we were entertained by a troubadour who sang the song of Elise and Abelard.

"I have thought about what you said this afternoon. I may have misjudged Henry Bolingbroke. I thought he sought my crown." I did not say that he would happily have the crown but would not do anything to take it by force. "Perhaps I have been ill-advised. It is just that Parliament seems to forget that I am King. I have the right to revenue! We need the coin to pay for our armies! We fight France!"

"Remember, Majesty, that the country has been ravaged by the plague. People have to work harder for there are fewer of them to do it. When they see their taxes being taken it makes them question the reason for it."

"I have tried to be a good king. It is just that I am surrounded by enemies and I know not whom to trust. Even my uncles seem to be against me."

"You are your father's son, King Richard. I believe that you are a good King. Your father was never put in the position of King. You cannot compare yourself to him. He did not have to ask Parliament for money. He had lands which provided that coin. Perhaps England will recover her lands."

He smiled, "I hope so and I feel that we are both safer with you here." He lowered his voice. "They tried poison blades and then attempted to murder him in battle?" I could tell that the attempted murder worried him.

"They did and they were household knights who did this. He is now protected by some of those who protected you."

"I should never have dismissed you. It was a mistake and I am sorry but Robert meant well. He comes from a noble family and does not see that someone raised to the rank of a gentleman can have a natural nobility within them. I learned much from you." He sipped his wine and it was as though a thought came to him. "Perhaps the new Duke of Ireland may find finance from that land and then I will not need Parliament."

"I have heard it is a poor country."

"It is but they have to pay their taxes too. It costs money to civilise a land."

I did not think that the Irish would see it that way but I did not wish to spoil his increasingly good humour. When the troubadour had finished the Queen said, "Tell us, Master William, of the battle you fought against the Castilians. Henry here tells me that they outnumbered you and the Earl of Derby and Northampton many times!"

"They did but we had that which they did not. We had the yeomen of England. Our archers and sergeants, as they did at Crécy, proved to be too good."

Keeping my part to a minimum I told them the story of the battle. I glanced at the King and saw that he wished he could have such a glorious battle to his name. His greatest victory was over the peasants at Smithfield five years earlier. None of his lords had managed a victory since then. I suspected that was why the French and the Scots were becoming bolder. They sensed weakness.

The food was good and the wine flowed freely. I did not drink as much as the King nor anyone else. I had promised the Queen that I would keep watch and I would. During our talk, I had learned that the Captain of the Guard had been appointed by Robert de Vere. I did not like that. Most of the guards, however, had been chosen by the King. When he was in his cups he told me that he tried to choose them as I would have. If I was going to keep watch then I needed to get to know them.

Captain Raymond Mavesyn was waiting to escort the King and Queen to their chamber when they rose. I walked with them. The Captain was Norman and he did not like me. I knew it from his look. "Thank you, Master William, I will escort their majesties to their chamber."

"As mine is on the same floor I will accompany them." I smiled, "After all, I was the first Captain of the Guard. I do not think I will have forgotten how to protect the King from all enemies; foreign and domestic."

The King giggled a little drunkenly and said, "Well said, Will!"

The Captain had no choice and he and his two men walked behind the three of us. When we reached the door, the King put his arms around me and embraced me. "Thank you for returning!"

"You are welcome, Majesty."

Anne of Bohemia mouthed, "Thank you!" and led the King within.

The two guards stood on either side of the door. I knew that the Captain wished me to go but I did not oblige. "Do you two stand watch all night?" They made the mistake of looking at the Captain. "Answer me or shall I ask the King to return to the door and explain my position here?"

The Captain screwed up his face and then said. "They will be relieved at dawn. I will bring their relief."

"What happens when you need to make water?"

"We go and make water!"

"And leave the King with just one sentry? Not good enough. I will return in the middle of the watch. First one and then the other can make water. There will be two men on duty at all times. From now on Captain, have a third man available. You are all paid well and have an easy life here. I know for I enjoyed it. Do I make myself clear?"

The three of them nodded and I left. I knew how to wake myself up. I would be there and I would ensure that the King was safe. I was, temporarily, back on duty and he would not be harmed on my watch.

Chapter 12

I woke after a couple of hours sleep. I managed to strap on my weapons and slip out without disturbing the other two. They had drunk more than I had. The two sentries were on watch when I walked down the dimly lit corridor. It was too dark. I saw that there were a couple of empty sconces. I would have them lit. The two men did not look like warriors. They lounged. One looked too young to have been a soldier while the other was overweight. He might have been a soldier once but that had been long ago. I nodded as I approached. The older one seemed to know me. "I will wait while one makes water."

"Thank you, sir." The older one scurried off to the nearest garderobe.

I turned to the other guard, he was the younger one. "What is your name?"

"Tolly, sir."

"And the other?"

"Alan of Ham."

"Have you been a soldier?" He hesitated. "The truth. I have good eyes and I know soldiers. You are too young to have been a warrior."

"My father worked at Windsor. He died of the coughing sickness and I replaced him."

I could understand why it was done but it did nothing to inspire my confidence. "Have you trained with your weapons?"

"I can use a sword, sir."

This was not a sentry for the King. This was a night watchman for a merchant. Alan of Ham returned. Tolly hurried down the corridor. "You have been a guard long?"

"All my life sir. I have seen thirty summers. I came here after serving the Earl of Arundel."

"He let you go?" He said nothing. I remembered the Peasants' Revolt. "Were you at Smithfield with the Earl?" His head went down and he looked shamefaced. I remembered that some of the Earl's men had not been willing to draw their swords on their fellows. Some because they agreed with the rebels and others because they feared to fight. I took Alan of Ham to be one of the latter. I said nothing more because he knew that I knew his secret. I had been there with the King.

When Tolly returned I said, "Neither of you are fit to be guards for the King. If I were a killer then you would both be dead as would the King and Queen."

Alan of Ham began to object, "Sir I..."

In a flash, I had the rondel dagger I had taken from Sir Jocelyn and my ballock dagger at the two men's throats. "And you would both be dead. I would slide your bodies down the wall and enter the chamber." I sheathed my weapons. Tolly was shaking. I poked Alan of Ham in the gut. "You need to be fitter. Get rid of the excess weight." I turned to Tolly. "Practise every waking moment. Show me your dagger."

He shook his head. "I do not have one."

I drew his sword. I ran my finger down the blade and then showed the young guard my hand. "My finger should be bleeding and it is not. Put an edge on this sword so that you can shave with it. Get a dagger. If a killer comes here then he will be able to get close to you. Your sword may be of little use. Have a dagger and find out the best place to stick it." I turned to Alan of Ham, "Have you ever put your blade in a man's flesh?"

"No, sir."

"Then if a killer comes then you will die for you will hesitate and a killer will not."

Just then the door to the chamber opened and I saw the King. He was smiling, "I should listen to Captain Will for he knows his business and, William, if you are going to instruct my guards I would that you did it during the day. Much as the Queen and I have enjoyed the lesson I do need my sleep. There are affairs of state which need my attention on the morrow."

"Sorry, Majesty." He slipped back inside.

Alan of Ham said, quietly, "I am not certain I could stick a man, sir."

"Then this is not the place for you. I will walk to the main doors and then return. Listen for my feet. If you cannot kill then you can at least warn. I will be trying to be silent." I walked to the stairs and down to the door. Two guards were playing dice. I was behind them before they knew. They leapt to their feet. "Who is captain of the watch?"

One nodded, "Me, sir, Peter of Lussac."

I saw that he was older than the others. He was the sergeant who had tried to deny me access to the King. "And you fought at Lussac Bridge?" My voice displayed my disbelief.

"I was with the army, sir. I was there when the Blue Company defended Sir John."

"Why are you called Peter of Lussac? You were not on the bridge with us."

He hung his head, "When I returned I said I had fought at the bridge with Sir John. I meant only to get free ale but the name stuck and I liked that men thought me a hero."

"You were not there with the brave men who died!"

"No sir, I was with the baggage train and I left the Green Company soon after."

"And now you dice while you are supposed to protect the King."

"I am sorry sir but there is no danger."

"There is danger and the King's life is in peril. I will be staying with the King for a short time. If you wish to keep this post then you will serve as though you had fought with me at Lussac Bridge."

"I will, sir, but this is the first time that any has checked on us."

"How many other guards are there?"

"Two outside the King's chamber and two in the kitchen."

"Where they will be sneaking ale and eating no doubt. Do your job Peter of the Baggage Train and use the edge of your tongue for I fear that the blade of your sword is blunt."

"Aye, sir. I will change I swear."

I was within six paces of Alan of Ham before he knew I was there. I shook my head, "Use your ears and your nose. Your eyes can be deceived at night. You know where my chamber lies. Wake me if there is danger!"

I half slept for the rest of the night. When I woke it was almost dawn. I went down the stairs and waited with the captain of the watch for his relief. When the six of them walked in my heart sank. None looked like warriors. "Which of you is captain of the watch?"

An older man with a grey-flecked beard said, "Me sir, Richard of Norwich. You are William Strongstaff are you not?"

"I am. Do you know me?"

"I have heard your name, sir. It is an honour to be in the company of one who has risen so far."

I nodded, "And you know how I have managed that? I did my duty. From what I have seen England's King could be murdered at any time and his guards would be powerless to stop his killer. You two command five men each. I would have those five men worthy to be the King's guards. It is not just a surcoat which marks you as the King's men. It is the ability to fight and give your lives for him if necessary. I saw that they had not thought that through. "Where does Captain Mavesyn sleep?"

Richard of Norwich pointed to the door. "In the hall by the main gate. It was the old warrior hall."

I left with Peter of Lussac and his men when they had been relieved. A growing unease filled me. Mavesyn was de Vere's man. The King had said he had chosen the guards. I now saw that Mavesyn had guided his judgement. The guards were all asleep. Richard of Norwich pointed to a chamber with a curtain across it. I strode to it and tearing the curtain down entered. The Captain was sleeping on a cot. I picked up the cot and deposited the Captain on the floor.

"What!" He leapt to his feet. "I could have you whipped for that!"

I laughed. He was naked. "It is all that you can do to stand on two feet. You said you would relieve the guards in the morning. It is morning and yet you lie abed. I could have killed your sentries and the King and Queen had I been an assassin. When the King rises I will ask him to dismiss you!"

"You cannot do that without the permission of the Earl of Oxford!"

I walked close to him and said quietly, "The King makes decisions and not your master. I know what is in your heart. I know what the Earl plots. I am returned and I will stop him." I saw the truth flicker in his eyes. I had it aright.

I walked from his chamber. Many of the men had heard the commotion and risen. I shouted, "Those who are still asleep, wake. This is a new day. Today you begin to become warriors again! When I have broken my fast I will return and all of you will be tested by me and my squire. My squire has little experience and any one of you should be able to best him. Let us see if that is the case eh?"

I heard groans and moans. Peter of Lussac shouted, "And any who are tardy shall answer to me. Now rise and obey Master William!"

I stood with my hands on my hips to watch the sorry apologies for guards as they stumbled from their bed. I had not expected to have to train the King's Guards. I would not have a rapid return home and the Earl of Derby and Northampton would need to wait for me to rejoin him. The men began to dress.

"Sir, look out!" Tolly's voice was strident and he pointed behind me.

I whipped my head around. Captain Mavesyn had his sword in his hand and was swinging it at me. The noise in the hall had distracted me and but for Tolly's cry, I would have been sliced in twain. I stepped towards him and gripped his right hand with my left. He was a big man but he had become soft. I bunched my right fist and hit him hard in the ribs. I did it three times and I heard ribs crack. He was not wearing a helmet and so I head-butted him. His nose erupted in blood and cartilage. He dropped his sword and, as he fell backwards I used the heel of my right boot to smash onto his knee. The knee folded back on itself and he fell to the ground, screaming in pain.

Leaning down I took his sword and threw it to the side. "You are as poor a killer as you are a captain. I will go and speak with the King."

The King and Queen were in the Great Hall. I bowed. The King smiled, "It was good that you were on duty last night. We slept well."

"I believe, sire, that Captain Mavesyn should be dismissed. He is incompetent and he has misled you about his men." I explained what I had learned the previous night.

"You may be right William, but he was appointed by the Earl of Oxford and I would not dismiss him without first speaking with the Earl."

I shrugged, "It is a mistake for I do not trust the Earl either."

The King's face darkened, "This was the cause of your departure last time William!" It was a threat but this time an empty one.

I nodded. "Then I will gather my things, lord. I would visit with my family before I return to the service of the Earl of Derby and Northampton."

I turned to go. "I have not dismissed you!" I faced him and said nothing. "I am King!" It sounded petty and the Queen grabbed his arm. The King turned to her and said, "You see, there is only Robert that I can trust!"

"No husband, you can trust William. He has done nothing wrong. He seeks to protect us. You said yourself you are more comfortable knowing that his sword guards you."

"But I am King! I will not be gainsaid."

"Sire, I do not question you. The quality of guards is not good enough and the captain is at best incompetent and at worst a traitor."

"A traitor?"

"He is putting your lives in danger."

Just then Richard of Norwich appeared in the open door. The King looked irritated, "Yes Sergeant? What is it? We are busy!"

"I came to tell Master William that Captain Mavesyn has taken his war gear and fled west!"

King Richard slumped in his chair and his wife put her arm around him. I turned, "Richard of Norwich, organise the guards. I will speak with them. Make certain that the Captain did not take keys with him!"

"Aye, sir!"

The Queen waved to the servants, "Leave us and close the door." When they had gone she spoke quietly, "Husband, William was correct. You must listen to him."

He nodded, dully, "What can be done?"

"I will spend a week with your men. I cannot be Captain of your Guard for I owe fealty to the Earl of Derby and Northampton but I will ensure that the guards who watch you are able to do so. I believe there are three sergeants?" He nodded. "Then I will see if one of those can take the position of Captain. Tell me, sire, how long do we stay here?"

The King seemed to have withdrawn into himself. He was a creature of moods. One moment joyous and the next in the depths of despair. The Queen answered me. "The King is summoned to Parliament and he will not go. Here he is safe from the mob. Until the Chancellor manages to secure the money for the war then we have to stay here."

"We are effectively besieged. I would suggest, Your Majesty, that your steward ensures that we have enough supplies for a month in case we are cut off."

"You are a good man, Will. Leave the King with me." The Queen held the King's hand.

I went out of the hall and up the stairs. Peter and Henry were dressed and waiting. "I think, Master Henry, that you are going to get a serious lesson in leadership sooner than you thought," I explained to them both what had happened. "So we have a two-fold task. The three of us must train the guards so that they can resist an attack on this castle. At the same time Peter, I want you to discover the true nature of the men. Which of the sergeants might make a good captain and which of the guards will never make a warrior? Do not worry I will be doing the same but you can perform this task in a less obvious way."

"Aye Captain. I can do that."

"The three of us will also share the duty of bodyguard. This will just be until we leave here but there is a killer out there and, at the moment, the King is unprotected."

We went down to the warrior hall. The two of them stood behind me. Sergeant Richard of Norwich had organised the men and they stood with their weapons. They were ready. "Sergeant, go and join your men and guard the King. I will speak with them at the end of their duty."

"Aye, sir." He hesitated, "I for one, sir, am happy to be following your orders."

"Thank you but I should warn you that I am not returning as a captain of the guard. I am here to perform a task." He nodded and left. "First you should know that I was the first captain of the King's Guard. The rules you should have been following were laid down by me. Captain Mavesyn was not a good captain. If you wish then you can leave now and follow him. If you stay then you obey every order I give." No one moved. "Good. That is a start. Who is the third captain?"

A younger man than I expected raised his arm. "I am Dick of Craven, sir."

"When I have done with the men I will speak with you and Sergeant Peter separately We need to understand each other." The two sergeants looked at each other. "Last night's watch can sleep until noon then they train. Peter and Master Henry, along with me, will test and train you with your weapons. Now all of you should be able to defeat easily Peter and my squire. Peter is no longer young and has an old wound. Master Henry is a callow youth but I am wagering that none of you will be able to defeat them. Even when you can defeat them you will still not be ready to defend the King and his wife. Out there is a mob and from what I understand their mood is ugly. You have to defend these walls in the event of an attack. I am here for a month and I have that month to make men of a rabble." A few flashed angry looks in my direction. "If any question me then I will fight them now and I will just use my left hand!" They had all seen the way I had disposed of the captain without a weapon. They might grumble but none would question me. I did not like it but to turn them into warriors I needed to become as cruel as my father had been. I did not have the luxury of time. "Get your weapons and assemble outside. Peter divide them into three."

"Aye Captain!"

The watch who were to sleep curled up in their beds as the others left. I said to the two sergeants, "Now you two and Richard of Norwich are the three contenders for the post of Captain. If you do not wish the post then speak now for I have little time to waste."

"Do not consider me, Captain. We both know that I sail under false colours."

Peter of Lussac went up in my estimation. I nodded. "Then you may rest. One more thing. I will need another man to become a sergeant. I would have your recommendations. I will be watching too." I went outside with Dick of Craven. "What is your tale?"

"You are blunt, sir."

"I have little time to be other."

"I wished to join a Free Company. I came to London but I fell in with a bad crowd and was arrested. Captain Mavesyn found me and offered me a post."

"He thought you were a bad man." He looked shocked but nodded. "You are not and you did not like the way the Captain ran the guard."

"Aye, sir, but I could do nothing."

"Well, you can now." Peter and Henry had the four wooden swords we used to practice fighting. "We need more of those making. For now, let us see how the men cope. Begin!"

I saw that a hulking brute of a man was dwarfing Henry. He hefted the wooden sword easily and the look on his face made me think he intended to do Henry harm. All of them were wearing their arming caps but not their helmets. Dick said to me, "Ham has broken a man's jaw in a fight before now. He is a streetfighter. The young man might be hurt."

"Good. Let us see if he is any good at fighting a half-trained squire." Henry had come a long way since I had taken him from his home. Today would be a test of him as much as anything. Ham hurled himself at Henry who deftly stepped out of the way and smashed his sword into the back of Ham's right leg. The guard crumbled and Henry brought the wooden sword around to crack into the back of his skull. He fell like a sack of wheat and lay unconscious. Henry picked up the wooden sword and, holding it aloft, shouted, "Next!"

Sergeant Dick said, "I see what you mean, sir." He walked over and took the wooden sword from Henry. I guessed that Henry would not have it so easy.

Peter had already disarmed his opponent and was gesturing for the next one. I watched the sergeant. He was more cautious in his approach. His stance, however, showed that he had not been taught to use a sword properly. Henry was more balanced and was ready on the balls of his feet. Dick brought his sword down to strike at Henry's head. As Ham had discovered an arming cap would not stop a wooden sword. Henry lifted his sword to meet it but did a trick I had taught him. He twisted his own sword and the wooden sword flew from Sergeant Dick's hands. The wooden sword was at Dick's throat in an instant. Henry was doing better than I had thought. He had watched and he had learned. The King had two young squires but John and Ralph were even less experienced than Henry. They were but thirteen years old and were decorative squires rather than functional ones. Had they had any skill then I might have had them join in the training.

That evening I dined with the King and Queen. I could see that he was still unhappy with me. His mood was not helped by the fact that his Chancellor had still to return from the meeting with Parliament. The mood was strained. Queen Anne came to my rescue. "I heard the swords of the guards practising. How did that go, Captain?"

"Better than I had hoped. There will be bruises and cuts but they are improving. By the end of the week, we might have made progress." The King glowered at me. "Your Majesty, the men are not bad. They were presented to you as plausible guards by Captain Mavesyn because he thought to make you weak."

"Then that must have been done without the knowledge of the Earl of Oxford. I will write to the Earl and ask him to visit with us. I need his support. I cannot have Parliament telling me what to do! He has soldiers and they will restore order!" He was deluding himself.

A day had passed since he had been smiling and happy. He was a creature of moods. The Queen turned to Henry. "And how did you enjoy practising, Master Henry?"

"I surprised myself, my lady. The Captain has kept me from harm since he took me from my father's hall but he has worked on me as a potter works in clay. He has fired me. I thought I was fragile and I would break but I survived and defeated men who were older than I."

I warned, "They will get better, Henry!"

He laughed, "And so shall I!"

The week passed quickly but there was still no sign of Michael de la Pole and the King was increasingly anxious. Nor were there words from the Earl of Oxford. That did not concern me. There was no sign of the mob and the men had responded well to the training. Now Henry, Peter and I coached them in their techniques. They were all better swordsmen. Their weapons were sharp and they each had a dagger. I had issued pikes too for if we were attacked they would be a weapon which could keep men from our walls. Each of us was mailed from the moment we rose until the moment we retired.

When the Chancellor, the Bishop of Durham, and his officials arrived back at the palace his face told me that it was not good news. Surprisingly I was not dismissed when the Chancellor reported to the King. "Well, Chancellor? Do I have my funds?"

"Wine!" A servant hurried over with a jug of wine and poured some in a goblet. He downed it in one and then sat. In the presence of the King, this was unprecedented.

"Well! Chancellor?"

When he spoke, it was in a small, tired voice. "My liege they say that the sum of one hundred and fifty-five pounds is unprecedented. They seek to impeach me and the Earl of Oxford. They demand that you dismiss me and the Earl. Further, they demand that you appoint your ministers in Parliament from now on."

I saw the Queen as she gripped her husband's hand. I could see him becoming red and angry. He stood and shouted, "I would not dismiss as much as a scullion from my kitchen at Parliament's request!"

"Husband, you upset yourself."

"Who are these common ingrates to tell a King what he can and cannot do? Chancellor, you will return to Parliament and..."

"Majesty, if I return then I will be arrested. This time they mean business. Your uncle, the Duke of Gloucester, as well as the Bishop of Ely and the Earl of Arundel, are leading the opposition to your councillors."

The King turned to me, "What can we do, Will? Who is loyal to me?"

I could not answer him truthfully but I would not lie to him. "Majesty there are many men who are loyal to you. I would wager that more than half of the country is. However, here is the south and close to London there is a mob. They are easily roused. Your best troops are in Aquitaine and Castile. Your uncle has an army which could quell this trouble. Perhaps you could send to Henry Bolingbroke. He should be back in England now."

I was not sure if he had heard me. He smiled, "Robert will come and save me. I can trust him." He turned to his wife. "Now you will see the wisdom of giving Ireland for the Earl to rule. His army will be loyal!" He waved over Walter Skirlaw, the keeper of the Privy Seal. "Walter return to Osney. Ask for a delegation from the Commons to meet with me here. Tell them that I will discuss the matter further."

"As you command, Your Majesty." The official did not look happy but he turned and with his escort left.

"Chancellor, when they arrive we will arrest them and hold them hostage. Then they will pay the money I demand."

"Is that wise husband?"

"I am King. It is my right to do so!"

"Sire, I have but forty men to guard you. This will not be easy."

"You too, Will? Remember when I faced down the peasants? This is just like that. They think to break my will. They will see that they are wrong." He smiled at me. "It is good that you had the steward lay in supplies. We can laugh away a siege now. The training you have given the men will stand us in good stead! Well done, William!"

The problem with the King was that he saw one world and it was not the world we lived in. He could no longer demand of Parliament. That horse had left the stable. I would do as he commanded for I was loyal but he was wrong.

The next two days were a maelstrom of action. While the castle prepared for a siege I had to finish training the men and ensuring that we had sound defences. When I had brought the letter from the Earl it had set me on a path I wished I was not treading.

My guards were kept busy with people coming and going. It was hard to keep track of who had entered and who had left. In the end, I put Peter and Henry at the gate with Richard of Norwich and they made it difficult for people to get in. I stayed with the King, Queen and the Chancellor. The King was in a bad place. He was promising to pay back all those who had crossed him. The Bishop of Durham, who was the Treasurer, counselled caution. The Chancellor just feared for his life.

The Commons and the Lords wanted a scapegoat. They needed someone to punish and the Earl of Suffolk was the one most likely to be singled out for punishment.

The King was back in good humour. He was convinced that Robert de Vere would arrive with an army and restore his power. "Chancellor, do not fear. We have William Strongstaff here." He turned to me. "You will be my champion will you not?"

I was confused, "Champion?"

"Of course, champion! When my father made you swear to watch over me it was with this in mind."

"But who would I fight, sire?"

Even Queen Anne looked confused. "You are not thinking straight husband."

"Whoever comes for me will be challenged by me and I will have them fight my champion, Will. Trial by combat will defeat our foes and I shall have my money and power will be restored to the monarchy!"

The Queen looked at me and I gave the slightest shake of the head. This would not work. The days of trial by combat were long gone or so I thought. I did not argue with him. I just allowed him to rant for a while. When he had calmed a little I said, "My lords I will have the gates closed at dusk. No one enters or leaves in the hours of darkness. We cannot risk the King or any other lord coming to harm. There are desperate men out there." I did not mention the assassins who still sought the King's life. The King was already in a high state of anxiety.

"Good, William, and we are secure within these walls."

I went to the lesser gates and ordered them closed and barred. The men I commanded were now a better force of fighting men. They had more discipline, self-respect and skills. Many, such as Tolly, had been disappointed in the regime run by Mavesyn. However, I had too few to defend the walls. If we were attacked then we would withdraw to the keep. I headed to the main gate. A group of men approached. There were nine of them. Their cloaks hid any weapons they might be carrying. They were dressed as though they were just folk from London but I saw that they had tanned skin. They had been in hot climes.

Peter, Henry and the four men who stood guard had not seen me. I reached the gate just as they were arguing with Peter. "We have a petition to deliver to the King. He must see us."

Peter said, "I cannot allow any in without the permission of the Captain."

One of them growled, "Then get him, cripple."

When my voice roared it made everyone jump, "And you watch your mouth spawn of the gutter! I am the Captain and I tell you to begone."

I think that they had planned carefully what to do. I had played into their hands by identifying myself as the Captain. It was no secret that I was back and protecting the King. The nine of them suddenly threw off the cloaks and ran at us. Dick of Craven was at the gate and he had his sword out even before I did. Peter was also fast. The axe which came towards Tolly would have taken his head had Dick of Craven not brought his sword down to hack through the wrist of the first man. None of us had shields and I whipped out the rondel dagger from my boot. I knew that these men would be mailed.

"On me!"

Part of their training had been obeying commands and instinctively all formed a line. Henry was the slowest but even he was in line before the eight unwounded attackers could react. The seven of us filled the gateway. What I worried about was that there were more men waiting to enter. We needed these dispersing and the gate closing. With the bridge up we were safe. I brought my sword over my shoulder and aimed for the neck of the man ahead of me. He was an old soldier and his dagger came up to block it. Without shifting my eyes, I lunged at his head with the rondel dagger. He tried to block the blow with his sword but the narrow head of the dagger penetrated his hand and he dropped the sword. Even as I hacked again with my sword one of them tried to stab me. The tip of his sword was too wide and although he hurt my side my mail held. I sawed the sword back and blood spurted from the man with the punctured hand. I pulled back again and swung at the bearded man who had stabbed me. He blocked it with his sword and I stabbed with my dagger. He blocked it with his own.

All down the line my men were engaged with the tanned warriors. I heard boots running across the cobbles inside the outer ward as Richard of Norwich brought reinforcements. I had the chance to study the man I was fighting. He had a long scar down his cheek and his sword was an old fashioned one. There was no fuller. It was broad almost to the end and it was very heavy. His dagger was almost like a short sword. Our swords and daggers were locked. He was strong but I was stronger. I pushed and his feet began to slip for there was a slight slope on the cobbles leading into the castle. He tried to spit at me. I moved my head but I smelled garlic. The man was French. I brought my knee up but he was wise to the move and he blocked it with his own. When Peter slew one of his men and Dick the other my opponent shouted, "Run!" Even though it was just one short word it was said with a French accent. Four men fled.

I looked and saw that Ralph was dead or soon would be for he was bleeding from a stomach wound and Tolly had also been wounded. "Get everyone and the bodies inside. Close the gates!"

Richard of Norwich and the four men he had brought fetched in the dead attackers and we slammed the gates shut. "Search them for clues as to their identity. Then take their heads and put them on pikes on the battlements. I would have all know the penalty for attacking us!"

"Aye Captain."

I went to Tolly. He had been stabbed in the left arm, "How is it, Tolly?"

He smiled, "I might be wounded, Captain, but I feel like a warrior now! I will live and I will be better for it!"

Later, as the bodies were thrown into the moat, I reflected that we were now under siege. The King was at war.

Chapter 13

It was dark by the time I reached the hall. We had discovered little from the clothes and coins of the men. They had Spanish and French coins but that was not a surprise. Most of us did. Unlike those we had discovered in Spain none were fresh-minted. They had served abroad. Two had been in the Holy Land and the rest had been in Spain. We deduced that from some of the items of clothing they wore. Their weapons were the weapons of sergeants and not knights. To get close to Henry Bolingbroke they had used knights. They could use anyone in an attempt to kill the King for he did not surround himself with knights. Anyone we did not know and many that we did could be suspect.

I gathered the three sergeants around me. "From now on we have two men guarding each entrance to rooms which the King and Queen occupy. If a killer thinks he cannot escape then he might be reluctant to risk his life."

Dick of Craven said, "You are forcing them to act at night when the castle is asleep."

I nodded, Dick was quick thinking. "And that is why we are all operating a two-hour shift. I want all of us alert. Until this problem with Parliament is solved we are stuck here and we do not have enough men. It appears that the King has few friends."

Peter of Lussac said, "But there are many people who support the King!"

"Sadly, few of them are lords. We do not worry about that. Our task is to keep the King safe. While he eats we just need one watch on the walls and four men guarding the doors. Peter, Master Henry and I will be at the table. I do not think there will be an attempt there but we will be ready if there is. I will watch during the night too. For the time being, I become the cat and take sleep where and when I can. Remember, the only ones we trust are our men. All else are suspect. Better to upset a suspicious looking priest than lose the King."

I sent Henry and Peter to rest and I joined the King and Queen in the Hall. The Chancellor and churchmen sat together. They were deep in discussion. Everyone knew of the attack. They did not know it was an attack on me rather than the King. Pages and servants were kept busy serving wine and small bites of food. The Queen's ladies in waiting all chattered like magpies and the King and Queen were seated alone before the fire. They looked lonely. How many people dreamed of being in their position and yet the present incumbents were not enjoying it at the moment.

I walked over to them and the King said, "William, sit. The Queen has chastised me for my treatment of you. Forgive me." He held out his hand. On it was a ring with a blue stone. "See she has given me this ring to remind me that you are a true warrior and I should trust you. You have ever served me true and yet I doubted you. What happened at the gate?"

I decided to be honest with them both. They deserved that. "I believe it was an attempt on my life. Someone sent malefactors and hired swords to bring me forth and kill me. They failed."

The Queen looked shocked, "Why kill you?"

I said, flatly, "For without me you would both be easy to kill."

"Surely not."

"Yes, King Richard. If I was a killer I could easily hide in this castle until dark. If you know what you are doing then you can hide almost in plain sight. Your guards are better than they were but they do not have the experience to sense when an enemy is close. Perhaps Captain Mavesyn was involved in this I know not. Certainly, his practices left the two of you vulnerable. I have changed all of them. If he is advising the killers then he will be in the dark about what we are doing. The sooner we can get to Windsor the better, lord. It is a stronger castle and there is a larger garrison." I stood. "My men are watching you. I will go and wash. I have blood on me. We will sit at your table and when you retire this night then so will we."

I think they were shocked into silence at my dire predictions. I hoped they would not come true but Henry had sent me to warn the King because he believed there would be an attempt. I was now convinced of it.

Henry was asleep when I entered the room. "You should sleep too, Peter."

"I am like you, Captain. I can live off short sleeps. The lad has done well. If I am to be truthful better than he should with grandparents who sheltered him for too long. I know they lost their son but every man deserves the chance to live his own life. He will make a good knight."

"Aye he will but we have a few more days of danger to endure."

"Days Captain?"

"I believe this crisis will come to a head soon. This is not like a battle where a few brave men can determine the outcome. There will be a storm which we must ride out. Tonight, watch for any who behave differently. If you see a servant you do not recognise then challenge them. The Steward will know their names. Make sure that you and Henry wear your mail. It will be uncomfortable but had I not been wearing mine earlier then I would now be dead." I took off my bloody surcoat and put on a clean one. "We had better have our surcoats washed tomorrow. If the Commons come here we will need to look like warriors and not vagabonds."

I washed and then combed and oiled my beard. It refreshed me as much as a sleep and then I descended. I left Peter gently waking Henry. It was almost a maternal gesture. The old lame warrior cared deeply for the youth.

The table was not the normal one. Usually, there were loud conversations. This time men and women ate and drank as though this was their last meal. As I walked in I noticed that the conversations were subdued. Heads were close together as though the words they spoke were not to be heard. When I walked in all heads turned. Only the Queen smiled, "Master William, we were waiting for you to begin. You and your men have worked hard this day. Come and celebrate that we are all alive!"

I saw some shocked looks from the churchmen but the King smiled. "Yes William, you give us all hope. Sit."

Henry and Peter followed me. We tried to be jolly but it was hard. We had lost Ralph today. Peter and Henry had trained him. There was guilt that they had not done a good enough job. I told them that war was like that but it had hit them hard. Few others would have even known his name. He was a face beneath a helmet holding a sword. I was just pleased that the King had been dragged from his dark pit of despair by his wife. When Robert de Vere had arrived, it had taken away the better parts of the King. Anne of Bohemia had the opposite effect. I just felt sorry that the people of England had not taken to her. She was a good woman but had been portrayed as the cause of England's woes by Richard's enemies.

The evening ended sooner than most. All wished to be in their chambers with a barred door. The three of us escorted the King and Queen upstairs. Peter of Lussac was waiting for us with James and Alfred. The Queen giggled, "Six men to see to my chamber and the seventh is my husband. I am a lucky lady to be guarded by seven such gallant gentlemen." It was the perfect thing to say and I saw James and Alfred grow taller by a handspan.

When they had gone inside I said, "All is quiet?"

Peter of Lussac nodded, "I checked all the sentries and each of the gates. All are barred. I will go and ensure that the outer doors are all barred, Captain." He smiled, "You can rest easy. I am not the laggard I was when first we met."

"I will watch when I can." I smiled, "First I make water!" This was where I missed men like Peter the Priest and Red Ralph. One of them would have made a joke at my expense. I missed the banter. Here I was Captain. I was beneath the lords, ladies, kings and queens but above the men, I led. It was a lonely life. I went to the garderobe and then headed to the main gate. One of the changes I had made was to have burning brands placed outside the castle. They helped the sentries see any who approached. All were alert. In a short time, the lax life encouraged by Captain Mavesyn had been replaced with order and purpose. I descended the stairs to examine the outer ward. All was quiet and I wearily climbed the ladder to the gate which led to the inner ward. Here all was quiet. On the main gate and the fighting platform around the outer ward, there had been the noise of London which lay not far away. The higher walls seemed to hide the sound and I stopped. All was quiet. The servants' quarters were silent. The fact that the feast had finished early gave them the unexpected pleasure of a little longer in bed. In a few hours, they would rise and prepare food for the household. The bakers would have left their dough to rise. The baker's assistant would be up within an hour to light the bread ovens. He would be woken by the Captain of the watch's cry to change the watch. That was another change I had made. In Captain Mavesyn's time, some watches had lasted longer than others and it led to resentment. When the watch was to be changed it would be announced. That would not happen for two hours. I headed back to the royal quarters and my bed.

Matthew was the sentry who walked the walls around the inner ward. His was a lonely watch. He saw no one and so I stopped to speak with him on the fighting platform. "Is it all quiet, Matthew?"

"It is Captain. I think you deterred any who might do the King harm at the gate."

I nodded absentmindedly. That was the general opinion of all of the guards. Was it true? So far the attempts to kill both Henry and Richard had been purposeful and in numbers. It seemed that those who conspired to murder the king and the one who would be king did not rely on one means. In Galicia, they had used de Ufford and Sir Jocelyn. Then it struck me. The attack on the gate had been a diversion. It was to distract me and my men. Sergeant Richard had brought the men from the inner ward to help us. When they had done so then the gate to the inner ward had been left unguarded. Now it was locked but had we locked a killer inside?

"Matthew, leave your pike here. Come with me."

"Aye Captain."

I drew my sword. I raced into the royal quarters. The top floor was occupied by the royal guests and we quickly descended the stairs to the royal apartments. We hurried down the corridor which housed the Chancellor, the Bishop of Durham, and the royal squires. At the corner of the corridor, I saw a pool of blood. Opening the door to the squire's chamber I hissed, "John, Robert, treachery! Fetch your weapons!" As I neared the King's apartment I saw that it was Peter of Lussac's blood. The quantity told me that he was dead. Even as I turned the corridor I saw Alfred die. A killer held his mouth and one of his two companions slit his throat. James lay dying next to them. "Awake! Awake! Treachery!"

The three killers were all mailed. One pushed Alfred's body towards me and then pushed open the door to the King's chamber. The other two turned to face me. I had Matthew with me and he was mailed but John and Robert were not. It could not be helped. I ran at the two men who obliged me by rushing towards me. One lunged with his dagger. He had been the one who had killed Alfred. The ceiling was low and that prevented a blow from above and the two filled the corridor. Behind them, I saw Peter and Henry emerge from our chamber and run towards us. I punched with the hilt of my sword even as I felt the blade strike and enter my mail. The man fell but I felt the prick of his dagger as he pierced my flesh. If the blade was poisoned then I had a short time to live and the lives of the King and Queen were in great danger.

Steel clashed as Matthew, John and Robert hit the other killer. The two squires were brave but I feared for their lives. I burst into the room. The King had a dagger before him and he had placed his body between the killer and the Queen. Perhaps the would-be killer had thought his companions would have delayed me more for he had yet to strike at the King. I did not hesitate and, as soon as I had cleared the door, I swung my blade. It was more in hope than expectation. The man was an experienced warrior. He blocked my sword with his but the movement turned him from the King. Outside I heard shouts and cries as the battle raged. I trusted that Peter, Henry and Matthew would be able to deal with the two killers.

"You cannot escape! Surrender!"

The man spat and when he spoke it was obvious that he was French or Norman. "And be hanged drawn and quartered? I will do that which I intended and then kill as many of you eaters of beef as I can! I am a warrior!"

I drew my ballock dagger, "You are nothing more than a knife in the night! You are a killer!"

He suddenly lunged at me with both his sword and his dagger. I barely blocked them with my blade and the force of his attack knocked me backwards. The door slammed shut and we were in complete darkness.

His face was close to mine, "And now we are in my world. I will kill you and then your King and Queen. As you lie there bleeding to death know that you have failed!"

The wound in my side was now bleeding freely. Soon it would weaken me and he would succeed. Those outside could not get in for I was pressed against the door. I felt him push his sword against my dagger and my left hand gradually came towards my neck. My hauberk did not cover my throat. I pushed back as hard as I could. I think I would have died had not the words of Red Ralph come to me. When I had been a scrawny boy and others had bullied me, he had taught me how to use the strength and weight of others as a means of defeating them. I suddenly kicked my legs out and his weight and mine dragged us to the ground. I was supported by the door. When a man falls he instinctively puts out his hands. So it was with the Frenchman. His sword struck the door and not my neck. Even as he fell across me I lunged blindly with my dagger. Had it been the rondel dagger in my boot then I might have ended his life but it was the ballock dagger. I found flesh and sliced across his hand. Unfortunately, he also slashed blindly with his dagger and he ripped down my cheek. Blood spurted and he shouted triumphantly. I punched with my sword and rolled from beneath him.

"Captain! Are you alright?" Henry shouted and hands banged on the door.

I did not shout for I was still in the dark. I could see nothing save for the shadow of the man. I rose into the crouch aware now of the blood seeping from two wounds. It was the Queen who saved me. She flicked the flint to light the candle. The sudden spark made his head turn and I lunged low. My sword entered his thigh. He shouted in pain as the blade scraped along bone. The room flared into light as the Queen lit the candle. The Frenchman turned to swing his sword at me. Even as I raised my sword to block the blow the King's dagger slashed across his throat from behind and the assassin died.

The door burst open and Peter and Henry stood there bathed in the light from the corridor. The Frenchman lay bleeding to death in a pool of blood. Even as I looked the life went from him. I regretted his death. Had we taken him alive then we might have learned much. "Thank you, sire, I owe you a life."

The King was shaking. I do not think he had ever killed anyone before. The Queen came to me with a piece of cloth. She held it to my face, "William, you owe us nothing. Had you not come when you did then Henry Bolingbroke would now be King. Fetch the doctor!"

The slash to my face required many stitches. It would be an ugly wound. Poor Robert and Matthew had both been killed before Henry and Peter could get to them. The King was saddened by the loss of his squire. The survivors were all better warriors for the experience but the memory of that night would live long within us. The King and Queen had been within a handspan of death.

The Chancellor and the Bishop of Durham were even more shaken. That killers could enter the castle made them fear for their own lives. It showed me that they were driven by self-interest. It was the King who had been the target. The Parliament and their demands were forgotten. The King and Queen had been within a sighing breath of death. After the room had been tidied and all had been dismissed the King and Queen sat with me.

"William, I have treated you badly. I should not have dismissed you. The Earl of Oxford is a good man but he was wrong about you. I needed you. I will not make the same mistake again. I would have you choose for me another twenty guards before you return to your home. You are an honourable man and it is good that you serve my cousin. I know now that he is not my enemy. I was told that he sought my crown. I can see now that while he wishes it upon his head he will not try to take it. If he wished that he would not have sent you to warn me. And now we must prepare a story. This was not an attempt on my life. The killers were friends of those you killed at the gate. This was for revenge. They were trying to kill you and your guards. We have all those involved swear an oath that this attempt on my life will remain a secret."

I nodded, "Aye, sire, for an attempt on the life of a King might encourage others to regicide. Then, when I leave, it will be seen not as desertion but as an attempt to make your lives safer." I smiled, "Your wife has helped to make you wiser, sire."

He nodded, "My wife is the better half of me that is true and I bless the day we were wed."

The doctor had had to shave my face before he would stitch the wound. It made the wound look even worse. I would bear the scar to the end of my days. It looked worse when he had finished for it stood out on my newly shaven face. I would have to regrow my beard else I would terrify my children and my wife.

The rest of the day was sombre. We buried our dead and disposed of the bodies. It became clear that the three killers had entered when we were distracted at the gate. One of the servants remembered cloaked men hurrying across the outer bailey but thought nothing of it. There had been many people coming and going and he was but a servant. The sentries had been watching for danger from without. The killers had hidden in the castle until we retired and then came to do their deadly deed. I now saw that they could have escaped. They merely had to rid themselves of Matthew and they could have slipped over the wall. It was my suspicious nature which had spoiled their plan.

If I thought that life would become easier I was wrong. Two days later the Duke of Gloucester, the Bishop of Ely and the Earl of Arundel arrived at the castle. Parliament had decided and the King would not like their decision.

The Duke of Gloucester, Thomas Woodstock, was an uncompromising man. Just a year younger than myself he had been the last of King Edward's children to survive to adulthood. I do not know if he resented his nephew but there was no love lost between them. The other lords just followed him. As he represented England's Parliament King Richard had to receive him. I knew that the King was intimidated for while he made the parliamentary delegation wait outside he sent for me. "I know that you are still healing from your wounds, William, but in the absence of the Earl of Oxford, I need someone with a military reputation. The Chancellor is a man of coin."

"But I am just a gentleman, sire."

"A gentleman who is well respected."

And so I stood to the side of the two thrones as the delegation approached the King. "So, uncle, have you come to tell me that my Commons and Lords have agreed to fund the army we need to defend England?"

I saw the look of pleasure on the Duke's face as he said, "No, sire, I have not. As you have consistently refused to meet with us and, so I hear, threatened to have the delegation we planned to send arrested, I am here to deliver an ultimatum."

"Ultimatum!" I saw the Queen squeeze his hand. "I am the King!"

"You are the King so long as the people are willing to fund you and your circle of leeches."

"Is that a threat, uncle?"

He shrugged, "If we do not grant you any funds what will you do, nephew? Had you come to Osney you might have done as you did with Wat Tyler and his mob. You might have used your charm to bring them to your point of view. However, I fear that horse has bolted and the

promises which were not fulfilled will not be believed a second time."
The King was silent. I knew that he had not made good on the promises
which he had made. "So here is our ultimatum. The Earl of Suffolk,
Michael de la Pole, is to be dismissed and his lands confiscated. He is to
be imprisoned and tried for treason. The Bishop of Durham and Walter
Skirlaw are also to be dismissed from office with immediate effect. The
Earl of Oxford is to be brought before Parliament to answer charges of
corruption and murder."

"That is preposterous!"

I noticed that the three men who had been dismissed hung their
heads in acceptance of the sentence. The King was going to lose.

"I have not finished. You will come to Parliament where you will
have new councillors appointed to guide you."

"You would choose those who counsel me?"

He smiled but it was a cold smile, "No, nephew. You choose your
council and Parliament will either say yay or nay."

I was the only ally Richard had for his councillors had deserted him.
His wife continued to squeeze his hand. He looked around at me. I
smiled at him despite the fact my new wound hurt me. It was a
pathetically helpless gesture. I was telling the King that he had my
support. When his shoulders sagged and his head drooped then I knew
that he had lost.

"I am bereft of nobles who will defend me and I am forced to accept
your decision but I would have you know that God is watching how you
treat his anointed servant and like all such sins there will be
punishment."

I know the Duke of Gloucester thought it a melodramatic gesture
from the King but I knew that King Richard would never forgive his
uncle. I saw the King look along the line of those who had delivered the
ultimatum. One day the King would make them pay. He would have
vengeance for this betrayal. I was suddenly tired of this life at court.

"It is eighty miles to Osney, King Richard. If we leave by noon then
we need to spend just one night at St. Albans."

"And my safety? Can it be assured?"

"Of course, but will you not be bringing your guards and the
redoubtable Captain William?"

"I will. Now leave us so that we may make arrangements." When
they had gone he turned to me, "Will, you have suffered enough for me
but I would have you go to the Earl of Derby, Henry Bolingbroke. Tell
him of the attack on my person. It is a secret but he should know. Tell
him that I need his support. Do this for me, Will."

"But what of your guards? Who will lead them?"

"They have shown that they are worthy of my livery. You choose a captain."

"And the Earl of Oxford?"

"He must have been delayed. Once he knows what has happened he will rally to my side. With him and my cousin we can end this rebellion."

"Aye, Majesty. I will tell Dick of Craven. He is the better sergeant."

We left an hour after the sun was at its zenith. The Duke of Gloucester wisely skirted London and the mob. We reached St. Albans after dark. As we were in unknown territory Henry, Peter and I slept in the King's chamber much to the amusement of his wife. She was the one light in the King's life and lit up his darkest moods of despair. As we rode to the Parliament I spoke with the king. "I will try to get you more guards. I know the type of men you will need."

The Queen said, "Do you think the threat is still there, William?"

"I know not. All the killers who have been sent have died. From the coins in their purses, they were well paid. Perhaps the King's enemies will have to think again." I did not mention that I was sure Robert de Vere was involved. The King still would not believe me.

The King nodded. He had grown in the last few weeks. "I will start to choose knights in whom I can have complete faith. I would have more men like the Earl of Oxford around me. When this is over, my love, we will travel my land and seek support. England loves their King and I will prove it. My uncle thinks I am defeated but I am not. This is a setback only. I have sent to Dover for Sir Simon Burley. He is ever loyal."

My heart sank. Sir Simon had been one of the causes of the revolt by Wat Tyler. Sir Simon had been given the Cinque Ports and Dover. He had had enough men under his hand to come to the King's aid but he had not.

We parted at Osney. We stayed with the King for the first night to ensure that Captain Dick was happy about protecting the King. As we left the next morning the King was almost tearful. "I have learned much in the last month, William. No matter what happens you are a true friend and I will never forget what you have done."

The Queen gave me a small ring with a blue stone. "William, I give this to you. Wear it in memory of a Queen who regards you as her champion. You may not be a knight but in my mind, you are greater than any knight in the realm. Your wife is a lucky woman."

Chapter 14

We did not have far to travel. Our destination was less than a day northeast. We had our spare horses with our treasure which slowed us down a little. I had been away less time than I had told my wife but it still felt like a lifetime. I knew I would have to visit Stratford first and that would delay my arrival home by half a day. I would have to stay a night with Sir Robert. The last few miles, as we rode through what many considered the most beautiful part of England, I sensed that Peter and Henry were not ready yet to part company.

"Captain, if you need Master Henry again then know that I would gladly serve." I saw Henry nodding vigorously.

"Your lives have both been in danger. The fate of Robert, Ralph and Matthew could so easily have been yours."

"But we are alive, Captain, and serving you we felt so too."

Henry nodded, "Peter is right. We were in danger and we were alive. We served an Earl and a King. How can I go back to learning how to tally figures and balance books? I have fought against Spaniards and defied assassins. I have rubbed shoulders with Kings and Captains of vast armies."

I shook my head, "I have a message to deliver to the Earl. That message may determine that he no longer needs me. Part of me hopes that is true for I tire of this deceitful world where men struggle for crowns when ordinary men fight merely to live."

Peter smiled, "You do yourself a disservice, Captain. I watched and I listened. You have done your best for those ordinary men. If you are not there then the land will be fought over by the nobles."

I sighed, "I will take you home Master Henry. You now have the skills to fight as a knight. As for the rest? Learning the rote, reading, writing, composing a ballad, holding a vigil? All of that is a foreign land to me. Your grandfather can teach you. When you are a knight then you will not wish to associate yourself with a mere gentleman."

He said, quietly, "That will never be true, Captain."

The braziers outside his grandfather's hall beckoned us and ended our conversation. It should have been a joyous reunion but Henry wanted more time with me. I felt sorry for his grandparents. His grandmother burst into tears when she saw him and embraced him so long I feared he would not be able to breathe.

Sir Robert put his arm around me. "He has grown and he looks like a man. You have brought him back to me safely and you have earned your bounty."

"He is a good man. He left a boy but he is a man. He has killed, lord, more than once." The look of shock on Sir Robert's face almost made me smile. What did he expect? "More than that he has protected and saved the life of the King. King Richard will be forever in his debt."

"But there is talk of rebellion!"

I turned to face him and my words became harsh. This was a merchant. This was someone who worried more about piles of coins than the heart of a country. "Put those thoughts from your head! King Richard is King of England and your grandson will support him. You mention rebellion and you drive a wedge between you and your heir. He does not wish to be a merchant. You set him on a path and now there is no turning back. He will go to war. My suggestion is that you have him tutored so that he can pass the rites of knighthood. He has come back rich. He does not need your support."

"He has his own coin?" I heard the incredulity in the knight's voice.

I pointed to Peter who was unloading their chests. "As does Peter. If Peter is a freeman then he may choose to leave your service."

The knight looked crestfallen, "Had I known this…"

"You could have done nothing about it. Henry takes after your son. He would be a soldier."

His eyes were sad as he said, "You are right. We opened the box and now must live with it." His wife took Henry inside the house. "And you, what of you?"

"I fear that in serving you I have opened my own box and it is infinitely more dangerous than yours. I will say no more for the less you know the better. I will go home for a few days and see my wife and then I will leave. The Earl of Northampton is happy that you fulfilled your promise and you will be safe but your grandson will leave one day and your choice is to make it easy or hard." He nodded. "It is late and…"

"Of course! How rude of me. You are our honoured guest. I must seem churlish to you. You have done all that I asked and yet I carp on about matters which are nought to do with you. Come. We will feed you this night and hear my grandson's tales."

I felt inordinately sorry for Henry's grandmother. She was desperate to have her grandson back home but he had already left and she did not know. I watched his grandfather as Henry animatedly spoke of events in

Castile and Eltham. I thought, at one point, that he might speak of the attempts on Henry and Richard's lives but he did not. He had grown. Peter was not invited to the feast and for that, I felt sad. The two had been so close for so long that the absence of Peter seemed almost a crime. It was, perhaps, no wonder that Peter wished our lives could continue as they had.

As Henry spoke of the meeting with the Duke of Gloucester and my presence at that meeting Sir Robert said, "You are a more important man than I thought, William."

"I was at the meeting but I could not alter the outcome. It is important men who shape the world in which we live. Men like me are used to alter outcomes. There is a difference. No one ever asks my opinion."

"You are not the man I expected when I invited you to take Henry under your wing. You have earned your one hundred pounds and more."

"You need not pay me. Henry is a good squire and he has helped me immeasurably."

"I may not fight from a horse nor do I have the courage to do as you do but I am a knight and my word is my bond. The money I promised is yours and it is small enough payment for the return of my grandson. I am in your debt and it is a debt I can never fully pay."

The journey home was the shortest of journeys. I had my five horses and they were laden. Henry and Peter had done well but my rewards were so great that I almost feared that I might be attacked by brigands. When I reached the Earl, I would have more coin coming my way from the proceeds of the last ransoms and treasure from the campaign. I was rich and I felt empty. I had let King Richard down and yet I knew not what I could have done to change things. It was the Earl of Oxford who was the problem. He had changed Richard from the boy I had trained. I knew that when he returned King Richard would fall under his sway once more. As I neared my home I wondered about travelling to Wales and instead of returning to Henry Bolingbroke of killing the Earl. It would make an enemy of the King but it might save him and save England. It would mean the end of my life as I knew it but was it the right thing to do?

I had been away long enough to see a change in my son. He was less chubby and his running was more confident. He hurled himself down the track which led to my hall. I saw my wife and daughter waiting by the door. I dismounted to sweep him up into my arms.

"I have missed you!"

"And I you, son! You have grown!" I lifted him and put him in the saddle. I retained the reins.

"Is all this the treasure you took?"

"Aye, son, it is."

"And you won!"

I put the deaths from my mind. Soldiers had to do that or risk madness. You buried your dead and hid their bodies in the dark recesses of your mind. You prayed that their spirits would not come to haunt you. "Aye, we won." And yet in the winning, there was no victory for me. I would have a brief interlude at home and then I would have to obey the orders of my King and make an unlikely alliance with Henry Bolingbroke. I would be deserting my son and my family, again.

My son looked down at me. He saw my scarred face. "Did you kill the man who scarred you?"

"Aye son, I did." He nodded as though that satisfied him.

My wife was genuinely pleased to see me. As a servant held the reins of my horse she threw her arms around me and kissed me hard. She said, huskily, "I have missed you!"

As she stepped back I laughed, "Is this the way for the wife of a gentleman to behave before the servants."

She giggled, coquettishly, "I care not for…" she suddenly saw my new scar, "what has happened?"

"I was doing my duty. I am a soldier." One of my wife's women had been holding Alice and I took her from the servant. "And have you missed your father?" In answer, she burst into tears and began wailing.

My wife laughed and took her, "Do not terrify her husband. Our son may not mind the scar but this little one barely knows you. Hush, hush sweetheart. It is just your father." The wound I had received felt as nothing compared with my rejection by my daughter. It was as though someone had used a ballock dagger to disembowel me. "Come let us go inside and I will quieten her. John, fetch in the master's baggage."

I turned to pick Tom from the saddle. At least my son was not afraid of me. Was I a monster?

My wife had fed our children herself. Unlike the ladies of knights and other gentlemen, she did not use a wet nurse. Alice began to calm as she sucked at her mother's breast. My wife smiled. "From the baggage, you have brought you have done well!"

I was desperate to show my family that my absence had been necessary. I grinned and took out the purse of gold from Sir Robert. "One hundred pounds from Sir Robert!" John had brought in the chests. I took the small one and emptied it on the table. Coins tumbled out. Two gold pieces fell to the floor and Tom raced after them. He found them and raised them triumphantly. "I also have other treasures in the chests which may appeal more to you. There are spices from Spain, cloth and pots. We were successful."

Her eyes widened, "You are the best of husbands! Why I think that there is none save Sir Robert within fifty miles who has as much coin as we do! We could buy the village!"

I laughed. Tom held up the two coins, "And with these, I could buy a horse and armour!" Alice's tears were forgotten and I briefly basked in the affection of my family.

Later that evening, when the children were abed and we had eaten I sat by the fire with Eleanor and told her all. She was my wife and she deserved to know what her husband had been doing. When I told her of the attempt on the King's life she made the sign of the cross, "To kill a king is a mortal sin!"

I nodded, "To die in battle is one thing but to be stabbed in your bed is quite another."

"You liked the Queen?"

"As would you, my love. They are desperate for children but God has not granted them any yet."

She frowned, "That is not natural. You are sure that the Queen wishes to have children?"

"Of course. I am convinced."

"Then there is another explanation. The women who work in the inns as doxies and whores do not want children. There are draughts they can take which stop babies being born. I do not know what they are but I know they exist. Old Gammer Gurton who lived in Buxford was a woman who made potions. She was a horrible old woman with no teeth and breath like a pig's behind. Once, when I went for a potion for my mother she told me of such potions. I was terrified and thought that she meant to frighten me with stories of things untrue. My mother confirmed what she said. Someone may be secretly giving the Queen a draught. From what you have told me there are people who wish this line of kings to die out. You said she has ladies in waiting?"

"There are ten of them."

"Then any one of them could easily give the draught to the Queen. Even now it might be too late. The draughts, even when they are no longer taken, can change nature. The Queen may now be barren."

I was appalled. This was like the murder of an unborn child and went against God and nature. The name of Robert de Vere sprang into my head. This had all the hallmarks of one of his plots. When next I saw the King, I would have to discover whence came the Queen's ladies. Even now it might be too late.

Eleanor snuggled into me, "And you go away soon?"

"The King will need the help of Henry Bolingbroke. He is in Monmouth and I must go there."

"Surely you can spend a few days here in your home." I looked down and smiled. She giggled, "I take no draughts and we now have enough coin for a houseful of children."

I kissed her on the top of her head, "But my scar!"

"It will be dark and it is not your scar that I will see."

In the end, I spent five days with my family. They were five wonderful days. The nights were passionate and the days filled with laughing children. I was content.

"You will need a servant when you travel west. You are a gentleman now and we can afford one."

"Aye but I need one that can handle himself and I can trust."

"How about John son of Jack? He helped you train Master Henry last year. He enjoyed the work and I think he is less than happy to be a farmer. Perhaps he needs to travel away and then he will realise that he can work the land."

"A good suggestion, wife."

"And I will have you more tunics and surcoats made. We have enough females who can sew and I can buy the cloth at Stratford market."

Tom piped up, "And you can make one me, mother!"

Eleanor laughed, "Listen to the cockerel! Just because he no longer trips over his own feet he thinks he is grown up!" She picked him up and hugged him, "It is a good job you are so adorable. Aye, I will make you one if only to make you enjoy church!"

My wife was clever. Tom had to be dragged to church and wearing his father's livery might just make it a more pleasurable experience. Church had rarely been an option for me as I tramped Aquitaine and Spain behind my father. Even now I felt uncomfortable in church. Father Abelard seemed to understand me. In the end, we were delayed by almost a week by a sudden violent storm which flew in from the south-west. Trees were brought down and rivers flooded. Even had I wanted to leave my farm I could not have done so. By the time the storm had passed and we had cleared the damage it was All Saints Day. John and I took a sumpter for I was unsure of the accommodation we might find on the road. The storm had been so powerful that it might have struck other parts of the realm.

The roads were in a terrible state. The one hundred miles took three days. Had John not been such a good rider then it would have taken us longer but he was a natural horseman and got the best from his palfrey.

The hard journey helped to make us close. He was just a little younger than Henry but he knew more of the world than did Henry. He was the son of a tenant farmer. Henry had been the cosseted grandson of indulgent grandparents. John's hands had laboured. He had the chest of an archer for he had practised at the butts with his father. He had had run-ins with other youths. He knew how to use his fists. Most importantly he knew what he wanted from life and it was not the life of a farmer.

On the second day, as we headed for Tewkesbury, he opened up a little to me, "Had you not asked me to help work with Master Henry, sir, I might have ended my life as a farmer. I think I would have been unhappy. My father worries about the crops which do not ripen, the frosts which come early, the storms which come from nowhere." As if to illustrate his point he waved an arm at the fallen trees which lay next to the road. "Then I saw you and realised that I could have a life which was not on the land. My elder brother Jack enjoys the farm. He can take over from my father. I would be a soldier."

I shook my head, "John, the life has more worries than those of a farmer. You worry that you will not be paid. You often have to search for food or boil leather belts and baldrics to ease hunger pains. You risk being abandoned by a lord. You fret over the animal you ride in case it goes lame. There are worries when you are a soldier."

He smiled, happily, "I know, Captain. There are other reasons I would follow in your footsteps. When I held the shield for Master Henry to charge and when I sparred with him with the wooden swords I knew that I had more skill than he did. He is a noble! He will be a knight but I knew that unskilled as I was I could best him. You were an ordinary soldier and yet you became a gentleman and rub shoulders with a king! My father can never do that. If Sir Robert calls the muster my father will be called and he will stand with the other archers but there will be no reward for him. I would follow you, Captain. I would take my chances there."

He seemed to have thought it all through, "When we return from Monmouth we will talk again and I will speak with your father. It will be his decision; not yours and certainly not mine. I will not come between a father and his son."

We spoke over the next two days and nights about my life as a soldier. He was genuinely interested. I gave him a version of my life but kept secret those parts which were precious to me. I gave him the story that others knew. I told him of my time with King Richard and with the Free Companies. I told him of the recent campaign in Galicia.

When I had finished he smiled, "See, Captain Will, you have proved my point. You say the campaign was badly planned and organised and yet you came back with riches! I would follow you and take my chances."

Monmouth Castle was a magnificent structure. It rose from the river and dominated the land. A town wall had been recently added so that the castle, a favourite of Henry Bolingbroke, would be very hard to take. I could see why the Earl had left his family here when he went to Galicia. Even if the Welsh rose they did not have the siege engineers to destroy such a magnificent castle.

We reached the town in the late afternoon. As we passed an inn I spied some of my men as they emerged. "Captain Will!" It was Roger of Chester and some of my men at arms.

"How are the men, Roger?"

"Desperate to return to your service, Captain." There was a message beneath his words but I knew this was a public place.

I dismounted and led my horse, Jack. "Come we will walk to the castle. I take it the Earl is within?"

"Aye Captain. He dotes on his new son, Henry."

Then there was an heir should Richard die childless. Henry had been convinced there would be one. Did this change things? Would my message for Henry Bolingbroke to come to the aid of King Richard fall on deaf ears? The sound of our hooves covered the sound of our voices and so I said, "Come, Roger, what is amiss?"

"The Earl is a good man, Captain, but we are treated as mercenaries. His knights and captains command us as though we are servants. Captain, we are your men and you treat us well. The men grow unhappy."

I nodded, "And I have been tardy. Yet you are paid and the contract lasts but a little while longer, does it not?"

"It does but we hoped that you might find more work for us."

An idea began to form in my mind. I could serve my men and serve my King. As we were escorted by my men we were not stopped at the gate. I sent John and our horses with Roger of Chester while I went to speak to the Earl. Geoffrey, his page, smiled when he saw me, "His lordship will be pleased to see you, lord. I will tell him you are here. If you wait without."

I did not have to wait too long. The doors opened and Henry Bolingbroke stood grinning, "Master William! I have a son! Henry of Monmouth is a healthy boy! It is good news is it not?"

I nodded, "It is lord, congratulations. I also have news."

He frowned, "Do not bring a rain shower here, William. The storms of the last month hurt us badly enough as it is."

"I come from the King."

He sighed, "Come. There is an antechamber where we can speak in private. Richard, guard the door." Once inside with his squire watching the door, he poured two goblets of wine. "You are a good fellow but your sense of duty can be tiresome." He gestured to the seat and I sat. "On with your tale!"

I told him of the attempt on the King's life, the ultimatum from the Duke of Gloucester and the plea from the King.

When I had finished he nodded, "You were right to come so quickly. I like not this curbing of the King's powers. It smacks to me of my uncle being vindictive. He will never be King nor will his son. My son, Henry of Monmouth, puts his son even further from the crown. I am pleased that you were able to prevent the murder of my cousin. I know people think I would take the crown from Richard but I would not. I believe in here," he tapped his heart, "that one day either me or my son shall be king. I am young and I am healthy. I have time. You may tell Richard that I will not fight him but the same does not hold true for Robert de Vere."

"The King sets great store by his friend, lord."

"And he is mistaken! We both know that. Would you fight alongside Oxford?"

"No, lord, he is an evil man and he has some sort of power over the King."

"Then we have an accord. When the weather improves, after Christmas, I will go to London. I have been away from these lords for too long. Gloucester, Arundel and Mowbray gain power at the expense of the crown." He looked at me. "You are my liegeman but I would have you swear an oath."

I hesitated, "Lord, know that I am loyal to the King. I will never do anything which might lose him the crown."

"And I would not ask you for such an oath. I would have you swear an oath to keep what I say secret, even from the King. He is, at best, naïve and at worst, well perhaps he has an ailment hidden deep within."

"Then do not tell me anything, lord, and then I have no need for an oath."

"But I need an oath for if you do not know what I am to tell you then we might come to blows at some point and I would not wish that."

I looked into his eyes and I made a decision. It was one of the most important ones I ever made. I trusted Henry. I believed that he would not harm Richard. I nodded, "Then I so swear."

"Good. I will pretend that I am in agreement with these lords who seek to undermine Richard but know you that I am not. I seek to find out their plans. If I can stop them I will and if not then I will go to Richard and side with him. Does that conflict with your oath to Richard?"

"If you mean it then no, lord."

He frowned, "You are an uncompromising fellow. That will have to do." He took my arms and we clasped. We had fought together. There was a bond of blood between us. "How long do you stay?"

"A day or two only, lord. The King wishes to go upon a gyration around the country to seek support. I would loan him, my men, for he has perilous few guards."

Henry looked disappointed, "I had thought to keep them about me for they are good fellows."

I did not say that they wished to be gone. "When the King has finished his tour then they will be available."

He shrugged, "There will be no need for warriors for a while. It is just that their presence helped to improve my own sergeants and archers. No matter." As we left the chamber he said, "I would be wary when you leave Monmouth, William, for the Earl of Oxford is north of here in Powys raising men. I do not trust his motives. Thanks to my cousin giving him Ireland, the man is rich. He sees himself as King of Ireland. He is a dangerous man and I have heard that he hates you. He seeks your death. Beware him."

"Thank you, lord, and I will."

"Now let us go and see my wife and my most handsome son! When he is of an age I would have you make him a warrior. The lessons I learned from you live with me still."

Lady Mary was a lovely lady and I could tell that she would be a devoted mother. Unlike many ladies, she seemed happy to nurse her child. The babe was simply that, a babe. He did not cry overmuch and I am not certain he even opened his eyes in my presence but I said all the right things and pleased the doting parents.

In the end, I stayed for three days. Part of that was the influx of visitors who came to see the Earl's son. Some were friends, others were not. They appeared not to notice me and I blended into the background. The Earl was true to his word and gave my men their full pay for the six months. They were happy. He also mentioned to me, again, the knighthood he had promised. "When next I am in London I will dub you and find you a manor. I am Earl of Derby as well as Northampton. I would do this for you. The service you have done for me deserves a reward." I did not get overly excited for I did not wish to be disappointed when it did not materialize.

We left to head east and my home. There we would drop off the horses my men had captured in Galicia and I would take them to Windsor to meet with the King. John son of Jack was in awe of the men. He knew Dick Stone Heart but the others were new and he could not do enough for them. Knowing that the Earl of Oxford was to the north of us we kept scouts out and we watched as though we were on campaign. Someone might have told the Earl that they had seen me or he might even have a spy in Monmouth. The Earl now had enough money to be able to afford an army of spies.

It was Lol son of Wilson who spotted that we were being followed. We did not just have scouts ahead of us, we kept a couple behind and a couple on the flanks. From my journey west, I knew that we would not be able to have accommodation all the way east and I guessed our pursuers did too. Lol told us that there were thirty riders following us. He was too clever a scout to give himself away. He knew their numbers but not their make-up. As we neared the end of our day's ride he nudged his horse next to mine.

"Captain, there are thirty riders behind us. It may just be a coincidence but I think they are following us. When I stopped they did too. They tried to escape observation but I counted thirty horses or so."

My men were not given to either exaggeration nor unfounded fears. I nodded. "You have done well. Ride ahead and tell Stephen the Tracker to find us a good campsite in the woods. It needs to be one we can defend."

"Aye Captain."

Roger of Chester had overheard Lol's words. "Do we turn and scatter them, Captain?"

"That is not enough. We must lure them into an attack and then hurt them. I think our men will have more skill than they do. We will test their mettle."

The road, west of Oxford, climbed through a wooded area. There might be a lord of the manor but I knew of no castles which were close by. During the civil war of Stephen and Matilda, there were many adulterine castles which sprouted across this part of England. King John had had most of them demolished. The plague had further decimated the population. We would be alone.

Roger and Lol spread the word amongst my men so that they all knew there would be action in the night. The campsite which Stephen chose was a mile or so from the road and close to a stream. It was the sort of place experienced men would choose. It was, however, easy to defend. The hollow by the stream was a perfect place to disguise the presence of horses and keep them safe. The bushes and undergrowth at the edge of the clearing, which looked to have once been the domain of charcoal burners, made a natural barrier which would mask our positions.

When we stopped, the men made the camp as normal but, at the same time, they made it easier to defend. While apparently making water my men were also laying traps to trip unwary men seeking to do us harm. They cut saplings just a couple of fingers up from their base, covered the stumps with leaves and used the sapling as an obstacle. Poor John son of Jack seemed confused by our actions. I had him collect firewood. The stormy weather of a while ago had been replaced by scudding clouds and the promise of a chilly night. A fire would seem necessary.

My men all had mail. Even the archers had managed to acquire a brigandine each. Garth of Worksop had bought or traded a mail hauberk. They all had a good sword and while the food was being prepared they surreptitiously sharpened their weapons. I waved John son of Jack over. "Tonight, we may come under attack." He started. I smiled, "You must learn to control yourself and your face. Pretend I have just told you that we eat rabbit. Just nod and smile."

"We are being watched?"

"Not yet but this is a good habit to get into. The men you see around you are the best at what they do. None of us fear an attack for the night is our friend and the woods are our ally. You must pretend to sleep when the camp goes quiet. The others will too but if we are attacked then you just stay out of the way of my men. You do not have any experience and they do. Can you do this?"

He smiled, "Regard it as a test for me, Captain, and I will impress you." He suddenly laughed, "See, Captain, I laugh at the joke you have just told me."

I nodded, "You will do, John son of Jack, and I can see promise within you."

As the sun began to set for the days were getting shorter there appeared to be a great deal of activity in my camp. That was because four of my archers, led by Stephen were heading into the woods. Once it was dark they would wait for these potential enemies to pass them. The men in the camp made a great deal of noise and moved around the camp making it hard for a watcher to keep track of numbers.

Roger came to join me while I ate. John son of Jack squatted at our feet. It looked natural for John was little more than a boy. "All in place, Roger?"

"Aye Captain. Joseph and Wilfred will appear to be the sentries and they will talk close to the fire. If any who approach see them then the attackers will assume that they can no longer see well in the dark. The archers will feign sleep close to the fire and the rest of our men will be close to the traps."

"Good. And who is with the horses?"

"Dick Stone Heart."

John said, "But Captain how do you know that men will come this night?"

"We do not know for certain, John. It may be a coincidence and they happen to be on the same road. If that is the case then my men and I will lose a little sleep. Better lose sleep than a life. If you would join the ranks of warriors then know that the ones who survive are the ones who are cautious. The reckless die fast. Now eat. This is a good stew."

I saw Roger smile. My sergeant had no family. I could not see a reason why not for he would have made a good husband and father. If John joined us then he would be under Roger's wing and my sergeant would keep him safe. After we had eaten I walked to the bushes and made water. I could see nothing but I knew that four of my men were hiding and they were watching. If there was an enemy out there they would see me. If they had an archer or a crossbow then I was a dead man for with the glow of the fire in the dell I was a clearly silhouetted target. I finished and shouted, "Keep a good watch, Wilfred!"

"Aye Captain."

"We leave early on the morrow. I can smell a change in the weather." The little play was for the benefit of any watchers in the woods.

I went back to the blanket and cloak I had laid on the ground. I was far enough from the fire to be slightly in the shadows. I laid my bare blade and dagger next to me and I rolled in my blanket with my back to the fire. Then I waited. My men all made water and retired to their beds. A couple chatted first. That was natural. Roger was the last one to turn in and he lay just five feet from me. We waited. Autumn had made the trees shed their leaves. They would be a natural warning in the woods. A good woodsman, like Stephen and his men, could move through them and not make a sound. I couldn't. I would be more silent than most but even I would make a noise. There was silence. The rustling in the branches would be roosting birds. The rodents and animals who lived in the woods would steer clear of the smell of men and woodsmoke. Their scurrying would be in the distance.

There was no way to tell the passage of time but when I heard John son of Jack making the snuffling noises of sleep I knew that we had been feigning sleep for some time. Joseph and Wilfred had stopped speaking but I knew they still stood by the fire. The difference now was that they had turned so that they had their backs to the fire and their faces were concealed by the hoods of their cloaks. The noise I heard was in the distance. The night made it hard to determine the true direction but there was a noise. Having heard one I soon heard another. There were men approaching. They crunched leaves. Their visit could still be innocent. They could approach and call to the camp that they wished to share our fire but, in my heart, I knew that these were enemies and they were coming for us. My hand slipped to grasp the hilts of my dagger and my sword. The noises grew. From the stream one of our horses whinnied in the night and was answered by another far to the west of us. The guard with their horses would be cursing the animal which might have alerted us.

The traps we had made were simple ones. Old and worn bow strings were strung between trees close to sharpened stakes. They would not kill but when they were tripped they would wound and it takes a strong-willed man not to cry out when his thigh is punctured by a sharpened stake. The saplings and their stumps would trip a man. We would hear their stumbles. I heard the sound of the fall and then the cry as the hidden warrior sprang the trap. He cried out and I jumped to my feet. I heard the whizz of a crossbow bolt and then the snap as it struck the shield which Wilfred of Loidis had pulled before him. Arrows flew from the dark but this time they were sent by my archers and they struck the attackers in the back for Stephen and his men were behind the warriors. I moved towards the shadow I saw heading towards me. Our men were spread around in a circle and I knew it was not one of my men. I pulled my sword back and swung it hard. The man ran at me for all he saw was a silhouette before the glow of the fire. I blocked his swinging sword with my dagger. The firelight's glow glinted off the helmet he wore. My sword struck him hard in the side. I heard him grunt in pain. My dagger was across the hilt of his sword and I twisted it as I lunged at his eye. He screamed as it was pierced and then fell silent when it entered his skull.

All around me was the sound of battle. My men were masters of the night. I saw Roger of Chester used his gauntleted left hand to hold his enemy's sword while he rammed his own sword up into the man's neck. My archers had laid down their bows and were using their hatchets and short swords to deadly effect. I heard screams and cries as men died. Then I heard a horn. Men ran west.

"After them!"

I did not want to be looking over my shoulder all the way home. We would kill as many as we could. I saw the back of a man and knew it was not one of my men. I used my long legs to catch him and brought my sword down hard. Although he was wearing a brigandine it was one which fastened at the back and straps are always a weakness. My sword split the straps and laid his back open to the spine. He screamed, fell twitching and by the time I had passed lay still.

We reached their horses just as fifteen of them escaped. I looked around for any of them who had survived and there were none. "Bring back the horses and their dead. Let us examine them by the firelight. Are any of our men hurt?"

A voice came from the dark, "Lol has a dagger thrust to the leg.

"Geoffrey of Gisburn has his face laid open."

"Then see to them. We have been lucky!"

Stephen the Tracker ghosted next to me, "Not lucky, Captain, simply better than the dogs they sent after us! They were the men of the Earl of Oxford." He held up a surcoat. There were three crowns quartered but the white star on the red quarter was the most obvious sign that Robert de Vere had sent his men to kill us. Now I did not care if the King approved or not. The Earl of Oxford was now my enemy and I would oppose him with every fibre of my being.

Chapter 15

We buried their bodies before we left. I did not know the people who lived close by but they could do without carrion feasting on the flesh of the dead. John son of Jack was shocked when he saw the wounds we had inflicted. As we rode east I said, "Do you still wish to be a warrior?"

"Aye Captain, but I can see that it will be a hard journey to become as accomplished as your men."

Roger of Chester nudged his horse next to me. "It seems you have annoyed the Earl of Oxford, Captain."

I nodded, "When the King sent the messenger to him he must have spoken of me. The Earl regards me as a danger to him."

I did not speak of the attempt to murder the King but in my mind, there was now no doubt that the Earl of Oxford was in some way implicated in the murderous plots on Henry Bolingbroke and King Richard. I knew now that there might come a time when I would find myself fighting against those who supported the King. I could not and would not fight alongside the Earl of Oxford. I wrestled with the dilemma all the way back to my farm. As we came east we saw increasing signs of the approach of winter. I would have to ride with my men to King Richard sooner rather than later. I did not know when he intended setting out but Roger and my men would need time to get to know Captain Dick.

It was dark when we reached my farm. I had no warrior hall but I had a good barn and my men were happy to use that. My wife had not been expecting us and so I ordered the slaughtering of a couple of older sheep and my men set to making their meal.

"Master Henry came a few days since. He was less than happy with you. He said you had not finished training him."

"But I had! The rest of his training requires a knight to do it and, as yet, I am not a knight." As much as I liked Henry I had enough to worry about without having to fear for his life too. I had too many enemies and my position was becoming more dangerous by the day. Allied to the King, what was becoming known as the Lords Appellant, the Duke of Gloucester and his camp would regard me as an enemy. The Earl of Oxford and those who ostensibly supported the King thought me a threat for my connection with Henry Bolingbroke. My only ally appeared to be the son of John of Gaunt and by his own admission, he was going to play a dangerous game of duplicity. The quiet life of a farmer appeared not to be for me.

My wife made my welcome a warm one for she knew my mood and gave me comfort. The result was that I woke in a better humour than I went to bed. After I had broken my fast I went to the barn as my men were rising. They were all warriors and knew that weapons needed to be kept in good condition. Roger of Chester and Stephen the Tracker came to speak with me.

"Captain, how long do we stay here?"

"I thought to leave for Windsor in the early morning."

"Good we will be ready." Roger walked off leaving me with Stephen. The archer appeared to have something on his mind.

I smiled, "Come, Stephen, speak. Better to let that which is on your mind out than allow it to fester within."

He nodded, "Wise words, Captain. It is this. My men and I are happy to serve the King but we are not sure that he will need archers."

"He needs good men to watch over him."

"But what if he does not need us? We have enjoyed our employment. Regular food, a roof over our heads and coins in our purses mean we cannot go back to the life under the greenwood."

I had not thought of that and he was right. The King would have no battles to fight. He just needed men around him whom he could use as a wall of metal twixt him and danger. "You have a point. How about this, if you are not required by the King then I will retain you as my archers."

"That would cost you coin, Captain."

I did not say that Henry Bolingbroke had promised me a knighthood. When that happened, I would be given a manor. A manor meant I needed a retinue. "Let me worry about that. Besides, I will need a hall for warriors such as yourself. I will pay you to build me a hall and you shall live in it." He looked relieved. "But if the King wishes to retain you then he will have the first call upon your services."

"That is fair, Captain."

When we had cuddled I had told my wife that I would be leaving for London. She had been eminently sensible about it, "Then better you leave as quick as you can. I would have a Christmas celebration this year for we have much to celebrate and Christmas is a time for a family to be together. Your son is growing and he misses his father."

She was right and we prepared. John son of Jack now understood what would be needed on the journey. He had watched the others and taken lessons from them. It was an easier task for me. Master Henry arrived with Peter and his horse the night before we were due to leave.

"Master Henry, what brings you here?"

"I do not wish to sit in my grandfather's hall and wait until I am ready to be a knight. I am learning the rote and I can already speak the languages. I can practise just as well in your hall as well as my grandfather's and I will learn more."

"Master Henry I have a poor farm and your grandfather has a mighty hall. You would be more comfortable there and your grandmother misses you."

"She smothers me, Captain!" He pointed to my men in the barn as they prepared their mounts. "And you are going on a journey! Let us come with you."

I had no time for an argument. "You may come with us but you will spend Christmas in your home. I would have mine with my family!"

If I thought to hurt him with my words then I failed for he grinned, "Excellent, Captain. Peter and I will sleep in the barn with the men. I would discover what their journey was like."

We headed south and east while there was still a night's frost on the ground. Owls still hunted. The King has said he would spend Christmas at Windsor and so we headed there.

My poor horse had had to deal with the heat and arid nature of Galicia and now had to contend with autumn storms followed by bone-chilling cold. They were hardy horses. Jack was like an old friend. He was the best horse I had ever owned. As we rode through the start of winter I wondered just what the future held. We rode down deserted roads. The fields were empty and the towns we passed appeared deserted. I could see why the Duke of Gloucester had opposed the levy on the people. They could not afford it. The war would be to regain land lost by the King's great grandfather. The lords who would benefit were the ones who had lost land in France. I found myself changing my views as we neared Windsor. We did not need a war. We needed a stronger England with people who were not overtaxed and were well fed.

Dick of Craven greeted us at the gate. His welcome was a little muted, "You bring a large number of men, Captain. Do you mean well?"

Dick was doing his job. It was exactly what I had told him to do. "The King asked me to return and I have. However, there are ten of my men who would serve the King on his gyration."

He looked relieved, "I am sorry if I offended you, Captain, but there is unrest in the land. The journey from London was fraught. The Queen was abused by the people as we rode through the city. It was not right and the King was angry."

"I will speak with the King. Is there room in the warrior hall for my men?"

"Aye, Captain. You have come when the King is meeting with his supporters. Sir Simon and Sir Thomas Mortimer have been here for some time."

I took Master Henry with me. I felt dirty from the road but I was anxious to conclude my business and return home. Windsor felt like a besieged fortress. I saw the liveries of many lords. The King was in conference. We were made to stand without and I wondered at that. Was this a council of war? Was the King planning on plunging the country into civil war?

It was her perfume which alerted me to the presence of the Queen. She appeared behind me, "Captain William and Master Henry, this is an unexpected pleasure." She frowned. "You are being made to wait?"

I shrugged, "The King is closeted within. I do not mind."

"Come with me." She turned to the page who waited without. "When the King has finished fetch us. We will be in the south chamber." She took my arm and we headed down the corridor. Her six ladies fluttered behind us like a gaggle of geese. "This is a more agreeable castle than Eltham. Here there is room and we are far from the mob. If we had a family…" I heard the despair in her voice. Then she shook her head, "God will grant us children when he deems it right. We have our health and we should not complain." We turned a corner. I saw guards at each corner and alcove of the corridor. Dick had heeded my words. "I see that Master Henry is with you."

"He needs the courtly skills of a knight. I cannot teach him those but I thought that being in the company of the King and Queen might rub some of the rougher edges from him."

We reached the chamber which had the luxury of light as well as a roaring fire. She gestured to one of two seats, "Sit, I pray you. Ladies, entertain Master Henry while I speak with the Captain."

I saw Henry flush as the giggling ladies surrounded him and took him to a padded couch by the window. He gave me a pleading look. I just smiled. This was part of his training as a knight. He had thought to come to me for action and now he would see a different side to knighthood.

When the servant had poured the wine, she waved him away. "So Will, was your mission a success?"

"Partly, my lady. Henry Bolingbroke neither opposes nor wishes to usurp your husband. Of that I am certain. As for open support?" I sighed, "May I speak openly?"

"Of course."

"It is Robert de Vere, the Earl of Oxford, who is the stumbling block," I told her of the attack in the woods. "I know the King appears to be blind to the Earl's faults, but it loses him support in the land."

"De la Pole is incarcerated in Corfe Castle. Is that not enough?"

"We both know that de Vere has more ambition than the Chancellor."

She shook her head, "You are right, Will. I have tried to make the King see but he appears to be under some sort of spell." She suddenly looked at me. "You still support the King!"

"Of course, but I oppose his servant, de Vere. I would fight de Vere but not the King."

"Then you are in an impossible position."

"I know. Perhaps the King's uncle, John of Gaunt, will return and bring order."

She shook her head, "I fear not. He is too busy in his new Kingdom. Henry Bolingbroke is our only hope of reconciliation."

I was now in an even worse position. I could not tell the Queen that Henry Bolingbroke might appear to be opposing the King when, in fact, he was supporting him. I was saved from further interrogation by the arrival of the page.

We hurried to the hall. Sir Thomas, Sir Simon and the other lords were just leaving. I saw the looks of disdain which came my way. They did not like me! I was not a lord. I thought that the Queen would stay with me but, when we entered, she took Henry's arm and said, "Come, Master Henry, there is a rote in my ladies' room we will hear you sing eh?" She was teasing him and I heard him groan.

The King was eager to speak with me and he wasted no time, "Well?"

"Your cousin will not oppose you, majesty. I have to tell you that he is as concerned about this attack on the monarchy as you are. He believes that the King should rule and not Parliament."

The King looked relieved, "Good. Then when does he bring his men to my aid?"

"He does not."

The King looked deflated, "Then his support is worthless."

"So long as Robert de Vere has your support, King Richard, then your cousin cannot bring his men to your side. The Earl is very unpopular." I sighed. "I agree with your cousin."

He was stunned. "Had you not saved my life I would have called you a traitor."

"Lord, if the Earl of Oxford is so loyal why is he in Wales? Why is he not here?"

"He is raising an army for me!"

"And using them to attack those he deems to be his enemies."

"They are my enemies!"

"Then why did his men attack me when I was returning from Monmouth, sire?"

I could see the genuine shock on his face, "Are you sure?"

"They wore his livery."

"Then when I see him I will speak with him." He poured some wine for us. "You know I begin my gyration after Christmas?"

"Aye lord and I have brought ten of my best men to augment your guards. I have ten archers too but …"

He shook his head, "Men at arms are what I need and if you vouch for them then they will be good. I will need them until the early summer."

I nodded, "They are happy for that commitment. Will you need archers too?"

"No, not until I am ready to face my uncle. Have them ready for me by summer." I nodded. "By then I will have my army and we can return the government of this land to me! Sir Simon raises an army from the Cinque Ports and Sir Thomas is mustering Lancashire and Chester. There the men are loyal to me. Then will my uncle, Gloucester, and all the other traitors feel my wrath." He emptied his goblet. He had a wild look in his eyes. Was he unwell or was this simply his character? The threat in his words worried me. He was still young. His uncle and those who sought to weaken his position were older men who knew how to play the game of politics. "You will dine with us this night?"

"Of course."

When I left the King, I had to pass through the Great Hall to reach the warrior hall. As I passed through the milling lords, barons and knights I was aware that I was under scrutiny. Thomas Molineux was Constable of Chester. I had seen him before. He was a close confederate of the Earl of Oxford and I saw him glowering at me. He spoke with two knights who were close to him. When a finger jabbed in my direction I knew that I was being identified but I did not know the reason. I knew that I had some notoriety. The story of Sir John Chandos at Lussac Bridge was often told and inevitably my name came up. Added to that was my service to King Richard. I understood the interest but this appeared to be different. I put it from my mind.

I walked across the inner ward to reach the warrior hall. I realised I should have fetched Henry but the ordeal of performing before the Queen would do him no harm. Inside I heard shouts and cheers. When I entered I saw Silent David. He was arm wrestling with Ham. Ham had been the huge man at arms so easily bested by Henry. I knew him to be a strong man. He had overmatched himself for my archers all had arms like young oaks. I stood with Stephen the Tracker, Dick of Craven and Roger of Chester. They were grinning. I saw piles of coins on the table. I knew my three leaders would not have bet but the rest would. It was almost a rite of passage.

As Silent David slammed down Ham's hand a cheer went up and I saw my men greedily grab the coins from the table. I turned to Dick and Roger. "The King wishes you and your men at arms to accompany him on his tour of the land. He is paying your stipend until the early summer and then you return to me."

"Thank you, Captain. Ten such good men will make my life easier. You know yourself that some of the men under my command while willing are not the warriors to protect the King in strange castles."

"Then you should make them worthy of the honour."

"We do not have enough time to practise and to train, Captain. We have more visitors here than at Eltham. It is a harder castle to watch."

"I do not envy you. When I had the duty I just had the Tower and the King was unmarried."

"And us, Captain?" Stephen had not heard me mention archers.

"You stay with me. The King does not go to war. He goes for show. Roger, you will wear the King's livery."

After leaving my men to discuss the new arrangement I went to rescue Henry. The Queen was laughing, "Your squire will make a fine knight, Captain William. He is both a fine singer and can tell an amusing story or two. My ladies found him a pretty young thing. He has the face of a boy still."

I smiled at the blush which rose up Henry's cheeks. "Then he has learned neither skill from me!"

She leaned in, "Yet he has learned much more useful lessons from you. He admires you greatly." I nodded. "You will be at the feast?"

"We will."

"Good for I will have someone to talk to. My husband's men only plot and plan!"

As I led my squire back to our chamber I worried about that. The King was dabbling in murky waters. He was an unpopular King. His enemies were appealing to the ordinary people and promising them that which would enhance their lives. I was close enough to those people to see the attraction in their words.

My wife had managed to make me one new surcoat and I took it from my bag. I guessed that the lords who flocked around the king would be rich and well-dressed men. I did not wish to embarrass myself before them. I would have one more night of pretending to be someone I was not and then I could return to the bosom of my family and enjoy Christmas. The King would be away for months and I could just be William Strongstaff, gentleman.

When we reached the hall, many lords had already arrived. They jostled for a place close to the King and Queen. A servant brought us drinks and I waited to one side with Henry. He was still excited about his time with the Queen and her ladies. "Captain, do you think the Queen meant what she said about my having a good voice?"

"I cannot see why she would lie. You and I are the least important men in this whole room. I waved my arm. This will be your world when you are a knight. Are you ready for it?"

"I am not sure but I do know that I would be a knight and support the King. I have learned much with you, Captain."

I nodded. A servant came over to us. "The Queen has reserved seats for you, Captain and your squire. If you would follow me."

He led us to the high table and we were seated by the Queen's right hand. It was the most prestigious of positions and I saw many knights casting covetous and hateful glances. It did nothing to increase my popularity!

The King knew how to keep his lords on his side. The food and the drink were superb and the quantities were prodigious. I thought back to the time when I had been with the free companies. Sometimes we had not eaten as much in a month as I ate in that one night. Henry proved to be good company. Knowing that he was well thought of by the Queen seemed to make him more confident and he kept her laughing all night. I had counselled him about his drinking and he did not drink too much. Many of the lords around us became very drunk. Some were just a little older than Henry and I saw one or two fall face first in their food.

Henry went to make water and the Queen shook her head, "He will break some hearts when he wins his spurs."

"He is a well-meaning youth."

"At least tonight you need not sleep on the floor. Here we are safe."

"There are still enemies out there, Majesty. Dick of Craven knows his business. You will be well cared for."

"And that is just as well for some of the young nobles who are supposed to protect us are obviously incapable."

Henry came back and looked a little flushed. I knew something was the matter. "What is amiss Henry?"

"It is nothing lord."

The Queen frowned, "Speak, I command you."

He lowered his voice. When I returned from the garderobe I was accosted by a young knight. He asked me how much were my services! He thought I was a boy for hire!"

The Queen said, "That is intolerable. Which is he?"

"I will not say, majesty. I am just a squire and I have no standing."

It was obvious who it was for a knight came in and pointed a finger at Henry and spoke to the knight next to him. They laughed. The Queen turned to her page, "Robert go and fetch Sir Hugo Vernon to me."

"Yes, my lady."

She shook her head, "He is an unpleasant man. His elder brother is one of the Constable's lieutenants. I do not like him nor his master, Sir Thomas Molineux. At least Sir Thomas can pretend to be polite. I have had cause to speak to Sir Hugo about the way he speaks to my ladies. He does not speak to them in an honourable way."

I saw the page bend down to speak to the knight. The laughter left his face. He made his way towards us. I could see that he was a powerfully built knight. Although young, he had the look of a tournament knight for his right arm looked to be larger than his left. It often happened that way when men used the long jousting lance.

"Yes, my Queen."

"Do not my Queen me! You are an unpleasant knight with no manners at all. You owe this squire an apology."

He feigned surprise, "I owe him nothing! He made lewd approaches to me. I should have had him whipped."

Henry coloured, "My lord! I did not."

Sir Hugo laughed, "Lies and deception! What can you expect of a country bumpkin who has to follow a jumped-up serf and villein?"

The Queen started, "Sir Hugo!"

I said quietly, "You lie. Apologise as my lady told you."

"I will do no such thing and unless you apologise for your very existence then I will have satisfaction."

All eyes were turned to us for Sir Hugo's voice had become louder. I should have realised that this was deliberate. He had been put up to the provocation and I had bitten. Henry was a squire and could not fight a knight. If he had he would not have lasted two exchanges. If I had remained silent then the Queen would have censured him. I could not allow my charge to be insulted.

The King said, "What is this that disturbs our feast?"

Sir Hugo said, loudly, for the benefit of the hall, "I demand satisfaction from this creature. He has insulted me."

I saw the King was on the horns of a dilemma. He did not wish his knights to fight but Sir Hugo served a most important lord. Sir Thomas commanded most of the men of Lancashire and Chester. He was also a close confederate of the Earl of Oxford. The King could ill afford to alienate him. In that moment he made a choice and I was abandoned for the men Sir Thomas could bring. It showed me my true position. "I will not have any of my knights hurt!" It was a weak reply and I felt disappointed in him. There was no need to fight and yet I would have to. "It will be a combat to first blood."

Sir Hugo roared, "Till the morrow! Upstart!"

The Queen's hand pressed on mine and she gripped my hand. She whispered, "He is a tournament knight! This is wrong! I will speak with my husband."

"You cannot put the carrot back in the ground, my lady. The King has spoken and if he were to go back on his word then he would risk losing his allies. If I lose then the King has lost nothing."

Her eyes were like deep pools. "Will Strongstaff you are a good man. If England had more like you then we would not be in this position. Good luck!"

I stood. I would need to prepare for a combat. I was guessing it would be on foot. Tournaments were not fought in winter. As I turned Henry look shocked, "I am sorry Captain! I should have said nothing!"

"You have done nothing that was wrong. You have behaved with honour." Men parted before us as we left. "This was planned. I was identified earlier on. There are men here who seek to weaken the King while there are others who think that my presence also makes the King weak. I should have stayed away but I had a duty and I performed it."

Instead of going to our chamber I went to the warrior hall. My men needed to know what was going on. The warrior hall was in direct contrast to the King's feasting hall. Men chatted and drank. It was almost quiet by comparison. I stayed at the doorway and my leaders came to me. "What is amiss, Captain?"

"I have been forced to fight a combat to first blood with Sir Hugo Vernon." They both nodded. "He will have men at arms here. They may be loose-lipped. Without giving too much away or putting yourself in danger find out what you can. I will send Henry at dawn and you can tell him what you know."

Roger said, "We heard this Vernon mentioned as we ate. He has won many tourneys. They say he has become rich by unhorsing many men.

He is said to be the best with a lance in the land and there are few, even in France and Italy who can match him."

"Then I hope it will be on foot."

As we walked back I said, "Wear your mail from now on. I fear for your safety. I would not send you tomorrow but I need to know as much about my foe as I can."

He nodded, "What does first blood mean, Captain?"

"Just that. We are not supposed to kill each other but, as we will be mailed, then any wound which draws blood could potentially be life-threatening. Sir Hugo thinks to kill me tomorrow no matter what the King says. If he does then he will be reprimanded. If I kill him then I will be punished for I am a mere gentleman and he is a knight. There are few endings to this in which I come out well."

"Have you fought like this before, Captain?"

"I have fought to the death many times but it was on a battlefield. I lived on my wits. I hope that those wits will see me safely through this tomorrow."

As we prepared my armour and mail I knew that my enemy would have a full-face helmet. My open bascinet would make it easier for him to claim first blood. He would be completely mailed and if he was so good with a lance then his right arm would be powerful indeed and it would be unlikely that he would tire. Unless my men discovered another weakness, I would have to use the speed of my feet. I did not think that he would be used to moving quickly on his feet. A tournament knight rode to battle and his cantle held him in place. The more I could make him twist and turn the better the chance that I might survive and that was all I was trying to do, survive!

That night I said my prayers, as I always did, but I asked God to watch over my family. My wife was a practical woman and we had coin. If I died she would remarry and she would choose a good man. I had hoped to be a better father than my own but if things went badly then that was unlikely to happen. I was glad I had not drunk as much as others and I fell asleep quite quickly. My body woke me when it was still dark. Nights were much longer. I made water and washed.

I woke Henry. "Go find Roger and Stephen! Bring Peter and John from the warrior hall."

I began to dress. I pulled on my chausse and tied them. I donned my aketon. It was a good one and was well padded. I would need help to don my hauberk. When Henry returned he would fasten it. Most of the plates I would wear required Henry to tie them but I was able to don my sabaton, poleyn and cuisse. I only had cuisse for the front of my shins and thighs. The backs of my legs would be protected only by my chausse. I waited for Henry.

"I am sorry I took so long, Captain."

"No matter. Help me with my hauberk while you tell me what you learned." The three of them made short work of slipping the hauberk over me and tying it at the back.

"He uses a long sword. It is longer than yours by a handspan, Captain. It is sharp up to the hilt. When he fights on foot he relies on strength and the speed of his blows. It is said he is like a blacksmith. He can pound at the same spot for a long time."

"Does he use his shield as a weapon?"

Henry frowned, "Roger did not say so and so I guess not. His man knew that he would be fighting. He said that he had boasted of killing another man and adding to his reputation."

Then it was planned. He had told his men. He was overconfident. I liked that. Henry and Peter fitted my cannons. My hauberk did not have mittens. I wore gauntlets. Many knights used ones which were made from metal. They were expensive but they protected the hands. The disadvantage was that they did not give a man the feel of the sword. I had leather gauntlets. The palms and underneath of the fingers were made from softer leather while the backs were hide and were covered by metal strips. I placed my rondel dagger in the sheath inside my shield. It was close to my hand and if I had to then I could draw it quickly.

There was a tap on the door. Henry opened it. A page was there. "Master William, the herald says it is almost time."

"And where do we fight?"

"In the outer ward, sir."

"Thank you."

Henry held my helmet and John son of Jack my shield. I knelt and prayed. When I had spoken to God and asked him to watch over my family we rose and went to the ward. We headed down to the door which led from the Great Hall. Dawn had not truly broken. The King must have decided to minimise the number of spectators. Was that for his benefit or mine? I saw the white on the cobbles. There had been a frost and it had yet to melt.

The Queen and her ladies were waiting at the door. "I will not come to watch. It is unseemly. I have prayed to God that you will win. Sir Hugo is a beast and needs taming. You may not be a knight but I know that you have the heart to do so." She took a piece of blue cloth. "Here is my favour. It is little enough but it may help you. God speed."

Despite the early start more than a hundred knights and lords were gathered in a circle. Henry would not have to fight if I declined for I was not a knight but I saw Sir Thomas' squire as he grinned at us. He had hoped to inflict some sort of pain on Henry. Sir Thomas had engineered this whole situation. His squire's face showed me that. I knew that Sir Robert's grandson had not anticipated this when he had sat down to feast the night before. The world of lords and barons was a dangerous one and he had had a lesson. The King was there along with a smirking Sir Thomas Molineux. He had put the knight up to this but I could not work out the reason. I did not like Sir Thomas but he was as loyal to King Richard as any man. I was out of my depth. I also saw that my men at arms were there too and, as I glanced at the fighting platform, I saw my archers. They had their bows and they were strung. I smiled. If anything treacherous looked likely then a flurry of arrows would descend from the walls. For some reason that made me more confident.

The King and his herald approached. The King said, "I am sorry about this, Will."

I nodded curtly. I had been abandoned and all words of what he owed me were forgotten.

The herald said, "We await Sir Hugo. Before the contest begins I should tell you that you can cry quarter at any time. I will end the battle."

"And I will be adjudged to be in the wrong." I turned and looked at the King. "I did not begin this but I swear that I shall end it and then return to my manor for all debts will be paid!"

The King knew what I meant and he nodded. I heard a cheer and looked around. Sir Hugo appeared. He was in full plate. The backs of his legs and arms were protected. He also wore his spurs. I could not fathom why. His squire carried his visored helm. When I saw that I spied hope. He had eye holes out of which he could peer. The snout point was useful in a tournament but not in battle. I saw that the sword was a long one. Most men would need two hands to wield such a blade but if he was such an expert with a lance then he would have no problem with the sword. My rondel dagger might be the difference between life and death.

He strode arrogantly up to me and stared at me as though he might intimidate me. His visor rose like a unicorn's horn. I had faced fiercer enemies before. The herald spoke. "I will be the arbiter of this battle." He held a mace in his hand. "If you fail to obey my instructions I will smite you with this!"

I nodded and so did Sir Hugo but he nodded with a smirk.

"Step away from each other and arm yourselves. May God give the right!"

I walked to Henry who donned my helmet. I tied the leather strap beneath my chin. He handed me my shield. As I slipped it on my arm I gripped the rondel dagger and I turned. Sir Hugo had lowered his visor and I saw that he was eager to get to me and, I assumed, end it quickly. I was a common soldier elevated to the rank of gentleman. If it did not end quickly then it would reflect badly on him. He came quickly across the ward to get at me. I stepped more slowly. The cobbles in the ward were still slippery from the frost. I held my sword slightly behind me.

I braced my left arm for the blow which was coming. His longer sword would hit me before I could make a swing. The open helmet I wore helped me to judge distance a little easier than if I had had a visor. I saw him pull his arm back and begin his swing. I pushed my shield towards the blade. Then he slipped. It was only a slight slip on the slick stones but it was enough to take some of the force from the strike. It hit my shield but not as hard as he had intended. More importantly, he had been forced to slow. I suddenly swung, not at his shield, but at his aventail. He lifted his shield to block the blow and even as my sword cracked into his shield I punched at his head with my own shield. I struck the side of his helmet and pointed visor. He reeled.

From the walls, I heard a cheer from my archers and a groan from the lords. I heard a shout of, "Cheat!" from those who supported my foe.

I balanced myself again. Sir Hugo's slip had shown me the dangers of the frost. His face hidden behind a mask meant that I could not see his reaction. His next action showed me that he was angry. He swung a long sideways blow at me. I deftly stepped back to the place where I had already cleared the frost. Sir Hugo's sword struck nothing but fresh air. He stepped forward and tried a backhand swing. I stepped back again. There was a limit to the number of steps I could actually take. There was a wall of knights behind me and they would hem me in. Perhaps Sir Hugo thought that I was afraid to take a hit for he came forward and swung again.

I had the advantage that I could see where the cobbles were white and slippery and where they were black and merely wet. Even as he swung I saw to the knight's left a patch of black where he had slipped. His feet had scraped the frost from the stones. Instead of stepping back I stepped on to my left and crossed his path. I began to swing my sword as I did so. When I had cleared his body, I stepped back with my right foot. As I turned his back and side were towards me. My sword swung into his side and it ripped across his short surcoat. He had a cuirass and back plate but they were held by straps. As my sword rasped back I saw that I had weakened one of the straps. There was a scar where my sword had cut the leather.

There was another cheer from my men and another groan from Sir Hugo's supporters. This battle was supposed to be over. I was not doing what he expected.

A surcoat is there mainly for decoration. It also hides the armour and the mail. As Sir Hugo moved his sword and shield he aggravated the tear. His belt, riding up and down also made the rip worse and I could see his mail. I could not break the plate but I could use my dagger to pierce the mail. He turned to face me. He was having to move more than he had expected. I had fought on foot more than I had on a horse. For Sir Hugo, it was the opposite. I decided to make him make more unnecessary movements. My open helmet kept me cooler than he would be enclosed in his bascinet. I feigned a strike at his shield and when he presented his shield I switched and used my sword to lunge at his head. I hit the point of the visor and the blade slid down the side. The point caught in one of the eye holes. My sword was too big to enter but it jerked his head around a little. I suspect it might have unnerved him too for he swung blindly at my shield. We were so close that he could not generate enough power and I barely felt it.

If this had been a battle then it might have been all over. When there are men all around you fighting and when the ground is covered in bodies, broken spears, blood and guts then it is easy to become distracted. We were both tiring. I saw that in the knight's movements which were slower. The bottom of the surcoat was getting lower and lower. Soon it would become a hazard. He could not see that because of his visor. Sir Hugo was a clever man and a cunning fighter. My blow to his helmet had shown him a way to end this combat quickly. He stepped back. I was not so foolish as to follow and I balanced myself once more. I noticed that the crowd of knights were now silent. I had silenced them.

When I did not step forward Sir Hugo stepped off on his right foot and brought his sword from behind him. He made the mistake of turning his sword too early. It was a feint. He was going to lunge his longer sword at my open face. Instead of using my own shield I brought my sword from above. I saw the tip of his sword as it came towards me. My shield was before me and close to my chest. My sword hit his halfway down. He did have a strong right hand but so did I. Sparks flew from our blades as the metal clanged together. It sounded like a blacksmith making a sword. His sword scraped down my shield. I knew that he would have torn the leather but also partly blunted his edge for there were metal studs on my shield.

We were close together and I brought my knee forward. I wore a poleyn and my knee cap was protected. It rammed into his thigh. When I had been younger I had fought another camp boy, Alan of the Fleas, and he had used his knee in the same way. For a while after, I could barely move my leg. It felt dead. I knew that I had inflicted just such an injury on Sir Hugo for he had to step back. I knew that now was the time to strike. I could see, at his left side, exposed mail where the straps held the back plate and cuirass together. I swung my sword hard at his shield and, gripping the rondel dagger, lunged at his side. The rounded blade slid into the mail. The sharpened tip penetrated the aketon and then I felt it enter soft flesh. I pushed and twisted. As I pulled it out I stepped back. Blood dripped from my dagger and I shouted, "First blood!"

Even as the King's herald came over towards us Sir Hugo lunged at my head once more. As I stepped back my foot slipped on some frost. It saved my life for the sword merely glanced off my bascinet. The blood was now flowing from Sir Hugo but he was not ending the contest. I was helpless for my left knee was on the ground. I used my sword as a crutch to push me to my feet. He raised his sword to bring it down on me.

I heard the herald cry, "Sir Hugo! No!"

Sir Hugo's sword came down. He intended to kill me! I raised my shield in a vain attempt to block the blow but my slip made my movements awkward. Suddenly an arrow sprouted from the knight's hand. The arrow had found a gap between the articulated plates of metal and the sword was dropped. I turned and saw Stephen the Tracker. The arrow could easily have struck me or even killed the knight for it was a bodkin. Only an archer of the green wood could have made the strike.

I heard cries from the knight's supporters. Then the King's voice silenced them. "Sir Hugo! God has punished you for breaking the rules. William Strongstaff has won fairly. He claimed first blood."

Sir Hugo flung his shield to the ground and broke off the shaft of the arrow. He raised his visor and leaned down at me. "One day you will die at my hands spawn of the gutter! I will have your family butchered and all of your archers crucified."

The herald appeared and pushed the knight away, "For shame, Sir Hugo! For shame! The King commands that you leave his court. You are banished for half a year!"

Ignoring the herald Sir Hugo pointed his bloodied right hand at me. "Keep a close watch villein. When my hand is healed I will be coming for you!" He turned and stormed off towards his squire. Henry, Peter and John son of Jack ran to me as the herald lifted me to my feet. I now had another enemy!

Chapter 16

Sir Thomas had to endure a diatribe from the King about the conduct of his knight. He conducted it before all of the assembled knights. The King was using the incident to re-establish his authority. I had, inadvertently, served the King once more.

The Queen came to my side. "I fear, Will, that you have made a dangerous enemy."

I shrugged, "It seems to me that I had little choice in the matter, my lady."

She nodded, "If I were you I would leave quickly. The King will ensure that you are not followed."

I nodded, "Thank you, my lady. It will be good to get back to the bosom of my family."

The King did not speak before we left. He waved from the gate and the Queen hung from his arm. Queen Anne was the hope for England. It was she kept her husband from following the path of the Earl of Oxford. I was glad to be free from court.

Stephen the Tracker rode next to me. "I owe you a life, Stephen."

"No, Captain, for you gave me a life when you took us from the forest."

Henry asked, "How did you manage to hit such a small target?"

Stephen laughed, "I was less than eighty paces from the combat and on the wall. The target was bigger than you think Master Henry. I had the hand, the arm and the sword. An arrow has all the power of the yew and my arm." He took a bodkin arrow from his arrow bag. "See the tip. It can pierce mail. Gauntlets are the weakest part of a knight's armour for, to enable the fingers to move, there are many rivets which hold the plates together. It was an easy strike but God guided my hand for the Captain had the right. He drew first blood."

"And now we have to watch for Sir Hugo in the spring. His estates are close to Chester but he will feed this grudge over winter. He will feel slighted and become not cooler but hotter. He promised dire consequences for you and your archers Stephen."

He laughed, "And we lived with those threats when we were outlaws. I do not fear Sir Hugo."

We pushed hard and reached my home after dark. Even as we rode up to it I knew that when spring came I would have to make it defensible. Sir Robert was the lord of the manor but if Sir Hugo came to attack my home then it would be up to me to defend it. Ironically, I would now be even more beholden to Henry Bolingbroke. As Earl of Northampton, he was the one man who could thwart Sir Hugo.

My wife looked relieved to see me. "You will be home for Christmas!"

"Aye, my love and right glad am I to be here. Henry will stay the night and then I will escort him home tomorrow."

"Do I have to?"

"Henry, Christmas is a time to be with your family. Your grandparents are no longer young. How many more celebrations will there be?" I saw realisation crease his face. "When February is here then come back if you need more training but I think you are ready to be a knight. You just need to practise and Peter can help you with that."

Peter nodded, "Aye Master. The Captain is right and he has a family. He deserves some time with his children." I heard the envy in his words. Peter had no children nor would he ever have them. Henry was as close as he would come to having a son.

On the way home I had discussed with Stephen the prospect of a warrior hall. He had come up with a quicker solution than the one I had. The ground would be too hard to dig effective foundations and so Stephen had suggested building a floor halfway up the barn. The animals could remain on the ground floor and the archers could make the upper floor their warrior hall. All that it would lack would be a fire and as Stephen had told me after winters under oak trees a roof and the heat of animals from below would seem like a luxury. That way they could build a warrior hall and attach it to the barn in the spring. While I went to Stratford they would begin their conversion.

It was cold and the days would be incredibly short. We wrapped up well. I knew that it would take all the short day to reach Sir Robert. My practical wife gave me a list of items which I would need to purchase at the market and town of Stratford. We were largely self-sufficient. We had cereal, vegetables, meat and fowl. We had a fish pond. We had our own bread oven and we had men who could tan so that we could turn the hides into leather. What we needed was more material so that the female servants could produce more clothes over the winter. The winter weather might keep us indoors but it would not make us idle. I would still practise with my weapons. My archers would make arrows and practise their art. We would hunt. We would forage.

As we rode Peter said, "What you need, Captain, is a smith. You have horses which need shoeing, ploughs which ought to be repaired or replaced and then, of course, the mail and weapons he can make."

He was right of course. The village had been a busy one before the plague and it had had a mill and a smith. We had repaired the mill and used it to grind our barley, oats and wheat but we really needed a miller. However, the fire in the forge had not been lit for many years. The roof had crumbled and we had no one with the skill to make and to shape iron. The plague had made such skilled men even more valuable and it was hard to find one. Most served rich lords like Henry Bolingbroke.

We arrived at dusk. While his grandmother fussed over him I spoke with Sir Robert. "I believe that I have done all that I can for your grandson. He still wishes to spend time with me and I find that flattering but he needs to begin to stand on his own two feet."

"I know but I have been delaying."

"He is old enough and if he is to inherit this manor he will need to learn how to do so as his own master."

"I have a small manor, it is a mile from here. Shottery would suit my grandson for there are just a few houses in the village and six tenant farmers. It would need a hall but that would be no obstacle."

I nodded, "And you would have to ask the Earl of Northampton for permission to dub him. I do not think that would be a problem as your grandson has done the Earl no small service."

The knight still looked unhappy, "I would not wish my grandson to go to war without you close by."

"If he is knighted then I will be beneath him in rank. It would make life difficult. But it is not a problem at the moment. The King did not get the funds for his war in France and the Earl of Northampton is preoccupied with his new son. We have six months before that situation might arise."

I was feted by both the doting grandparents. Since I had first met with Henry he had changed. Physically he looked like a man now rather than the gangly youth I had first encountered. However, he had also matured. He had been around men at arms and archers. He had bantered with them. He had learned their curses and their language. He had killed a man. He had fought for his life. He had entertained a Queen and her ladies. The man I left with them had been made in the time he had spent with me.

John and I were up early and at the market to buy that which we needed. We headed along the road before most people had arrived at the market. As we rode back to my home the attacks upon us and the danger of Sir Hugo made us ride as though we expected an ambush.

John son of Jack might have lacked experience but the ride from Monmouth and the combat in Windsor had made him realise that serving William Strongstaff would not be an easy task. We rode quickly and reached home before dark. As the door was closed I felt relief. I would not need to stir again until well into the New Year.

It was a joyous Christmas. The snowstorm which came on Christmas Eve lasted a full seven days and the land was coated in a blanket of white. It mattered not. We had laid in great quantities of food. The puddings and the cakes my wife and her women had made would last for a month and the animals we had hunted would feed us into January. We were lucky for our campaign in Galicia had allowed us to bring back treasures from that land. The spices and oils we had brought back were only found in the halls of great lords. We had jugs with preserved fruits such as lemons and oranges. Used sparingly they made even the most mundane of Monday cakes taste special. I knew that we were lucky. None in my village would suffer but there would be others who would.

My son and daughter enjoyed their father being around. Tom enjoyed the presence of the archers and John son of Jack. If Henry had been changed by his time with me then it was doubly so for John. He had been right. He would never be a farmer. He was a natural warrior. He reminded me of me. He did not have the finesse of a lord but like me, he knew how to win a fight. My archers were all skilled with a sword but by the time Henry returned, in February, John could defeat all of them. He could not come close to beating me but I knew that I had special skills. When I defeated Sir Hugo I realised just how good I was.

We were outside for although the air was cold it was a bright day. I believed that cold fresh air was beneficial and stopped illnesses. The plague still swept the land and I was sure that it was visited upon those who spent their lives indoors. We turned to look when Henry and Peter rode up. His arrival had not been expected. They reined in.

"You wish to continue your training?" He nodded. "And your knighthood?"

"The Earl sent a letter to my grandfather. The King is still on his gyration and the Earl intends to knight and give spurs to all the squires from his lands at the same time. It will be when the King returns to London." I nodded. "I thought that I might use my time usefully. Shottery will be my manor but only when I am wed."

That was news indeed. Henry Bolingbroke was a clever man. A mass dubbing would make a statement to friends and foes alike. It would tell them that the Earl was a force to be reckoned with. He would soon be twenty-one. His father was still in Castile and showed no sign of returning. He had lands in England and those knights not serving in Castile could be called upon by his son. I had put the Earl's words about my knighthood behind me. Perhaps I would be dubbed then, too. I had not mentioned it to Eleanor. I knew she would be excited. I did not wish to disappoint her.

When Henry rejoined us it seemed to spur us all on to improve our skills. The King had said he would be away until the summer. I was in a unique position. I knew that the King resented the men who had tied his hands, the Lords Appellant. I also knew that he was building an army in the west under the guiding hands of the Constable of Chester and the Earl of Oxford. The King's gyration was to gather support so that he could make war on his uncle and his enemies. When civil war came we would be involved and yet I knew not which side I would be on. If the Lords Appellant or Henry Bolingbroke attacked the King then I would offer my sword to the King. If, on the other hand, it was Molineux and de Vere who attacked the Lords then I would fight them. This would not be a war where I could sit in the middle.

March brought us both news and help from an unexpected source. My wife was with child. She said it was a Christmas gift from God! To celebrate my men and I went hunting. It was good training for both John and Henry. In addition, it culled the animals. The older stags could be taken and the older females too. Stephen the Tracker had found the herd and the next day we left to hunt.

We hunted on foot. My archers had their bows while the four of us had spears. It was a challenge to get close enough to the deer to make a kill with a spear but if we failed then Stephen and his archers would complete the work. The four of us acted in unison and trailed the herd. We headed down the stream with the smell of the herd blowing toward us. Our archers lay almost a mile downstream. We each had three spears. They were not the ones we used for wild boar. These were for throwing. Narrow-headed, they had a barb close to the bottom of the head. Peter had complained that if we had hounds our task would be easier. He was probably right but I had little experience with dogs nor had my archers.

When the smell of the deer grew really strong I held up my hand and we stopped. Sure enough, after a few moments, there was movement as the herd moved upstream. I daresay the stag had smelled my archers. They were a distance away but a stag would be cautious. There were many young with the herd. This was a big herd. The young would be safe. None of us would take an animal which would grow into a better meal over the next few years. I raised my hand and we moved slowly. I had hunted more than the others and they were behind me.

I spied, as the herd came towards me, an old hind. She was less than thirty feet from me and drawing closer. She was favouring one of her legs. She would be an easy target for one of the others. There was also an old stag. Although rare for there to be two stags with a herd it did happen and I saw that this one had had his left antler broken some time ago. He was moving close to the old hind. Perhaps the dominant stag allowed these two older ones to stay with the herd. I saw one of the immature males raise his nose and sniff the air. It was time. I pulled back my arm and, as the young male snorted an alarm, I hurled at the older stag. My spear caught him just behind his neck. He turned and bolted. Peter and John threw their spears at the hind. Henry threw his at the immature male. He missed completely for the male had already turned to run away from the danger. I threw a second at the stag and hit him in the rump. The herd was gone. They would thunder down the stream to my waiting archers. Our work was done.

"Come let us finish these two." I turned to Henry. "Why did you disobey me? You went for a young, healthy male!"

He hung his head, "I am sorry Captain but the older pair reminded me of my grandparents."

Peter laughed, "As good a reason as any for sparing them, Master."

The old female had two spears in her and she had stumbled just forty paces into the forest. She was still alive when we reached her and Peter ended her suffering. "You two gut her and John and I will follow this blood trail."

The old stag was tough. He was bleeding to death and the blackening blood was easy to follow. I saw him. He stood panting close to a large oak. I handed my spear to John and drew my sword. The animal snorted and blood came from his nose. He was dying. I spoke as I approached, "You have had a good life and your young are evidence of your being. Your seed will fill this land. Now I will send you to a better place old man." The animal tried to raise its head and that allowed me to bring my sword in a long sweep up into its neck. It died instantly and fell in a heap. The animal would not have survived another winter. Perhaps the hind had been its mate. I liked to believe that the two would be reunited somewhere. My father would have laughed at such nonsense, "When you are dead you are dead! This life is all we have!" I now had children and I did not want to believe that.

I cleaned my sword on some grass and sheathed it. I had a gutting knife in my belt and John and I began to cut open the belly. I heard a noise in the woods. It was close. It was not one of my men. John had not heard it. I drew my sword and pointed to the left. John was a clever young man and he nodded and drew his own sword. He moved to my left. I smelled humans. I heard a sob. I moved a little more and heard some leaves rustle.

"Whoever you are, show yourselves!"

A female cried and then I heard a man, "Do not harm us, lord, we mean no harm!"

"I am not a lord! Show yourselves."

Ten feet from me a man rose. He was broad and looked to have seen perhaps twenty summers. He had no sword but held a long-handled hammer in his hand.

"Drop the weapon, friend. There are two of us. If you mean us no harm then you are safe. I am William Strongstaff and I do not lie." The hammer dropped. "Who is with you?"

"My wife, sir."

"Then have her rise." Slowly a young woman, perhaps seventeen summers old, rose. I could see that she was weeping. Behind us, I heard the noise of Peter and Henry approaching. I held up my hand. "Hold." I gestured to the couple, "Come closer that I may speak with you." As they did I said, "John, fetch the hammer and whatever else they have."

The young woman was shaking and looked terrified. The man had his arm protectively around her. As they made their way through the undergrowth John picked up the hammer and a small bundle of clothes.

"What is your tale?"

The man, now that I saw him close up, was bigger than I was. He was a powerful man. He looked belligerently at me. "We have done nothing wrong, sir. Why do you question us? Is this your wood?"

"Speak softly friend. This is my land and I would know what you do upon it."

Just then the woman who looked pale swooned. Had she not been held by the man she would have fallen to the ground. "Henry and Peter, fetch the horses. What is wrong with your woman?"

"She is my wife and we have not eaten well." He hesitated. "She is with child."

"John, your ale skin." I sheathed my sword and took the skin. I took out the stopper and held it to her mouth. I allowed some to dribble in. When I deemed she had had enough I replaced the stopper and took off my cloak. "Here wrap it around her and then tell me your names. I will try to be of help but I must know who you are."

He wrapped the cloak around her and held her tightly. "I am Edgar of... I am Edgar the Smith and this is my wife, Edith. We have been wed for three moons. It is a week since we had a decent meal and we last drank yesterday."

"And why are you in the woods?"

"The green wood is the only place we can afford to live, sir." The woman, Edith, opened her eyes. They widened in terror when she saw me above her. "He will not hurt us, Edith."

I heard the sound of horses as Peter and Henry brought our mounts, "Stephen the Tracker has finished hunting, Captain. They are bringing the carcasses to us."

"Edgar the Smith, put your wife on the horse. We will take you to my home. It is our Christian duty to help those who are in distress."

"Thank you, sir."

I turned and looked him in the eye, "But know this I will discover your story. You are hiding something from me. If you are to be helped then we will know all."

The man was strong and he lifted her on to Jack's saddle as though she was a feather. Edgar led my mount and I followed. When we reached the archers, I saw the questions in their eyes. "We had a good hunt then, Stephen?"

"Aye, Captain. We have collected the offal too. Do we give it to the poor of the village?"

"We can. The winter has not been as harsh as some but it was bad enough."

The woman kept her hand on her husband's head. I could not fathom their story. From their accents, they were not local. There was a hint of Welsh in their words but Wales was a good seven days travel to the west. I looked at her feet. She wore wooden clogs, galoshes. These were poor people and yet, when I looked at the clothes they wore, although dirty and showing wear, they had been well made at one time. Smiths were highly paid. What would make one leave his home and drag his wife across the heart of England in the middle of winter?

We had some of the children of the servants collecting the wood which had been torn from the trees during the last storm and when they saw us they ran to my hall to warn my wife of our return. All knew that we hunted and that meant a bounty for everyone. We would all eat well and when the meat had been taken the bones would be used for stews. Then we would use the rest. The antlers and bone could be carved. The hides would be tanned. The hooves rendered down for glue and sealant. We wasted nothing. Lol took the offal into the village. There were one or two poorer families there. They rarely went hungry for my wife sent food to them whenever she could but the offal from the hunt would be like treasure to them. Deer heart, kidneys and liver would sustain even the weakest of folk.

My son ran to us. He had been keen to join the hunt but he was still too young. Next year I would let him hold the horses. "You have done well, father!" He looked up at Edgar the Smith, "You have animals for us to eat and guests to share our food!"

My wife stood in the doorway. The child within her was barely showing. I guessed that Edith was at a similar stage. We stopped and I pointed to the pair, "We have guests, wife. This is Edgar the Smith and his wife, Edith. She, too, is with child. They have been living rough in the woods and eaten little."

My wife's face clouded over, "Then what are you doing keeping them out in the cold! Come, my dear. Men! They have not the first idea of being a mother. This must be your first."

Edgar helped her down and my wife took her hand, "Why your hand is like a piece of ice. Nanna, put the poker in the fire to heat it and a ladle of honey in a jug of ale. We need to warm this little one through." She turned to Edgar. He towered over her but she cared not, "And what kind of a half-wit has his wife living as outlaws in the forest in winter! Fool!"

It was her words which told me that I was the fool. Edgar had done something terrible and had to flee. Nothing else would induce a man to have his pregnant wife travel through England in winter. That reassured me. I had feared he was one of Sir Hugo's men. Having a wife as a disguise was the sort of thing lords like Sir Hugo encouraged.

We went to the room we used for dining. A fire was blazing away. I tossed another log upon it. Nanna had disappeared with Edith and my wife. Alice had tagged along with her mother. "John, fetch another jug of ale and the honey." I turned the poker in the fire. It was becoming hot enough. "Peter, beakers. My wife has a vicious tongue sometimes but it is a good suggestion." John and Peter disappeared. Edgar was a big man but I saw that the journey had weakened him too. "And you had better sit before you fall!"

My wife had beehives and our honey was of the best quality. Some might think it a waste to put so much in the ale and then plunge a hot poker into it but for us, it was a treat. The poker hissed and I swirled it around. I poured the hot ale into the beakers. I watched as Edgar the Smith drank deeply and then smiled as the sweet, steaming liquid slipped down his throat. "Thank you, sir! That is almost as good as a meal."

I filled up his beaker and he drank again. A replete smile of joy went from ear to ear. "Tonight, you will eat well. I can see that you need a good feast. It is a long way from Wales."

"Aye, sir, and winter is still biting."

"You have done well to make it thus far. Your wife must be hardier than she looks for I know of strong men who might have faltered."

"Aye, sir."

"Especially with men pursuing you. Was it hard to remain hidden?"

"It was sir…" He suddenly seemed to realise that he had allowed his loose tongue to reveal almost all. He put the beaker to one side as though that had been the cause of his undoing.

I leaned back and spread my arms, "You fled Wales. You left your forge and brought a pregnant woman across England in the heart of winter. It does not take a learned man to piece together the solution to this puzzle. You are an outlaw. I know not what crime you have committed but your wife is being cared for and I would appreciate honesty from you."

"But…"

I held up my hand, "I will listen to your words and make a decision but know you that the archers who now serve me were all outlaws. I know why men choose to be an outlaw. My judgement will depend upon the crime."

He nodded. I poured some more ale and, giving me a wry smile, he drank. "I killed a man."

He deserved it?"

"I believe so. Let me start at the beginning and then you can judge. You seem like an honest man. That has not always been my experience of lords. I come from a village in Powys. We still use its Welsh name and you will not have heard of it. That is no matter. The lord of the manor is Sir Bohemund Ratcliffe. He is an evil man. He serves the Earl of Oxford and men who complain about Sir Bohemund do not receive justice from the Earl. I confess that he did not bother us overmuch. As I say it is a small village. I earned enough to get by. We were lucky for the plague passed us by. It was when I married Edith that trouble came my way. Edith is English. She lived close to Nantwich and the manor of Sir Hugo Vernon."

My eyes opened wide.

"You know him, sir?"

Henry answered for me, "Aye Edgar we do. He made accusations against me and the Captain fought a combat to first blood."

"It was you maimed him! Thank you, Captain!" He drank some more ale. "As I say Edith did not come from my village but her uncle did. He had a farm. Last October she came to stay with her uncle for Sir Hugo wished her for his woman. Not his wife, you understand but his woman, his plaything. Her uncle hid her. I went to shoe his horse and when I saw her…" he shook his head and suddenly looked like a boy again. "I had always been shy around women. I was an only child and had neither sisters nor aunts. My mother died when I was but ten and my father four years later. Edith's uncle saw the joy in us and we were married at the end of November. It was quiet and only the priest knew of the marriage."

I filled up the beaker, "So far I can see only joy in your life."

"Sir Bohemund had been away and he arrived back at Christmas. The priest was invited to the feast and he mentioned the beautiful young woman who had come to live in the village and married the blacksmith. I suppose we were lucky in that we had thick snow until the end of January. He sent his men for Edith. There were three men. Her uncle came to warn me that we were being sought. He came to my forge and gave me a bag of coins. He implored me to leave and save her from Sir Hugo. Even as we packed a bag they arrived. We begged them to let us alone but one, he was the leader, laughed. He said when his lord wanted something he took it and blacksmiths could go hang. I pushed him from my door. He came at me with his sword. I hit him with the only weapon I had, my hammer. One of them tried to stab me but Edith's uncle pulled a dagger and slit his throat. For his pains the last one slew him. I smashed his hand with my hammer and he fled. Edith's uncle was dead. We took the coins and our clothes. I set alight the forge and hoped that when they found the three bodies they would think two were ours."

"And you fled."

"We did. We could not go north for there lay danger and so we went south and east. I had heard that the King was touring the land. I thought to appeal to him. We kept from the main roads and travelled the little known byways. We used the coin to pay for food and a bed but people realised we were in trouble and charged us more. Two weeks since we spent the last of the money. I bought some ham and bread. We lived on that and water." He sat back and stared into the fire. "That is my story."

His story smelled strongly of the truth and I knew Sir Hugo. God had sent him to us. "And you are no outlaw. Had there been justice where you lived and made a living then Sir Hugo would have been brought to account. I have need of a smith and there is both a forge and a house. The house needs work but it is yours and welcome."

"And if Sir Hugo seeks me here?"

I smiled, "Sir Hugo wants me far more than either you or your wife. He may well come here but if he does it will be to hurt me. So you see my offer is not as generous as you might think. I cannot promise you safety, just a roof, a job and the protection of my men."

"And I will take both, Captain." He clasped my arm and I had a blacksmith.

Chapter 17

My wife would not allow Edith to leave our hall until she was much stronger. The blacksmith's wife had been open about the events which led to their flight and Eleanor was angry. She took her anger out on me, "It is not right that lords are able to abuse such precious and fey young things. Why does the King not protect them? I would that you were a lord for you would be a good one. I hope that Henry will be a good lord too but…"

I put my hand on my wife's. "He will. Henry is as angry about this as any but I must warn you my love, this Sir Hugo is an evil man and he already holds a grudge against me. We may be attacked."

At first, she showed shock and a little fear then she squeezed my hand, "You are first and foremost a warrior and a fighter. I may fear the plague or some horrible illness blighting our children but if you have a sword in your hand and good men behind you then we will be safe."

Edgar would go to the damaged smithy in the village and he would rebuild his home there. The hunt proved a happy accident. My hall was full but it was full of joy and love. My men, when they heard the story, were more than happy to repair the former blacksmith's house. There were few tools in the forge. The dead blacksmith's anvil remained, probably because it was too big to be stolen. The most important item, the fire and the chimney remained. We all shared in the work.

That first day after toiling all morning we ate and rested. "This is a good place, Captain. There is water close by and that is always handy. The fire and chimney remain. The anvil embedded in the tree trunk is all I need to shape iron and I have my hammer!"

"What of the tools you will need? The wood with the holes to draw through the metal. The formers to shape the metal? The tongs to use in the fire? The snips to cut the steel?"

He had smiled happily at the problems I presented to him. "I can make them. Some will be harder than others to fashion for I will need metal but it is a start and it will be safer than where we were."

Stephen the Tracker said, "Captain, there is a chest of old metal in the barn. We fetched it from Galicia. Much of it is rusted but it could be used."

Edgar seemed happy. "That will do for the tools but the better-quality ironware will need iron ore." His face darkened. "Close to the land of Sir Hugo, they mine it."

"Forget that land. It is gone, Edgar! Besides, there are iron workings to the south of us. When the weather improves we will go and buy some."

"But Captain I am already in your debt! Will I become your serf and be in servitude?"

I said firmly, "Never! We have no serfs here nor do we keep slaves. We pay our people that which is right and proper. They are not fettered and may leave at any time. We will come to some arrangement, Edgar the Smith. You are good at your trade?"

He grinned, "Aye Captain, the best!"

"Then you will earn your keep and your surplus can be sold. Now let us get back to work. My wife has a venison stew enriched with ale on the fire. We owe it to the dead deer to have a good appetite when we devour it!"

We had news from Stratford that Lady Anne was unwell and Peter and Henry returned home for a few days. She recovered and they returned. While they were away we had a spring storm which brought down trees and made roads impassable. When they did come back, it was with the news that the bad weather had slowed the progress of the King on his gyration. My men, led by Roger of Chester, would be frustrated. I knew they would rather be with me and my archers. Henry also brought fifty pounds with him. "My grandfather said that this is a bounty due to you for what you have done for the villagers in Stony Stratford."

"I needed no such bounty. You did not tell him about Edgar and Edith, did you?"

Henry looked disappointed, "Am I so shallow a creature that I would do that, Captain? I had thought you would have thought better of me."

"I am sorry but that couple need time to recover and the last thing I want is Sir Hugo or Sir Bohemund arriving here."

"I doubt that they will Captain. We had visitors who were passing through from Wales. The snowstorm caught them unawares and they spent the storm with us. They knew of Sir Thomas, Sir Hugo and Robert de Vere. Those lords are in Chester where they are building an army."

"An army?"

"Sir Jasper, the lord who stayed with us, told us that the Earl of Oxford says it is an army to save England."

"England and not the King. I fear that Henry Bolingbroke is right. This de Vere plays for high stakes. He is gambling for a kingdom."

"He cannot usurp the King!"

"Henry, I was there when the young de Vere first came into the life of King Richard. I know not how but he has a power over the young King. Only the goodness of Anne of Bohemia prevents the Earl from ruling through the King. If I am honest I believe that de Vere has something to do with the barrenness of the Queen. She is healthy in all other respects and yet she cannot bear a child. Still, you bring good news. If Sir Hugo is in the north-west then he cannot come knocking at our door and we have the opportunity to prepare for him."

By the time it was April the smithy was working and the house repaired to the satisfaction of my wife. Edith was now showing the child she was carrying. The weather had improved and the news that Sir Hugo was raising an army meant we had delayed long enough on the improvements to my hall. I dare say if I had asked him then the King might have given me permission to build a castle but that would take time and alert my enemies to what I was about. Stony Stratford was a backwater. I would have it kept that way. We had an extra fifty pounds to spend and so I sent Peter and Henry to buy cartloads of stone. While they were away my archers and my men began to dig the foundations for my new wall and defences. Edgar was worth three or four men when it came to the digging of the ground.

I could not build a castle but I could build a wall around my hall and the homes of my tenants. We planned on one twelve feet high with a fighting platform and but one gate. We dug the foundations and a ditch around it. The ditch would improve the drainage of the ground and the spoil was piled against the walls to make them stronger. John son of Jack knew the land around us better than I did. He took me to the stream which lay just forty paces from the ditch. "Captain, if we divert this stream we will have a moat. It will dry in summer but the ditch will still be an obstacle. It will also help to increase the power of the stream in the village. One day you could hire a miller and grind once more."

He was right. My wife was unhappy with having to grind by hand. While we waited for the stone we began to dig the channel for the water. We did not break through. We needed the wall completing first. When it arrived we sorted it. Henry and Peter had managed to buy a great deal of good stone. There was some which was not so good. In addition, we had stones we had discovered when digging the ditch and the channel for the moat. We had no mason but it was just a wall we were building. We embedded tree trunks in the bottom of the foundations and then laid the largest stones there. We left a gap between the two rows of stones. With almost twenty men working we soon had the lower courses of the wall laid. I realised that we did not have enough stone to make it as high as we might have wished and so we hewed logs. We would need a palisade for the top six feet. We toiled until May. We might have finished the wall sooner but my farmers had animals to tend and crops to weed.

All the time we toiled we heard news of the King and his progress. He was in the north of the country, in the land of the Percy's. They were loyal but so far away and busy defending against the Scots that they would not be able to give him material support. And all the while the Lords Appellant ran London and the Earl of Oxford built up his army. It spurred us on.

By June we had the wall and palisade finished. We had a fighting platform and we had two small towers over the gatehouse. Stephen the Tracker designed and made them. They would accommodate two archers each and, with a roof above, would enable the archers to clear any enemies away from the walls. We built a bridge. We made it so that we could draw it up by means of ropes and add an extra layer of defence to the gate. That done, we piled the spoil around the base of the walls both within and without. The walls were solid. We then put the clay we had dug into the bottom of what would be the ditch. We were almost done. The last task on this part of the improvements was to break through to the stream. I feared that we had miscalculated as the water gushed and rushed towards the newly dug moat. The water came alarmingly high and then, after the first rush, settled. We had defences. Sir Hugo could come and we could hold him off.

We had not ignored the training of my men. Until Roger of Chester and his men returned I would have no men at arms but we had tenant farmers who trained as archers. John, Peter and Henry helped me to train the mighty Edgar to use a sword and shield. There would be five of us who would fight thus and thirty who would fight with bows. Each Sunday we rested from the walls and we toiled at the butts. We bought iron and Edgar began to make a mail hauberk for himself and for John. John was so keen to have one made that he worked the bellows and helped to drawn the hot iron wire through holes until it was the right thickness. Edgar showed him how to wrap the wire around a piece of wood and then cut it. The hardest part was to teach him to make holes in the links so that Edgar could rivet them.

All the while my wife and Edith grew. The end of summer would be the time when the babies would be born. Most children were born at this time. The long nights of December were a time when folk did not venture forth. We had also been lucky in the winter. Not only had we not lost any animals, the ones which had born young all delivered healthy ones. There were twins and triplets for the sheep. We had the biggest herds but my tenants also had good fortune.

One Sunday, at the butts, I spoke with Richard Stone Heart. We were watching John's father, Jack, as he herded his flock of sheep towards the new pasture. Richard was looking wistfully at the flock. "If you wish to have a farm again Dick, then ask. There are empty ones."

He shook his head, "No Captain, I am content with my life. I am looking enviously for had God not taken my wife and child from me then that would be my life and I would be content. You can never go back. You gave me a new life and I am resigned to my new one."

"But you sit alone too much."

He nodded, "That is my nature. I was ever that way. My wife was the one who brought out the smiling side of me. She was the better part of me. I am not unhappy, at least I am no unhappier than I was before I met my wife but, being solitary, I can think of her." He lowered his voice. "I talk to her Captain and, sometimes, I swear that I hear her in my head. Does that make me simple?"

"No, Dick, for I met my mother just a few years ago and that was the last time I saw her but when I am drifting off to sleep I often hear her voice and, in my dreams, she comforts me as though I was a bairn."

His face creased into a smile. "That is exactly how it is with me. Do not fret about me, Captain. I can loose a bow as well as any of the others and I will not run when things go badly. You are a good man and a good Captain. I will not let you down."

There were other changes as June came and went. Some of my archers had succumbed to the lure of the servants my wife kept in our house. Three were married on midsummer's day. It was always seen as a propitious day to be wed. It meant we had to build three houses for them. That also helped for both the newly built warrior hall and my home had more space. For a time we had seemed to almost be bursting the house at the seams.

Tom was more active now and he was growing. He had helped us to make the walls and dig the ditches. He had carried stones to infill and he had happily stomped down on the clay. He was desperate to be a warrior and so I taught him how to use a sling. It would develop good skills and I had used one when I was his age. Standing before the men at arms it had given me my first taste of war. I still remembered my first victory, hitting the Spanish man at arms on the helmet and felling him. I did not kill him but I had helped the company to win and that was important. Once I had shown him how to collect the smoothest of stones and how to swing the sling he was happy to spend hours each day practising. He came back one day in July exultantly. He had killed a pigeon. From that day onwards not a day went by when he did not go hunting and return with a rabbit or crow or magpie. He had learned not to harm the doves who used our dovecot. Their eggs in winter were a valuable source of food.

Stephen the Tracker liked Tom. I did not think the leader of my archers would ever marry. Tom was like an adopted son. Stephen was more than happy to show him how to make a scabbard for his dagger or a new sling. It was he who used the hide from one of the deer we had killed to make Tom his first brigandine. It had no metal upon it but it was tough and when we went hunting it would protect him from the brambles through which we hunted. The summer was a glorious one. I believe it was the happiest I could remember. There was no war for us. The King was at Chester as was the Earl of Oxford. I suspected he would tarry there longer. That was disturbing but no more for as long as the Earl was in Chester there was no civil war.

The Duke of Gloucester, the Earl of Arundel and Thomas de Mowbray ruled London. Henry Bolingbroke was in Northampton although I did not doubt that he was in touch with his uncle. So far the Earl had kept his word. He had not bothered me and for that I was grateful. I knew that I had been promised a knighthood but once that happened I would be his man. I would no longer have the freedom I enjoyed.

Edith's child, Edward, was born first. It was the third week of August and as hot a day as I could remember. My wife and the mothers from the village attended and we waited with Edgar. He was philosophical about the weather. "This is good, Captain. If he is a smith he will need to get used to the heat. My father told me that being a blacksmith was the one trade which prepared a man for Hades. I hope not to go there but if my sins send me hence I shall be ready!"

When the boy was born healthy with all of his parts intact and a cry which could be heard in Stratford we cracked open the birth ale. We had another such barrel ready for my son or daughter. This was special ale made with burned barley. As black as charcoal, it was a powerful ale. It was not one for a workday. It was a beer for a holy day or a celebration.

My own son, Harry, was born two weeks later in September. Like Edward, he was healthy and whole. My wife, on the other hand, had a hard time. As she nursed our son she said, "Three is enough William!"

I smiled. It was the pain of childbirth. She loved children. There would be more.

As September passed we began another end of the year. It was a busy time for all. We needed to pollard the trees. Every piece of fruit was collected, no matter how bruised. Each vegetable was picked. The best of both would be stored. The rest would either be eaten or, in the case of apples and pears made into cider. The cull of the older animals would begin soon and then we would have our bone fire at the start of November. Pigs were turned into fields to make the most of any stalks or stems which might be eaten. My archers went to collect ash and yew for arrows and for bows. When the land was beginning to sleep we were working harder than ever.

We had visitors who passed along the road and it was from them that we learned news of the outside world. The King was heading back to London and he had made de Vere Justice of Chester. He was already Duke of Ireland. King Richard seemed determined to make him the most powerful man in England. He appeared blind to the dangers therein.

The third week in November saw the return of my men at arms. Stephen the Tracker and his men had built the new warrior hall and my men at arms would be comfortable. Although they came back with full purses they were not happy. I feasted with them and my archers in the warrior hall. A newborn babe required quiet at night. Henry, John, Peter and Tom joined me.

Roger of Chester was in expansive mood, "Captain this is the first time that any of us have been able to talk freely. We had to guard the King and were unsure who was a friend or a foe. Poor Dick of Craven does not know if he is coming or going. The King has moods, Captain. One day he is everyone's best friend and on the next, he may have a guard whipped for smiling. If it was not for the Queen I think that all of us would have quit before now and returned home."

"But did he gain support?"

Roger downed his ale and shook his head, "The support for the King was the same before and after we left. His visit did nothing to encourage it. The lords with whom we stayed resented the expense of the royal visit. The men of the north were the most loyal and the ones least able to help. The Scots are being encouraged by the French. There were skirmishes even when we were there. The only places which gave the King total support were Lancashire and Cheshire and none of us liked the men there. The Earl of Oxford made my flesh creep. He fawned around the King but even a blind man could see that it was empty flattery."

"Then I am sorry that I committed you to such an ordeal."

"No, Captain, we all asked for the commission. It was a lesson and it was not all bad." He laughed, "The best part was when we saw Sir Hugo Vernon." I frowned. "Oh do not get me wrong, Captain, he is a man I would happily slay but Stephen the Tracker's arrow means that his right hand has a weakness." He raised his beaker, "Stephen the Tracker!"

We all chorused, "Stephen the Tracker!"

My archer bowed, "You are welcome!"

Roger said, "It is good to be home Captain but can you afford to pay us? If you cannot..."

I shook my head, "I will find some way to fund you."

Edgar was seated at the table, "You have taken on much, Captain. There is much expense in paying for my smithy and your new wall..."

I stood, aware that Tom was taking in every word I spoke, "Listen, friends, for that is how I view you. I have been successful as a warrior. I have husbanded my coin. I still have money from Galicia. My wife knows how to farm. It could well be that we have a disastrous crop next year or that we have weather which takes our animals but now, as we come to the end of this year, all is well and you are all welcome here. I will continue to pay you and, hopefully, like Lol, Alan of the Wood and Jack War Bag, some of you will marry and live here on this manor. As for the future? I am no seer and can not see past the end of this month. Let us enjoy our lives now. Let us relish our friendship, the food and the ale!"

They all cheered.

Two days later Henry Bolingbroke sent for me. He needed me and my retinue. I had spoken too soon and we were going to war."

Chapter 18

My wife was philosophical about it all. "You have to go for the Earl is our liege lord but I pray do not take Edgar. His wife needs him."

"I will not but our son has asked to come and I cannot gainsay him. I went to war when I was younger than he is."

She bit her lip and then nodded. "He is the son of a warrior. You will watch over him." She was feeding Harry. "And we have another son." She shook her head, "It is you I worry about. You are a marked man. I pray you come home safely to me."

"I swear I will." I did not say that I might return as a knight. The Earl might have forgotten his promise. Powerful men had short memories.

As we neared Northampton Castle it was obvious that the Earl was mustering his men. I saw the standard of the Earl of Nottingham too. Henry Bolingbroke greeted me like a long-lost friend. "William. It is good to see you. The troubles of this land may soon come to an end."

We were alone in an antechamber when he spoke with me, "Lord, you know my feelings on the matter. I will not be involved in any rebellion against the King. If that means I lose my lands then so be it."

He laughed and clapped his arm around my shoulder. "You have more nobility and honour in you than any man born of noble blood. Nothing could be further from the truth. The Duke of Gloucester wishes for his nephew to be free from the influence of the Duke of Ireland. You feel the same way, do you not?"

"Aye, but why are we gathered here? Do we mean well by this?"

"Thomas, Duke of Gloucester, the Earl of Arundel and Thomas de Beauchamp, Earl of Warwick are all coming here. The King is safe in London. The King was confronted by those three powerful lords who were supported by loyal men of the church. They brought an appeal of treason against de la Pole, de Vere, Tresilian, and two other loyalists: the mayor of London, Nicholas Brembre, and Alexander Neville, the Archbishop of York. The King is safe and protected by the Earl of Arundel's men. He and the Queen will be unharmed. When those who have duped him come to trial then his power will be restored. We do not rebel or arm ourselves against the King except in order to instruct him." He leaned in, "My father has been informed of all of this. He will return home soon and he will take charge. My uncle means well but my father is a King and knows what my cousin ought to do."

This all sounded very plausible but I was cynical enough to see a sinister side to it all. It sounded to me like John of Gaunt was returning to claim the throne.

"Of course, my father cannot return quickly. He still has much to do in Galicia."

"Then why are we here, lord?"

He smiled. It was the smile of a wolf which spies a sheep wandering into its territory, "De Vere has grown even more arrogant. He is heading south from Wales. He has with him Molineux, Vernon, and Ratcliffe." My eyes lit up. "There, now you are with us. It is the very same Vernon whose brother you fought. Now, do you see? If de Vere gets to London there will be war. The King is in the Tower and is guarded but if de Vere joins him then there will be bloodshed. We intend to stop de Vere." He stopped, "That is why I have summoned you. The men you bring are as but a beaker of water in this sea of warriors but your men have skills that none other has. You can scout and track de Vere. You can shadow him so that we know where we can stop him. We go from here to speak with Nottingham. On the morrow, you leave for the west. We believe he will pass through Stratford. You know the area well. It is not far from your own home. When you find him send word to us. I will give you four good men to act as messengers. If he is at Stratford then we will move south and west. Our aim is to stop him before he reaches the Thames."

"But your army is not yet mustered?"

"No. The Lords Appellant have had to leave some of their army to protect the King."

"And how many men come south with de Vere?"

"That is for you to discover but we think there are more than three thousand men."

"And you have?"

He paused, "Fifteen hundred."

"Then you lose."

"We have more men coming and now you see the importance of your task. If you can find the foe then we have the advantage. There are many places he could cross the Thames. It could be anywhere from Castle Eaton to Oxford or even as far east as Reading! There are many miles and many bridges to watch. We think he means to surprise us. If we can surprise him then we can negate his numbers."

I nodded, "And we mean well by this?"

"You want de Vere stopped?"

"I do."

"Then we mean well." I nodded. "Come and I will bring you to my messengers."

The four young men were all squires. Two I knew: Edward and Geoffrey. "I see you are no longer a page."

"No Captain. I have been rewarded by my lord. And Richard now has his spurs."

"You will have time to talk when you are on the road. Here are John and James. They are brothers. They have good horses and they are clever. You just need to tell me the direction the enemy takes and if you can predict the bridge or the crossing then so much the better."

"We will do our best, lord."

We had brought spare horses, armour and weapons. We would not be able to take them and so I sent Henry and my men at arms back to my hall. It was on the way and we headed for Stratford. As we rode I discovered that the brothers came from close to Stratford. Henry vaguely knew them. I asked them where was their home and they told me, Loxley. It was just a few miles from Stratford.

"Could we hide close by there?"

"Aye Captain. There is a wood to the north of it and the Banbury road is just to the south of the wood."

"Then we will camp there. Peter I would have you shed your tunic and wear some old apparel. Go to Sir Robert. Tell him not to oppose the Earl but go along with whatever plans he has."

"I should go, Captain. They are my grandparents."

"Have you forgotten Master Henry that Sir Hugo knows you? He knows of your association with me. Peter will be invisible. Lords like Sir Hugo do not notice the likes of Peter and myself. When I was in the Free Companies none knew me."

"Aye Captain I will."

We reached Loxley Woods and made camp. After changing from a warrior to a common man Peter rode to Stratford and Sir Robert's Hall. He knew of a place he could leave his horse. We waited and ate cold rations. It was hard for it was almost freezing and we needed a fire and hot food but we did not wish to give away our position. I sent Stephen and Lol to watch the Banbury road in case our foes sent scouts there. Peter did not return until the sun was up and thin wintery sunlight filled the sky.

"Well?"

"I waited until dawn to return as the Earl of Oxford had not arrived. I heard horses and spied his scouts. I waited long enough to hear them demand accommodation for the Duke of Ireland and his lords."

Henry said, urgently, "And my grandparents know they have to dissemble?"

"Your grandfather is no coward, Master Henry. He knows this is for the King and he will feign support. All will be well." Henry looked relieved and nodded. Peter said, "There is something else, Captain." His voice sounded worried. "I spied Captain Mavesyn. He was in command of the men in the hall."

I saw the look of terror on Henry's face. I put up my hand. The Earl would not harm your grandparents. Mavesyn is an evil man but he will not hurt them." I was not sure that I believed my own words but we could do nothing about it.

Knowing that the enemy were at Stratford was one thing but knowing their route was another. They could pass to the north of us and head for Oxford. I still expected them to take the Banbury road. The river west of Oxford had fords as well as bridges. This was winter and the river was higher than in summer. I guessed that the Earl of Oxford would not have chosen to march except that the King had sent for him. He had not obeyed the King the last time that he had been needed. He had been forced to march. As dusk fell I went with John and Stephen the Tracker. I left the men under the command of Roger of Chester. Henry wanted to come but I needed men who could be invisible. The rest of the men waited in the woods on the Banbury road.

I had been to Sir Robert's hall enough times to know the quiet ways in. However, I had not anticipated the host I saw camped by the River Avon. We would not be able to reach the hall for the army was camped south of the river. We stopped in the closest cover we could find. It was in woods close to the eastern end of the river. We tethered our horses and walked to the edge of the wood. We would have to count fires. Most camps had ten men to a fire. Some had more and some had less. This would not tell us the number of lords but we would be able to estimate the men. We counted the ones before us and I used a tally stick to keep a record. Then we headed west. The most dangerous part was crossing the Banbury road. When we reached the river again I had the tally. I did not try to count, I could do that later on. We headed back to our horses.

We were less than half a mile from our horses and had just crossed the road when we heard voices. I jammed the tally stick in my tunic and drew my sword. Stephen slipped his bow from his back. John had a short sword. We did not move. We listened. It was men on horses and they were moving down the Banbury road. We then moved and headed back to the road. The two were speaking.

"At this rate, it will take a month to get to London."

"Does that matter just as long as we get there unseen?"

"How can you keep a host this size hidden? As soon as we leave, Stratford, the doddery old man will send word to his master the Earl of Northampton."

The other man laughed, "And that is why there will be men left to guard them. Captain Mavesyn served the King. He will watch them. The Duke is no fool. He knows that the old man was lying through his teeth. When this is over he will pay the ultimate price."

Their voices were fading as they headed south. "Just kill them both I say. Dead men tell no tales."

Then they were gone. We hurried back to our horses. We now knew that they were taking the Banbury Road and I had a dilemma. Did I tell Henry that his grandparents were in danger? All the way back to the camp I debated with myself. As soon as we arrived I sent James back to the Earl with the news that they were taking the Banbury Road. We would leave before dawn and camp close to Stow. I knew there were woods there and we could hide. De Vere was being clever. He was travelling through forested land where his mighty host would be well hidden.

Once again, we had cold fare and a frozen night. I sat with Henry and Peter. "I think that your grandparents will be held by some of the Earl's men once he has left Stratford. I tell you this but I hope you will not do anything to jeopardise the Earl's plan."

"Are they in danger? Captain Mavesyn is a bad man."

"I confess I do not know. It would take a hard-hearted man to hurt two old people but he may."

Henry looked at his servant. "What do I do?"

"What your heart tells you, Master Henry. If you wish to go back and wait until the Earl of Oxford and his army have left then I will come with you."

Henry looked into Peter's eyes. "And you believe we would die?"

"That is a certainty. If the Captain and his men came with us then we would have a good chance of survival but the Captain will not. He has sworn to scout the enemy and warn the Earl and he will do that."

The others around the camp heard the words and knew the dilemma faced by my squire. "It is unfair, Captain."

"Life is unfair. What I promise is that once we have fulfilled our obligation we will ride to Stratford and secure the release of your grandparents."

"If they are still alive."

"I will not honey my words. If they are still alive."

"Then I will follow you until this evil man is destroyed."

We left before dawn and I risked the Banbury Road. We had not heard hooves during the night. If we met the scouts returning then we would have to deal with them. I intended to make good time while we could. We left the road at the Chipping Norton crossroads. There were woods to the south of us and my intention was to head through them. We had no sooner left the road when we heard the sound of hooves. It was the scouts we had heard the previous night. We had barely made it under cover in time. We saw them as they halted at the crossroads. They had come from Stow. We could not hear their words but we saw them debate. They rode a little way down the Chipping Norton road and then, turning back on themselves, headed north. That decided me.

"We will stay here the night. Geoffrey, ride to your lord. Tell him I think that the enemy will cross the Thames at Radcot Bridge."

The Earl's squire, Edward asked, "How can you be so certain, Captain?"

"They came from Stow. There are two bridges which are close. The one at Chipping Norton and the one at Radcot. The one at Chipping Norton is a longer road to the bridge and the river is shallower at Radcot. It is but a guess. Your master is using me because of my experience." I turned to the other messenger, "John, go with Geoffrey. This message must get through. If the bridge can be held then we can trap de Vere by the river."

As we made our camp I saw that poor Tom looked exhausted. When I had been his age I had done as much but perhaps I had been tougher. I pulled him to me and wrapped him in my cloak. "I am not tired, father."

"I know but I am. You and I will have an early night and let the others watch." I caught Roger of Chester's eye and he nodded. My men would let me be a father that night. I hoped that I would be able to keep him safe when the battle came. Had I made a mistake?

We woke to silence and it remained that way for some time. The rest helped our horses and us. Tom looked much brighter. We had two archers on each of the roads, Stow and Chipping Norton. Two returned at noon. "Captain, they are approaching down the road."

I went with them and Roger of Chester. I left Tom with Henry and John. We hid far enough back from the road so that we would not be seen. We heard their noise long before we saw them. They were like a huge colourful snake which slithered along the road to Stow. They were heading for Radcot Bridge. Estimating their speed told me they would have to camp at Stow and would not be at the bridge until the morning. The baggage train passed us and we returned to my men. There was little point in trying to get ahead of them. If my messages had reached the Earl he would be racing down the road to reach us.

"Stephen the Tracker. Follow them and let me know where they camp."

We mounted and I led my men down to Chipping Norton. The castle still stood but it was empty. It was one of the ones first built by the Conqueror all those years ago. A small village, it had no river to guard and the main road now ran through Banbury. It was of no importance. I led my men up to the deserted castle. We tethered our horses within what had been the bailey and we waited. Part of the fighting platform remained and I had men keep watch. They spied, in the late afternoon, the retinue of Henry Bolingbroke as they headed down from Banbury. I mounted Jack and rode, with Edward, John, Tom and Henry, to meet with him. We met on the outskirts of the village.

"Well, Will?"

"They were heading down the Stow road, lord. Stephen followed them. He has not returned."

"You are certain about Radcot Bridge?"

"It is less than twenty miles from Stow to the bridge. They will cross there but, lord, they have five thousand men."

"My uncle is heading for the bridge even as we speak. He has three thousand men and they can deny him the river." I turned my horse and we rode towards the village. "Are your men rested?"

"They are, lord."

"Then when your archer confirms their direction ride to the bridge and tell my uncle and the lords. I will close the jaws on this trap tomorrow."

"Lord, you have less than eight hundred men with you."

He smiled, "It will be enough. If you taught me anything when you trained me Will it was that a resolute leader who leads good men will prevail over one who has weakness. We both know de Vere has weakness."

I knew that but I wondered how Henry Bolingbroke did. He saw the confusion on my face. "Will, you are a good man and the best of warriors but you saw just one side of de Vere. You saw the ambitious, power-hungry man who seeks a crown. I know him to be a weak and vain man. If he had been any kind of leader and friend to King Richard he would have come last year when you guarded him at Eltham. He did not. He has spent almost a year gathering this army. Why? He hoped that the French would invade and he would be called upon to rule. He is not confident about his own ability to win a battle. I have enough men, for when he sees that he is surrounded he will try to bargain."

We reached the castle and the village. Stephen rode in, "Captain, my lord, they are camped at Stow."

I nodded, "Then I will see you on the morrow, my lord." I turned to Edward, "We did not need you as a messenger but I thank you for your company."

"And I yours, sir. I learned much. You shared the hardships with your men and I can see why they are so loyal. God speed, sir."

We had twenty miles to ride and would not reach the bridge until well after dark. I had Simon and Walter Longridge ahead as scouts. We clattered over it as the cold began to bite. My scouts rode back to tell me that there was an army camped just half a mile from the bridge. I frowned. They should have had guards upon the bridge. What was the Duke of Gloucester thinking?

We dismounted and led our horses to the camp. The lords had spread on both sides of the road. The ground close to the bridge was a little marshy. They had no sentries out. I heard the murmur from the fires and we had almost entered the camp before there was any sort of alarm. Men jumped up and grabbed weapons. I held up my hand. "We are friends. I am William Strongstaff and I serve Henry Bolingbroke." My name was known and swords were sheathed. "Where is the Duke?"

A sergeant at arms pointed, "The lords are lodged at the farm."

I turned to Roger and Stephen, "Find us a camp. Send John to me when you have found a suitable site. Henry, come with me. And you, Tom." I handed my reins to John and strode with Henry and my son along the road. I said, "If you are still worried about your grandparents..."

"I am but if this de Vere wishes them harm then he will have to defeat the lords and then send a messenger. Tomorrow will decide my grandparents' fate. This lesson has been one I did not expect to learn. I had been so concerned with becoming a knight that I had forgotten what gave me the chance to become one. I will not neglect them again in the future."

As we approached the farmhouse sentries approached us. "I have come from the Earl of Derby! I have intelligence about the enemy."

The sentry opened the door and I heard the hubble and bubble of conversation. The heat from the interior hit me after the cold of the night. I realised I had not eaten for some time and the smell of food made my stomach ache. Faces turned as we entered the room. The Duke of Gloucester frowned and then recognised me, "You are the fellow who guarded the King." I nodded. "Bolingbroke sent you?"

"He did lord. Your enemy, Robert de Vere, is camped at Stow eighteen miles from here. He has over five thousand men. He will be here by noon. Your nephew guards the road north. He cannot escape but he has five thousand men."

The Duke jumped to his feet and smacked one fist into the palm of the other, "We have the slippery eel!" He took a purse of coins and threw it at me. "You have done well!" he suddenly seemed to see me. "You once served with my brother, the Black Prince, in Spain."

"Yes, my lord."

"As I recall you were handy and I hear that the cutthroats you lead are also handy."

I did not like the appellation he afforded me but I nodded, "They are good men, lord."

"There is a small ford a little way west of the bridge. I would have you and your men guard the eastern approaches to it. We intend to put our force on the river. He outnumbers us but I hope to daunt him with the mettle of the men I lead."

Sir Thomas Mortimer, a knight who was a close associate of the Lords Appellant jumped to his feet. "Lord, let me challenge de Vere and I will fight him. Then he will see that we are men of steel."

The Earl of Arundel, whom I knew favoured Sir Thomas pulled his friend down to his seat, "We both know that de Vere will do anything to avoid having to fight anyone. He will hide in the rear and it will be Molineux, Vernon or Ratcliffe who come to face us beard to beard!"

The room laughed and the Duke of Gloucester waved his arm. I was dismissed. I confess that I did not like the men I had just met. When I had been in the free companies I had seen groups of ordinary warriors who were like them. They thought themselves exclusive. They mocked others and thought only of themselves. The Blue Company had not been like that. My men were not like that and I hoped that Henry Bolingbroke was cut from a different cloth.

John awaited me and he led me to the camp. My men had chosen somewhere close to the river and they had a fire going. For the first time in many days, we would have warm, if not hot, food and we would not be chilled to the bone. Already a stew was being prepared and as the fire took hold the pot was placed on top. We drank from our ale skins and I told them what we had learned.

Henry said, "I did not like the man who leads us."

I laughed, "Nor did I but men like us do not choose who leads us. We choose our sides. We lie in bed with the Duke of Gloucester and the enemies of King Richard but it is only to scotch the snake that is de Vere. When de Vere is gone and the King free from his spell we may well be the enemies of the Duke of Gloucester. We fight one battle at a time, Henry!"

We rose, as was our way, before dawn and breakfasted on meat cooked on a skillet over the coals. We could have eaten the ham cold but warmed through it seemed to fill a man better and the smell of ham cooking added to the pleasure. We led our horses beyond the bridge and secreted them in the woods. The bank was lined with willows and bushes. It was easy for us to wait there. I knew that it was unlikely that our enemy would arrive much before noon.

"Tom, I will be busy this day. If we have to fight I want you near to the horses. If it goes badly with us then flee."

"I can fight!"

"I know my little cockerel, but for today watch the horses eh?"

"Yes, father!"

Some of my archers threw old bowlines in the river. There were fishes, even in December. My men were expert foragers. We had our shields and helmets by our horses as we waited. The archers had their bows ready but not strung. I looked north of the river and saw that marshes spread on that side. They lay behind us too and we occupied one of the few dry areas. The Duke of Gloucester had made a wise decision to use the road and bridge for defence. This was not a good battlefield and he had chosen the better ground. I thought back to when I had first met Robert de Vere. He had been young then but he had known what he wanted. He was ambitious and saw friendship with the King as a means to gain power. I could not remember him fighting a battle save against the Irish and they were so wild and reckless that they did not count. I wondered when he had decided to try for a crown. The Earl was correct, de Vere threatened the stability of the crown. So long as he lived then King Richard could never be the king his father hoped.

There was a shout from the river and I looked up in alarm. I smiled. James Warbow had caught a fish. Noises began to come from the camp as the Duke of Gloucester began to send his men to their positions. He and his lords stood on the south bank of the Thames. We were close enough to the bridge to see that he was surrounded by his closest knights: the Earl of Arundel, Sir Thomas Mortimer and the Earl of Warwick. They were mounted but surrounded by dismounted knights. The marshy ground meant any knight who fought on a horse was doomed.

Noon approached and we heard the sound of hooves on cobbles. I did not think we would be involved overmuch in the battle for the marshy ground opposite precluded its use by warriors. We would, however, have a good view of the battlefield. I saw the banners first and then the leaders of de Vere's army. He led and I saw, next to him, Molineux, Vernon, his brother, Sir Hugo, and Sir Bohemund Ratcliffe. I prayed for the opportunity to lay alongside Sir Hugo. I did not want the threat of him hanging over my family and my farm. If this came to blows then he would be fighting at the bridge but I would be ready.

"Archers!"

My archers pulled in their fishing lines and grabbed their bows. They strung them and then jammed arrows in the soft earth next to them. There might have been a frost but the thin December sun had turned it to mud. The marsh ruled once more. Horns sounded from de Vere's army and they began to array. I saw horsemen on the bank opposite. They were going to risk the marsh. De Vere was a bigger fool than I had taken him for. Both commanders were showing caution. They shuffled their men around. I saw crossbow men approaching their right flank. They would be opposite us. My archers would anticipate a duel with crossbows. De Vere came to the western side of the bridge. He was accompanied by Sir Thomas Molineux. Were they going to be so foolish as to attack the marshy side, our side?

The Duke of Gloucester saw the movement and he sent Sir Thomas Mortimer and his retinue to join us. There was a gap between my men and the end of the Duke's line and perhaps de Vere had seen it as a weak point.

Sir Thomas grinned, "Master William, we may have need of you and your archers yet. Are your horses handily placed?"

"Aye, lord. We can be mounted in a heartbeat."

"Good."

Just then Stephen the Tracker said, "Captain, look, to the north!"

I shaded my hands against the thin sun and saw the banners and pikes of Henry Bolingbroke and his men. I knew how few they were but the enemy did not and a large contingent, at the rear, began to drift away. De Vere and the Constable of Chester had not seen the movement yet and de Vere raised his sword. They were going to attack.

"Ready men, on my command!"

The mounted horsemen rode into the water. Sir Thomas lined the banks with his knights and men at arms. They were armed with pikes. As crossbow bolts began to fly, striking the shields of Mortimer and his men, I shouted, "Kill the crossbowmen!"

Stephen the Tracker had been waiting for such an order. I only had ten archers but soon their deadly missiles began to hit the crossbows and their operators. Some fell and the others moved out of range. My son hurled his stones too. Most fell short but I was proud that he tried. At the same time, de Vere must have realised that not only were his men not advancing most were fleeing. The Constable of Chester and his men were having to face the pikes of Sir Thomas Mortimer and they were having the worse of the exchange. Suddenly de Vere raised his visor and shouted, "All is lost! Flee!"

As he turned to look at his leader the Constable of Chester fell from his rearing horse. His men fled. Sir Thomas Mortimer shouted, "Captain, get de Vere!"

I ran back to the horses. Over my shoulder I heard Sir Thomas shout, "You are lost, will you surrender?"

Constable shouted, "I will not flee. Will you come down and fight with me here?"

"Tom, stay here and guard the spare horses. We will return."

"Yes, father. Be safe!"

We mounted our horses and made our way to the river bank.

I saw Sir Thomas say to the Constable of Chester, "Come from the river."

"Will you save my life?"

"I promise nothing."

The Constable looked down the river where de Vere and ten of his men were swimming their horses to a place where they could clamber to dry land. As my horse entered the water I watched as Sir Thomas reached down and, pulling the helmet from the Constable drove his dagger into his throat. It was not an honourable thing to do. I kicked Jack and we kept to the south side of the river. There the water only came up to Jack's withers and we began to gain on the Earl of Oxford. I knew that there was a ford downstream and he would be able to use that to escape. To my amazement, I saw him throw his helmet, shield and lance into the water. He was lightening the load his horse had to carry. Behind me, I heard the wail as the men de Vere had been leading realised that he had fled. They joined the flight north. They had a choice of the pikes of the men of the Earl of Derby or marshes.

I saw the ford just ahead. We were closing. The Earl of Oxford turned and saw us. He shouted something to his men and, as he did so, managed to fall from his horse. Perhaps the horse lost its footing or maybe he jerked the head around too quickly. The result was that he was dumped into the water. I spurred on Jack as the retinue of the Earl turned to defend their lord. His squire rode to help him. I drew my sword. My shield still hung from my cantle as did my helmet. I would have no time to don them. I rode at the leading sergeant at arms. He had little plate but he wore good mail. I did not slow and he was stationary. He was trying to make his horse turn and he concentrated too hard on that. He swashed his sword rather than hitting. I put all of my effort into the blow and my blade hit his chest hard. He fell backwards into the water. His mail dragged him under for the water came above the horse's stirrups. My other men were already fighting with the remaining retinue and I urged Jack to get at the fleeing de Vere. His squire had given him his horse and stood facing me with a shield and a spear. De Vere scrambled up the ford and disappeared into the bushes which lined the north bank of the Thames.

I did not want to hurt a squire doing his duty. I needed to stop the Earl of Oxford and end his reign. The squire, as I neared him, suddenly hurled his spear at me and my horse. He was just ten feet away and the spear hit the armour on my leg. The plate turned the spear and it scored a line down Jack's side. He reared and deposited me in the river. We were nearing the ford and I did not sink far. His squire ran at me with his sword. He saw his chance of glory. I barely blocked his blow as I was having to fight the river. My feet found purchase and as I stood I raised my sword. The squire attempted to block the blow. I swung my fist around and knocked him out. He fell backwards into the water and I dragged him out by his coif.

Jack was standing in the shallows and I hurried as fast as I could to get to him. Sir Thomas Mortimer had sent two knights; Sir Tristram and Sir Geoffrey. They joined me and my men. "Where did he go, Captain?"

I pointed west and mounted Jack. The two knights and their squires galloped off. I shouted, "Wait!" They did not heed my words and I cursed them. Their hooves would hide his tracks! By the time I caught up with them they had muddied any tracks, there might have been.

"I cannot see him! Which way Captain?"

I shrugged, "Had you followed the tracks we might have known. As it is he is lost but I would guess that he would head west."

I guessed that they were annoyed at being spoken to like that by a mere gentleman but I cared not. We spent almost until dusk searching the river. We were about to turn when we heard the neigh of a horse. I drew my sword and waved my men in a half circle. The knights and their squires looked confused. Roger of Chester shouted, "Captain, I have found his cuirass and sabaton."

Just then his horse wandered over. It was injured. One of the knights, Sir Geoffrey of King's Lynn said, "He is dead then."

I turned and gave him a scornful look. "And how do you arrive at that conclusion? Did he stop his lame horse, take off his cuirass and throw himself in the river?"

"Well, where is he then, Captain?"

"He is escaped. He is now in his aketon and he will be hiding. We might as well return for we have lost him now. The Earl of Oxford has escaped!" I was angry and weary as I turned Jack to head back to the bridge at Radcot. If Sir Thomas had not sent the knights to help us then de Vere would be captured or dead!

Chapter 19

Henry Bolingbroke was waiting for us with his uncle. "Well?"

I told him what had happened. "He stripped off his armour and disappeared."

"Perhaps he is dead."

"No lord. Just because we wish it does not make it so."

He nodded, "At least we have our victory and now we head to London. You and Master Henry shall be knighted. You have deserved it."

I shook my head, "Lord, the Earl left men in Stratford. They hold Sir Richard and Lady Anne hostage. We need to ensure they are safe. We will join you in London within the week."

He shook his head, "Any other man would jump at the chance of knighthood."

"Lord the men they left were not knights. They were mercenaries. Henry's grandparents are in danger!"

He waved an arm. "You are a strange man. Go!"

We had no chance of reaching Stratford soon but I decided to ride as far north as we could. We managed twelve miles and reached the village of Rissington. It was more of a hamlet than a village. There was neither inn nor alehouse. The farmer who had the largest farm offered the use of his barn for twelve pennies. It was too much but he promised us some soup his wife had made and so I paid.

Roger of Chester saw to Jack's wound. It was a superficial one but it needed to be tended to. My men at arms and archers were appalled at the behaviour of the Earl of Oxford. "The man never even attempted to fight, Captain. He ran! Even worse he discarded his armour and weapons."

I smiled at the indignation of Natty Longjack. Others voiced their disapproval of such a craven lord. As we had ridden north we had seen the men slain when they had fled and met the Earl's pikes. We saw others who had fallen foul of the swamps and pools which lay close to the river.

Wilfred of Loidis shook his head, "Better to die facing a man with a sword in your hand than to sink into a swamp and drown."

John said, "And what about his poor squire? The coward loses his horse and takes his squire's whom he expects to slow down the Captain. It is a good job the Captain is a fair man. He only knocked him out."

Natty laughed, "Remind me never to annoy you, Captain. That was a mighty blow!"

My son Tom loved the way the archers and men at arms spoke. His eyes lit up with their words. I did not regret bringing him now. When we reached Stratford, I would leave him with the horses. He would be safe.

The farmer and his wife brought in the cauldron of soup. We each had our own bowls and wooden spoons. It was one of the first lessons we learned in the Free Companies.

Henry had been silent since before the battle and I sat next to him and Peter as the soup was ladled out. The farmer's wife had also made rye bread. It was a couple of days old but it worked well with the soup. I had finished and Henry was still moving his soup around as though it was too hot.

"Eat! I do not think that arriving home half-starved will help your grandparents at all."

"But Sir Hugo and the others all fled the field. They could be at Stratford by dawn!"

"They will do as we do. When they think the pursuit is ended they will rest. Their horses will be tired. They marched from Stow and ours rested."

He nodded and ate. Peter gave me a grateful smile. I was also worried about Sir Hugo and those who had fled the battle of Radcot Bridge. My worry was Edgar. I feared that they might head to my home. I had promised Henry that I would ensure his family was safe and I would do so.

I waved over Lol. He and the other archers who had married were worried about Sir Hugo and his vengeance. "Lol, when we ride for Stratford I would have you go to our home. It may be a waste of time but have the tenants and villagers come within my hall. Let us protect them from Sir Hugo. Take Tom with you. He will be safer there."

He nodded and I saw the relief on his face, "Captain I will go now. I have a good horse and the food has filled my belly. Alan and Jack will sleep easier knowing that I will be there."

I waved Tom over. "I have a task for you. I fear bad men may come to our home. I want you to go with Lol and protect your mother."

"I would rather stay with you."

"You can be home in a short time and we will have to fight a battle. I cannot watch over you and defeat our enemies."

"Then I will do as you ask."

Lol had brought Tom's horse, "Come, young Tom. You and I will get to know each other on this ride through the night!"

"God be with you." I felt empty as my son and archer disappeared into the night. It was for the best but I still worried. We had already prepared our beds. As I rolled into my blanket I wondered if I should have sent more men to my home. It was too late now but the sound of Lol son of Wilson's and Tom's horses' hooves disappearing in the distance was the sound of hope.

We left before dawn and pushed our horses so that it was dusk when we approached Stratford. Reassuringly we had not passed any others from the battle. Perhaps they feared the retribution of the Lords Appellant and kept away from the main road.

Peter knew the hall better than any and he and Natty Longjack crept close to the house while the rest of us prepared to use force. The two scouts returned to us silently. "They have guards on the doors and they are an unsavoury band. They wear no livery. We glimpsed the Reeve, old Harold, and he had been beaten. He had a bandage upon his head."

I nodded, "It is my decision. We go in hard and we go in fast. We cannot allow these men to hurt any more people. If we have to kill then so be it. Do we know how many men there are?"

"No Captain. We counted three men at the front gate and two at the back. From the noises we heard, there are more within."

Roger, take three men and two archers. Go around the back with Peter. By the time you get there the rest of us will have taken the front gate. Stephen, I would have those three guards dead and without making a noise."

"We will do so, Captain. Henry, you and John get to your grandparents. We will follow but leave us to deal with any men between you and the lord and lady. If you see Captain Mavesyn then leave him for me."

"Do not worry, Captain. My blood is cold and my eye is sharp. This night will show if I have the mettle to be a knight." We left the cover of the outbuilding and headed towards the gate. The wall next to the gate was more decorative than functional but the gate was substantial. The three men lounged inside warming themselves on a brazier. I had my sword and dagger in my hand. I did not even look at my archers for they knew their business better than any. Stephen must have given them a signal for four arrows flew and three guards fell. One was still moaning as we leapt over him. We did not need to worry about him. The gate to the hall was not barred and we opened it silently. I waved to the right for a corridor led to the kitchens. John Bowland led two men there. The main chamber in the hall was to my left. I had Walter of Loidis and three archers with me. I opened the door. There were five men there. They had two terrified serving girls half-naked. I could only guess what they intended. I knew that Henry and John, along with a pair of archers, would be racing to get to his grandparents but I guessed that these five were the leaders.

I gestured with my sword, "It is all over. The Earl of Oxford has fled and the Constable of Chester lies dead. The army you served is now speared over four counties. You have two choices, flee now or stay and suffer the consequences."

It could have been that the five men were simple and did not understand but I thought it more likely that they thought they could take the five of us. They were all big men. They grabbed weapons and ran at us. There were two terrified girls in the room and I wanted no accidents. The obvious leader swung an axe at me. It can be a terrifying weapon but I had seen them used before. I deftly flicked the axe aside and, stepping in, rammed my rondel blade into his side. It punctured the mail and struck something vital. Blood began to pour from his mouth and his dying hands clawed at me.

Just then the door burst open and Captain Mavesyn limped in. Since I had seen him last life had treated him badly. He drew his sword and dagger. All around us men fought but it was as though we were the only two, "I will have you now, lickspittle of the King. You will not trick me this time."

He swung his arm and brought his sword from the side and above him. Sir Robert had a higher ceiling than most and the Captain was able to generate a great deal of force. I used my ballock dagger and the angle of the blow to twist the blade towards the floor. I lunged at his boot. I had a sharpened tip and the sword pierced the leather and his foot. He screamed and swung again with his sword. This time he went directly for my neck. I ducked and rammed my dagger upwards into his skull. He died instantly. I realised that the sounds of fighting had ended. My men had been outraged by the half-naked girls and only one man survived the encounter.

"Bind his hands, Walter, and you two cover the girls. Silent David, come with me."

I could hear shouts and screams in the hall. They seemed to be coming from upstairs. I reached the landing on the first floor in three strides. I saw Garth of Worksop. He had a wound to his leg. He waved me to go on. There was a clash of steel from the bedroom. When I entered I saw John and Henry engaged with two men. Henry was losing and John was disarmed. Even as the brigand brought down his axe I lunged and my sword tore into his throat spraying blood in the room. Silent David launched himself at the back of the man who had driven Henry into a corner. Silent David's huge arms enfolded the body of the bandit and Henry slew him.

I turned and saw Lord and Lady Stratford. They both had a look of absolute terror on their faces. They gripped each other tightly. I think that their fear was for their grandson. "Henry, can you and John take charge here? I would search the rest of the house."

By the time I reached the ground floor all was over. The bandits had either died or they had run. We had one prisoner. Roger of Chester said, "I will shackle him in the stables, Captain." He shook his head. "These have behaved as animals. Four of the male servants lie dead and there was a serving girl..." he shook his head as though to expunge the memory of what he had seen, "It is not right what they did to her."

I nodded, "Then do not waste time shackling the prisoner. Let him confess and then hang him."

It was summary justice and it was necessary. Sir Robert was a magistrate and he could confirm my sentence afterwards. I sheathed my sword and sent men into the woods to fetch our horses. Henry stayed with his grandparents and I sent for Roger and Stephen. "I am worried about Edgar and my home. We leave after we have had some food and the horses have eaten grain. Henry can stay here with Peter and Garth of Worksop. They can keep the doors barred and summon help from the town. Lol should have the village and my hall warned but Sir Hugo and Sir Bohemund may think they have nought to lose."

"Aye Captain."

When we were ready to leave Sir Robert and Henry came to see us off. We had learned of the way these twenty men had behaved. They were men who served Sir Bohemund. I was glad that we had done what we had done. Sir Robert confirmed my sentence. "I fear that my wife will never recover. I have sent for the doctor for she cannot move her left arm. I fear the shock has hurt her. Had Henry not returned when he did she might have died."

"I would not leave if it were not necessary. I fear for..."

"My grandson has told me. Go and may God be with you."

We were fewer in number now and we rode faster. We were spurred on by the memory of what we had seen at Stratford. The men there had been the sweepings of the gutters. Sir Hugo had men who were equally foul and yet would be better armed. Even if Lol had reached my walls then there would be a handful of farmers and their families to defend my walls. Apart from Edgar and Lol, they would have bows only. Most would not have bodkin arrows and Sir Hugo and Sir Bohemund, encased in armour, would be safe from their missiles.

We had a long forty-five miles to ride and we pushed hard. We were lucky that, for most of the way, we rode down the old Roman road which went from Wales to London. When we stopped it was for our horses and not for us. We ignored the chafing saddles and the hunger pangs. We ate and made water when we watered our horses in the village troughs. I do not think we had ever made such a fast journey. It was when we stopped at Syresham, just nine miles from home, that John son of Jack said, "Captain do you know that it is almost Christmas?"

I shook my head. I had forgotten. "And last year we had such a celebration that we thought we lived in a perfect world. How wrong we were."

Dick Stone Heart said, "Not so, Captain. When I lost my wife and child I felt as you did. It has taken time but I now spy hope. When you took in Edgar and Edith and they had their son that was a glimmer in the darkness. They were saved from a fate they did not deserve. God took my family for a purpose. I am too insignificant to divine what that is but I am content. I can begin my life again. Life is not perfect but we make our own lives to be the best that they can be. God made a perfect world and it is man who spoils it." Those words of hope from one who had lost all made the last ten miles fly.

We heard the fighting long before we saw the battle. My house lay just half a mile from the road. The river we had used to make our moat was to the south of it and there lay the bridge. As we crested the small ridge which overlooked my hall we saw men advancing towards the walls. The walls were defended but I saw that there were more than thirty men trying to scale them.

I shouted, "Stephen, take your men and flank the attackers. The rest of you don helmets. I know we are weary and our horses gone but we cannot allow our people to suffer."

"Aye Captain!" While we donned helmets and swung around shields my eight archers galloped down the road towards the river. With my helmet and shield in place, I dug my heels into Jack. We had no time to form line. We would have to plough our way into them and hope that our sacrifice would divert them and allow Stephen and his archers to destroy them.

Roger of Chester nudged his horse next to mine. He shouted, "Captain, these are bandits we fight. We take the head of the snake and they will break. Let you and I engage the two knights!"

"Aye. Sir Hugo is mine. There is bad blood between us."

As we neared the walls I saw that Lol and his bodkin arrows had made a difference. Two sergeants lay with their mail pierced. On the walls, Edgar with a pot helmet upon his head swung his hammer at those who tried to scale the walls. The two gate towers had, within them, Lol and my three tenant farmers. Their bows had accounted for three horses and I saw some of the attackers wounded. I saw stones flying and striking those attacking. That would be Tom.

The sun was setting behind us and the ground was hardening with a December frost. Our hooves began to thunder and, above the cacophony of battle, Sir Hugo must have heard us. I saw him turn and wave his sword at us. He shouted something and Sir Bohemund, along with their squires and ten sergeants, the only ones who were still mounted, turned their mounts and moved towards us. His squire handed him a lance and Sir Hugo sheathed his sword. I could see that Sir Hugo had misused his horses more than ours.

Lol, in the tower, had seen the movement. An arrow flew and I saw a sergeant plucked from his saddle. With their backs to the men on the wall, they were vulnerable. Then I saw arrows from my right as Stephen the Tracker led his archers against those assailing the walls. Some of them sent arrows towards the mounted men. Once we closed with the mounted men then those on the walls and our archers would not be able to risk arrows for fear of hitting us. The twelve of us would have to prevail.

Sir Hugo had his visored helmet. The sun was setting and soon we would be fighting almost in the dark. A visor would inhibit his ability to fight. He would still be harder to beat than when I had fought him in Windsor. He now had a lance. All had told me that he had never lost when fighting from a horse and using a lance. As we closed I pulled my shield a little tighter and braced myself for the impact. I was grateful that our closing speed was slower than Sir Hugo would have wished but I saw him pull back his arm. He intended to punch me hard. It was the uneven ground which saved me but not my mount. The half-frozen field must have had a small hole for Jack's foreleg went into it. He was weary and not as surefooted as he normally was. I heard the snap and my horse's head dipped and swung to the right. Sir Hugo's lance ended any suffering my horse might have felt. The lance entered his head and snapped. I kicked my feet from my stirrups as I began to tumble from the saddle. My dying horse forced Sir Hugo to swerve. I hit the ground with my right shoulder. It was a hard fall on the half-frozen ground and it hurt but my aketon's padding saved me from worse injury. As I jumped to my feet a sergeant galloped at me. I was still raising my shield when Dick Stone Heart's arrow struck him in the neck and he fell from his saddle. I had no time to thank my archer for Sir Hugo wheeled his horse around to charge me with the stump of his lance. That was his undoing. He should have drawn his sword.

His weary horse lumbered towards me. He was but ten paces from me. I feigned fear and pretended that I was frozen to the spot. Sir Hugo pulled back his lance. He had no tip but a splinted lance could blind me. He was aiming for my head and reliant on me raising my shield. He had a courser and it would trample me into the ground. I waited until the last moment and as his lance came at me I jumped to the right and swung my sword into his leg as he passed me. He wore poleyn and plate but my sword hacked into the leather binding behind the knee. My sword wounded his horse and tore into his tendons. I heard a feral scream from within the visor and, in the darkening light of dusk, I saw blood on the blade.

A cry from behind made me turn. I saw Sir Hugo's squire galloping to his master's aid. Sir Hugo would have to turn his horse. I braced myself for the spear which was coming towards me. Dick Stone Heart sent an arrow at the squire. It hit his shield and made the squire flick his face to the left. It was enough. Holding my shield before me to make his horse flinch I hacked into the horse's neck. As it fell it threw the squire from its back.

Dick Stone Heart pulled back his bow to end Sir Hugo's life and shouted, "Captain!" Even as the arrow flew Sir Bohemund's squire's spear skewered my archer.

I turned and saw Sir Hugo bearing down at me. The arrow had struck his horse but still, it came at me. It was a war horse and it was angry. It did not matter for I was angrier. Dick Stone Heart had found hope and it had gone with the spear thrust from the squire. This was down to Sir Hugo. He had drawn his sword and rode directly at me. This time I would not move. His horse was so weary that it could no longer gallop. It was doing a fast walk and so the knight tried to make the horse rear. Its two wounds made it a feeble attempt but it allowed the knight to have greater momentum with his blade when it came down. I held up my shield to block the blow and, as he came down, thrust up with my sword. His blade almost broke my left arm. My shield dropped to my side held only by my shoulder strap. My sword went beneath his cuirass and into his mail. His downward movement drove my sword deep within him. I pushed harder knowing I had to end this quickly. When blood flooded down my blade then I knew he was dead.

Behind me, I heard the clash of steel on steel and a horse whinny. As I turned I saw Sir Bohemund catch Roger of Chester in the chest with his sword. As Roger's horse wheeled around, Sir Bohemund hit him across the back knocking him from his saddle.

As Roger lay struggling to get to his feet Sir Bohemund pulled on his reins to allow his horse to trample my sergeant. I ran at the horse and rider. As the hooves came up I hit the horse's hindquarters with my shield, the edge of my blade and my body. Already off balance, the mighty horse tumbled to the ground. I slipped my shield from my shoulder and allowed it to drop and walked over to Sir Bohemund. He had fallen to the ground and the impact had knocked the helmet from his head. He was spread-eagled on the freezing earth. His horse struggled to its feet and one of its hooves caught the knight's knee. He screamed. I was weary and I was hurt. I held my sword in two hands above me. The knight saw me approach and shouted, "Yield! I yield!"

I inverted my sword and as I drove it into his skull said, "Tell that to the Devil when you meet him."

I turned around. Having seen their two leaders slain the rest of the men began to flee. Edgar and Lol led the men from my walls to encourage their departure. I ran to Roger. He shook his head, "I am hurt but a little. I am slipping Captain. Time was I would have had that villein for he was all strength."

"Are you hurt?"

He put his hand to his chest and it came away bloody. "I will need a new hauberk!"

I laughed, "Then take that of Sir Bohemund and his armour too. You have earned it." I put down my arm and helped him to his feet. I surveyed the battlefield and counted my men. Some had died. Joseph Woodman and Robert son of Tom would no longer ride behind me and James Warbow had escaped the woods of Sherwood only to die in the garden of England. He and Dick Stone Heart had both been killed.

John son of Jack had survived. He stood over the body of Sir Hugo's squire. He had a wound to his cheek but it was not mortal. He grinned, "Do I get to have his mail, Captain?"

"Take all for you have earned it." Edgar and Lol strode towards me. "Are all safe within?"

"Aye, Captain, for you came just in time. The attack began shortly before we spied you. Had you not sent Lol here to warn us then it might have gone ill." Edgar grinned, "Your wife is a force of nature, Captain. She had all of the women armed and ready to fight on the walls!"

"Have the wounded and our dead taken within the walls. Strip the enemy of mail and treasure. Fetch kindling and we will burn the dead before the carrion come."

I passed the body of poor Jack. My horse had carried me faithfully for a long time. He had died to save my life and I would honour him by naming my next horse, Jack. As I walked through my gate my wife ran to me. She ignored the blood and gore on my tunic and hands and she embraced me and then kissed me. "You are a good man! Welcome home!"

I said, "I fear this Christmas will not be a merry one."

She shook her head, "It may not be a merry one but it will be cause for thanks. We will feed the whole of the village this Yule for God has brought us all together for a purpose. Let us celebrate life and the man who keeps his word and has honour intact. You are a great man!"

My wife was right, I had kept my honour and my word but at what cost? Four of my men had died and my horse was slain. The Earl of Oxford still lived and I had work yet to do.

Epilogue

I do not think that the Earl of Northampton and Derby was happy when we did not reach London until the end of January. I cared not. We had had dead to bury and walls to mend. Henry's grandmother had died and it had saddened us all. I did not take all of my men to London. But ten of us rode into the city. We stayed in 'The Blue Company' inn. The Duke was staying with his uncle at Westminster. I did not ride directly there, we had an evening in the inn. It proved informative. John and Tom knew a great deal about the events in London. The King had been forced to accept that he would still be guided by his Council, the Lords Appellant. He had little choice for his only hope, the Earl of Oxford, had fled to France. The suspicions I had seemed justified. He had been stripped of all his titles. There would be no Duke of Ireland. So many men had been lost that no one mentioned Sir Hugo and Sir Bohemund. It was assumed that they had perished in the marshes.

When we reached Westminster the Earl of Northampton greeted us as naughty boys who had stayed out too late. "I thought you had ignored me! I wished you here almost a month since!"

"Sorry, lord, but we had many matters to deal with. Master Henry here lost his grandmother and we had men to bury."

He frowned, "But we won the battle!"

"There were other battles to be fought. They are fought and we are here." I sounded enigmatic. I did not care.

"As it happens this is fortuitous. There is to be a dubbing of knights in five days' time at Westminster Cathedral. You and Master Henry will be knighted. You have both done all that was asked. Now can we build England again and, perhaps, retake France."

"And the King?"

"I have hopes for him now that de Vere is gone. We have spoken to him and I have also done so privately. You need not fear, William, we are friends. He greeted me warmly. He would not do that if we were enemies. You and Henry must stay here with me until the ceremony."

"Lord we have rooms in an inn and our men are there."

"Good, then they will not require chambers here. I insist!" There was steel in his voice. "When you are dubbed then you can leave."

He was keeping us close and I could not work out why.

The ceremony was an impersonal one. The Earl of Northampton dubbed ten of us. I saw that some of those he knighted were not warriors. He was building up those who would support him. We feasted in the palace but Henry, Sir Henry now, and I drank little.

The next morning, he drew us apart. "Sir Henry you have Shottery but when your grandfather passes on you shall have Stratford. Sir William I have a manor for you but it is a delicate situation. The lord who died has a relative who claims it."

I shook my head. "It matters not, lord, I am content with what I have."

"Good, then I will send to you when I need you again. You are a man of your word and now that you are a knight then my enemies and those of the King will fear you! Enjoy your title Sir William!"

When we reached the inn Harold Four Fingers said, "Captain…"

Henry said, "He is a lord now."

Harold looked delighted and grinned, "Sorry, lord, it is not before time. Three days since we met Dick of Craven in the inn. He came yesterday to tell us that the King wishes you to visit with him when you return."

I nodded, "Prepare our horses. I will visit with him now and then we will leave for home. Henry, you had better come with me. Peter and John, you shall be our squires for the day." John would be my squire but I did not know if Henry would have such a low born man for his. I was not even sure that Peter would enjoy the position.

The King was eager to speak with me. When we arrived at the west gate we were taken straight away to the Tower and the Great Hall. The King and Queen sat on their thrones and they held hands. They rose when we entered. He gave me a sad smile when he saw our spurs, "I see that my cousin has bestowed that honour which we hoped would be ours."

Now I understood why we had been kept in the palace. Henry was still plotting. He might not harm the King but he would keep him weak.

"I am sorry, sire. I would that you had been the one to lay the sword on my shoulders."

The Queen beamed, "But I can bestow upon you the title of Queen's champion. That the Duke cannot steal." She handed me a ring. It had upon it the Queen's sign.

I bowed, "Then you have given me the greater honour."

That seemed to please them both. The King said, "You have always been loyal to me. It is a pity that you and the Earl of Oxford did not get on. He has deserted me you know?"

"I do, sire."

He grinned and leaned forward, "They think that I am beaten but I am not. There will be vengeance. Mowbray murdered my Constable and he will pay. My uncle executed some of those who advised me and imprisoned others. There will be an accounting for this but you, my wife's champion and most staunch of friends, will ever be our rock. Know that when I send for you that you must come. Now is not the time for vengeance. Now is the time for King Richard to play a part as other dissemblers have played one before. When the time comes then I will need you."

I saw the look of fear on the Queen's face. She was frightened of the changes in her husband.

I dropped to my knee, "Know, your majesty, that I swore an oath to your father and to you both. Sir William Strongstaff does not break his word. When you need me I shall be here."

Sir Henry dropped to his knee too, "And I swear that I am your man unto death."

The King stepped from the throne and, taking our hands, lifted us to our feet. "Then on this dark winter day, you have brought summer sun and hope. Thank you, my friends!"

As we headed north from London up Watling Street I wondered what the future held. I had two cousins both of whom were relying upon me. One day I would have to make a choice and I prayed it would be the right one. One thing was certain. I would not have the peaceful life my wife dreamed of. I had been born into the world of warriors and that was still my path.

The End

Glossary

Ballock dagger or knife- a blade with two swellings next to the blade

Begawan- a metal plate to protect the armpit

Bishop's Clere -Highclere Castle

Chevauchée- a raid by mounted men

Galoches- Clogs

Hovel- a simple bivouac used when no tents were available

Mêlée- a medieval fight between knights

Pursuivant- the rank below a herald

Rondel dagger- a narrow-bladed dagger with a disc at the end of the hilt to protect the hand

Sallet bascinet- medieval helmets of the simplest type: round with a neck protector

Historical Notes

This is a work of fiction. There is no evidence to suggest a plot to murder either the King or his cousin. Equally, there is no evidence to suggest that men did not try to kill them. Anne of Bohemia was the love of Richard's life. When she died, he changed. I could find no reason why they could not have children but they did not. For a medieval king that was a disaster. I have made up the plotline involving some sort of potion to stop her conceiving. They had such treatments. I chose a sinister motivation.

Castilian Campaign

John of Gaunt sailed from England on 9 July 1386 with a huge Anglo-Portuguese fleet carrying an army of about 5,000 men plus an extensive 'royal' household and his wife and daughters. Pausing on the journey to use his army to drive off the French forces who were then besieging Brest, he landed at A Coruña in northern Spain on 29 July.

The coinage was pounds shillings and pence. Older English readers might remember how it worked but for those unfamiliar: twelve pennies made up a shilling, twenty shillings made up a pound. A penny could be divided up into four farthings and two half pennies. A groat was a coin worth four pennies. The sixpenny piece and the threepenny bit had yet to be created.

The Battle of Radcot Bridge

This is Holinshead's 16th-century account of the battle.

In 1387, King Richard II. sent secretly to Robert de Vere, Duke of Ireland, who was levying troops in Wales, to come to him with all speed, to aid him with the Duke of Gloucester and his friends; and commissioned at the same time Sir Thomas Molineux de Cuerdale, Constable of Chester, a man of great influence in Cheshire and Lancashire, and the Sheriff of Chester, to raise troops, and to accompany and safe conduct the Duke of Ireland to the Kings presence. Molineux executed his commission with great zeal, imprisoning all who would not join him. Thus was raised an army of 5,000 men. The Duke of Ireland, having with him Molineux, Vernon, and Ratcliffe, rode forward "in statelie and glorious arraie." Supposing that none durst come forth to withstand him. Nevertheless, when he came to Radcot Bridge, 21 miles from Chipping Norton, he suddenly espied the army of the lords; and finding that some of his troops refused to fight, he began to wax faint hearted, and to prepare to escape by flight, in which he succeeded; but Thomas Molineux determined to fight it out. Nevertheless, when he had fought a little , and perceived it would not avail him to tarry longer, he likewise, as one despairing of the victory, betook himself to flight ; and plunging into the river, it chanced that Sir Roger Mortimer, being present, amongst others, called him to come out of the water to him, threatening to shoot him through with arrows, in the river, if he did not. "If I come," said Molineux, "will ye save my life?" "I will make ye no such promise," replied Sir Roger Mortimer, "but, notwithstanding, either come up, or thou shalt presently die for it." "Well then," said Molineux, "if there be no other remedy, suffer me to come up, and let me try with hand blows, either with you or some other, and so die like a man." But as he came up, the knight caught him by the helmet, plucked it off his head, and straightways drawing his dagger, stroke him into the brains, and so dispatched him. Molineux, a varlet, and a boy were the only slain in the engagement; 800 men fled into the marsh, and were drowned; the rest were surrounded, stript, and sent home. The Duke of Ireland made his escape to the Continent; and the King returned to London.

I have been as free with my interpretation of Holinshead as Shakespeare was. Three men killed in battle and eight hundred drowning sounds like a historian ingratiating himself in the good graces of a royal family!

The battle of Radcot Bridge happened almost exactly as I wrote it. De Vere stripped himself of armour and fled. The Constable was killed as I said.

King Richard was a complicated man. Some modern writers call him bi-polar. Certainly, his wife, Anne of Bohemia, was the greatest influence for good. The story will continue. Henry Bolingbroke will become Henry IVth and his son, Henry of Monmouth will become Henry V[th]. However, this story is really about the ordinary folk of England. The archers and sergeants. William Strongstaff represents those people and it is his story which I tell.

For the English maps, I have used the original Ordnance survey maps. Produced by the army in the 19th century they show England before modern developments and, in most cases, are a pre-industrial revolution. Produced by Cassini they are a useful tool for a historian.

I also discovered a good website http: orbis.stanford.edu. This allows a reader to plot any two places in the Roman world and if you input the mode of transport you wish to use and the time of year it will calculate how long it would take you to travel the route. I have used it for all of my books up to the eighteenth century as the transportation system was roughly the same. The Romans would have been quicker!

Books used in the research:

- The Tower of London -Lapper and Parnell (Osprey)
- English Medieval Knight 1300-1400-Gravett
- The Castles of Edward 1 in Wales- Gravett
- Norman Stone Castles- Gravett
- The Armies of Crécy and Poitiers- Rothero
- The Armies of Agincourt- Rothero
- Henry V and the conquest of France- Knight and Turner
- Chronicles in the Age of Chivalry-Ed. Eliz Hallam
- English Longbowman 1330-1515- Bartlett

For more information on all of the books then please visit the author's web site at http://www.griffhosker.com where there is a link to contact him.

Griff Hosker
October 2018

Other books
by
Griff Hosker

If you enjoyed reading this book, then why not read another one by the author?
Ancient History

The Sword of Cartimandua Series (Germania and Britannia 50 A.D. – 128 A.D.)
Ulpius Felix- Roman Warrior (prequel)
Book 1 The Sword of Cartimandua
Book 2 The Horse Warriors
Book 3 Invasion Caledonia
Book 4 Roman Retreat
Book 5 Revolt of the Red Witch
Book 6 Druid's Gold
Book 7 Trajan's Hunters
Book 8 The Last Frontier
Book 9 Hero of Rome
Book 10 Roman Hawk
Book 11 Roman Treachery
Book 12 Roman Wall
Book 13 Roman Courage

The Aelfraed Series
(Britain and Byzantium 1050 A.D. - 1085 A.D.)
Book 1 Housecarl
Book 2 Outlaw
Book 3 Varangian

The Wolf Warrior series
(Britain in the late 6th Century)
Book 1 Saxon Dawn
Book 2 Saxon Revenge
Book 3 Saxon England
Book 4 Saxon Blood

Book 5 Saxon Slayer
Book 6 Saxon Slaughter
Book 7 Saxon Bane
Book 8 Saxon Fall: Rise of the Warlord
Book 9 Saxon Throne
Book 10 Saxon Sword

The Dragon Heart Series
Book 1 Viking Slave
Book 2 Viking Warrior
Book 3 Viking Jarl
Book 4 Viking Kingdom
Book 5 Viking Wolf
Book 6 Viking War
Book 7 Viking Sword
Book 8 Viking Wrath
Book 9 Viking Raid
Book 10 Viking Legend
Book 11 Viking Vengeance
Book 12 Viking Dragon
Book 13 Viking Treasure
Book 14 Viking Enemy
Book 15 Viking Witch
Book 16 Viking Blood
Book 17 Viking Weregeld
Book 18 Viking Storm
Book 19 Viking Warband
Book 20 Viking Shadow
Book 21 Viking Legacy
Book 22 Viking Clan

The Norman Genesis Series
Hrolf the Viking
Horseman
The Battle for a Home
Revenge of the Franks
The Land of the Northmen
Ragnvald Hrolfsson
Brothers in Blood

Lord of Rouen
Drekar in the Seine
Duke of Normandy
The Duke and the King

New World Series
Blood on the Blade
Across the Seas

**The Anarchy Series England
1120-1180**
English Knight
Knight of the Empress
Northern Knight
Baron of the North
Earl
King Henry's Champion
The King is Dead
Warlord of the North
Enemy at the Gate
The Fallen Crown
Warlord's War
Kingmaker
Henry II
Crusader
The Welsh Marches
Irish War
Poisonous Plots
The Princes' Revolt
Earl Marshal

**Border Knight
1182-1300**
Sword for Hire
Return of the Knight
Baron's War
Magna Carta
Welsh Wars
Henry III

The Bloody Border

Lord Edward's Archer
Lord Edward's Archer

Struggle for a Crown
1360- 1485
Blood on the Crown
To Murder A King
The Throne

Modern History

The Napoleonic Horseman Series
Book 1 Chasseur a Cheval
Book 2 Napoleon's Guard
Book 3 British Light Dragoon
Book 4 Soldier Spy
Book 5 1808: The Road to Coruña
Book 6 Talavera
Waterloo

The Lucky Jack American Civil War series
Rebel Raiders
Confederate Rangers
The Road to Gettysburg

The British Ace Series
1914
1915 Fokker Scourge
1916 Angels over the Somme
1917 Eagles Fall
1918 We will remember them
From Arctic Snow to Desert Sand
Wings over Persia

Combined Operations series
1940-1945
Commando

Raider
Behind Enemy Lines
Dieppe
Toehold in Europe
Sword Beach
Breakout
The Battle for Antwerp
King Tiger
Beyond the Rhine
Korea

Other Books
Carnage at Cannes (a thriller)
Great Granny's Ghost (Aimed at 9-14-year-old young people)
Adventure at 63-Backpacking to Istanbul

For more information on all of the books then please visit the author's web site at www.griffhosker.com where there is a link to contact him.

Made in the USA
Middletown, DE
03 October 2020

21066416R00137